THE
LOST ARK
OF THE
SACRED
MOVEMENT

Ron Osborn

In the beginning was the Word, and the Word
was with the God, and the Word was God. John 1:1

❧

1.2 billion people believe
the Bible to be the inspired word of God.

Many of the same words which appear in
that work appear in this one.

Draw your own conclusions.

The Present: Monday, April 5ᵗʰ, 8:52 p.m. – Paris

Mikhail Samanovananonvich should have read his horoscope for that day. Not that it would have warned that he was about to be violated in a James Dickey *Deliverance* sort of way. But then horoscopes always did tend to sugarcoat things. All that morning's astronavigation advised was to "venture somewhere new and exciting." Still, had Mikhail Samanovananonvich seen fit for the first time at this autumnal age to heed such superstitious offal, he might have avoided the average male's second worst nightmare; and one that a select niche pays extra for.

Mikhail Samanovananonvich, as strong and solid as the oversized Napoleon III ebonized writing table he was hunched over, cluttered with pages of notes and various tomes, was the sole occupant that evening in the musty *Bibliotheque Historique de la Ville de Paris Antiquities.* But his heart was pounding, his face flushed, his body surging with adrenaline; he had barely been able to sleep the previous night after he'd made the call to Cardinal Thomasina at the Vatican.

"Your Eminence...I discovered a lead today that will focus our search dramatically. For over six decades the church has been looking in the wrong direction like a fly hitting against the window. All the fly had to do is turn around. All *we* had to do was turn around...the answer was closer than any of us realized. I believe I will have it for you when I call tomorrow!"

Was it possible? Could a desperate search spanning

much of his lifetime actually be approaching the end? A search for the greatest theological find in two millennia that was so valuable. So historic. So potentially shattering if it fell into the wrong hands. It could only be expressed in fragmentary sentences? The profundity of Mikhail Samanovananonvich's claim was reflected in Thomasina's three-word reply. "I will tell him."

Mikhail Samanovananonvich was deaf and dumb to the world this night. *Oh my God,* he thought, poring over his notes, *I am right! I AM RIGHT! I AM BLOODY WELL RIGHT! HA! HA-HAAAA! HA-HA-HA-HAAAAAAAAAAA!* Granted, Mikhail Samanovananonvich's unusual jocosity was due in part to a transcendentalist joke he'd heard earlier that day.[1] But it was mainly the discovery thing. In his euphoria, Mikhail Samanovananonvich never heard the iron door latch lift behind him. He never heard the footsteps on the two-hundred-and-seventy-four year old peg-and-groove floorboards. An arm shot around his neck and yanked his head back against a body, his air supply dangerously reduced. "Where is it?" the assailant demanded in a voice that was, if possible, even more off-putting than what was to follow, a whiskey-tenor-on-helium reminiscent of a Chuck Jones animated character.

"I...I don't know what you're talking about!" Mikhail

---

1   Henry David Thoreau, refusing to pay a poll tax, was imprisoned in the local jail. Ralph Waldo Emerson happened by, saw him behind bars and said, 'Henry, what are you doing in *there?*' To which Henry responded, 'Ralph...what are *you* doing out *there?*' One of the reasons given for Transcendentalism's truncated lifespan was its refusal to go blue with its humor.

Samanovananonvich strained to reply.

"You most certainly do."

Mikhail Samanovananonvich had kept the paper trail of his search to a modicum, the key revelations written in his unique and unintelligible shorthand. Kill him and the search would be set back decades.

"Where is it?" the voice persisted.

Mikhail Samanovananonvich was prepared to die rather than tell. He was not, however, prepared for what followed. His head was slammed hard onto the table. Suddenly he found himself face down on the surface, his wrists and ankles secured to the legs of the table with plastic restraints. The click of a switchblade was followed by the sound of his pants ripping. He was beginning to review this whole rather-die-than-tell ultimatum since, y'know, it was a personal choice really, like quitting smoking or cutting carbs.

"Where...is...it?"

No, he could not waver...he *dare* not waver; the very fate of the Church of Rome hung in the balance. "I don't know what you're talking about!"

"You told Cardinal Thomasina otherwise."

Mikhail Samanovananonvich began to repeat the *Pater Noster* with the urgency of a mantra. It was not the answer his attacker wanted to hear. Whereupon, with an object not intended for such use, the attacker began to inflict upon his victim the male equivalent of giving birth.

In his diary for that day Mikhail Samanovananonvich's entry would read, "Ate squab dinner, took walk, admired Eiffel Tower." Had he kept a diary.

Tuesday, April 6th, 12:35 a.m. – Paris

Inspector Renault – handsome in that non-threatening second-tier leading man sort of way – stood beside a forensic medical analyst in the 8th *arrondissement* hospital clinic, leaning over Mikhail Samanovananonvich's exposed buttocks, which were now as numb as the rest of his body thanks to a three-hundred-pound needle-wielding nurse.

"I shall never use that phrase again," sighed Inspector Renault.

"What phrase?" asked the forensic analyst, not really caring, as he measured the size of Mikhail Samanovananonvich's violation with a set of calipers.

"*I'm going to tear you a new asshole.* Because every time I do I'll see the results of just such an act wrought upon poor Mikhail Samanovananonvich."

"Why do you do that?"

Renault looked at him, baffled. "Is it not common to witness something traumatic and forever associate it with a—"

"No," said the analyst curtly, "why the pretentious need to say both the forename and surname of a person who happens to be of Russian descent? It is the mark of a sophist who reads Tolstoy or, worse, of someone of negligible intellect who wants his listener to *believe* he reads Tolstoy when he does not. In either case, both have the exact opposite effect that the speaker intends, illustrating in truth that he may have a passing acquaintance with the author or, more likely, reads too many hackneyed authors who may or may not have read Tolstoy themselves but feel that the repetitious use of forename *and* surname of any

Russian character, along with ungainly run-on Tolstoy-like sentences, gives their commercial tripe the patina of literary urbanity."

Having studied enough French in high school to attain the part of "Bistro Patron #3" in the French Club's production of *Cyrano*, Mikhail Samanovana ...that is, Mikhail... concentrated hard to pick out any familiar words he could which, as near as he could tell, were: *hydroplane...eggplant...* and either *Keith Richards* or *giant panda*. Surprised he was still alive, he awoke to learn that he had been rescued by the elderly Sister Laudare who, arriving just before closing to shoo out anyone remaining in the library, walked in mid-*acte indélicat* and never knew such a feat possible. Screaming, she promptly ran and told the gendarmes of an act unnatural to God, man, and the unsaved Arab states, her focus of the event making her unable to describe the assailant from the wrist up. Thus, since neither victim nor witness could describe anything of the assailant, Mikhail was forced to assume the facedown position again, as the scene of the crime was inspected for clues.

"What do you conclude?" Renault asked the lab-coated troll.

"Conclude? My job is not to conclude. Since that is your occupation, inspector, what do you notice out of the ordinary about the victim's back porch?"

"His...?"

"...derrière, rumble seat, nether cheeks, parking place, chocolate goldmine, pressed ham, moneymaker—"

"I understand!"

"No," sighed the little man wistfully, "you most certainly

do not. I wanted to be France's greatest thesaurist, in French *and* English, a feat never before accomplished. Until... well...in the elimination round of the televised nationals, I heard the judge give me the noun 'constellation.' I quickly listed all manner of descriptors regarding heavenly bodies. The audience gasped audibly, I assumed, at my verbal acuity. Until I was told the judge had said 'consternation.' Thus here I am today, on a Saturday night no less, when I should be out with fellow phraseologists and etymologists enjoying the company of women of great pulchritude and pneumatic talents...instead of inspecting a grown man's exhaust pipe." He thought a beat and then corrected himself. "No...make that 'servants' entrance.'"

Renault remembered that famous Thesaurus Finals crash-and-burn[2] on primetime television, though he failed to grasp how the incident led him to this unpalatable occupation. Renault returned to studying the victim with the experienced eye only someone with twenty-plus years on the Parisian beat could bring to bear. "What do I see out of the ordinary," he mused, running his gaze over Mikhail's exposed countryside. "Those depressions that corkscrew inward...whatever was used was twisted as it was inserted. Odd, too, that the assailant, intent on inflicting pain, would mitigate matters with what appears to be a petroleum-based lubricant...perhaps to spare the offending object more than the victim," concluded Renault. The rat bastard's silence came as close to agreement with Renault as the analyst would allow.

In the cool fluorescent lights of the precinct hallway

---

2   Otherwise known as an "Icarus" in the word trade.

Renault perused the statement Mikhail gave earlier through an interpreter. Which was as follows: Mikhail, researching a book reconciling the differences among the four gospels, had come to the *Bibliotheque Historique de la Ville de Paris Antiquities* for its original Hebrew, Aramaic, Greek and Latin vulgate biblical documents. He had spent the day translating a fourth-century fragment from the Gnostic Apocryphon of James. Suddenly Mikhail was attacked and robbed of all his money. Tied up as he was, he felt like a helpless sheep about to be defiled in one of those eight-millimeter, one-Euro-for-two-minutes'-worth-of-loop one hears about and can see in private booths in certain parts of Denmark (this Mikhail did not elaborate upon). Whereupon Mikhail underwent the deed.

Renault stared at his notepad. Nothing in this perfunctory statement shed any light on matters, though a visit to Denmark, purely in the interests of research, might be necessary. He noticed a medical-alert bracelet on Mikhail's wrist, though for what he didn't know. Renault sighed, disappointed. When the forensic analyst was finished and the on-call physician pronounced Mikhail satisfactory, he would be free to go, one more crime that would remain as open as Mikhail's orifice.

But matters were about to escalate to an unfortunate though dramatically compulsory new level.

At 7:09 a.m. the on-call physician pronounced Mikhail fit to leave and dispensed an oral sedative. Mikhail – against doctor's orders, taking it immediately instead of waiting for the anesthetic to wear off – was given an oversized pair of trousers to replace his ripped ones, from a morgue stiff who apparently expired from the criminal defilement of an all-you-can-eat buffet. He was also given his file of notes, retrieved from the *bibliotheque*.

When the heavily sedated Mikhail stepped out into the bright Parisian morning, he was met with a blurred, overexposed image that refused to settle. Mikhail braced himself against the wall lest he do an Icarus. He spied a taxi stand not fifty yards away. He carefully ambulated toward the stand, which seemed to get no closer the further he ventured, all the while pondering why American streets could not be made of such marvelous deep foam as these Parisian boulevards.

Suddenly Paris listed steeply starboard, but a hand gripped his shoulder to steady him, Mikhail greatly appreciative of this French Samaritan. "*Merci*," he said. But Mikhail was roughly steered into an alley that reeked of the mandatory tang of rotting food, stale urine, and Thunderbird wine or its local equivalent. A dumpster shielding them from the street, the Samaritan turned Mikhail around and stiff-armed him against the wall.

For the first time Mikhail saw his assailant from the night before. Six-foot, four inches tall (minus his Prada thigh-high black leather boots that give him panache *and* height), wearing a matching full-length black leather duster (for just that extra touch of villainy), his tormentor cut an impressive figure even without his zebra striped black-and-white Mohawk.

"Mikhail...where is it?" he asked, picking up exactly where things left off the night before.

"Wow...déjà vu."

"Where...is it?"

"I feel pretty."

A swirling black and orange funnel of monarch but-terflies descended to the alley bricks, revealing another figure as the monarchs suddenly flittered away. (It's pos-sible Mikhail imagined some of that.) This new arrival approached and looked into Mikhail's hubcap-sized pu-pils. He opened a small leather case, removing a syringe. "Mikhail," the newcomer said in a honeyed, measured voice, "once and for all...where is it?"

Sadly, Mikhail Samanovananonvich failed to read his horoscope for this day as well. It counseled that to live long and prosper, it was a propitious time to tell the truth.

Tuesday night, April 6th, 11:49 p.m. – San Francisco

Five thousand, five hundred and fifty-eight miles away, thir-ty-eight hours earlier, someone named Mickey Samanov was also in a police station, this one in San Francisco, hauled in on a physical altercation charge. A uniformed female with swimmer's shoulders and natural red hair in a gelled water-fall, sat across from him. He found her quite fetching, not just in that Stockholm-syndrome sort of way; Mickey wasn't all that current on the nuances of global warming, but for him the world just got a little hotter. She, on the other hand, was looking at him with an expression best described as Osama Bin Laden staring at a naked tranny in his cave.

"Just to be sure I heard correctly," she asked, "...you want to run that by me again?"

"I said, yes. I hit the woman. Tossed in a knee to the

stomach and finished with a roundhouse kick to the ribs. Think I hurt my instep," Mickey said, rubbing the stubble on his sun-burnished jaw. "Because I happen to subscribe to the immortal words of Ike Turner...you gots to control your bitches." He paused. "Or was it Joseph Smith?"

She turned from the keyboard and leaned forward for emphasis. "Mr. Samanov..."

"Please...call me Mickey."

"...in this job I'm certain I've met someone more repugnant, distasteful and misogynistic than you. I just can't remember when."

"Wow," he nodded, "it's not every day I top the list."

"Don't be modest, I'm sure you've topped plenty."

"I'm guessing afterwards we're not gonna do shooters and play connect the dots with my tongue and your freckles."

"I'm guessing you're a lot of fun during skin shedding season."

"I'll pencil you in for Spring."

" Mr.—"

"Please, call me—"

"Shut. The Fuck. Up."

Her perfect jaw clenched, lips forming a taut line, she took an angry breath causing her attractively small but exquisitely proportioned-for-her size breasts to press against her uniform. "Let's start again. You seem to enjoy waving red flags in front of bulls. Meaning you are either profoundly moronic to a degree heretofore unknown in law enforcement, or there's a side to this situation that I fail to comprehend."

Damn, thought Samanov, *she's steamin' in neutral...but she's smokin' in gear. Wonder how she'd look at the moment of orgasm? Mine, for instance?* He got lost in her piercing hazel eyes. This could be wife number six...or was it seven?

"I'm waiting," she said.

"Whahuh...?"

"For your explanation."

Mickey decided to dial down the charm. He sat a little straighter and squinted at her nametag. "Of course. Y'see, Officer Furburger—"

"Farburger."

Smooth. "Farburger...it seems in my occupation that women are a cross to bear."

"What do you do?"

"I'm a minister and a couple's counselor."

"Very impressive."

"Not if you have the calling."

"No, that you could say it with a straight face. What denomination is your ministry?"

"I prefer to not limit my audience."

"Could we narrow it down to a general faith?"

"Isn't that religious profiling?"

"Where's your church?" she pressed.

"Any Heart, U.S.A."

"And the name of this unspecific, non-brick-and-mortar, line of worship?"

Mickey retrieved from a pocket a crisp white card, handing it to her. "Mickey's A-A-A-A-A-A-A1 Pool & Spa Service," she read.

"Shit." He searched and produced another card, this

one creased and linty. He smoothed out the folds and handed it to her.

"'The All-Encompassing Church of the Unified and Omnipotent Being,'" she read. "That pretty much covers all the bases." Mickey shrugged agreement. "I assume those are your vestments?" She was referring to his faded denim shirt open down to the top of his just-starting to-protrude belly, his worn Army-green fatigues, and huarache sandals.

"Clothes do not a cleric make."

"No, but a degree of divinity does. You got one?"

"How long have you been an officer?" he asked.

"Four years, three months."

"And in that time how many people have asked to see your degree in police sciences?" She didn't have to answer. "And yet you are free to ticket, arrest, mace, and taser the average taxpayer's ball sack at will. Simply because you wear the vestments of a police officer. But when someone without a miter, staff, and tabernacle choir behind him claims to be a man of God, everyone and their mother is Pontius Pilate."

"You wanna see my degree? Here's my degree," she said, pointing to her badge.

"Your left tit?"

"Funny, really, you should take this on the road."

"I'm beginning to think this interrogation is not by the book," he said.

"Speaking of the book," she said, "name the four gospels."

"I refuse to dignify that."

"Is the Koran Taoism, Islam, or Buddhism?"

"This the best you can do?"

"Was Joan of Arc Noah's wife?"

"When you throw the heat I'll step up to the plate."

She regarded him, amused despite herself. That he could construct a complete sentence and didn't reek of regurgitated Jim Beam and Twinkies put him in the top five percentile of her precinct's interrogation pyramid. Shaved, moussed, clothed in Brioni, he was probably not unattractive. Not to her, of course, involved as she was in a committed relationship. But to another female, around last call, six appletinis to the wind...?

"One question, Mr. Samanov...and whatever your answer, I will accept without condition that you are the universally recognized pope of the All-Encompassing... whatever." His expression accepted her terms. "You're here for hitting a woman. Just what kind of man of God are you?"

"The kind who doesn't judge," he answered forthrightly "who knows that one man's sin is another man's sacrament...who knows that to be acquainted with sin on a first-name basis is to respect its power...who knows that God dotes more on the one fallen than the ninety-nine saved...and that the highest redemption comes from the lowest depths."

Farburger, unprepared for anything deeper than *the kind who would like to worship at your Y*, could only stare. If Samanov were a boxer, she thought, he'd be pre-draft Muhammad Ali, winning rounds by footwork and feints. He gave his age as 44, but had he said 40 she would've bought it and had he said 50, the distinguished crow's feet and the healed facial scars would have given that credence, too. He somehow maintained a slightly weathered tan even though it was the tail end of winter. She suspected he surfed or used to surf, which would account for his solid chest and a kind of easy, leonine sexuality. She had to remind herself that he was here for possibly laying hands on a female, and not in the faith-healing sense. "You were saying...felony assault as occupational hazard."

Mickey tiredly ran a hand through his mane of blond-grey hair. "It's not so much the minister part. It's the couples counseling. By the time a husband and wife come to me, they're usually in desperate straits."

"I would agree. And where do you do your 'counseling?'"

"In my church offices."

"You have no church...but you have church offices." His demeanor betrayed no contradiction. "How do your customers—"

"Parishioners—"

"—find you?"

"Word of mouth. And, of course, I advertise."

"Where, the Pennysaver? The laundromat bulletin board?" Off his stutter-step, starting to respond until his brain caught up with her question, she knew. "Son of a bitch...I'm right, aren't I?"

His dignity had barely been dinged. "Shall I continue?"

"Oh, please."

"In my experience I've found that the number one issue among husbands and wives...the root cause of ninety-five percent of couples' problems...is not money...family...

communication. Which leaves what?"

"Something to do with the toilet seat?"

"A couple's been married long enough, they either live in quiet desperation, or take the Edward Albee approach picking at each others' emotional scabs to cause the death of a thousand cuts."

"You should write for Hallmark."

"They confuse existence with living, assuming whatever life they have beats the alternative. Sure, their problems are money, family, communication. But those are the symptoms. The why, the *reason* these couples are marital zombies, is that they dwell on the missed opportunities of the past, or the diminishing returns of the future, and they've forgotten how to live in the *now*. The moment. The very instant that exists in the blip you experience it."

"So…if I understand you correctly," ventured Farburger, feeling very much like a character in a novel whose job was to make sense of ill-conceived and/or threadbare sections of exposition, "you're saying…forget how sucky your relationship used to be and may continue to be…and just live blissfully in the here and now."

"Very good, cricket."

"I think it's 'grasshopper.'"

"Whatever. Only in the moment can we manifest any semblance of command over the universe. I'd like to think I came up with it, but St. Augustine was the one to posit that all humans were damned at birth no matter how good they were, saved only by the gratuitous grace of God."

"And what part does grace play in your counseling?"

"Doesn't. But I really dig the damned-at-birth part."

Officer Farburger, almost twenty years his junior, had never been married, or in a relationship beyond two years. Her own parents had divorced bitterly when she was thirteen. She had never read a book on interpersonal relationships nor had she ever watched Dr. Phil. But still, Samanov's slant on relationships seemed so counterintuitive as to turn back on itself more times than a fakir's cobra.

"Couples actually pay you for this insight?"

"Pay? No-no-no-no…I only accept donations."

"Of course. Being a non-profit. And this short-sighted, nihilistic approach to marriage gets results?"

"There's a bit more to the approach than meets the eye," he said, then anticipated her next response. "But does the Colonel give out his secret herbs and spices?"

Shifting back into work mode, she returned to her keyboard. "As to the assault charge…"

"Many times, after I explain to a troubled couple the philosophical underpinnings of my approach, the wife will request a one-on-one with me. And much progress can be made in these sessions."

"And why do I think this cost-free, donation based, one-on-one tutoring to live in the moment is no doubt expressed through sexual congress?"

"Because by your *question* you know that one cannot be more in the moment than during sex and, like most people, you've probably invoked Jesus Christ more times on your back than you have on a pew."

Huh, she thought, *that's probably true.*

"As to the incident," he continued, "both husband and wife came to a counseling session and, probably because she came early the week before when I was…counseling a Brazilian foreign exchange student…she chose to confess in front of her husband our independent study. He was damn fast for a handicapped veteran, and was out of his wheelchair and on me before I could tell him I supported our boys in Iraq, just not the cocksucker who sent them there. I felt bad pulling his prosthetic arm out of the brace and hitting him with it, but it's probably covered by insurance. At some point the wife joined in, forcing me to bear arm against her as well. And when the dust settled," Mickey said, not without a touch of pride, "I was the last man standing."

If one opened a Funk & Wagnall's to the definition of "slack-jawed," the tome could not do better than to include the image of Office Farburger reacting to this. Which is when the Watch Sergeant sauntered by with a cup of over-franchised coffee that would rank as product placement if this were a film.

"He's free to go," he said without stopping

"Wait, free, but…why?"

From over his shoulder, "Charges dropped."

Farburger would later find out that husband and wife, joined in combat against a common enemy, had rediscovered their passion for one another.   Amazingly for this couple, Samanov turned out to be just what the doctor ordered.[3]

3   Unknown to Samanov and Farburger, however, the couple's reconciliation would be a Pyrrhic victory. They went on to join the sadomasochistic subculture and continued their passion for each other through the sex and violence first kindled by the counseling incident; which, per the wife's admission two years

All this time spent on his paperwork, listening to his outlandish and misanthropic abstractions, jabbing, sparring, dancing, going into the championship rounds…and it was a no-fucking-contest. Even worse, Samanov now had the demeanor of the guilty party *not* chosen in the line-up who just had his faith reconfirmed that crime does indeed pay. And now he was free to go, to ply his self-serving sexual healing philosophy that would no doubt continue to get results in a world where morons were willing to wire money to deposed Nigerian royalty with frozen assets, vote for term limits, or find their marriage counselors in the want ads between "machine contractors" and "massage parlors." *Mickey Samanov is just what I need tonight,* thought Farburger, a plan shaping up in her mind. It was time for his karma to pay some dividends.

"So," he smiled, "are we done?"

She would feel no guilt for what she was about to do.

Tuesday, April 6ᵗʰ, 10:15 a.m. – Paris

Mikhail's killer left the alley, carrying Mikhail's notes file, stopped at a phone booth near the always-noisy Rue de Presbourg, dropped in some coins, and dialed. After three rings someone answered but said nothing.

"You wanted word when it was done," the mohawked caller said in his falsetto-sandpapered voice. "It is done."

"And this is…?" whispered the listener.

---

later in her trial for accidentally decapitating her husband during sex, was probably a factor in her now being an incarcerated widow.

Apparently one of two million, four hundred, sixty-seven thousand three hundred and fifty-five fucking contract killers in Paris who sound like this. "The Fist of God." He dare not say his name, Aaron Zworkan, lest this line be tapped.

"One can never be too careful," said the listener as if reading Aaron's mind, "when the stakes are this high."

"Mikhail Samanovananonvich had the information. And he is dead."

The speaker's voice trembled in excitement. "And now you have it?"

"Mmm...not exactly. Mikhail Samanovananonvich did not divulge it," said Aaron.

"You mean to say," began the voice, barely audibly, "that you killed Mikhail *before* getting information only he possesses...information we've been in search of for *decades*... information that will lead us to the find that will rock the very foundation of Christianity and make us wealthy beyond all measure?" His voice was now at a fevered falsetto just below Aaron's.

"More or less."

The pounding on the other end was either a fist or a forehead hitting a wooden surface; you'd think by now evildoers who hire psychopaths to precisely execute their plans should expect this sort of thing.

Aaron remained calm. "Our cohort whose name I dare not say lest your line be tapped, chose to play his or her hand and show him or herself to Mikhail Samanovananonvich. It produced nothing. If Mikhail Samanovananonvich would not tell me last night, or tell him or her this morning, our options were limited. Especially since Mikhail Samanovananonvich could have identified us both."

The pounding stopped. "What now?" the voice asked weakly.

"Mikhail Samanovananonvich may be dead...but he will still lead us to what we seek."

There was, for now, a mollified silence. "Do you read Tolstoy?"

"Yes, why?"

"Never mind. Godspeed."

Wednesday, April 7ʰ, 6:52 a.m. – San Francisco

Brian Johnson bleated *Highway to Hell* over and over, the Brothers Young churning out the pumping riffs, until Farburger awoke, found her cell phone on the nightstand, and looked at the caller ID – bolting upright as if being waxed by an untrained Filipino illegal her first day in the shop. She sat there, unsure whether to answer, until AC/DC finally left the stage. She flung her head down on the pillow, unable to enjoy the magnificent nineteenth-century four-poster that sat upon an imported wormwood floor taken from a sixteenth century Austrian stable, in this bedroom the size of her apartment. Brian Johnson and crew came back for an encore and Farburger knew it would be a day of encores until she answered.

She opened the cell phone without speaking. Someone said something. "No," she answered in a monotone, "I didn't make it home last night...how observant of you... when'd you notice?" The voice on the other end was playing defense. "Bullshit, Nick, why do I finally hear from you this *morning*, where the fuck were *you* last night?" Defense scrambling, broken field running. "Nick...*Nick*...you were the one who said we were 'soul mates' when I caught you emailing your old girlfriend, you were the one who set up a 'lunch date' with her that I found out about after the fact, you were the one who wasn't at work last week on a supposed double-shift when I stopped by to surprise you with..." She abruptly stopped, began rubbing the bridge of her nose to stave off a sharp pain. "How long you been see-ing her?" Whatever the answer, it wasn't what she wanted to hear. "Jesus." She continued to rub, listened. "No, I'm not alone...none of your goddamn business." The tone on the other end was pained. "No one you know." There was a long silence. A small fissure cracked in her resolve. "It's nobody...just some guy."

"If I had any self-esteem I'd be pissed," Mickey said beside her, naked, his hair a starburst. He looked relaxed, intertwined in the sheets, arms stretched up behind him in a pose of morning-after gratification...until one noticed his wrists in handcuffs wrapped around a post.

"What, you don't believe me?" Farburger said, now the one playing defense. "Say hello," she said to Mickey, hold-ing up her cell in his direction.

"Nick, she's right, I'm nobody, brau," he said affably.

She put the phone back to her ear. "I dunno, Nick," she said, dispirited. "I keep saying this is it, this is the last time, and what do you do? Same goddamn thing. Then you call and expect me to just...to just...we talked about buying a house, for crissakes...about..." She trailed off.

"Just tell me this, Nick...that you're never gonna see her again." Samanov couldn't hear the answer, but caught the vibe. "I gotta go." She snapped the phone shut then threw it as hard as she could out the bedroom door. A shattering noise followed.

"That sound like a fifteenth century Ming vase to you?" asked Mickey. No response. She slumped, glowering into middle distance, contemplating acts found only in books printed in Denmark. "Sounds like someone could use a good couples' counselor." Still nothing. "Give ya the police discount."

"Three people you don't wanna piss off, Samanov," she said without looking at him. "Your lawyer...your food handler...and the woman next to you when you're cuffed and your dick's hanging out."

Good advice, he thought. He let Farburger stew for a while. Then a little while more. After an appropriate amount of stewing, Samanov said, "Do I get to post bond?" This warranted a glance. "Even the overnighters're let out at seven." A snort from her. Figures he'd know that. "So... couldn't help but hear. To break it down, Farburger...you came to work yesterday ready to screw two people, Nick and Not-Nick. Nick was playing musical beds, you were gonna respond in kind. Then you saw me coming all the way from Oakland. I saved you from having to cruise some face-place or embarrass yourself with a co-worker. So you promise me a night of indoor sports the likes of which caused Yahweh to destroy entire cities, and would so deplete me that for the next day or two, I'd be unable to produce anything *close* to a money shot."

"You lay awake nights thinking up this stuff?"

"Granted, I should've seen the hook, the ten ounce sinker, but a woman like you offers bareback rodeo, I tend to let my guard down. I take you home, you suggest we play naughty cop and criminal, handcuff me to the post, and here I am…a revenge fuck without the fuck." She was completely unmoved. "You get a place to stay, I get a night of blue balls a Smurf would covet."

She foraged through a pile of clothes by her bedside, came up with the key, and unlocked the cuffs. He rubbed his wrists with abandon. "So who's Nick…?"

She exhaled, considering whether he was worth the answer. "My partner."

A claxon sounded in Mickey's brain: *Ohhhhhh shit. Oh-shit-oh-shit-oh shit. Shit-shit-shit-shit-shit, did she say…is it actually:* "Your partner…? You mean like the, uh…other cop in the car? Pissed-off dude with a badge, a shotgun, my address?" Mickey's dick did the receding turtlehead.

Farburger let him twist in the wind, this being the most entertaining part of her morning. She hated to break the truth. "My domestic partner."

The claxon shut off mid-wail. *Nick…as in Nicole… Nikki…Nicolette. Domestic partner…as in one who appreciates the poems of Sappho. Carpet baggers. Scissor sisters. Dutch Boys.* Nick not being a testosterone claymore, Samanov's turtle began to venture back out. And given that Farburger was such a petite piece of perfection, this duo was definitely worth getting a visual on, thought Mickey, to serve in those times when, uh, y'know…no one else was around to serve him. "Gotta say," he began, paying out his own hook and ten ounce sinker, "Nick sounds like a real ball buster...a flannel-shirt, crew-cut, Jabba the Hu—"

"She strips at the Crazy Horse in North Beach."

Samanov silently took that in. He and his Ego nodded thoughtfully, silently, supportively. Inside? His Id was doing the Riverdance. *Fuuuuuck me. Fuck me. Mickey, you just hit the trifecta, this is a five-alarm stiffy, like that so-called lesbian in Marin with the rock grotto spa who was "in a committed relationship" but turned out to be bi and her significant other turned out to be committed to watching, dude, like, it's a home run, a slam dunk, a sports cliché of your choice that one of two possibilities will loom larger than your Johnson: Either this relationship of hers does a crash-'n-burn like whasisname and she needs a shoulder or equivalent body part to cry on, or she and Miss Lap-Happy make nice again and she's so grateful that you were part of the plan, and she feels so bad for the bait 'n switch that gave you a dose of imploding nads, that she and Mustang Nikki'll be willing to make up for it with a Samanov sandwich. Stranger things've happened on Planet Mickey. Play this one right, Mick, think long-term, don't force it, be, um, y'know, what's the word? Thoughtful? Tactful? Yeah, one of those. Actually listen to her, be caring, take this one slow, real slow...unless of course she* wants *to go all freaky on your ass, in which case score a keg of Jagermeister, a Colin Farrell-sized tub of KY jelly, two, three dozen reservoir tipped con—*

"And you know the really half-assed part of all this?" she continued.

"Whahuh...?"

"She doesn't care if I fuck a guy. Another female, she would've had an aneurysm. But I punked out...blew it...I should've let her think..." She trailed off, sinking into a black hole so strong that it threatened to suck Mickey and the whole room into it.

"Look," he offered tentatively, "Farburger...I'd really like to be able to call you something other than...well... Farburger."

"What's it matter?"

"I like to know all my jailers."

"It's not like we're gonna be friends."

"I'm not looking for that either," he said, wondering if they should hyphenate their last names after they get married.

Screw it, she sighed, resigned. In one hour she'd be gone and he already knew more intimate details of her life than most of her co-workers. "Danica."

Danica...

Danica, Danica, Danica.

DAY-ni-ka. Day-NI-ka. Day-ni-KAAAAH. It rolled off the tongue like silky iambic pentameter, as arresting a name as the visage it described, as if the Almighty had made this female to fit the sound, as right a combination to Mickey as Sam Cooke singing *A Change is Gonna Come*, as beautiful a combination as Monet and water lilies.

"Nice," he said honestly. "Very pretty."

"Samanov, just to be clear...when you do that? You make my skin crawl."

"Completely understood." Nikki could be their best man.

Danica shook her short red hair into place, the sheet sliding off her breasts and falling just below her diamond-pierced navel. Arching her back, arms at ten and two, she stretched mightily, every muscle and sinew on that 6% body-fat physique pulling taut. Watching, Mickey's blue balls turned cobalt.

Danica rose, walked idly past the Parian marble fireplace and out the door onto a second story balustrade that ringed a three-story circular foyer of this 1912 mansion. She didn't know from Ming pottery, but she could see the shattered remains didn't come from Vases R Us. She looked up at the leaded glass skylight. The only way someone couldn't be impressed by this was to not have a pulse. She wandered to the next door, a study of floor-to-vaulted-ceiling shelves, with more books than she could ever read if she murdered Nikki tonight and as punishment were confined to this room for life. Punishment indeed: Tomes by Aristotle, St. Augustine, Thomas Aquinas, St. Jerome. Bindings that included such titles as *Ancient Greek Syntax and Idioms*, *Utopia*, *Gnostic vs. Agnostic Gestalt*, *Proto-Orthodox Christianity*, *Tertullian's Arguments Against the Valentinians*, and *Origen and Pseudepigrapha*. Not a Tom Clancy, Judith Krantz, Dan Brown among them. However, one book caught her eye: *Heterodoxy and the Council of Nicaea*. It wasn't the title. It was the author: Mikhail Samanovananonvich. It jumped out to her but she couldn't put her finger on exactly why.

"Your silence frightens me," Mickey called from the bedroom.

Boom, that was it, the nudge to the frontal lobe releasing the frustrated neurotransmitter that jumped the dendrites. "Samanov," she called.

"Mm."

"Where's your family hail from?"

"Russia."

"And was the family name…more Russian?"

"Samanovananonvich."

"Mikhail" equals "Mickey;" whatever-he-said equals "Samanov." Which suddenly added one more ingredient to the over-seasoned gumbo that was Mickey Samanov, this strange – if strangely compelling – blend of highbrow intelligence and lowbrow attitude, someone quick on his feet but slow to catch on, at ease in this mansion or skimming pool scum.

She noticed a framed photograph on the wall, a family portrait. Most prominent was a striking patriarch, handsome but allergic to smiling. Ramrod straight, he stood behind his equally as handsome seated wife; a wife who had just the hint of a smile that suggested an independent streak that this husband, no doubt, did not suffer lightly; a wife who, with a child of three or four in her lap, seemed less a mother and more a model to sit in for the mother, but unable to strike a nurturing pose. The studio portrait was in color – the woman's hair a natural bright red, her eyes an arresting green – but it could have been taken by Matthew Brady. "Picture in the hall," she called back to the bedroom, "is this the happy family?"

"You're half right."

The next door opened into the smoking room, complete with a glass-walled walk-in humidor. "Gotta say," she said, "I didn't take you for someone who lived in these kind of digs."

'These kind of digs' happened to be in Pacific Heights, a.k.a. the gilded non-hoi polloi of San Francisco where the nouveaux riches of Silicon Valley drove criminally inflated prices even higher before the bubble burst; where the priciest views had the best unobstructed sight lines to Alcatraz and, ironically, the best sight lines from Alcatraz toward Pacific Heights were from solitary confinement. This particular address was just a few blocks off the "Gold Coast" of Broadway and Divisidero, a Victorian styled, or "painted lady" (that is, ho-ish, to the early 20th century architectural cognoscenti) palace. It was built by an industrialist who made his fortune in leather tanning, which was why the walls of the smoking room were padded in leather that retained the superior aroma of rich Cuban leaf. Danica Farburger had never experienced the Freudian joy of a good cigar, but the ghost of evenings past in this chamber suggested that there was more to life between orgasms than waiting for Nick to call; or for Nick to come home; or for Nick to remember their anniversary. Then there was the tactile nature of the leather itself, impossible to resist, her hand caressing the supple, buttery surface.

"You wanna fondle aged skin, let's go back to bed," Mickey said, suddenly behind her in his nonchalant birthday suit. "Where'd you figure I lived?"

"A double-wide...dangerously leaning...family of raccoons underneath."

He smiled, scratched an impolite itch. Actually, she only saw his business card, he never said he himself plied the water and chlorine arts; that was something she assumed from his directionless 40-something pool cleaner appearance. "Guess bullshit's a growth industry these days," she said. He gave her the RCA dog look. "Your so-called marriage counseling," she clarified, "must be a license to print money." He didn't say it wasn't. Still, she found it harder to believe than Nikki's excuse for being M.I.A. last night (too drunk to drive, slept on a couch in the Crazy Horse office, blah-blah-blah) that Samanov could afford a crib like this based on his rut-for-the-moment approach to relationships.

"Funny…one would think your degree of divinity would be hanging somewhere," she said, scanning the walls.

"It's at my Marin address," he said. She tried not to act impressed. "In any case, right now? I'm thinking Denver."

"As in your summer retreat?"

"As in to eat. I flip a meaner omelet than I do a red-head." Somehow that seemed plausible. Still, she hesitated. "Don't worry," he lied, with an earnestness that would have made Bernie Madoff proud, "there is absolutely no future between us past breakfast. It is the last meal Danica Farburger and Mickey Samanov will ever eat together."

It turned out to be the last meal Danica Farburger and Mickey Samanov would ever eat. Period.[4]

Tuesday, April 6th, 3:17 p.m. – Paris

Time was of the essence. Aaron the killer would have a difficult time blending into the Hotel Meurice on Rue de Rivoli where Mikhail Samanovananonvich always stayed while in Paris.[5] But Aaron the dog groomer in his lilac

---

4   In this house.

5   First opened in 1816, it was visited by the likes of Melville (who was inspired to write *Moby Dick* after trying in vain during

faux military jacket and matching lilac spandex pants, was a familiar *accessoire nécessaire* in such an establishment.

Aaron breezed through the lobby, got on the elevator and went up to Mikhail's room, a receipt for which had been among his papers. At the door, he zipped open his grooming kit to reveal no scissors or brushes, but tools of quite a different trade. He slid a blank magnetic card through the door swipe, swiped it again on a portable electronic reset, punched in new numbers and *voila*, entrance was gained more easily than Scheherazade talking to a rock.

Aaron found the room's safe in the closet, also secured by magnetic interface that was soon breached. He removed a briefcase that contained several inch-thick files. On Mikhail's desk were some personal papers, Aaron snatched those as well. Those were the only items he took from the room (besides the chocolate on the pillow, two bars of soap, some shampoo – and of course you can't have shampoo without conditioner – hand crème, the plush robe and, naturally, the slippers to go with, as well as the entire contents of the mini-bar…and obviously a suitcase to pack all this in). Oh, and the snacks basket.

What Aaron couldn't know as he exited the suite was how close he had come to death. Someone else was in there, someone who had arrived ahead of him by minutes and was concealed by the beaux arts divider that Aaron had not

---

a two-week stay to find the rude albino concierge), home of Salvador Dali for thirty years (who invented Surrealism after a plate of bad *repand le flambé* in the Le Meurice restaurant), and the headquarters of Commandant General von Cholitz (who refused Hitler's orders to burn Paris at war's end because, seriously, *der Fuehrer* was crazier than a shithouse rat).

looked behind as he wasn't searching for a person; a person who had also waited for Mikhail Samanovananonvich that same morning outside the police station but who did not expect Aaron to intercept Mikhail first; a person who, soon after Mikhail's death, went to the police to describe a missing person very similar to Mikhail, and was then allowed to view the body in the morgue; a person who, while viewing, deftly removed the hotel card key still inside a jacket pocket; a person every bit as deadly and skilled as Aaron Zworkan, and then some.

Aaron drove his Peugeot 207CC[6] to his second-floor Montmartre flat, within view of the *Basilique du Sacre-Coeur*, where priests still pray twenty-four hours a day for atonement as regards the uncivilized screwing the French gave the enemy in the Franco-Prussian war.[7] Aaron entered the Spartan dwellings, double-latched the door, then sat down to peruse the contents of the briefcase. Even for someone like Aaron, whose most-read authors included Sun Tzu, Machiavelli, Ayn Rand and political theorist Ann Coulter, it was arcane and exceedingly slow going. Afternoon became evening and then night; in fact he didn't realize how late it was until his body, denied a ritual it had grown to crave, began to tingle in anticipation.

---

6   *Elegant design, high quality finish, and a drive to match…Puegot… the drive of your life.*

7   Even though it was the Prussians who crucified Pierre-Charles Debray on the blades of his nearby windmill-cum-tavern-cum-dance hall that would later be known as the Moulin Rouge; no doubt they were unhappy about arriving a few decades early for the original girls-gone-wild stage show.

Unable to deny himself any longer, Aaron put on the teapot and disrobed. Naked, he turned off the lights, lighting exactly seventy-seven candles that gave the quarters an eerie devotional glow. Whereupon he prepared 1.89 liters of steaming chamomile tea, poured it into an enema bag, and administered the contents to himself, blurring pleasure and pain, as if to flush out demons more than the contents of his colon as he bit into a rubber baton to silence his shrieks. After feeling returned to his jaw and innards, he went to his refrigerator to reveal carton upon carton of fresh buttermilk. This he poured into his bathtub, then lowered himself into the ivory thickness as an hourglass marked time. Exactly one hour later, he entered his bedroom that contained only a hard wooden frame with no sheet or blanket, and a cinderblock for a pillow. Standing before a full-length mirror, he watched as he flagellated himself with an olive branch resulting in huge welts that raised all over his torso. This he did every night and twice on holy days.

That Aaron Zworkan marched to the beat of a troubled, discordant drummer could not be denied. What could be denied, however, was that Aaron Zworkan was anything like his percussionist. Assuming Warhol was correct, Aaron was preparing for his upcoming fifteen minutes. If this story and his position as antagonist was to ever come out (and who are we kidding, these stories *always* come out) Aaron had constructed compelling pathological elements to make him a rich man, elements that had no bearing on any aspect of his personality but would make for fascinating analysis to the lucky biographer who won a premium bid for the life rights to a killer who performed such unnatural acts so open to phrenic interpretation; acts, too, that would spare him from harsh judgment for a reduced sentence in a hospital ward. But most important to Aaron, serial killers with no sense of style or ritual were like, well...American light beer. All the horror but half as satisfying.

Covered in cross-hatchings of blood, he donned his late mother's purple silk robe[8] then pulled up several floorboards to expose beneath an ancient oak box with pewter hinges. He lifted it out, opened it, and revealed a velvet depression awaiting that which conformed to its contours. From his previous day's labors, Aaron came forth with said object wrapped in a chamois. He reverently unwrapped it, then used soft, freshly laundered 800-thread Egyptian cotton towels to wipe the object's glistening surface of petroleum jelly and any evidence of Mikhail Samanovananonvich. He then lovingly oiled every square millimeter of the object to defend against time and moisture. Finally, he placed the object into its place of repose in the box. Were this a cinematic moment, it would call for a memorable music sting to complement an overhead shot as the box, still open, was returned to its hiding place, catching just enough candlelight to be identified:

A twelfth-century metal glove.

The right hand metal glove of a knight, to be exact.

The right hand metal glove of a knight named Jacque de Molay to be perfectly exact; a knight whose story was so disturbing, whose end was so grotesque, whose part in this

---

8   Granted, a bit too Alfred Hitchcock, but *imagine* the field day they'll have with that!

Passion Play was so central that it could not be revealed for another two-hundred and fifty-six pages.[9]

Aaron closed the box and replaced the floorboards. He then poured himself a glass of pomegranate juice as purple as his mother's robe[10] and resumed the perusal of Mikhail Samanovananonvich's papers. This time, however, it didn't take him long to find something of – memorable musical sting – extremely interesting value.

Still throwing on clothes, Aaron rushed into the streets, coming to a phone booth some blocks away outside a boisterous nightclub. He dialed. Three rings. An answer with no welcome.

"It is the Fist," huffed Aaron.

"Which Fist is that?"

Apparently one of six hundred thousand, four hundred and fifty fucking killers in Paris who call themselves the Fist of God and sound like a castrato with a mouthful of razor blades. "The Fist of God," he said edgily.

"One can never be too careful," said the listener again, "when the stakes are this high."

Yeah-yeah-yeah-yeah. "Mikhail Samanovananonvich did not have the information we seek among his papers. But he has something that will no doubt get us to it." He paused dramatically. "A son."

Momentous music sting.

"How do you know?"

"A photograph among his papers…Mikhail beside a boy in secondary school, the picture possibly taken at graduation, holding some award."

_____

9   Give or take.

10   No special significance, he just liked antioxidants.

After a profound non-response that told Aaron the listener did not take the news as momentously as he did: "How can you be certain the son can lead us to what the father no longer can?"

"The photograph is old and dog-eared from handling. Only a father who loves his son would carry this picture so long afterward. The award appears to be for scholarship. Which makes perfect sense, as any father as learned as Mikhail Samanovananonvich would not have suffered a son who was anything less."

There was a not unmollifying logic to this. "You seem confident in finding this son."

"I have Mikhail's address. Mikhail Samanovananonvich *fils* is as good as ours."

Which in any other story would *demand* a slam-cut to said son in the narrative…if not for that irksome but deadly other person in the hotel room today. Which requires that we make a slight literary detour…

The start of World War II – Antwerp, Belgium

Jean-Henri Vandersmissen was not his real name nor the name Interpol had for him in its Odessa File;[11] nor was it

---

11   "ODESSA" is an acronym for the German phrase "Organisation der ehemaligen SS-Angehörigen", or the "Organization of Former Members of the SS". Said to be a fictional Nazi organization to protect SS military personnel and their collaborators after the war, this is yet one more case of fiction writers trumping pointy-headed East coast nay-saying so-called intellectual historians who still refuse to believe that the moon landing was completely fabricated on a sound stage in Van Nuys, California, that

the name the OSS, the FBI and later the CIA had for this person when, after the close of World War II, they sought to bring him to justice.

Ironically, before the war young Jean-Henri had done nothing afoul of the law that couldn't be erased in a confession booth. An orphan who by age ten realized with his limp he would never be adopted, he traded the regimentation of the nuns for freedom in the streets of Antwerp, stealing food to eat, siphoning gas to sell, and taking advantage of any situation that allowed the smallest net gain by sundown that he might survive to do the same the following sunrise. Certainly survival in the eyes of God was no crime. Indeed, God made him clever by half, as he became street-conversant in French and German besides his native Flemish. As for the war spreading like typhus across the globe, nothing would change for him whether the Axis or Allies won. This is not to say that Jean-Henri was a poster child for Hannah Arendt's banality of evil. But his moral compass pointed to another north, in which God was irrelevant not because He didn't exist to Jean-Henri, but because Jean-Henri felt *he* didn't exist to Him.

Jean-Henri's road to riches was begun by the Nazis when they opened an industrial-strength can of blitzkrieg on Belgium, France and the Netherlands. The Port of Antwerp was overrun by frantic Europeans willing to give half their fortune for a skiff that might or might not make

---

Bill Clinton has been and is still killing associates who got in the way of his career, and that Snopes.com, which debunks the Bill Clinton Body Count is in fact run by Hillary.

the crossing. Where all saw the End of Days, however, young urchin Jean-Henri saw the beginning.

As in any seacoast city, the prevalent culinary fare among restaurants became seafood, and a common emblem on their facades a round life preserver. Amid the frenzy, Jean-Henri set free a good two dozen such wooden emblems, taking a few at a time down to the docks where he sold them as actual flotation devices to those boarding overcrowded rowboats. Bidding broke out around him, the faux devices going for thirty, forty francs; by day's end his last few went for over a hundred.

That night, he allowed himself the luxury of his first hotel room, a suite with a view of the bedlam below; it went for a fraction of the cost and room service was spotty. But it was his first taste of extravagance and the appetite would never leave him, his appetite only growing until, decades later, his narrative would intersect ours in a most impactful way.

Why bring all this up now? Because just as Jean-Henri's talents and appetite grew in the rich loam of hostilities, a narrative begins modestly and grows just so under the proper conditions...think of this detour as story fertilizer.

Wednesday, April 7ᵗʰ, 7:21 a.m. – San Francisco

If Mickey had known this was his last meal, he would have made waffles.

While Danica considered her night with Mickey as much fun between two people as a bone marrow transplant, the romantic in Mickey liked to think of it as a first date…except, y'know, for the part about actual penetration. His mornings-after usually ended at the front door with a parting tongue wrestle, a little grab-ass, and, if the night before she did that thing most husbands only get on their birthday, cab fare. This date, however, would lack such a Jane Austen-like conclusion. In fact it's fair to say in the history of embarrassing mornings-after, this might rank in the top ten.

Mickey had proposed breakfast. He and Danica made their way down the circular staircase, crossing the grand foyer into a surprisingly intimate kitchen, as unaware of their nakedness as pre-fruit Adam and Eve.

"What'd your father do?" she asked off-handedly.

"Still does. He's an author."

"What kind of books?"

"Didn't the interrogation end yesterday?"

"Just curious."

"Why?"

"Small talk."

"Sounds more like interest."

"The same interest I have for a two-headed cow fetus at the fair."

"Stop with the compliments."

Samanov pulled out a mixing bowl, whisk, eggs, ham, various garden-grown spices and vegetables, and began dicing an onion with the skill of a seasoned sauté chef. Finally he said, "You saw his work in the library. He's written twenty-some books on religious esoterica, any one of which could make God himself nod off in the foreword. He's also a consultant to the Archdiocese of San Francisco, a board

member of the Catholic League, and teaches biblical studies at Stanford." He was whisking the eggs with more vigor
than required.

Down this path lay the answer to Samanov versus
Samanovananonvich. "So what's the story?"

"Of...?"

"You and Mick Daddy."

"No offense, but I'd much rather be swapping spit than
history."

"Pardon me while I wash with lye and a wire brush."

"Why you wanna know?"

"Maybe the cop in me."

"Bullshit, the cop in you checked out—," he looked
to his wrist at the only accoutrement covering flesh on
his body, "—ten hours ago with the immortal words, 'So,
Samanov, got some etchings you wanna show me?,' then
proceeded to inflict your own brand of cruel and unusual
punishment."

She loathed admitting he was right. Not about the
punishment, he had that coming. But why was she so
intent on being the equivalent of a second-billed star in the
umpteenth sequel of an action franchise who was *finally*
going to be the one to get under the lead's moody, lone-
wolf psyche and get him to spill his soul before she died in
a hail of bullets? Was it just because the Mickey she almost
booked last night was not the Mickey who clearly grew up
amid affluence and academia? And perhaps this bruised
apple couldn't have fallen far from the tree? The clatter
of a plate in front of her and the aroma of artery-clogging
animal fat finally snapped her to.

"Okay, Samanov," she said, "I'll tell you why I wanna know." She took a bite. "Damn, where'd you learn to cook this good?"

"Fourth wife was a chef."

She swallowed, finished her thought. "Because you're pathetic."

Mickey smiled, and opened his arms to indicate their surroundings. "Everyone should be this pathetic."

"True...if you lived here." Mickey had led with his chin and got tagged with a straight right. "There's not a single picture of you in this place beyond that family picture, which, given your bloated sense of self would show a level of restraint worthy of Ripley's. And most people don't hang pictures of people they can barely talk about. Table by the front door, it has a six inch stack of unopened mail, at least a week's worth, if you lived here you would've have opened it. The name on the top letter's out of a Russian novel, meaning your father's. I'm betting your family name didn't change between the old world and Ellis Island, it changed between senior and junior, which means if this house is his address it sure as hell ain't yours. My guess is while the cat's away, the mouse wanted a cubbyhole upgrade to impress his date and I'd shit in my hat if it's the first time you've done it." Samanov was Mike Tyson crawling on the canvas groping for his mouthpiece, a voice above him tolling *five...six...seven*. Then, just to make sure he stayed down for the count, "And by the way...your dad's in France." His look asked the conspicuous question. "Top letter on the stack, Air France frequent flyer club. Where is he, Paris?"

Mickey's cornermen were dragging his whupped ass from the ring but, just to squeeze one last drop of dairy from an already over-milked metaphor, he had the final word with Larry Merchant.

"Since you feel free to shoot from the lip, allow me." She shrugged, ready for whatever he was about to throw. "You're a lesbian who goes home with a man, *doesn't* sleep with him but wants her partner to *think* she has when said partner doesn't give a shit. Meaning you were pissed off enough to do something stupid, but not too stupid to do it right, with another woman, which would push your partner hard enough and get a real test of her feelings...a partner who already has a pretty good test of yours. Which tells me you don't have enough self-esteem to bail on a world-class bitch who has the balls to use a cliché like 'soul mate' 'cause she can't be bothered to come up with something original, and she'll eventually break your heart into a thousand little pieces. Whereupon she'll move on to someone else. And the person who finally tests her, who finally pushes back? That's her," air quotes, "'soul mate.'" Mickey shook his head. "You'd rather live in hell *with* her, than live with an ounce of self-respect without her. Which makes you slightly more pathetic than I am."

Danica was witness to the unthinkable: That Samanov was abso-fucking-lutely on the nose. How could someone so proudly ignorant of his own shortcomings be so insightful about someone else's? It couldn't possibly be...that as a counselor... (dare she say it?)...he actually *knew what he was doing?* Jesus, that'd have to be one of the seven signs of the Apocalypse.

Mickey, having the good sense not to be a sore winner, remained silent. As did Danica. Finally, quietly, she just said, "…yeah." That was it. But in that soft answer he sensed the nascent rumbling of strength that she knew was there to draw upon. And in the silence that continued, he knew some small reserve of good sense had phoned her ever-diminishing dignity and this time, *this* time, it answered. Danica wasn't one to believe in fate, in some cosmic calibration that kept the universe in balance, but maybe, in her and Mickey's random meeting, there was some larger purpose; and maybe she needed to hear the truth from the person she least expected to hear it from, and in hearing it from so unexpected a source she could finally —

Brian Johnson interrupted matters like a lobbed grenade. Danica's head whipped toward the phone hard enough to require a lawyer. "Don't answer it," Mickey said. "Do…not…answer." But it was like telling the ocean not to make waves…the moon not to rise…Elvis not to eat a chocolate éclair. Before he could think of a less clichéd simile, she was running up the stairs. Then tentatively, hopeful, he heard, "Hello…?" (Was that a sniffle?) "Hi, babe…" Mickey felt his psyche sag. Whoever said 'tis better to have loved and lost blah-blah-blah, he'd like to pop a cap in his sorry ass. Even if he was already dead. He'd like to dig up his coffin, pry it open, and shoot his sorry pile of dust in the ass.

Mickey stood, scraped the plates, put everything in the dishwasher and decided to go through a rinse cycle himself. He sauntered toward the stairs, egg and ham reasserting itself in a belch…which almost masked a noise from the kitchen that sounded amazingly like the scrape of a glass cutter on a fulcrum making a perfect circle large enough for a hand to reach through and unlock the door.

Wednesday, April 7ᵗʰ, one hour-seven minutes earlier – San Francisco

The Fist of God had arrived.

Stepping for the first time on American carpeted airport, he was disappointed to see that his zebra Mohawk fit more seamlessly into San Francisco than it did in Paris. He brought none of his tools with him, all would be provided. Though his two suitcases did raise an eyebrow leaving De Gaulle, filled with cartons of buttermilk packed in dry ice, boxes of chamomile tea, an enema bag, candles and olive branches.

"What is this for?" asked the skeptical x-ray security agent.

"My legacy, sir," was the tart high-pitched reply.

"And…what legacy would that be?"

"In due time," Aaron smiled insidiously, "you'll read the news. Then you'll read the international bestseller based on the news. Then you'll see the movie based on the international bestseller inspired by the news. Then you'll be able to tell your snot-nosed children that in your otherwise meaningless job and pointless existence that on this day…you actually met…the Fist of God. Remember that, sir. The Fist…of God."

"Okay. You're free to board." One could overdo this post-9/11 suspicion thing.

As Aaron awaited his American contact, the aroma of baked buttery croissants wafted his way from an airport concession. He smiled. In this *nouvelle terre* that wasn't even as old as some Left Bank restaurants, in this, the birthplace of fast food, in a country that viewed obesity as the birthright of first-world over-consumption, it was comforting to know that a little French culture managed to sprout in a society which valued pleasing the palate with the mass production of sodium-laced, corn syrup-rich, empty-caloried brand-name placebo food grunted onto a conveyor belt from the sphincter of a mechanical intestine, that would only be processed again through consumers' intestines to their detriment. Aaron approached the concession and made his first purchase in America: Three flakey, air-filled pastries that, upon contact with his lips, transported him back to summers spent at his grandfather's just outside Orleans, and their early morning walks hand-in-hand to the *La Bonne de la Boulangerie d'Orléans*. There the two would watch the croissants come right from the oven as the baker picked one off the sheet and handed it to the excited little boy; a little boy who loved to read the classics and was normal in all ways (if one overlooked the missing neighborhood cats, his collection of American Tab Hunter movie posters and the five straight wins that would later follow in the annual village Edith Piaf Look-Alike Contest, still a record), who in eight more summers would intern at his uncle's veterinary hospital where one day he would place his glass of ginger water next to a beaker of carbolic acid, reach to slake his thirst, and forever change the way the world heard and perceived him. But such unpleasantness melted away as the layered Eucharist met his tongue, this sacrament of all that is sacred to French gastronomic worship, and took him back to a point in his life when food was a simple pleasure for a simple time; a reminder that in France, sometimes its greatest manifestations are its most basic pleasures.[12]

"Aaron Zworkan?" Aaron turned to face the pleasingly handsome speaker. "You are here on the private matter of all men?" he asked. Aaron smiled. This was his American contact.

Tuesday, April 6th, 2:07 p.m. – Paris

The file landed on his desk with the thud of a gravestone. Inspector Renault opened it to find that Mikhail Samanovananonvich had been murdered. But then Mikhail *was* working on something of a religious nature, in the city of international religious thrillers. Still, there were curious anomalies surrounding his death, per the report. First, that the murder was so close to the police station, not a hundred meters away, seemed to indicate that whoever

---

12   Ah, sad, tragic Aaron! For all his learning, what a poor bastard to not know that the croissant was not French in origin, but Austrian; and that it was born in 1683 out of a siege by the Ottoman Turks on the city of Vienna; and that when King John III of Poland finally drove the Turks away, the bakers of the city celebrated by making a pastry in the shape of the Islamic crescent moon; and that the kipfel, as it was known there, would not find its way to France for almost a *hundred* years when King Louis XVI arranged to marry a fifteen year-old Austrian princess named Marie Antoinette, who brought with her a love of the pastry.

did it either felt that he or she could operate with almost complete impunity (no doubt a man), or else he or she had no sense of geography (clearly, a woman). Second, per the medical bracelet on Samanovananonvich's wrist, he was a diabetic; the coroner's report stated that he died from an insulin overdose, indicating that the assailant had some familiarity with his victim. Third, his wallet contained almost 700 francs. Mikhail claimed he was robbed the night before.

There was another piece of business worth noting that, however queer, actually had a certain logic. To wit:

Though Mikhail had been taken deep into the alley, after he was injected with insulin he almost made it back to the street. In one of those fortuitous twists of plot convenience,[13] Mikhail, staggering, red faced, just happened upon a fellow American strolling by, sipping a non-fat double latte extra foam from an over-franchised coffee chain that would rank as a second product placement if this were a film.

"You okay, man?" the backpacking tourist asked, recounting this to the gendarmes, suggesting that Americans are either masters of understatement or pretty goddamn slow to grasp the situation. When Mikhail heard the man speak English he knew he had fortuitously found

13   Why point this out? To beat many readers to the punch before they groan. It's worth noting that critics have forever given Victor Hugo free reign to traffic in much more egregious plot conveniences, apparently because he writes in French and had a hit Broadway play, but those same critics turn into a torch-carrying village mob in search of the stitched-together miscreant who dares try it in English.

one person in this foreign land to whom he could speak his very last thought. Whereupon the American heard the final utterance Mikhail would ever say before he disappeared into eternity. What he said, several times and in English, was..."mice."

In French, for the report...*souris.*

Why at the moment of death was he concerned with rodents? Having just been in a garbage-filled backstreet no doubt overrun with them, was it possible that Mikhail felt the need to warn others from entering?

"Inspector Renault!" he heard sharply, looking up to see Police Chief Jean-Claude Poujouly before him. Grey and jowly, Poujouly looked 63, which he should have since that was his age. The reason he looked it: City Hall. As police chief his ass was fodder for trickle-down blame from up top, and for once bad movies and television got it right. Which is why Renault was always careful to exhibit just enough job skill to justify his annual cost-of-living raise and bottle of Christmas cognac, but not so much as to elevate himself anywhere near ass-fodder proximity.

Renault was intrigued to see two priests flanking Poujouly. Both were surprisingly broad shouldered and fit – even a little intimidating. Per their vestments, Renault could tell that they were from the Order of St. Dominic. But your garden-variety clerics did not stand in the military at-ease position. Both had dark hair buzzed short, the only major difference between the two being that one looked more Mediterranean in his olive complexion.

"Inspector Renault, this is Fr. Rossellini and Fr. DeSica," said Poujouly. "They've come from the Vatican in regards

to the Samanovananonvich case and I have been commanded from the highest levels...," he couldn't help but
sigh, "...in city hall...to extend them every courtesy."

"Do they speak French?" asked Renault, already reaching for the phone to call an interpreter.

"We do," said the Mediterranean.

"I grew up reading your Victor Hugo," said the other.

Renault, raising an eyebrow, asked, "How may I help
you?" Poujouly, he noticed, walked away with the odd
urgency of a novitiate parked in the monsignor's space.

"We understand there are three documents as regards
Mikhail Samanovananonvich," said the Mediterranean –
Fr. DeSica – in a clipped, procedural tone. "A statement
he gave post-assault, a report after he was found dead, and
a coroner's statement."

"We'd like to see all three, please," said Rossellini, in
the same crisp manner.

"*Certainement*, though the files may not leave the premises." Both looked at Renault, silent. "That is, you may sit
here and read them under my supervision. You may not
take notes, however." The same passive response. Renault
shifted in his seat. "The press and his family know nothing
of this homicide, do you understand?"

"The documents please," said Fr. DeSica. *Jesus. Guess
these two slept in the day they taught the Sermon on the Mount.*
Renault placed all three folders in front of them. They
sat, each picking up a file, inspecting it...whereupon something suddenly struck Renault.

"If I may ask...as the press know nothing of this...how
did you hear of it in Rome?"

"He was doing research for us," said Fr. Rossellini from behind his file. Not that it answered the question.

"Research. For...?"

"The Holy Father," said DeSica, who also did not bother to look up.

"Regarding?"

An annoyed pause. "The blessed father has a new decree, *ex cathedra*, coming out and M. Samanovananonvich was making sure of historical context."

"Interesting," said Renault, nonchalant, "in the statement I took from M. Samanovananonvich, he said he was doing research for a comparative study on the four gospels." That met with a towering Babel of silence. "And I seem to recall from catechism that anything *ex cathedra* was infallible since it was channeled by the Holy Father as divine revelation."

One-Mississippi, two-Mississippi, three— "What are you implying?" said DeSica. Both were looking up.

Renault shrugged, certainly not equipped to go mano-a-mano with papal ambassadors on matters of dogma; furthermore, he feared this line of questioning might appear more ambitious than his station. But there was something about these two. "What need is there to fact-check the Holy Father if he is merely the mouthpiece for the Holy Spirit?"

DeSica and Rossellini exchanged a look – *we got us a live one* – then turned back to Renault. "With all due respect, Inspector Renault," said Rossellini, "we are not here to discuss theology."

Renault was aware that any sentence that began "with all due respect," even from sanctified foot soldiers of God,

really meant *you insignificant speck of ant shit.* He couldn't
resist a little spear to the ribs. "As he was in the church's
employ at the time of death, I will need statements from
both of you as to the nature of said employment."

"Not to diminish your authority," said Fr. DeSica (rough
translation: *Ask that again, dickwipe, you'll be demoted to sneeze
guard cleaner in the precinct cafeteria buffet*), "I believe our
superior will get your superior to overrule that." DeSica,
returning to his file and coming to the word *souris,* pointed
to it, showing Rossellini, asking uncertainly in Italian, "*molti
mouse?*" The other stared at it just as uncertainly.

When the two priests finished, they stood up as one and
bowed with stiff courtesy. "I sincerely hope you fall down
an elevator shaft," said Renault ("It was a pleasure being of
service"). "May you fry in a lake of fire as demons shove hot
coals into every orifice," Rossellini replied. ("The pleasure
was ours.") Renault watched them leave, and thought he
noticed something only a policeman might discern under
their cassocks.

Kevlar vests...?[14]

---

14   In 12th century Rome, word of *hashshaseen,* Shi'ite assassins formed by extremist poet Hassan-I Sabbah, as well as their
effectiveness filtered back via the Crusades to Pope Innocent
III, a papal misnomer if ever there was one. This is the pope
who condemns the signing of the Magna Carta as "contrary to
moral law," since England is a subject of Rome and no law of
man dare supersede the law of God (ergo his representative, Mr.
Innocent). This is the pope who launches the Fourth Crusade,
which stops in Constantinople to rape and pillage since the East-
ern Orthodox Church split with Rome a century earlier and was
overdue for a serious bitch slapping. This is the pope who orders

Wednesday, April 7th, 7:27 a.m. – San Francisco

Danica was shocked to hear that Samanov had a daughter. And that she was in the house. Upstairs, curled under the goose down comforter, phone to ear, the little girl's urgent shriek flipped Danica from scorned and vulnerable to armed and dangerous. "Call you back," she barked to Nikki, springing from the bed.

fellow Christians, the Cathars in France, to be put to death to the tune of tens of thousands for heresy. By the end of his papacy, Innocent in fact killed more Christians than emperors Diocletian and Nero combined, the Catholic Encyclopedia, summarizing this indiscretion with the succinct phrase, *Innocent was also a zealous protector of the true Faith and a strenuous opponent of heresy.* (Since the Church of Rome chooses to treat this as a footnote, so do we.)

This pope is rumored to do one more thing. Innocent apparently sees the P.R. value in such an organization as the *hashshaseen.* Not just for assassination per se, but for various and sundry odds and ends that are better dealt with on the down-low. And so he reportedly begins a secret group known as the Order of Extreme Unction. ("Extreme unction" a.k.a. "final annointing," is one of the seven Catholic sacraments, given to those who are old, grievously ill, or about to die.) These are priests who, it is rumored, are schooled in the deadly arts of their time, who have the ability – indeed, the license – to kill and then, conveniently, perform last rites on those victims who at least are Christian. These are priests who supposedly work under *direct* order of the Holy See. All that said, however, it is very important to note that it has never been proved whether they ever truly existed. And if they existed, it is just as important to note that it has never been proved whether they ever performed an actual mission for Pope Innocent III or any other pope thereafter.

In fact, forget they were ever mentioned.

With death imminent, triggering the mind to recap glorious victories, ignoble defeats, and recollections that defy category like spying on Manny Detwiler's older sister repurposing her electric toothbrush in a way not intended by its manufacturer, Mickey wanted only one image to take him into the light: That of five-foot-six, one-hundred-fifteen pounds, bikini-waxed Danica Farburger naked, stepping down the stairs, a taut sculpture with a .357 at the end of her extended arms pointing wherever those perfect, perky, untouched-by-Mickey breasts did. And being a true redhead was added value. If one had put a gun to Samanov's head – besides the one Danica would soon see already there – Samanov couldn't think of any anything better he'd *want* to take with him into eternity.

Danica advanced far enough down the spiral to see just inside the kitchen two assailants, one darkly handsome with day-old stubble and the *au courant* look from the Land's End Bad Guy Catalogue, a gun pointed at her; the other with the most perfect buttermilk skin she'd ever seen, made whiter by the abundance of black leather (the zebra Mohawk was old news, this being San Francisco), behind Mickey holding a gun to his temple in a hand, oddly, wearing an ancient chain-mail glove. Mickey watched her, hands raised, his dangling manhood confused between happy-to-see-you and I'm-a-gonna-die. Danica stepped from the stairs into the foyer, staking her ground. Samanov gave thanks to the law enforcement genius who came up with the wide-legged shooting stance.

Danica's unblinking game face would make most perps wet themselves. "Where is she?" she demanded. The two men looked at her, confused. "The little girl I heard scream." Realizing, the men burst into wracking, belly-grabbing laughter that threatened to render them defenseless. Mickey flushed red, giving her the answer. "That was *you?*"

"Hey...*you* turn and see *that*—," a nod to the Mohawk – "breaking in with a gun and backup, and see how excitable you get." She still stared in shock and amazement; more of the former. "Thanks for understanding."

Danica addressed the two behind her revolver. "What do you want?"

The Mohawk answered in his unique-even-if-it-weren't-gay-French-accented English. "That is none of your business."

Hearing him for the first time, resisting her own burst of abs-tightening laughter, she said, "As a lieutenant on the San Francisco police force, I'm making it my business."

"Even if I believed you, and this was the American style of arrest, I'm sorry to say it's wasted on me," Aaron replied. "Leave now, and you will not become a part of this."

Mickey put himself in her position...a North Beach stripper home waiting for her who had forgotten more ways to pleasure Danica with her big toe than Mickey knew with his six extremities. Tables reversed, in his heart of hearts, he knew what his choice would've been. He closed his eyes to make it easier on her.

One-Mississippi, two-Mississippi, three-Missis—

"I can't do that," Mickey misheard Danica say. He opened his eyes to see he didn't mishear at all. He felt his dingle tingle.

"I'm sorry?" said the Mohawk, not unpleased; the promise of bloodshed, even his, was a job perk.

"You're both under arrest."

And that's when things got really embarrassing.

Tuesday, April 6th, 2:06 p.m. – Italy

The big event...the theological Thrilla in Manila...was about to happen. Bishops, archbishops, cardinals were streaming into Rome for a defining *sancta synodus* to address once and for all where the church stood on whether a fetus was homosexual at conception, or was a product of free will and social conditioning; which would, of course, be a great aid in determining the nature of sin and how much penance to dole out to the pitcher versus catcher. Cardinal Thomasina, a social conditionalist, was to make the case that it was free will (however influenced by the Gay Mafia). The opposing argument, that same-sex love was all part of God's divine plan (in the Jobian sense), would be made by a conceptionist, Cardinal Michelle, author of the exercise book, *The Body of Christ in 40 Days!* How the synod decided would be a huge feather in the miter of either cardinal. Indeed, it could even prove the tipping point in the choice for the next pope.

The convocation of the synod was only six days away. Which was all the more reason Thomasina impressed upon Frs. DeSica and Rossellini that they could not fail. The reason why was not theirs to know. Or, put another way, yours.

Tuesday, April 6th*, 7:36 a.m. – San Francisco*

To return to our show already in progress:

That Danica chose to risk life and limb *without* benefit of a Samanov Love Hangover almost made Mickey forget that the only thing standing between two gun-wielding killers and a deputized gun-wielding killer of gun-wielding killers was, um, well...

...him.

The four stood stock still, three index fingers pressing ever more delicately on triggers to get that one one-hundredth of a nanosecond's advantage when the moment came, the room so silent you could hear Mickey's heart sinking. Whatever good might come from Farburger standing her ground, however much appreciation he felt, any way he sliced it this was a zero-sum proposition. Mickey was in a roomful of set mousetraps, each trap holding a ping-pong ball, and all it would take for an orgasm of white Taiwanese sweatshop-produced projectiles exploding in all directions would be someone dropping...

...that first...

...little...

...white...

...ball.

Which, of course, happened. Thanks to Mickey.

Mickey's gastrointestinal tract erupted in a mighty sirocco of the butler's revenge, a blunderbuss of high-density flatus causing his captors to choke like French soldiers inhaling mustard gas at Ypres. Danica, seeing the stench of opportunity, squeezed off one-two-three rounds in rapid succession, Samanov helping by getting the fuck out of her way, belly-flopping to the floor then making like a sand crab chasing the water line. Their return fire in retreat, random, in all directions, allowed Danica to dive behind an eighteenth-century Spanish settee, its Andalusian pine absorbing 9mm slugs from a pair of Glocks. The two flattened themselves against the walls in the kitchen on either side of the splintered doorway. As smoke and wits began to clear, the three found themselves, as before, in a Mexican stand-off (or, since this was above the Rio Grande, just a stand-off).

"Mademoiselle," Aaron said, allowing his English to take on a bit more Gallic flair, "I am impressed with your courage as much as your boyish figure. If you were a man, you might convince me to be more forgiving." Danica was too focused to answer. "Either way, the *mathématiques* are against you. There are two of us who came prepared with many clips apiece. You were not prepared. So unless you are hiding a clip in a most unsavory fashion, we have twenty times the ammunition you do."

She watched Samanov, out of their purview, continue his crab-scramble up the stairs to, she guessed, the bedroom where he'd perform an Olympic-worthy dive out a second-story window. Clearly he had a lot of practice doing it.

"Monsieur Nancy-boy," Aaron called to Mickey, assuming he was still within earshot, "give yourself up and I will kill your *amoureux* mercifully." Aaron didn't like the non-answer that followed. He peeked around the doorjamb and saw no Mickey. Whereupon, inexplicably, he began to unwrap and shove several pieces of gum into his mouth, chewing hastily.

Danica had seven rounds left in her Smith and Wesson M&P .357. Their Glocks had 33-round clips; with one or two extra clips apiece, they had at least 150 rounds between them, making her a likely contender for a closed casket ceremony.

"Monsieur Nancy-boy?" Aaron repeated as he chewed the large wad. Realizing their quarry was escaping, Danica heard urgent French, ejecting clips and fresh ones jammed into place, knowing in a matter of seconds that the antique Spanish chair she was huddled behind would remain in one piece longer than she would. She heard the countdown. "*Un....deux...tro–*"

A heavy metallic object bounced hard on the floor, for all combatants to see. Mickey stood at the top of the staircase, still naked, starting back down. "See that, gentlemen," Mickey said. "That's a police badge. It belongs to the redhead you didn't believe. You're about to kill a member of the San Francisco police force. If you've seen Clint Eastwood as Dirty Harry, you know what kind of the hornet's nest you're kicking."

Lucky for Danica that Jerry Lewis wasn't the only *acteur Américain* to win the French Legion of Honor. More urgent talk between the Mohawk and cohort.

"If it's me you want...she comes with, unharmed," he said, channeling Harry Callahan from *The Enforcer.* "Package deal."[15]

---

15 True, *The Enforcer* is much inferior to *Dirty Harry,* but more apropos insofar as Tyne Daly was the second or third-billed star

"Or what?" asked Aaron; Danica was wondering the same thing.

"Two ways to take me...the easy way...or the hard way. It's up to you." He was the picture of iron resolve...had not a small flatulence escaped him.

"The French share your love of the democratic," said Aaron. "We vote for the easy way." Then, to Danica, "Throw out your weapon." She knew she had no choice; all she could do was trust in the word of someone from the country that gave us the Statue of Liberty, champagne, and the croissant. Farburger put on the safety, then slid the gun toward the kitchen door.

She might have thought twice if she knew how horribly wrong she was about the croissant.

Tuesday, April 6ᵗʰ, 2:19 p.m. – Paris

The two priests burst out the police station doors, marching in urgent lockstep. "Mikhail's death could only be the work of one person," said Rossellini in Italian.

DeSica agreed, answering as if invoking Beelzebub, "The Fist of God!" Beethoven's 5ᵗʰ accented the moment; it blared from a passing car.

The two priests turned into the alley where Mikhail breathed his last, the stink of decay stifling, which would account for Mikhail's last word, Rossellini pointing to

_____

in a third franchise movie who was finally going to be the one to get under the lead's moody, lone-wolf psyche and persuade him to expose his own personal secret before she died in a hail of bullets.

multiple rodents declaring, "*molti mouse.*" They walked deep into the narrow space and approached the dumpster where it happened, regarding the spot somberly. Rossellini pulled out a vial of holy water and drizzled it over the area. Both bowed their heads as DeSica intoned, "O Gentlest heart of Jesus, ever present in the Blessed Sacrament, have mercy on the soul of Thy departed servant and let drops of Thy Precious Blood fall upon the devouring flames, O merciful—"

A door burst open behind them, DeSica and Rossellini spinning around, silver-plated Smith and Wesson .357 magnums pointed at a hapless minimum-wage restaurant lackey holding a box of spoiled cabbage. The priests maintained their bead on the man's forehead, their eyes boring into his soul, the moment frozen in time. Then, their quick-twitch instincts honed by experience telling them he was just a minimum-wage restaurant lackey holding a box of spoiled cabbage, they just as quickly slipped their guns into their cassocks. Fr. Rossellini blessed him, making a sign of the cross before the man's still bloodless face, intoning, "*In nomine Patris, et Filii, et Spiritus Sancti. Amen.*"

The two clerics walked to the street. The unfortunate kitchen worker added to the stench of the alley.

World War II – Antwerp, Belgium

Poor Jean-Henri Vandersmissen of Antwerp…not only an orphan and lame, he seems to be an orphan in this plot on his own lame story thread. But Jean-Henri was used to such challenges. Indeed, he thrived on them.

As the war raged, information became currency, making Jean-Henri a very rich man. Long of the boulevards and backstreets, he knew intimately which doors were locked and what was behind those that weren't; who was hoarding what commodity where; who the working girls were and where they plied their nightly arts; who their more prominent johns were and what they paid extra for; which *agent auxiliaire* or *inspecteur* was not above accepting "gratuities." After the Germans took control and order returned, Jean-Henri grew a fledgling mustache to appear older, bought two tailored suits, and negotiated a suite in the luxe hotel, much of his rooms taken up with boxes of Belgian chocolate liberated from a dockside warehouse during the chaotic exodus. With supply routes disrupted, Jean-Henri knew the last goods to return to shelves would be non-essential items that gave the most comfort. Thus he waited weeks to begin doling out his dark brown gold, making it more valuable than rationed gasoline, the rectangular slab providing a calling card to German soldiers who recognized a procurer when they saw one; a procurer whose slight stature and limp stripped away any pretense of threat. And if he had access to *this* dark delight, well…what other dark delights might he be able to provide?

Jean-Henri did not disappoint. A lonely corporal needing companionship knew Jean-Henri could not only provide it in provocative finery, but also the room with which to comingle – even if the officer didn't know he paid three times what it cost Jean-Henri. The owner of the small *pensione* Jean-Henri used for such liaisons was so grateful for the business that he would reward Jean-Henri with a

Haut-Médoc Bordeaux; which was the particular favorite of a certain German major who liked to have it with Camembert sweetened by just a touch of Swiss preserves; who in return might have an occasional gasoline ration ticket to give Jean-Henri. And so and so and so on.

Within six months Jean-Henri had moved into the hotel's penthouse, had cards printed for the business of import/export giving the phone number of the hotel's front desk, and began smoking clove-scented Moroccan cigarettes in an ivory holder to give him that international finish.

Before long Jean-Henri's contacts ranged from other street orphans all the way up to an *aide de camp* in the German High Command. His acquisitions expanded to misdirected Red Cross food shipments, illicit drugs Berlin expressly outlawed but were enjoyed by more than a few in the upper ranks, crates of rifles and bullets meant for the underground and, the *piece de resistance*, a commandeered railroad car of Northern Renaissance paintings hidden under framed canvases of cheap present-day landscapes, on their way to Switzerland.

Jean-Henri couldn't resist keeping a Frans Hals for himself. It wasn't the status of having an original master, he had never seen a Frans Hals before or knew anything about him. A striking portrait of a smiling tousled-haired, bearded man with sparkling eyes and wielding a jawbone, it hung prominently in his suite.[16] But it was the first acquisi-

16 Why a jawbone? The painting is believed to be a portrait of Pieter Verdonck, a prominent member of the most puritanical group of Mennonites in Haarlem, whose personal style was con-

tion by the orphan, who had known only institutions and streets and rented rooms, of something stable, something that existed long before him and would continue to exist long after, serving as an anchor in a world where nations and continents shifted in power overnight with the future very much in doubt. It would be the first of a very expensive habit.

A habit that might cost the lives of our protagonists. But then we're getting ahead of ourselves...

Tuesday, April 6th, 2:31 p.m. – Paris

Rossellini placed a defcon 5 call to the Papal Secretary in Rome on a scrambled frequency, requesting that His Holiness command the Archbishop of Paris to contact every parish in his archdiocese to assist in the search for the Fist of God.[17] Rossellini and DeSica had narrowly missed

---

sidered as strong as the blows that Samson of the Old Testament struck with an ass's jawbone. This was the 18th century painterly way of calling someone a stark, raving asshole without the subject knowing. In fact Pieter was said to have written that the portrait captured him perfectly.

17   This ecclesiastical all-points-bulletin first originated in the twelfth century to counter the spread of Catharism, a heretical religious sect originating in the Langeudoc area of France that revived certain Gnostic beliefs thought put to rest after the Council of Nicea. The effectiveness with which the church was able to use its ground-level organization to track down and bring to inquisition all of Catharism's adherents was the start of the Order of Ecclesiastical Adjudication which, to not a few objective observers, was a more unholy and toxic fellowship than the Opus Dei.

the Fist three years ago in Calais, bursting into his flat one night while a steaming pot of chamomile tea was still brewing. This couldn't happen again, especially if he was in possession of, or in knowledge or approximate knowledge of the whereabouts of that which he wished to possess, which was the same as that which DeSica and Rossellini wished to have possession of, or be in knowledge of, but were not. But then that goes without saying.

What the papal secretary was instructed to pass along *tout de suite* from His Holiness to all Parisian parishes, was the one odd bit of information the two were able to glean from Calais: A fine residue of buttermilk remained in the tub that came up to the overflow drain. Thus what went out to every parish priest was to find the closest creamery

---

The organization later fell under the supervision of the Dominican Order that, by the thirteenth century, was empowered to act in the name of the Pope as inquisitors of the church, and on their own could prosecute and judge heresy of any baptized Catholic without Vatican review (not that such review would have counted for a tinker's damn). During the Spanish Inquisition, the Office of Ecclesiastical Adjudication was given more jurisdiction, able to prosecute Protestant, Jewish, and Islamic *converts* to Christianity who might have lacked the – shall we say – true fervor of the faith (given that their choice at the time of conversion was either to accept Christ or become a perforated non-Christian in an iron maiden). The order eventually also became a secret police for the Spanish crown, reporting on secular matters. And in the seventeenth century during the Roman Inquisition, their most renowned prosecution was that of Galileo whose findings had the temerity to suggest that, strictly speaking, the Old Testament might not be a scientific text.

wholesaler and inquire discreetly after anyone who bought a regular allotment of buttermilk in volume. This was not, the parish priests were told, repeat was *not* to be handled by the local constabulary. And this was not, repeat was *not* any of their damn business as to why they need do this immediately. The double-intransitive verb stressed the utmost importance of the mission. To give them such dire information – i.e. "The fate of the world as we know it hangs in the balance" – would only serve to make an already melodramatic situation more so, besides sounding like the commercial thriller tripe read in airports, by pools, or on beaches.

But the fate of the world as we knew it did hang in the balance.

Tuesday, April 6ᵗʰ, somewhere over the Atlantic – time depending on time zone.

Mickey awoke with a filament of drool between lip and chest, in restraints, disoriented and naked. Which wasn't uncommon awakening protocol. Though in this case his hands were shackled to his waist, preventing them from rising above his navel. Reclined in a lounge chair, his ears popped painfully as he swallowed to moisten his throat. His left shoulder throbbed with a dull ache. He peeled his face off burgundy leather, looked around, and saw he was apparently on a private jet. A Citation Excel, to be exact. Above the seatback in front of him he saw the zebra-colored plume of the Mohawk. Mickey could hear the tinny buzz of Euro-trash techno-rock coming from the buds stuffed into the Mohawk's ears, his head bobbing wildly like a balloon on the string of an epileptic.

To his left Mickey saw Danica still asleep in a reclined chair. Whether it was that she, too, was still naked, or winsomely submissive in restraints, he couldn't help but feel a stir in his loins; a tumescence that, to his mild chagrin, would not be denied. He looked about for some kind of concealment, spotting only an airsickness bag in the seat pocket, but he didn't want to seem like he was bragging. With his captor dancing in the boy-toy disco of his mind and the object of his arousal still unconscious, Mickey just let the turtle sun on the beach.

Bits and pieces of what happened began to filter in... Danica and him on the settee at gunpoint...he and Danica injected by the Mohawk with a syringe...Danica, without a flinch, taking it like a lesbian...him sliding from the chair to the floor like a candyass just before blissful disconnection.

Mickey engaged in victim-required tugging on his restraints, but had he miraculously freed himself, strangled the Mohawk, then made his way to the cockpit, killing the pilot *and* co-pilot, Mickey had seen *Airport '75* and he was no Karen Black. Best to ride this one out then come up with Plan B. Which as of now was an Act of God.

"Why doesn't it surprise me," Samanov heard *sotto voce*, "that you can be sexually aroused right now?" He saw Danica awake, her still-blurry focus zeroed in on his perpendicularness.

"Blame evolutionary priorities," he said. "Us males wake up good to go."

"Males kidnapped at gunpoint and probably facing death, not so much." Danica took stock of their surroundings. "Samanov...who *are* these guys, what do they want?"

He could hear the seriousness in her voice. "I don't know."

Then, as much to herself as to him, "No one knows where I am...these guys are professionals...they probably found my cell phone, my clothes...took my service revolver. If they did, there's no record of my even having been at the house."

Mickey stared at her dumbly. "You're telling me that you, Danica Farburger, a trained San Francisco police officer, clocked out, went home with a potential felon, and didn't tell a man, woman, cat or *dog* where you were going?" Until now he at least held onto the slim statistical possibility that, missing one of their own, the SFPD would somehow come to their rescue. Then again, maybe he'd seen too many Dirty Harry movies.

She looked away, eyes beginning to mist. She very well could be right about his immediate future, meaning things weren't too promising for hers either. This was probably a time for Mickey to dig deep for that slender vein of selflessness that must be somewhere in his mother lode of narcissism. True, the night before she did try to seriously cripple him by testicular vasocongestion. But hell, he got to see her naked. That had to count for something.

"Danica...I honestly don't know anything. I clean pools. I don't live in a doublewide, but damn close. Granted, I've pissed off a few more people than your average pool cleaner-slash-spiritual couples' counselor...but," he said looking around in wonderment, "…no one in this tax bracket."

"Then they came for your father and took you by mistake," she tried. "Or they want to get to him through you."

"Not the smartest plan, me 'n dad haven't spoken since the days of vinyl records."

"But if they did—"

"I couldn't begin to guess why. All he does is teach, write and lecture about the faith. That's it. He's a bona fide tub-thumping believer that salvation only comes through the blood of a Jewish carpenter. Though I guess there's one enemy he's made."

"Who?" Danica had a straw to grab onto.

"The Anti-Christ's."

She couldn't be less amused if he sang show tunes out his ass. She turned away, confused, angry, unafraid to be afraid. Her stomach added its own two cents, letting out a loud, rolling grouse to be sated.

"If I could reach the stew light," he offered, "I'd get us some Chex mix." She remained turned away, silent. She suddenly seemed smaller…more fragile…not a person who walked down the foyer stairs without a trace of fear for her own safety to face two armed killers. Right now she didn't seem like she'd ever been that person; right now, she seemed like someone's daughter.

"Farburger," he began. She didn't acknowledge him. "Thanks."

Her back still faced him. "I didn't do it for you."

He admired her spine that ended in a lovely butterfly tattoo. "I know. You did it for John Q. Citizen."

"And I didn't do jack."

"Sure you did."

"…what?"

"You stayed." She just lay there. The white noise of the turbos filled the vacuum. Mickey let it go, pondered the stew light and whether he really could score some Chex Mix. He heard a sound from her direction.

"You did, too…stayed."

"The window was jammed."

"You're a worse bullshitter than you are a marriage counselor."

The Citation Excel banked left. Out the window Danica could see the nighttime establishing shot that has caused writers, painters, and directors the world over to thank the muses that such a visual shorthand exists allowing them to, as economically as possible, show or tell their audience what place on the globe their protagonists were located. The Taj Mahal for Agra, India; the Statue of Liberty for New York City; the Opera House for Sydney, Australia.

Or the Planet Hollywood for Paris, France.

Tuesday, April 6th, 8:49 p.m. – Paris

The door shattered inward, the two priests ready to pulverize anything that moved with .357 crossed-tip hollow points. They were in Aaron's Montmartre apartment. A section of flooring was pulled up revealing the hidden compartment beneath. DeSica and Rossellini knew what it had contained.

Pivoting in all directions with their guns, they entered and crossed to the bathroom. Rossellini reached in the bathtub, running his finger along the porcelain. *Yes!* He dropped to one knee, crossed himself, and gave thanks to God. The Fist may still be one step ahead, but somewhere in this flat was a clue to shorten that distance. If only they could intercept him within the next two chapters.

Wednesday, April 7th, 3:45 a.m. – Paris

The Citation Excel descended and kissed the tarmac as gently as a feather. *We may be dealing with international killers*, thought Mickey, *but they take pride in their service.* The jet taxied leisurely, Mickey and Danica exchanging looks that said they wouldn't have to worry too much longer about unreturned DVD rentals. Outside were a number of hangars housing private jets. Inside, in his seat, the Mohawk was still reducing his inner ear to marmalade with the electronic wail of a synthesizer getting its balls squeezed in a vice.

The jet rolled into a hangar like a diva making her appearance. Mickey saw a pristine Rolls Royce limousine awaiting them. Beside it stood two pituitary-active, black-clad valets who had that just-gimme-an-excuse-to-aerate-your-torso-wid-my-uzi demeanor that said they used to work for either Mossad or L'il Wayne; and the fact that the vehicle trunk was open led Mickey to guess that his bare ass wasn't going to be riding in the back seat of a Rolls anytime soon.

Danica noticed out her window another jet alongside, and a third one beyond that. Both jets had a logo on the vertical stabilizer, three identical, elongated lions flattened like road kill and lined up vertically. Below them were the initials FSL. "Samanov, look," she said turning to him. But Mickey's focus was elsewhere.

"Condition Mauve," he said tensely.

She followed his gaze to the Mohawk exchanging niceties with the pilots as they exited the cockpit; then he produced a silenced Glock and killed them. From a medical bag on the wet bar he then pulled out another industrial strength syringe. He turned and approached Danica. *"Les dames en premier,"* he said.

Ladies first. The French invented chivalry.

Wednesday, April 7th*, 4:01 a.m. – Paris*

Mickey had never seen an Angel of Death. But he was certain he was looking at two of them. With a Keith Moon-sized dose of tranquilizer coursing toward his heart, the valets carried him down the steps to the Rolls, his toes dragging on the hangar floor.

And then he saw Them.

Two silhouetted creatures in black, their wings flowing magnificently around them, boldly marched into the hangar. In time too elongated to gauge, they reached beneath their wings, outstretched their arms, and flashed hellfire, thunder booming against the hangar walls. Mickey felt the spray of gelatinous matter on one side of his head, turning to see the valet beside him crumple to the ground as if the body within the uniform had disappeared, beginning to realize he had just witnessed the Zapruder film up close and personal. The other valet had already released Mickey letting loose a continuous burp from his Uzi. The white puffs of direct hits on the angels' chests slowed them not at all. Mickey found himself supine on the cold cement before he was even aware how he got there. He attempted to rise up to watch, as it might not be until The Rapture before he saw such angels again, whereupon he placed a hand in the cottage cheese that was the dead valet's face. He decided it was best to wait for The Rapture. He felt fuzzy and good and wonderfully ineffectual, overcome with amniotic warmth even as the thunder pummeled him. Somehow he knew the Angels would pass over him, his door anointed by the blood of the sacrificial valet. Finally all was at peace as the second valet slowly fell into his purview and came to a leisurely rest on the cement, lacking a jaw. The thunder halted and leached away in weakening reports. It was about now that Mickey ceased to get reception.

Wednesday, April 7ᵗʰ, 10:14 a.m. – Paris

Mickey awoke to find he was still alive and relatively intact; he was also clothed. The bad news was, so was Danica... clothed; the alive part was good news indeed. Both were in hospital gowns, in hospital beds, sharing a non-HMO hospital room that to Mickey, unaware of the forward-thinking ways of French healthcare, was clearly going to require a mofo co-pay. He was already planning his egress before the bill came. On rollaway tables next to them sat the most saliva-inducing cuisine Mickey had seen in the last 30-some hours – a cup of ice chips and rectangle of green Jello – largely because it was the only cuisine he had seen in the last 30-some hours. But right now that looked like *foie*-fucking-*gras* marinated in cognac.

"Hello, Mikhail." Only one person besides his father called him Mikhail. Mickey turned, surprised and disoriented, to see such a familiar face standing in his doorway.

"Richard."

That would be Sir Richard Winthrop, silver maned and timeless, a Brit with that proper Brit bearing and nary a crease in his immaculate Saville Row suit, a criminal litigator who specialized in international law and had argued cases before the Hague on behalf of reason against Serbian butchers, Rwandan maniacs, and your Islamic extremist or two. It was said he had a *fatwa* pronounced against him, and that the Fourth Reich couldn't wait to brand a swastika on his chest in front of the revived head of Hitler in his Alpine hideaway. True or not, he never married or raised a family for fear of endangering a loved one. Knighted for service to Queen and country, he looked every bit the Sir but appeared to have a spastic colon whenever he was introduced as such.

A college chum of Mikhail Senior, the two met at Cambridge when Mikhail was getting his Ph.D. in Judeo-Christian philosophy. Though a devout Anglican, Richard bonded with Mikhail over spirited discussions of Luther, the Reformation, the Counter-Reformation, grace versus good works, Russian vodka versus British stout, and the best pick-up lines to get the attention of jaded mini-skirted mods. (Richard's guaranteed attention-getter: "I just returned from Fiji converting cannibals to Christianity... now they just eat fishermen on Fridays." Luckily comedy wasn't a prerequisite in his line of work.) Richard was best man at Mikhail's wedding and Mikhail would ask him to be godfather to his son.

"It's good to see you, Mikhail," Richard said. He approached and gave his godson a sincere hug. "I come, however, with terrible news." The moment Richard said it Mickey, as certain as a military wife opening the door to two uniforms, knew what that news was. "Your father is dead."

Danica had roused to hear this as well, and to see the first genuine display of emotion from Mickey. Which was no display at all. Unable to glibly toss this into the dustbin of the inappropriate with a quip, confronted with something he thought he wouldn't have to deal with for years, he was no longer a compelling paradox; he was now – just like Farburger not so long ago – reduced to being somebody's child. Despite his seeming disregard for his father, she sensed that whatever divided them had been repairable if either had made the effort; and that Mickey was mulling over that very same point, all this time having chosen the path of least resistance, as sons often do, ignoring the problem, expecting the parent to be the adult in the situation and make the first move. "I wish I could say it was from natural causes. But the truth is, your father was murdered. I don't have the facts, it was less than two days ago. Even worse, certain authorities believe your being here is directly related to his death." Richard's last statement began to give focus to the chaos that was Mickey's and Danica's last day-and-a-half. "I still haven't properly processed the news myself. I have business in Zimbabwe, was passing through, and your father and I were going to spend an evening together. Instead, the police called. They found my contact information on his person. I was asked to identify the body. I tried to locate you before I left for Africa. That's when I got the call that you were here." He paused then said, "I asked that you hear the news from me." Mickey seemed appreciative. "I understand you were spirited into the country without passports. I can call in some favors at the American consulate and expedite them for the two of you."

"Don't need it…just a one-way ticket home. Today and first class." The on-top-of-his-game Mickey would've requested Hooters Airlines.

"I…don't believe that's going to happen. You are to help in the matter of your father's death."

"Help…?" Finally he said, "I can't tell the police jack."

"It is not the police who demand your compliance," said a voice in English with a heavy Italian accent. Two priests entered; it slowly began to dawn on Mickey.

The Angels of Death.

Who they were he'd soon find out. How they tracked him down, especially from the Fist's empty apartment he'd never learn.[18] Fr. DeSica turned to Richard. "A moment,

18 For the curious: The questioning of a prostitute neighbor who found them quite fetching and had never done two clerics before revealed that, while having a post-coital cigarette on her balcony a few nights before, she overheard the Mohawk on a call arranging his flight back from America "sometime on Tuesday." Since there was an air traffic controllers' strike only the day

if you please." Richard was savvy enough to know a command. "I'll be outside, Mikhail." DeSica closed the door after him.

Foregoing even the pretense of caring about Mickey's loss, DeSica began, "Your father secretly was in the employ of the Vatican for many years on a matter of the gravest import. We need you to continue his mission."

Mickey took the proper amount of time to think about it. "No."

"The very future of Christianity depends upon it," said Rossellini.

"Yeah, well...first impressions notwithstanding, I'm really not someone who gives a shit."

"It is not a request," said DeSica.

"...Say again?"

"It is not—"

"I heard you the first time, chuckles, it's an American idiomatic phrase for 'what the fuck?'"

"You can either help us," said Rossellini, "or you can leave and we leak your whereabouts to the people who flew you here. You will not make it to the airport. And what they will do to you," he continued, indicating for the first time that Danica was even there, "...and to her...to get what information you may have...will be unpleasant beyond imagination."

---

before, it couldn't have been via commercial airline; since it was from the United States it had to be via private jet; there was only one non-commercial airport with a runway long enough to land a Citation; and as for the incredible timing of their arriving just after his jet did, well, that was chalked up to intense prayer and divine intervention.

Making her part of the equation gave Danica license. "Back off. Why do you think someone like *him* can help you?" It was meant to be supportive.

"Mr. Samanovananonvich Junior was second only to his father as a biblical scholar and helped his father research and write a number of his books," said DeSica. "That, plus the fact he was formerly a priest, makes him the most qualified person in the world to continue this mission."

Danica turned to Mickey. The look she gave him redefined the American idiom "what the fuck?"

Wednesday, April 7ᵗʰ, 12 ½ minutes later – Paris

The eighty-two year old Cardinal Thomasina, a plastic tube running from his Roman beak, pushed a walker with an oxygen tank into the room…and into every conceivable object in his path, eliciting a "*Christo Santo!*" every time.[19] The Cardinal finally made it to a chair and lowered himself into it with all the alacrity of a zeppelin docking at Lakehurst. Mickey would have been greatly annoyed by this if his arm didn't distract him, aching where the Mohawk's supersize-me needle had penetrated.

---

19   This was not a contravention of the second commandment because, a) a strict reading of the pre-King James Greek and Latin vulgate texts of Exodus show that the taking of God's name in vain referred only to oaths where one's *word* was given in His name and, b) the term "Christ" was the Greek term for the Hebrew word "messiah," which simply meant "anointed one," which could refer to a person born of natural woman as well as He born of virgin.

Finally, in a wheezing accent that demanded the listener's undivided attention (not to mention subtitles),
Cardinal Thomasina intoned, "Meeestah Sahhh-MAHN-
ovan-ANON-ah-VEEECH…ahm abow to tella you the raisin
you-ah fatha wassah wharking for-ah usssss." What followed
unfolded with all the narrative energy of Steven Hawking
reading Virgil. To summarize:

Thomasina began matters in the year 33CE at Christ's
last supper, in Jerusalem, on Mt. Zion, in an upstairs room.
And though Mickey needed no tutorial, Thomasina felt
the need to outline the context and importance of the
supper: Jesus as the descendent of the House of David in
fulfillment of the scriptures, Jesus offering himself up as
the sacrificial lamb, Jesus creating the miracle of transubstantiation, the Eucharist central to Christian communal
celebration, yada-yada-yada.[20]

However…it appears that after this meal Christ left
more behind than just his teachings. Thomasina described
one more act that had somehow escaped His biographers.
Mickey wasn't sure he'd heard correctly.

"Wait a minute. You're saying…after the Last Supper…
that Jesus pinched a loaf?"

Thomasina turned to Rossellini for translation. Then:
"Ah. Si."

Actually, as Mickey would come to learn, multiple
loaves.

---

20 It should be noted that the Cardinal avoided the whole
Christ-as-an-apocalypticist-preacher-whose-apocalypse-never-
came-in-his-or-his-immediate-followers'-lifetime issue, but then
99.9999987 % of Christians seem to overlook this one, too.

This most natural of acts went unreported in the gospels. Largely. Despite at least fifty other purported versions of Jesus's life and/or teachings floating around, the
synoptic gospels and John were the only ones to make it
to the bigs. All of this was painfully old news to Mickey.
Except for one thing: At the Nicene Council in the 4th
century, a three-verse edit was agreed upon in the Gospel
According to Mark. It was in fact the reference to Jesus'
post-supper activity. To wit:

*26 And Jesus then excused himself and went to an antecham-
ber where he knelt down and raised up his hem.*

*27 'Lord, go you to pray?' asked the brother James, 'and may
we join you?'*

*28 And the Lord replied, 'No, as the son of man I go to perform
the private matter of all men.'"*

Mickey sat up a little straighter. "Wait...what with
Abraham having concubines...or the twelve tribes of
Israel originating from various other women who were *not*
Jacob's wife...or Judah, one of the heads of those twelve
tribes, hiring a whore by the roadside who turned out to
be his daughter-in-law...or Lot's daughters knowing their
old man in the creepy sense...or David jumping the married Bathsheba and ordering Mister Bathsheba to the front
lines to be killed so that Israel's greatest king could increase
his harem...when Jesus takes a squat, *that* somehow offends
the Church of Rome's delicate sensibilities?"

But the elimination of the elimination, he was told, had
nothing to do with keeping the good book good. There
is much rich and varied storytelling that is scripture, the

Cardinal said. It was more a question of...of...? There was conferring among the three clerics.

"Inconvenience," translated Fr. DeSica.

"Inconvenience?" inquired Mickey.

"Si."

And that's when things got interesting.

It had to do with all these *other* gospels that were threatening to go viral, a few of which were particularly radioactive. The church worked overtime and had successfully made everything not Mark, Matthew, Luke and John irrelevant and unorthodox.[21] Mickey knew where Thomasina was going. "I'm guessing somewhere among the Marcionites, Ebionites, Gnostics, apocalypticists, Manicheans, and/or Mandeaeans there was corroboration for your three-verse edit of Mark."

Hearing Mickey use such terms, Danica felt like the carnival patron who got suckered into a midway sideshow by a barker promising a talking mandrill...and by God if he

---

21   Among the heretic gospels: The Gospel of Judas wherein he was really the good guy who fulfilled Gnostic scripture and freed the earthbound Jesus from his human vessel; The Gospel of Mary Magdalene who was really the one to whom Jesus spilled all his spiritual insider tips; and the Gospel of Shiloh, a little beagle who licked the blood off Jesus' face when he stumbled on the way to Mt. Calvary, the dog then barking incessantly at and ankle-biting Pontius Pilate until he had the little fella crucified, too, and now it's curled up at the collective feet of the trinity; other outlawed gospels denied us the Jesus who tanned himself on the shores of Galilee, and the Jesus who led the first conga line at the wedding at Cana.

didn't deliver. Nonetheless, she continued to watch the mandrill closely just in case it was an animatronic.

"*Essattamente*," said Thomasina, addressing Mickey's hunch. What the Church of Rome went through to become the Church of Rome was not pretty, especially with these offending gospels. But the church was pretty successful in putting them to the shredder...until 1945 and the jaw-dropping discovery of Nag Hammadi, Egypt. This was an amazing trove of biblical texts and heretic gospels that managed to slip through the cracks, discovered by several brothers out to avenge their father's death when they stopped on the way to dig for fertilizer (seriously...a blood feud was a blood feud, but good *sabakh*, found in the Jabal al-Tarif mountains, was hard to come by). Whereupon they happened upon a large earthen jar containing many of the suppressed texts.

Again, Mickey was ahead of the curve. "And they've all been published and parsed and picked over," he said impatiently, "what's the news?"

"Thee-ah noose ees thad they ees-ah three-ah gos-pulhs tha' hav-ah nev-ah behn poobleeshed thad no-ahn knows ex-eeests."

"Because...?"

"Any-ah-one outside-ah the Poop and the-ah College-ah Cardeenals whooo knowah ah-boud them...tend-ah to turnip dead."

If Thomasina said what Mickey and Danica thought he said, this was a good time for the conversation to end. Unfortunately, it did not.

Wednesday, April 7th, 4:05 a.m. – Paris

The .45 caliber soft-point exploded into Aaron's left clavicle, mushrooming in size as it did a two-and-a-half gainer through muscle and sinew, buzz-sawing bone, cartilage, and severing thousands of ducts for billions of corpuscles before a rude exit out his back more destructive than its entrance.   The force spun Aaron clockwise releasing a Jackson Pollock-worthy splash of crimson as he fell.

And then it was over.

A priest grabbed the gun from his hand and walked off. Aaron could feel life glug from his body, knowing he was going to expire sooner than buttermilk left in a tub if he didn't get proactive pretty goddamn soon.   Painfully, discreetly, he reached into a pocket, removed and unwrapped a stick of gum, and pushed it into his mouth; then a second, third, and fourth, masticating urgently.   He then pulled out a stretch and severed it with his teeth.   He rolled it into a musket ball and shoved it into the entrance wound; he repeated this with the larger remaining glob, into his exit wound (he found *Bulle Heureuse* gum worked best to stop hemorrhaging, plus it had a livelier taste).

The two priests were engrossed in a triage inspection of the over-medicated Mickey, who in all the excitement soiled himself and was giggling something about this being France, he was Pepe Le Pew.   Aaron looked around.   Within arm's length was the valet whose face resembled a casaba melon dropped from atop the Eiffel Tower.   He slid a hand under the valet's jacket and removed his backup snub-nosed .38.   Aaron then began the arduous crawl toward the open limousine.

Father DeSica noticed him. Amused, he stood up and walked toward Aaron. He and Rossellini were looking forward to getting him alone since the Vatican was not a signatory to the Geneva Conventions and they had a list of questions they intended to get answered in ways that would make Dick Cheney proud.

The purloined .38 changed everything. At the first report Rossellini threw himself atop their prize; DeSica, having left his magnum next to Mickey, dove to the floor. Aaron scrambled into the driver's seat, closed the bulletproof door and, tires screaming, weaved drunkenly out of the hangar. DeSica and Rossellini remained composed, knowing at the rate he was hemorrhaging, he would soon lose consciousness as his blood pressure dropped. But then they didn't know about *Bulle Heureuse* brand gum.

Wednesday, April 7th, 10:39 a.m. – Paris

Danica was a semi-lapsed Catholic. Baptized in the church, raised by holiday-practicing parents who were role models for what not to do in matters of faith and marriage, she received the sacrament of communion, and even made it to confirmation at the age of twelve.[22] After that, though, religion stayed below the radar in her life. Still, she considered herself a Christian even if, given her sexual pro-

---

22 For the unsaved and apostate among you, confirmation is the sacrament when the Holy Spirit descends upon the believer, giving him or her special strength to spread and defend the faith (or, the less politically correct description given the whole Crusades thing: That sacrament which makes you a soldier of God).

clivities, the church didn't.[23] But had she become a habit-wearing handmaiden of the Lord, nothing would have prepared her for this conveyor belt-view she was getting of how spiritual sausage was made.

Thomasina continued. This much the world knew about the Nag Hammadi discovery: The simple brothers who discovered the texts were not so simple as to not suspect that they had stumbled upon something of humongous significance. They brought their find home to mother. And here something strange happened. Mom mysteriously burned three texts in the oven "for heating." Why this woman destroyed ancient Coptic and Hebrew documents, at a time when the lowliest clay-digger knew such a discovery would be priceless in the thriving black market of all things ancient, has never been explained. But that was her story and she was sticking to it.

Thomasina told what really happened. Immediately after the discovery word got to the Vatican through its spies in the Coptic Church (Russia and America weren't the only adversaries engaged at the time in a cold war). With the possibility of the most dangerous banned gospels re-emerging, the Vatican dispatched two Dominican priests to the Egyptian brood, found their worst fears confirmed, and gave them a choice: Either give us three of those gospels and tell the world that you burned them for heating, or let us hear your confessions then free you from the shackles of

---

23   Technically speaking, scripture says in Leviticus 18: 22-23 that man shall not lie with man nor animal, nor shall a woman lie with animal. But it says nothing against a woman lying with a woman. If any proof were needed that God is a man, this should suffice.

earthly limitations and take the texts ourselves. The family made the prudent decision.

The three gospels were these: The Gospel of Thaddeus, who was also known as St. Jude, one of the twelve apostles; the Apocryphon of James, who was the brother of Christ; and the Gospel of Shem the Baker. This latter-most gospel was the testament of the purported caterer of the Last Supper; in fact the room Christ and the twelve used, it claimed, was above Shem's establishment somewhere on Mt. Zion. This gospel also had the added bonus of containing, almost word for word, the three-verse excise from Mark about the Christ taking a squat and was written before or about the same time as this earliest of the orthodox gospels, thirty years after the crucifixion.

All three texts, however made the following and, um, vexing to say the least, claim. Fr. Rossellini produced a sheet of paper and read the version from what was The Gospel of Shem the Baker:

"And the servant who had provided them the bread and the wine, returned and put before the Lord a platter with roasted animal of cloven foot, for he was not of the twelve tribes and knew not their ways.

"And Shem the Baker sayeth 'An offering to thee and thy followers, for many say you are the one who preaches truth and casts out demons, I bring a dish for which many come from afar to taste and return ever after; would that you enjoy it as well.'

"And the twelve chided him as one saying, 'Know you not whom you insult with your petty offering; such a meal is unclean and forbidden, try you to make him unworthy?'

"And the Lord rising up in anger sayeth, 'Rebuke him not, and know that an improper offering made in good faith is better received by the Father than a proper offering made with improper motive.'

"Whereupon the Lord took not one but many bites and said to Shem, 'Verily, I understand why many come from afar to partake.'

"And on that day Shem became a follower, and proclaimed to all with a stone tablet above his door that the Christ had eaten there."

Fr. Rossellini finished. Danica could see that Mickey, not easily dumbfounded, was dumbfounded.

"You're saying," he said, "that possibly...just possibly... the rabbi of rabbis...the king of the Jews...the purported son of He Who Is," and then, incredulous "...*ate pork?*"

"Si."

"Jesus Christ."

Wednesday, April 7ᵗʰ, 5:07 a.m. – Paris

Aaron had ditched the limo that would be traced back to the dead valets and not to him since the field dressing stopped his DNA from getting on the interior. He hailed a taxi and went straight to the recently finished magnificent *Centre Médical de Saint Denis.*[24] He stumbled into emergency

---

24   Besides the country of France, St. Denis is also the patron saint of hydrophobia and rabies. As if to confirm that St. Denis himself approved of such a mantle, one of the hosptial's first patients was a water-phobic dog bite victim. Naturally, the patient was French.

to see a busload of English Historical Society members already there, all of them stricken with food poisoning from the previous night's dinner at a popular Le Marais eatery, most of them certain it was a parting jab for either the first or second Hundred Years' War. Aaron pushed his way through the whining, vomiting Brits, approached the admitting nurse, and pushed aside a pasty-white, overfed twit who could stand to purge a few stomachs-full anyway.

"*Monsieur!*" snapped the admitting nurse, "If you will just wait your—"

Aaron threw down a card with a hand-written phone number. "Call this, now, tell whoever answers that it is a 'private matter of all men,' then pray you still have a job."

She sighed, then dialed. "Yes, Admitting, I have a patient who *ordered* me to call you, say this was a private matter of all—" End of discussion. Her face drained as she listened. "Yes, sir. Immediately. No, of course, I will." She hung up, shaken, and grabbed a form to take his information.

"Save your ink," he said, "and put me in your best suite, I care not whether it is already occupied. Then send up two liters of chamomile tea, an enema bag, and olive branches."

"*Mais naturellement!*"

Post-op, Aaron relaxed in a king-sized orthopedic bed overlooking a stunning panorama of the city of lights. A meal of trout almandine and sautéed julienne veg-etables with a dessert of double-chocolate mousse from the *other* kitchen had revived his spirits. He realized he could stand to use a little rest, perhaps lie low for a day or two. After all, given that he possessed the bulk of Mikhail Samanovananonvich's research, he had bought himself a little—

His reverie was shattered by a realization: Mikhail's briefcase was left in the limousine.

Aaron would be sure to make his chamomile flushing extra hot.

Circa 1951, Buenos Aires, Argentina

Jean-Henri Vandersmissen would escape Europe, wanted for collusion, theft, drug trafficking, white slavery, revealing the names of double agents; but then he always lived his life with an exit strategy. With collaborators everywhere, it was not difficult for him to blend into a refugee camp then make passage to Canada, courtesy of the Allies. From there he hopscotched down to El Paso, Mexico City, San Cristobal, Venezuela, and ended up in Buenos Aires, Argentina. Despite his tens of millions of francs, he decided he was going to keep the low profile of a dealer of antiquities, and when the real estate agent showed him the house in a quiet suburb on a narrow tree-lined street, he knew he had found the place he could hide with complete peace of mind. Named after a 19th century Italian who was, in fact, a hero in the Uruguayan battle for independence, what better place to avoid capture, thought Jean-Henri Vandersmissen, than to live on Garibaldi Street?

Needless to say, after the unpleasantness in 1960 with Mr. Eichmann two doors down, Jean-Henri thought it better to live in wealth and plain sight. And so he bought a twenty-six-room mansion on Himmler Avenue.

During this, his passion for things ancient grew exponentially. A Guttenberg- printed *Ars Minor* schoolbook sat in a Plexiglas case, never to be read; one of three handwritten copies of the Magna Carta, signed by King John himself, hung in his foyer. But his prize of prizes, his *Action Comics No. 1* if he was a Superman-iac, was a glass-encased piece of Aleppo pine, no bigger in length and width than half a pencil, one of the few authenticated relics from the sacrificial cross of Jesus himself.[25] This he kept stored in a safe deposit box at his bank.

He will never forget the day he got the call about this most sacred of treasures from his private artifacts dealer: Umberto Stefanelli. A capitalist without borders, Umberto crisscrossed the Levant on the bare whisper of rumor in search of that single discovery he could bring to light that would forever be tied to his name, much like Nag Hammadi no longer referred to that camel dropping of an Egyptian

---

25 Authenticated by news articles at the time of the same piece of wood in a glass case having been stolen from the St. Lucy Abbey in Czechoslovakia. While not the most daring of robberies, it was particularly dastardly in that St. Lucy is the patron saint of the blind and all clerics, groundskeepers and livery workers in the abbey were so afflicted. It was decided after the crime, since no one could identify the criminal, that such purity of dedication to St. Lucy was not in the wisest interests of the abbey, and a sighted cleric was allowed to join; that is, so as not to completely abrogate the dedication of their original charter, a newly ordained cleric with one eye. Sadly, the power this gave him went to his head, he began to rule as a king, and the order and abbey went to ruin shortly thereafter.

town but to the fifty-two religious texts found there. Jean-Henri had met him in the refugee camp. They bonded immediately with so much in common, and it was not difficult for Jean-Henri to grease Umberto's rails to freedom with a new identity and passport. In return, Umberto promised to give Jean-Henri first refusal on any valuable find henceforth.

Umberto was told to bring the piece of wood to him immediately. Holding the beveled glass cube that contained it, gently running his fingers over the surface, Jean-Henri knew he had come upon something ineffable.

And not a moment too soon.

Two months later Jean-Henri was diagnosed with amyloidosis, an incurable disease that was a death sentence. Jean-Henri became increasingly listless, falling into the blackest of depressions until one night he awoke with divine inspiration. *But of course!*

The next morning he was at the bank as it opened, retrieved his safe deposit box, repaired to a private room, took out the relic, and did the unthinkable: He slammed the cube on the table, shattering the glass case. He unbuttoned his shirt, jamming the sharp end of the Aleppo pine into his chest. Whereupon the faith drummed by rote into him at the orphanage, the faith he let slip away in his resulting riches, came flooding back into him like a transfusion of sanctified blood.

Over the next several days his depression gave way to hope. He waited a month to be sure before returning to his specialist, where the doctor confirmed what Jean-

Henri already knew: It was the first case of spontaneous amyloidosis healing in the annals of medicine.

It was nothing less than a sign to Jean-Henri. *This* is the reason he survived the vicissitudes of war, *this* is why God allowed him to amass an ill-gained fortune, it was for this very moment, this touch of the Holy Spirit, telling him to use his millions in the service of something. Which to most people would mean philanthropic acts and living a life of asceticism, or building churches in which to spread the faith, or in an increasingly godless world, airlifting thousands of bibles to the communist countries. But then any multi-millionaire could do that. To Jean-Henri it was a sign that told him the more such artifacts and relics he accumulated, the greater his chances he might live forever. Proving once again that true faith is not logical.[26]

But it was Umberto Stefanelli's *next* even more momentous find that would impact world events and set in motion this narrative. Unfortunately, this time he chose not to contact Jean-Henri first. On July 12th, 1951, Umberto stepped from the one hundred-twelve degree heat into the stagnant air of a Tehran post office, where he arranged to send a letter special delivery. The irony is that he had no idea he was mailing off his own death warrant, or that in sending it, this letter would reach back centuries and rock the very foun-

26   Jean-Henri would never find out that his medical file was accidentally switched with another patient who indeed had amyloidosis and was never diagnosed; indeed, given a clean bill of health, he left the hospital, and planned a world cruise. He would never take it, ironically, not because of the disease, but because he slipped on a freshly mopped floor at the supermarket, hit his head, and died.

dation of Christian faith, or, had he sent it rushed delivery instead of special, it would have taken approximately the same amount of time for $1.42 less.

It was going to a boyhood friend, a recently ordained cleric who worked as an administrative assistant at the Vatican, in the office of Secretariat of State, whom he affectionately called Gigo. It read as follows:

Hello, Gigo! I write you from Tehran, trust this missive finds you in good health. I have in my possession something of a curious nature and would be grateful if you would be so kind as to direct me to the proper Vatican office to see if I might get some corroboration on this most curious find.

The article in question is a papyrus of the Gospel of St. Mark, and it appears to be from the third century. It is not, however, written in Greek but in Aramaic as it was found in the Arasbaran Mountains of Northern Iran. For that reason, it has remained uncorrupted by later translation or liturgical tomfoolery. The curious part concerns Chapter 14, which is three verses longer than the orthodox text of Mark from mid-fourth century on. The addition begins at verse 26 after the last supper and refers to the Christ performing "the private matter of all men."

I hope someone there might be able to shed light on this. I will await word from you before I leave Tehran.

Yours, Umberto.

A cable returned immediately, instructing him to remain there, show his possession to no one, and representatives of the Holy See would come to *him* to inspect the manuscript.

Umberto's gambit worked! Had he sold the find to Jean-Henri, he would have earned a fraction of its real value. Had he announced his find in the press without going through proper Vatican channels, he risked the church declaring it a forgery if it in any way breached doctrine. By going through a lowly placed friend, in his dilettante-like way, it displayed an unthreatening naiveté that gave them the appearance of total control. The cable back was the exact reaction he was hoping for.

Three days after receiving the cable Umberto died in a fiery car accident. His remains were returned to his home city of Turin. Gigo said his funeral mass.

Wednesday, April 7ᵗʰ, 4:31 a.m. – Paris

Aaron abandoned the limousine in an underground garage, where it would sit to be found by the authorities. However, that is not to say it remained undiscovered.

He had barely left sight of the unlocked vehicle when footsteps clicked deliberately up to it. A door was opened, revealing the treasure the trespasser hoped was there: Mikhail's briefcase. Gloved hands opened it, pulled out a legal pad full of shorthand notes that made sense only to Mikhail, and it tossed aside; files filled with arcane documents were rifled through, as well as typed notes, and letters. Surely this was the trove of information long sought after that would forego the need for silly puzzles and ludicrous overwrought clues that would normally send two opposite-gendered protagonists across continents just a step ahead of those who would stop them. The door was closed, and the steps faded into the night.

Tuesday, April 5ᵗʰ, 4:34 p.m. – Paris

Something about *L'affaire Samanovananonvich* didn't sit right with Inspector Renault: The conflicting information between Mikhail's statement and those of the priests, Chief Poujouly's unusual deference to them, that they came from Rome despite the fact that no one outside this department had been informed of the death, Mikhail's claim that it was a simple robbery when too much money was on his person. Renault decided this needed the insight of a trusted and disinterested party. His parish priest knew him since he was a swaddled infant at the baptismal fount. He performed Renault's first communion, his confirmation, heard his confessions, married him and his ex-wife. There was no one he believed in more to give him an honest opinion. Renault gathered his notes and went to see the esteemed Father Marisol. That such initiative might put him up for promotion he would worry about later.

Wednesday, April 7ᵗʰ, what felt like six hours later from all this exposition but was only several minutes from the last chapter with Thomasina – Paris

Danica, again feeling like the character whose sole purpose was to advance vast swaths of unwieldy information, asked the obvious regarding the Christ's last meal: "So?"

Mickey turned to her. "If Jesus ate pork at the last supper...this would mean he wasn't an observant Jew, not likely a descendent of the House of David, and either way, not the anointed one. Which could undermine the very legitimacy of Christianity for 1.2 billion Christians."

"This is bad."

Mickey turned to Thomasina. "What's this got to do with my father?"

"Ahm-ah getting to-ah thad."

Before the second coming, Mickey hoped.

Returning to the last supper and its aftermath...this is where the Gospel of Thaddeus comes into play. Witness to the final hours of Jesus, Thaddeus realized that their meal above Shem's was indeed his last; and since this rabbi was not only his lord but clearly a figure of huge historical impact, Thaddeus hurried back to said room after the crucifixion to see if he might retrieve any and all things Jesus as hallowed mementos (in fairness he couldn't have foreseen the era of ceramic, plastic, and wooden sadomasochistic images of a tortured, bleeding, near-dead man nailed to a cross). Luckily Shem's daughter was a slattern lay-about given to knowing the customers and it had not been cleaned. Thaddeus was able to retrieve the fired dish from which Jesus ate...the crumbs of unleavened bread still upon it...and from the antechamber just off the main room...um...the final leavings of the Christ.

What happened to it after that, Thaddeus only records:

"And he buried it in an ark where no one would look."

"So lemme guess," said Mickey. "You're saying that my dad spent *years* of his life tracking down an ark that may not even exist. And that he was killed because not only *does* it exist, but that he was on the brink of finding it."

"*Precisamente*," said Thomasina.

Another silent pall over the room. The importance of that possibility was beyond words, at least to those in the know.

"*Okay*, I've got to ask," blurted Danica, exasperated at her outsider status. "You find this ark and it contains what you think it contains, you'll test it for traces of pork. But it's got to be damn near petrified. How can anyone tell what Jesus ate two thousand years ago?"

"A fecal odorgram," Mickey said. "You subject a sample to a gas-chromatographic analysis, that releases odors of the ingested food. It's been used on rodent scat as old as forty-thousand years and it's quite accurate." This talking mandrill just kept getting more and more remarkable, thought Danica. Mickey turned back to Thomasina. "This other party that wants it, who is it?"

Thomasina spread his hands, truly pained. "We-ah do-ah nawt know."

Fr. Rossellini amplified. "There may be more than one party. We know some of the minions of the party we're sure killed your father. But we do not know who that party is."

"How do you expect me to find what my father almost did?"

"We recovered this pad of his notes." Fr. Rossellini produced the legal pad that was left in the limousine and handed it to Mickey. Holding it, Mickey felt a slight stab, recognizing something of his father's that contained his personal and most important thoughts. Mickey flipped through the several pages of near-illegible scrawl; a jumble of single words or phrases; thoughts scratched out as dead-ends; a line drawn from a circled phrase across the waste-land of obsolete clues to a circled single word elsewhere.

"What do you need me for, this thing practically finds itself." Mickey saw they weren't big fans of sarcasm. "If people who know everything tend to turn up dead...and I'm going to end up knowing a helluva lot more....what's to keep *you* clowns from killing me?"

"You would have to trust us as emissaries of the church," said Rossellini, "when we say that in choosing the side of right, you will be choosing to live."

"Which I'm just supposed to believe."

DeSica shrugged. "That's why it's called faith."

There was a quick three-rap knock at the door. Rossellini and DeSica had their guns out and aimed before the third rap.

"Assassins usually don't knock first," said Mickey.

DeSica approached the door, cracked it...then yanked in the offender, an octogenarian priest who he pushed up against the wall and prepared to frisk.

That will not be necessary, barked Thomasina in Italian, *he is my old friend.* It seems the two of them were having dinner together.

I apologize, Father Marisol, said Thomasina.

The cleric bowed to his senior. *Good to see you, Gigo.*

Wednesday, April 7ᵗʰ, 11:15 a.m. – Paris

The sound on the other end of the phone was either a fist or a forehead hitting a wooden desktop. A moment of woozy silence, then, "Just to recap...you have killed the man most able to lead us to the ark. You have brought his son from America only to lose him. And you have lost the only files that might contain vital clues."

"Put that way," said Aaron, "the glass might appear to be half-empty."

"Half-empty?! No, you zebra-striped feather duster, the glass would appear to be completely shattered and devoid of all liquid whatsoever!"

"Not quite," purred Aaron, "a drop of moisture remains."

The voice so wished he had never extended the simile.

"Before I took him from the airplane I implanted the chip in his shoulder. Deliver the GPS tracker and I will locate him. And, I guarantee you, he will lead us to the prize."

A courier arrived at the hospital within the hour. Aaron turned on the tracker and a soft beeping announced Mickey's location. Aaron stared at it, the realization dawning. There are times when evil people actually laugh long, hard, and really evilly. This was one of them.

Per the GPS, Mickey was in the same hospital. Three floors down, it would turn out.

Wednesday, April 7ᵗʰ, 12:01 p.m. – Paris

If this were Victor Hugo, the moment wouldn't be doubly coincidental. As Mickey was being tracked from a few floors above by his father's killer, Richard Winthrop, who had the papers faxed from his London office, was going over Mickey's father's will with him.

"You're a wealthy man," Richard said. "His house... proceeds from his books that don't go to the Catholic Solidarity Fund...an annual trust he set up for you...they should provide for all your needs for life."

"You don't know my needs," deadpanned Mickey. Danica smiled to herself; she was thinking the same thing. "I don't get it," Mickey said. "Dad said I was disowned, cut off, unless I, and I quote, 'came back to God.'"

"I've reviewed the wording and he doesn't specify through which means. He probably assumed the Catholic Church, but nothing in this states that the 'The All-Encompassing Church, etc., etc.' doesn't qualify. And since you have a degree of divinity –" Mickey didn't have to look to feel Danica's bullshitometer go haywire again "— you are qualified under the tax laws of your state to form a church." Mickey winced guiltily. "I understand that was not your intention," added Richard hastily. Then, as much to change the subject, he asked, "As I was not privy to your conversation with His Eminence, what is your status as regards going home?"

Mickey looked over to the Angels of Death. Uh-uh. "I'm apparently staying on this side of the pond 'til further notice."

"Anything else I can do for you?" Mickey drew a blank. "You'll have your passports within twenty-four hours." With that, Richard was gone.

Mickey assessed his situation. He might not have been in control in a big picture sort of way but, as they say, the devil was in the details. He turned to the priests. "I dunno what your immediate plans are," said Mickey to them, "but you're up shit creek without my help. I'm so hungry right now I'd take communion just to get something in my stomach. So I'm not on the clock 'til I have an order of pheasant under glass, potatoes O'Brian, and an arrogant but insouciant cabernet." He turned to Danica. "Anything else?"

Danica would never encourage Mickey's view of the universe wherein Mickey was the center, but these were desperate times, being hungrier than a fiddler's bitch. "I've never had crepes suzette."

Mickey clapped his hands, the King of Siam. "Make it happen."

The clerics exchanged a Holy-Father-give-us-the-patience-not-to-pistol-whip-this-asshole look. Rossellini responded tightly. "Of course."

"Oh, and Gitanes cigarettes. I hear they go good after a meal."

"And..." began Danica tentatively, looking to Mickey; he gave her the go-ahead. "Could I have mascara...eye liner...a brush...maybe hairspray?"

"Chop-chop," said Mickey.

Rossellini, wound even tighter, left. Earlier, the priests had arranged for clothes from the nearby Catholic Thrift Shop. They arrived. When he had changed, Mickey looked like the one Parisian without a whit of fashion sense in brown wool pants and a purple frilly shirt in need of stain remover; this could not be accidental. Danica would've looked good in a burka. She looked stunning in jeans and a long-sleeved white blouse.

When Rossellini returned, Danica gladly grabbed the plastic bag from him and repaired to the bathroom to upgrade herself from stunning to heavenly. DeSica allowed in an orderly pushing a cart of food that triggered a serious Pavlovian response in Mickey. The orderly set the table, left, and Mickey started for it with a canine exuberance.

"No-no-no-no," said DeSica, stopping him. "Wait. It might be tampered with."

"You are shitting me."

"We do no such thing," said DeSica with nary a trace of amusement.

Mickey watched the two priests sit at the table and bow their heads in silent grace...the Stairway to Heaven version. Seven minutes later DeSica mumbled amen, they picked up their utensils then proceeded to sample every course... and, Mickey noticed, taking their sweet fucking time about it. They put down their utensils and sat back, neither moving from his chair.

"Funny stuff," said Mickey, his stomach grinding like an old transmission, "I'm laughing inside where it counts. You done?"

"Yes...with the first step," said Rossellini. "It certainly *tastes* safe."

"Indeed," said DeSica, "it tastes exquisite. Now...we must wait for the food to digest to *know* that it is safe." He glanced at his watch. They both sat there with a smugness that would make Bill O'Reilly look humble.

Suddenly, as if on cue, both closed their eyes, dropped their chins to their chest, slowly tilted forward, and each did a face-plant in his pheasant.

"Really, guys, a laugh riot, you could open for Carrot Top."

The door flew open as Aaron entered, closing it behind him. Dressed in medical scrubs he looked every bit the doctor, except for the Mohawk, the ivory smooth skin, the predatory demeanor and the silenced .38 that came from his waistband. He smiled, surveying his handiwork, "*tres bon.*"

Mickey could not be more dispirited. It was bad enough his repast was spoiled by a priest's five o'clock shadow *and* chloral hydrate. Now he had to deal with Mr. Joy Boy. His general love of his fellow man was beginning to be sorely tested.

"Where is your girlfriend?" Aaron asked.

"Probably beating the shit out of one of your boyfriends."

Aaron stepped forward, placed the gun to the back of Rossellini's head, and fired. The priest jolted, and died in the best pheasant under glass he'd ever tasted. Mickey went pale. Aaron came around to do the same to DeSica. "I will ask you again," he said before he noticed the bathroom. "Ah! Your own *toilette.*" A glance to Rossellini. "That was probably unnecessary." Mickey could only watch as Aaron crossed to the door and yanked it open.

A tongue of flame engulfed his head, Danica straight-arming the can of hairspray and disposable lighter that was with Mickey's smokes. Aaron yowled like a cat on a griddle, his gun clattering to the floor as he covered his now-eyebrowless face, knowing thousands of gallons of buttermilk had been for naught. The acrid odor of burning rope filled the room, his Mohawk turning into a brush fire.

Aaron bobbed, weaved, unable to get away. Finally he had no choice but to charge into the inferno, slamming her aside, and staggering out the door, his mewling growing fainter as he ran down the hall.

"He looked like he could use some color," she said to a grateful Mickey.

Wednesday, April 7th, 12:19 p.m. – Paris

Police converged on the hospital, Inspector Renault among them, hearing that one of the priests he had crossed paths with was now dead, a scrum of uniforms clogging the hospital room and the hall outside.

"Which one is Mickey Samanov?" Renault asked a beat cop outside the room.

"The one without a whit of fashion sense," the cop pointed disdainfully. Renault had to agree. He approached Mickey, with an unusually fetching redhead, and asked phonetically, "Mr. Samanov?" Mickey nodded. Through an interpreter newly hired from a progressive pass/fail college, the conversation took place, under a graduate who clearly wasn't class valedictorian.

"I am Inspector Renault."

"Inspector Reno?"

"No-no, Re-*nault.*"

"Re-naw…?" tried Mickey again

"*Renault.*"

"Like…the car? Pronounced with a cleft palate?"

"I have a speaking disorder…?"

"—the *car*, Renault, it sounds like the car, yes?" Mickey was trying.

"Ah. I see. So I sound to you like a car with a cleft palate?"

"Is it just me or are we both new to French?"

"But of course, Mr. Samanov, it is *I* who do not know how to pronounce my own name."

"Let's hit the reset button—"

"No, really," persisted Renault, "I am most curious how my quaint style of pronunciation is amusing to you."

"What's Keith Richards have to do with anything?"

"I know not *what* this has to do with a cockroach, but I find your rudeness consistent with the country that gave the world hip-hop."

"Hippity-hop?" Mickey, having just watched one man die in his plate and another get deep-fried, was running low on patience. "What's that, rap with a stutter?"

"You get amusement from speech impediments," snapped Renault, "I'll bet a hunchback leaves you breathless."

"I said nothing about Victor Hugo—"

"What I've always suspected is now blindingly clear," said Renault. "You Anglos suffer from linguistic inferiority. Unable to come up with your own language, you steal from the Romans, Celts, Germans, most baldly from us, and sew together this Frankenstein beast you call English. Where would you park your car if not for *garage*? How would your film students justify their self-indulgent hand-held claptrap without *cinéma vérité*? And how would your culture's idiocy be explained without a term *you* must be much acquainted with, *faux pas*?"

"Look, shamus," said Mickey, "we appreciate Marcel Marceau, the killer deal you gave us on Louisiana, and personally speaking, the French kiss, but that doesn't mean we have to keep dry humping you guys."

"You wish to perform simulated sex with me?"

"And while I'm at it, our California reds make your French wines their butt boys."

Renault turned to two policemen. "Arrest this man and bring him to the station immediately."

Whereupon Fr. DeSica picked up their conversation; he had awakened not ten minutes earlier to complete bedlam and a murdered partner. But whatever he felt, like the Marines, the mission came first. He didn't have time to mourn his partner beyond a soulful, abbreviated blessing before washing bird and potatoes off his face, then returned to the fray. "Arrest him on what charge?"

"Morals. And to investigate possible involvement in the murder of Mikhail Samanovananonvich."

Mickey watched DeSica and Renault go *mano a mano* and knew whatever the country, when a collar went up against a badge, the collar always folded. Big time. But when things built to a six-Mississippi stare-down, Mickey was shocked to see that it was Renault who blinked first. He turned curtly to Mickey. "You are a person of extreme interest," Renault said; Mickey didn't understand but knew he just made another list. Renault marched out. Could it actually be: a gun-wielding, Kevlar-wearing, above-the-law *priest?* Had he not seen it first hand, he would have thought this the domain of paperback thrillers written only for the quick buck and the gullible reader.

Meanwhile, Danica had seen something else. "Mickey," she whispered, "check this out." She walked him down the hall to a plaque. Though neither was a Francophile, it appeared to be an acknowledgment of *appréciation*, no doubt for generous funding to the hospital. The top benefactor on the list wasn't a name but a logo. It was three identical and elongated lions flattened like road kill and lined up vertically.

Wednesday, blah-blah-blah – Paris

Time was of the essence. The next twenty-four to forty-eight hours would be crucial. Perhaps seventy-two, seventy-fourish, tops.

Mickey approached DeSica who, Mickey could see, had a sense of urgency. "These bad-boy gospels," he asked the priest, "where do you keep 'em?"

"The Vatican."

"Let's go."

The four left for the airport where Mickey traded in his Parisian-dandy ensemble for a high-end warm-up suit and running shoes since a fair amount of running was in the forecast. Richard met them at the airport. He must have had grainy telephoto pictures of someone doing *something* as this British citizen was able to lean on the American consulate and get the two of them expedited passports in land-speed record time.

Richard said, "I'm delaying my trip to Zimbabwe one day. I'd like to see what I can find out about your father's death. Whom should I talk to among the *gendarmes?*"

"There was a cop at the hospital. Name of Renault."

Richard gave him a card. "This is my cell, do not hesitate to call for any reason." He leaned close and whispered, "There's no trust, no faith, no honesty in men, all perjured, all forsworn, all naught, all dissemblers." Most people would say, "Trust no one." Richard quoted *Romeo and Juliet*. Mickey and he shared a hug, and Richard left.

Danica, assuming she was here to be sent home, was in a no man's land of emotions. She served no ostensible purpose in a search only Mickey could navigate. Then there was Mickey himself, a piquant taste she had yet to acquire, and doubted if she ever could. Added to that was the Nikki factor; she still remembered every word, silence, and awkward moment of their interrupted make-up call that promised one of a kind, outside-the-box make-up sex that would make Jim Morrison blush. She hadn't had time to fantasize what that meant, but now that she did? She made *herself* blush. As for the countervailing arguments to stay – Paris, Rome, God knows wherever else this may lead were all beyond her pay grade – the exhilaration of having been shot at and missed literally and metaphorically, was a high few people knew.[27] And being part of an unnecessarily Byzantine religious mystery that might re-order the very way mankind viewed God did beat busting crackheads and cleaning vomit from the back seat of her cruiser. But did they outweigh Nikki? A Nikki who just got off work, her hair alluringly tousled, fragrant with sweat and musk and desire, who had just spent an entire night mechanically

---

27   Well, people who don't live in Arizona, Louisiana, and parts of Los Angeles...

arousing men and was now ready to come home and release all that passion she'd had to sublimate, to deny, on Danica?

Uh...nope.

Buh-bye, adios, ta-ta, toodle-oo, it was a hoot, love to stay but gotta run. Nikki awaited.

Whereupon she discovered she was *not* going home. It seems she had proved her mettle turning the Fist of God into a six-foot tiki torch; DeSica decided she was too resourceful to let go, that she would provide "an extra layer of protection," as he put it. She was beginning to learn what Lt. Renault already knew. "I had to do my job too well," she groused from her first class Air Italia seat.

"Don't dislocate that arm patting yourself on the back," Mickey said *sotto voce*, DeSica just across the aisle.

"Do I detect a case of protection envy?" she asked.

"I'm all for you being a layer on me. But seeing's how the French wanna throw me in the Bastille...the bad guys want the ark and want me in the past-tense...and the *good* guys would prefer anyone knowing as much as I do to not live too long afterwards? I'm guessing the same applies to anyone else in my party. You taking a bullet in the line of duty wouldn't be the worst thing to happen."

"You're saying they kept me here to die." He pursed his lips. "Sounds like I'm in for the second biggest adventure of my life."

"I'll bite...what's the first?"

"College, when I came out of the closet with a two-day all-girl threesome." Mickey's eyes glazed over imagining such a Letters to Penthouse saturnalia. She gave him a few moments to visit that castle in the sky then, allowing his heart to resume with the real reason she mentioned it, "Though I'll admit one thing...I'm waiting to hear how a priest and world-class scholar became a lowbrow, bottom-feeding lizardo."

"I'll tell you...after you tell me about that weekend."

"Quid pro quo?"

"I prefer tit-for-tat."

She settled back into her chair like it was a down mattress. They were somewhere over the Alps. She closed her eyes, trying to put a positive spin on life-as-she-didn't-know-it, this journey mere steps off the beaten path yet one very few others would ever take. And it would be one without Nikki. Had aliens come down and requested an example of the ideal object of sexual attraction, they couldn't do better than Nikki stepping out of the shower; or Nikki wrapped in sheets next to her in the morning; or Nikki with a cigarette blowing a perfect, languid ring. Everything about her – a stomach you could bounce quarters off of, full lips forever moist, perfectly proportioned breasts untouched by science, even her *elbows* – couldn't be reproduced. She simply was. True, they had fallen into that dreaded state of lesbian bed death, a condition usually hit around the two-year mark where bedroom time was more about forty winks than forty lashes. She'd been warned of it by the more seasoned, yet never imagined it would ever apply to her and the insatiable Nikki. But even they slipped into it without incident. If Danica could take solace in anything it was the fact that they were normal; it was probably nothing a good counselor – present company excluded – couldn't address.

She looked over to see Mickey thumbing through several manila folders from an accordion file in his lap, she guessed he'd gotten from the priests. He was studying the police and coroner's reports, the key points translated into penciled English in the margins. He was quiet. She knew it had to be unsettling, to see a parent's last moments reduced to measurements, times, clinical policeese. Finally, almost to himself: "His last word...the last thing the man says before he dies...the most important thing he needs to communicate. It's not 'rosebud'...it's not where Jimmy Hoffa's buried...it's not even 'burn my porn collection.'"

"What'd he say?"

"'Mice.'"

"Mice...?"

"Fucking 'mice.' You're the police woman, you gotta see shit like this all the time, what the hell's it supposed to mean?"

Danica wanted to be of help. "I'm sorry."

"It was rhetorical."

"No...about your father," she said. "You can drop the act...you two used to be close. You had a falling out. Given that you went from collar to chlorine, and that clause in his will, I'm guessing it had something to do with you not living up to your potential."

"Are all lesbians this irritating or do you come by it naturally?"

"Just one more service I offer."

He focused back on the file, pulled out a legal pad, and started making notes. His left arm continued to ache.

While Mickey was doing his job, the chip under his skin was doing its job...

Thaddeus had taken the limestone box to a memorial mason. "Verily, that is the legend you would have me inscribe?" asked the mason. Thaddeus nodded. "In Hebrew, Latin, Greek, or Aramaic?" the mason asked.

"Which is the least amount?"

"Latin."

"So be it." He would have preferred Greek but he was, after all, an apostle on a budget. The mason began to tap with mallet and chisel on the limestone. He was finished by mid-day.

Thaddeus waited until nightfall and for the moon to move behind the clouds. With the box concealed beneath his cloak, he went circuitously through the back alleys, padding lightly in his tattered leather sandals – sandals that had walked the sands of Judea and the muddy shoreline along the Sea of Galilee...that stepped among the five thousand as he handed out fishes and loaves...that Philip and Bartholomew tied together while he slept at Bethany and caused him to stumble and then they blamed it on Judas Iscariot... and when Jesus chided Judas for harming one of his sheep, Judas swore he would somehow get back at them. Thaddeus especially avoided Roman centurions who were in a heightened state of alert having crucified the Messiah during Passover. Finally Thaddeus arrived at his destination:

The Temple Mount. The most hallowed site in all Judaism... built by Solomon himself...the tabernacle that held the command-

ments written by the finger of God...where Jesus, in great agitation, overturned tables and chased away the moneychangers.[28]

With a chisel borrowed from the mason, Thaddeus pried loose some stones in the street at the base of the temple's north wall. He removed them, dug feverishly in the compacted earth, then placed the box in the hole. When he was finished he replaced the stones. It would remain and even survive the Jewish-Roman War, when the temple was destroyed almost forty years later.

The inscription on the box read: The Ark of the One True Excreta. The memorial mason correctly assumed the Jew could not read Latin. He found his customer's initial request beneath him to carve. "The Ark of the One True Feces" was too vulgar even for a pagan.

Wednesday, April 7ᵗʰ, 8:42 p.m. – Rome

The airplane slammed hard on the tarmac, bounced once, twice, then found terra firma as it arrived at the *Aeroporto Leonardo da Vinci di Fiumicino*, making Mickey long for the pilots of his abduction.

"How do you know all this?" Danica asked, re: the notes he'd made on the legal pad for the last hour, impressed as hell by what he surmised.

---

28 Depending on which gospel you read, Christ chasing out the moneychangers was either his first public act per John, or his last public act per everyone else, though that's not as vexing as the gospels' recounting of the actual day Christ was crucified, either on Passover as Mark recorded, or the day before Passover as John wrote; fact checkers were still a few millennia away.

"I'm guessing. I dunno what kind of box Thaddeus put it in, though limestone was common. I dunno if Thaddeus had *anything* inscribed, though on boxes holding revered remains that was common, too. And if he did have it inscribed, bodily evacuation was as coarse in the language of Paul as it was in the language of Lenny Bruce."

Danica was mildly deflated. "You sounded so authoritative."

"It's a gift."

"So you don't even have a thought as to where this thing was buried?"

"Actually, that's the one detail I'm probably right about."

A pinpoint of light. The sooner they found it, the sooner she'd be in the throes of passion in San Francisco. "You are?"

"I are. If Thaddeus wanted to put it where no one else would look, the Temple Mount would be the place. Christ died mid-afternoon on Friday.[29] The Romans knew the drill, were big on crowd control, 'cuz Pontius Pilate crucified thousands of troublemakers already. This one, though, might cause blowback. The Romans didn't know how many followers Jesus had, so there would've been extra security into the next morning in case of riots. But the one place they *wouldn't* have to keep tabs on was the Temple. This was the Sabbath, so that night all good Jews were home cheerfully celebrating their God under penalty of death. Furthermore, the Temple's the *last* place anyone would look for a relic of the very Messiah the chosen peo-

---

29   Well, give or take…

ple had rejected. And if you wanna go sardonic? There's even a not so subtle pox-upon-thee vibe to it, for a follower of Christ to bury a relic of Him in the hallowed ground of those who gave Him the collective finger."

"Then what the hell are we doing in Rome, I mean, okay, we're here, we see the statue of David, grab a slice of pizza, but then we pick up a couple of shovels and book the next flight to—"

"Because it's not there."

"But...you just said—"

"I said I'm pretty sure it *was* there. It ain't anymore." Slumping, she went from amazement back to deflated and decided to remain there until further notice. "I'm sure my father got to the same conclusion as well or he would've found it. Which means someone *else* got to it already. Maybe by fifty years ago, maybe a thousand years ago." He stared at his notes, unfazed. "But it's a place to start. And that's why we're in Rome."

Turns out they would have time for pizza. But not homoerotic sculpture.[30]

Over the course of the 1950s and 1960s, Buenos Aires, Argentina Jean-Henri Vandersmissen heard the news of Umberto Stefanelli's fiery death, had no doubt it was foul play...and that Umberto was on to a discovery of such magnitude that it was quite possibly the Find of Finds. Jean-Henri would not be denied. He still had his contacts, it was not difficult to find someone to travel to Iran and retrace Umberto's

---

30   Ed. note: Especially since the statue of David is in Florence.

last days. It confirmed all his suspicions – especially when the trail ended with a clerk in a Tehran post office who remembered an Italian sending a special delivery letter to the Vatican, something easy to recall since he could have sent it rushed instead of special and saved $1.42.

Unfortunately, Jean-Henri had no such contacts in Rome.

A generous donation of ten thousand dollars to the Catholic Foreign Missions Fund got him an audience with Cardinal Peralta of Buenos Aires, who suddenly remembered the contact information of someone in the Vatican's Office of Antiquities. Jean-Henri then inquired of the Vatican curator as to their most trusted scholar of antiquities. The priest was suspicious and not forthcoming. Until, for a generous donation of ten thousand dollars to the Vatican Antiquities Restoration Fund, he suddenly recalled the name of a young and recently acquired researcher:

Mikhail Samanovananonvich.

Wednesday, April 7th, 9:12 p.m. – Rome

Another stiff-backed priest waited at the airport to replace the murdered Rossellini. Every bit as cinematic, masculine, and Kevlared, this was Father Visconti. As the three entered the terminal, Visconti fell in beside DeSica without so much as a *ciao, padre!* DeSica and his new ride-along marched in silent quickstep through the terminal to a limousine out front. Danica was stopped short by their motorcycle escorts.

"We're being protected by four harlequins?" A not completely off-base assumption, given their uniforms were white-gloved, puffy-armed, ruffled-collared, red-gold-and-blue-vertical striped affairs.

Mickey whispered, "Those 'harlequins' are the Swiss Guard...mercenaries who have served the Vatican for over five-hundred years. They'd just as soon snap your neck as eat a piece of dark chocolate. Most speak several languages."

"Is one of them English...?" she said, hoping otherwise.[31]

Mickey and Danica were whisked to their destination with all the importance of a head of state. As they raced along the *Autostrada-Roma Aeroporto di Fiumicino,* crossed the flowing *Fiome Tevere* and sped down the vibrant night-time *Galleria Principe Amedeo Savoia-Aosta,* Danica could see why it was called the Eternal City. She almost wept, over-whelmed as she was by the juxtaposition of the moment against the ancient, of the ephemeral beside the timeless, of the hurried passing the everlasting, all of which seemed

---

31   Indeed, the Guard did begin as mercenaries, and are so effective there are only a hundred of them, and to this day take an oath to defend the Pope to the death. Recruits must have completed military training in the Swiss Armed Forces. They are further trained to handle swords and halberds, and are fully prepared in the ways of close-quarters fighting and counter-terrorism techniques. They must maintain peak physical condi-tion, and are tested regularly on their ability with the SIG Sauer 9mm pistol, the H&K submachinegun, and the Swiss Army knife. Their motto, translated from Latin, was roughly, "You want a piece of this?"

to have evolved over the centuries into proper and equal measure, organically, with a certain earthiness.

They rushed down *Via della Conciliazione*, still bustling at this late hour, until the motorcade seemed to pass through a narrow multi-story brick strait that opened into another world...a cavernous oval of Roman colonnades that led the eye to the most magnificent holy structure that Danica – and most visitors – had ever seen: St. Peter's Basilica, the collective vision of the greatest Renaissance and Baroque architects and artists, necropolis of saints, popes, emperors, and empresses, home and throne to the direct lineal descendent of St. Peter; and in the center of the oval, their vehicle pulling around the ancient obelisk that was a visual exclamation point aiming to heaven.[32]

Two Swiss guards approached in step, opened the doors, and stood imposingly as the four got out. Danica couldn't help but turn around and around, staring with the awe and wonder of a paleontologist happening upon an actual living brontosaurus casually drinking from her backyard birdbath. This was the power and the glory made real, the architectural approximating the spiritual on earth and coming pretty damn close to succeeding.

The guards marched them across the moonlit square, past column after polished column, until they came to a guarded door that looked no more impressive than that of a utility closet. Two guards stood there as well, one patting

---

32   Interestingly, the Obelisk was here courtesy of the decidedly not-so-Christian Caligula; he had imported it from Egypt in 40 CE and installed it in the middle of the Circus of Caligula (later Nero). Now it stood proud and erect in St. Peter's Square.

Mickey then Danica down, the other running an electronic wand over them head to toe.

"Soul detector," Mickey quipped to Danica as the wand passed over him.

"I notice it's not beeping."

The guards unlocked the entrance and opened it. DeSica led the way.

It was just a passageway, long, dark, nondescript, until they came to a set of steps that took them into the light as if from the stygian depths, Danica finding herself standing in a high-ceiling, frescoed, grand esplanade ringed with suites of obscene splendor. The priests moved matter-of-factly through this time-capture of the High Renaissance and encroaching Baroque periods, of the Borgias and Pope Julius II, of Donatello, Bernini and Raphael. Their heels clicked across travertine tile mined from the rich quarries of Tivoli, as well as inlaid Carrara marble that came from the hills of Northern Tuscany where Michelangelo personally found the massive deposits that would yield him three Pietas. This was, Danica would come to learn, the Apostolic Palace; two floors above them were the private quarters of the Holy Father himself.

"Your tithe dollars at work," Mickey whispered to her. The awe-struck Danica, for whom a glance in any direction revealed a new, even more inspiring expression of glory than the last, didn't hear. But DeSica did. Not one to care about the cynical opinions of others, he never saw need to counter them; but this one, by this person, in the very ventricle of Christendom, struck a nerve.

"It's so easy to believe in nothing," he said to Mickey.

"Or to ignore logic and reason."

"Ah, logic...reason...the hobgoblins of little minds trotted out when one can't comprehend faith. Your position might carry weight if you chose to be more than the obnoxious heckler in the gallery, only able to nay-say."

"And *your* argument might carry weight if you didn't feel the need to back it up with a gun."

"Faith has many enemies," he said, turning to Mickey, "and must be defended in many forms. I have committed my life to it. To what have you committed?"

Fifty-some answers sprang to Mickey's mind, all of them inappropriate and a waste of good humor on the humorless. Danica heard none of it, still unable to believe this was where they were staying. They crossed the majestic chamber to a set of double doors. Fr. Visconti opened them. "Your quarters."

A small sitting area served four plain, whitewashed rooms without so much as a velvet painting. Or a window. In each room was a single bed, a plain wooden cross above it. They all shared the same W.C.

"Great," said Mickey. "The Motel Sixtus." He turned to see Danica glaring at him. "What?"

"You weren't kidding about that soul detector. We're lucky to have indoor plumbing."

"An important ecumenical council is to begin in a matter of days," said Visconti, "and these are the only accommodations available." Then came the other shoe. "You may wash up, then you must get to work."

"Papal bull. You're kidding, right?" Mickey saw he wasn't. "Look, sky pilot...the only sleep I've gotten in the past few days has been under lock, key, and chemicals. I've crossed more time zones than Phineas Fogg and I'm not even getting the frequent flier miles. So turn down the bed, leave a mint, and I'll see you in the morning with a double shot cappuccino, extra foam."

"That cannot be."

"The mint or the cappuccino?"

"Mr. Samanov, we have an agreement that is valid only if we recover the ark. It greatly behooves all to do it sooner than later."

Mickey looked longingly at the single, white-sheeted mattress within flopping range, as if it was a king-sized circular sable-covered waterbed adorned with olive-skinned Italian lasses circa early Sophia Loren. One of them may have had a riding crop.

"Ooh, tough break, Mickster," said Danica who, as disappointed as she was by the prison-like accommodations, was more drawn to sleep, "but the sooner you get on it, the sooner I get on that." She was starting toward her bed.

Mickey's expression was of the unamused variety. He addressed DeSica, not taking his eyes off of her. "Father... what if I feel like I need an extra layer of protection?" What little color she had left to drain, drained. "I mean, sure, we're inside the Vatican and all...

"...you wouldn't," Danica began.

"...but I seem to recall a few popes back in the day died here..."

"...Mickey..."

"...usually at the hands of their next-in-line..."

"...when we get back to the city, I'm so gonna arrest your ass..."

"Would it make you feel better to have her with you?" DeSica sighed.

"You have no idea."

"Then she shall join you."

Danica stormed into a room, slammed the door and cut loose with a string of epithets that would have tested the bounds of free speech under Earl Warren.

Mickey shook his head at the priests. "I think someone needs to go to the red tent."

Wednesday, April 7th, 9:47 p.m. – Paris

A monster was born. Emerging from a chrysalis of medical gauze, he stared into his hospital room mirror. The red-black scar tissue that was his face, and the three-inch stripe of disfigurement that bisected his pate where hair used to be, gave him the appearance out of a 50s-era, black and white sci-fi movie starring John Agar, wherein the hapless protagonist wandered into the New Mexican desert unbeknownst to the bespectacled military scientists who were about to detonate the atomic-hydrogen-testosteranian weapon to end all weapons; and after said weapon successfully detonated, this is what wandered out. Hideous and evil, children he now passed would go to bed with their lights on; dogs would crouch and make themselves smaller; good Christian women would cross themselves.

And Aaron smiled.

This was the *piece de resistance*, the completion of his metamorphosis from Aaron the unfortunate croissant-eater to Aaron the Shakespearean tragic antagonist. *This* was that certain something he needed for so long. It was a look that screamed for visual treatment, that escalated his life rights by at least seventeen percent, and that elevated his evil factor by half. Now... *now*, he was truly someone to be reckoned with.

His threshold for pain having increased over time via tea and olive branches to a level that would make Von Sacher-Masoch wince, his still-raw disfigurement bothered him hardly at all. But having checked his GPS tracking system he could not afford to wait long to act. He dialed the phone. A voice answered with no welcome.

"It is I," rasped Aaron.

"I, who?"

Oh. My. Aching. PILES! "*I who could have solved this Goddamned mystery in the time I've wasted going through this inane charade whenever I call and have to identify myself when no one else since the dawn of <u>elocution</u> sounds like this!*" The voice waited. Aaron sighed. "The Fist of God."

"One can never be too careful when the stakes are this high. What is it?"

"Mikhail's son is in the apostolic palace. He will be taken to The Vault, where he will have complete access to private texts and hidden information. We must use our operative within the Vatican. Let Mikhail *fils* know even there he is not safe."

"By doing what?"

"Killing the girl."

One could almost see the voice on the other end of the line preparing to pound something on a wooden surface. "What, pray tell, would that accomplish? We only have to wait for him to discover what he needs and track him to the ark! To kill the girl would alert all that we know where they are, distract him from his search, and make the Dominicans even more vigilant."

"You miss the point," said Aaron. "Imagine you are reading a thriller. The situation has escalated and you are invested in the characters. But the threat of conflict has been completely nullified by the fact that the primary antagonist is over eleven hundred kilometers away and can do nothing. And what follows is twenty pages of talking heads spouting ersatz theology, backstory, and no violence."

"There's always sex."

"With two celibates and a lesbian?" Clearly the voice hadn't thought of that. "If you were reading such a thriller...what would you do?"

"I...I would put the book down for something more thrilling."

Aaron need say nothing more. The thought of non-being was too great to contemplate.

The voice's chair creaked as he leaned for his Rolodex. "I will make the call."

Wednesday, April 7ᵗʰ, 10:07 p.m. – Rome

Mickey, rendered mute, couldn't believe his eyes. He felt like the first child let through the turnstiles opening day into the

Magic Kingdom and didn't know where to focus his attention. Even Danica, seeing what she saw, thinking she and Mickey now might have to be killed, was still glad she saw it.

DeSica and Visconti had escorted them down more halls of Medici opulence,[33] Mickey in priest's robes and Danica in an altar boy's suplice and vestments. (It was realized after they showered that they had nothing fresh to change into; and when in Rome...) Mickey seemed comfortable revisiting this attire, which he inhabited without question for over a decade, which his father encouraged and husbanded him toward, and which he walked... no, ran, sprinted away from...for reasons only he knew. Most could not help but be impressed by the artistic, joyous expressions of salvation, sacrifice, and martyrdom celebrated from floor to ceiling in this palace; but Mickey now viewed even the greatest works of religious art – and virtually all art from the fall of Rome until the Renaissance was

---

33   The Medici family produced three popes, Leo X, Clement VII, and Pope Leo XI who were major patrons of DaVinci, Michelangelo, Raphael, and Donatello. The Medicis were responsible for the building of the Sistine Chapel and Michelangelo's frescos within. And in the ultimate irony, they were patrons of Galileo who named four of Jupiter's moons after four Medici children he tutored. Alas, the same church represented by the Medicis forced them to abandon the scientist when Galileo was later indicted under the Roman Inquisition during the reign of Pope Urban VIII, and all his works were banned. He died under house arrest. Galileo, though, would have the last laugh: in 1992, Pope John Paul II expressed extreme "regret" for how he was treated and finally admitted that the Earth was not stationary after a careful study by the Pontifical Council for Culture.

religious – as manifestations by geniuses in matters of creativity, but pinheads in matters of theology.

Danica, on the other hand, dragooned into duty by a spiteful Mickey, was now thankful he did so; still awed to be in the belly of the Catholic beast, she was nowhere near as awed as she was about to be, the altar boy get-up only serving to put her in an even more respectful and adoring spirit. Nothing could break this spell for her.

Well, almost.

Mickey glanced over, looked her up and down and said, "How do they expect us to keep our hands off you guys when you look so damn cute in that get-up?"

Her look would turn most men into pillars of salt.[34]

The four arrived at a set of polished steel elevator doors. Visconti pulled a key on a chain from his waist, placed it in a lock, and turned it. The doors opened, the four entered. Inside Visconti pushed one of only two buttons and they began to be lowered. It was perhaps two minutes, before the elevator came to a stop. The doors opened.

And there it was. The Vault.

The size of at least two soccer fields...twenty-foot ceilings...entombed in double-reinforced six-foot-thick concrete...a quarter mile below ground...self-sustaining air management utilizing the same system as on the International Space Station...low-wattage color-corrected diode light...the atmosphere humidified to within .00001

34 Lot's wife, who looked back at the destruction of Sodom and Gomorrah, was not, as most people believed, turned into a giant salt lick. The phrase "to turn into a pillar of salt" was an Aramic idiomatic phrase that meant to be scared to death. At this moment, either outcome would have worked for Danica.

percent of proper papyrus, palm leaf, or early pulped fiber preservation...able to survive a direct hit from a hydrogen bomb...survivors able to live as long as various freeze-dried goods lasted in an adjoining storage room. When that ran out there was presumably microwaved human flesh to sustain them (since a microwave was provided and none of the stored foods required microwaving).[35]

But it wasn't the room that rendered them dumbstruck. It was what was in the room.

The ceiling was veined with miles of small gauge track. Hanging from this on double cables were document after document after document...from credit card-sized fragments to entire pages...from every banned gospel or heretic text, of every surviving written page or piece of correspondence regarding such text...of alternate synoptic Gospels and John...of forged Pauline letters[36]...all sealed between pieces of thin, matte Plexiglas...row upon row of forever conserved treasures, to be perused by sliding them along their track, the actual fiber never to be touched by human hands for the rest of its considerable existence.

Mickey was awed to be in the presence of such history that redefined man's relationship with God; a history that would begat wars, redraw countries, and cause countless

---

35   Indeed, not such a stretch in a religion where Christ ordered his followers to eat his flesh and drink his blood. The First Crusades certainly took this to heart when a vanguard short on supplies descended upon the Syrian town of Ma'arra 50 miles south of Antioch and, after a hard day of massacring 20,000 town folk, enjoyed a menu of boiled and spit-grilled heathen.

36   Beyond the forged Pauline letters already in the Bible, such as Timothy 1, 2 and Titus.

acts of goodness and evil in its name; a history that for most
of his life ruled his moral compass. To stand before the
very documents, penned by the hands of iconic thinkers,
dating back to the time of Christ, some possibly handled
directly by the apostles and first Christians, it was Mickey's
turn to almost weep. Tired as he was, Mickey was now electric with the energy of a scholar's joy.

Mickey, Danica in tow, stepped from the elevator as if
in a trance, crossed the raised arrival area, ascended a set
of steps, and wandered the aisles, flipping among the documents, muttering recognition at this and that, pausing
to marvel at a document, expressing delight at ones that
demanded further inspection. If any question remained,
Danica had to admit this mandrill was the real deal.

Their escorts cared not for his fanboy exhilaration.
"The clock is ticking," said DeSica, herding them to the reference table where the accordion file with Mikhail's notes
sat. "Your father found what he needed here in a day,"
the priest challenged. But it was unnecessary. Mickey was
eager to apply those notes to what lay before him.

Visconti soon returned with a glass of clear liquid.
"Drink this."

"What is it?"

"Holy water," he said with a straight face.

A look to Danica asked whether he should. "I don't
care if it's bleach," she said. Mickey sighed, took the glass,
downed it. A wince and cough followed.

"Get started. We will bring dinner," said DeSica.

"Uhh, pardon my skepticism, but you guys and dinner
aren't my favorite combo. No games this time, right?"

"Games?" asked DeSica, as if it were a foreign word.

"No tricks, no teasing, no ten minutes of 'testing.'"

"Of course not."

"Okay, then...since we're in the birthplace of pizza...I want to order the best pizza in all Rome."[37]

"Then you shall have it."

Mickey was still suspect. "Under the eighth commandment on the second tablet given to Moses by God himself... you promise to bring us the most delectable, oven-baked creation by popular decree known to Italians?"

"Would you be happy if it is the very same pizza the Holy Father himself requests?" said Fr. Visconti. That was good enough for Mickey.

In the meantime, others were planning something for Danica that fell under the fourth commandment.

Wednesday, April 7ᵗʰ, 10:21 p.m. – Rome

The call interrupted Father Leone in his office, performing his nightly rosary before a particularly tortured Christin-all-His-beautiful-agony on the cross; which Fr. Leone approximated by baring his knees on a custom-made pew surfaced with broken glass. He wouldn't have even answered except that it came in on *that* cell phone.

"The private matter of all men?" he answered.

"Yes," said the voice in his French-accented Italian.

---

37   Okay, technically? The Ancient Greeks baked flat bread called *plakous* with flavored toppings and the Persians around the same time baked bread on their shields and sprinkled it with cheese. But at least the Italians invented the *word* pizza.

Fr. Leone stood up to his full six feet of Michelangelo-defined muscle, honed in the private Apostolic Palace gym.[38] "What is it?"

"The son of Mikhail Samanovananonvich is there now, in The Vault as we speak."

Fr. Leone felt his gut go taut.

"He is guarded by two Dominicans and has a female companion," the speaker continued. "You are to terminate the woman with extreme prejudice."

"…Do what?"

"Tuck her in with a shovel."

"I don't—"

"Rub her out, top 'er off, snuff her candle—"

"Are you saying—"

"*Kill* her."

"Ah. Of course." Then the obvious question: "And then the son?"

"No."

"Why not?"

"Long existential story. Do it tonight."

Fr. Leone hung up. He pulled another rosary from a drawer, its beads strung on piano wire, and tucked it into his cincture. He left his office and closed the door, on which was a plaque. If ever a plaque required a hard zoom-in, it was this one: *Father S. Leone, Aide-de-Camp to Cardinal Thomasina.*

---

38   Originally a chamber built for self-flagellation, it was later decided that weight training, step aerobics, and spinning were the new tortures.

Wednesday, April 7ᵗʰ, 4:51 p.m. – Paris

Inspector Renault stood in the empty lot that would soon be a new overpriced work/loft development that was the *rage du jour* of city planners but, for now, was simply an illegal mid-city dumpsite until construction began. Yellow tape and uniforms were omnipresent as Renault looked down at the beautifully flayed layer of alabaster skin, from head to toes, among the weeds that recently held together a twenty-something supermodel. As the third such remains found – there was no body recovered in any of them – this now qualified as a disturbing, lurid serial crime that warrant its own book with Renault as a spin-off character.

This is where Richard Winthrop found him.

As Richard approached, watching Renault do his job, he quickly summed him up as someone who was extremely competent, who had a great deal of potential, but who for some reason operated just below his full potential.

"And you are," the Inspector asked Richard after he inquired of him.

"Richard   Winthrop,   lawyer   for   Mikhail Samanovananonvich. And a family friend," he answered in one of his seven fluent languages.

Renault betrayed the slightest surprise. "You are the second friend of the family to visit me today. I hope you are not here to escort the body back to San Francisco. I released it to the first visitor."

"Who was that?"

"A Sister Agnes from the San Francisco archdiocese. I'm told he's to be buried in a cemetery not far from Joe DiMaggio."

Richard nodded somberly. "I would like to be of any assistance in the investigation of his death."

"No need. I believe he died of lung cancer in 1998."

"Not Mr. DiMaggio. Mikhail Samanovananonvich."

"Ah. What do you know of it?"

"Only that Mickey was in the hospital here a day or so after Mikhail was killed."

Renault regarded Richard; his gut told him he was sincere. Whereupon he asked, "What can you tell me about Mr. Samanov?"

"He was very close to his father, but they had a falling-out, the two hadn't spoken in years."

"A falling-out over…?"

"Mickey had been a priest but left the vocation, in fact he abandoned the Catholic Church. Mikhail was devout, traditionalist, and never forgave him."

"His father, was he well-to-do?"

"Yes."

"You say you're the family lawyer. Was the son in his will?"

"He was, but…he had been disinherited. Well, unless he fulfilled a very specific…" Richard stopped, this was not helping Mickey's cause.

"Please, continue"

There was no good way to sugarcoat this. "Mickey would only be reinstated in the will if he returned to the church. Mickey had devised…one might call it a sort of church… of his own making, to…" Richard stumbled, he wasn't sure *what* Mickey had devised it for, and knew he had walked into a damning cul de sac. "Well…it was technically valid to reinstate Mickey as beneficiary but I can say this church of his had nothing to do with his father's will."

"How can you be certain?"

"He told me."

"Well, then."

"Mickey didn't kill his father."

"You have proof."

"Mikhail was killed *before* his son was even kidnapped. He was rescued from the very airplane that brought him here!"

"*Monsieur* Winthrop...it's true he was taken from a plane that had just landed. But the pilots were killed and a flight plan had been filed to leave that afternoon for Switzerland. Samanov snuck into this country. Thus we don't know how long he had been here." Richard looked physically pained. "What else can you tell me?"

"I think I've said enough."

"I'm sure we'll have reason to talk further. May I have a way to reach you?"

Richard perfunctorily opened a silver cardholder, handing a card to Renault. The Inspector read the wealth of contact information. When he looked up, the otherwise formal and mannered Richard Winthrop was walking across the lot without so much as a farewell. How telling, thought Renault.

It was time to contact Interpol.

Two years, three weeks, four days after the last flashback to Jean-Henri...

Two years, three weeks, and four days had passed since Jean-Henri sent a letter to Mikhail Samanovananonvich, in regards to a potentially valuable discovery in Iran, and offering a great sum for any information about it. No reply had come. In that time Jean-Henri invested in a Venezuelan gold mine that made him even richer, confirming once again that God was rewarding him for continuing Umberto's search. As Christ had preached on the Mount, blessed are the patient.[39] And that patience finally paid off.

A letter finally arrived from Mikhail. Neatly typed, precise in margin and syntax, it revealed Umberto's find, what the curious addition to the Gospel of Mark was referring to, and that somewhere out there was the ark containing it. To simply say Jean-Henri was stunned would be a complete failure of one's ability to evoke his degree of excitement. But simply put, he was stunned.

39   It doesn't read that way today. By the time the Bible was translated into the King James Version, using less than perfect Greek and Latin Vulgate texts, it read "Blessed are the meek." The meek are certainly patient; the patient are not always meek. On the subject of translations, a few partial handwritten English versions of scripture had been floating around in the early 16th century. But it was Englishman William Tyndale who was the first translator of the New Testament, painstakingly made from Hebrew and Greek texts. He then had the good news printed, thanks to the recently invented printing press, and disseminated. For his troubles, Cardinal Wolsey, Henry VIII's cabana boy and one of more than a few church authorities uncomfortable with the masses having The Word in the vernacular, declared Tyndale a heretic and the latter was strangled then burned at the stake in 1536. It could have been worse; strangulation before burning was considered humane.

The letter claimed a Vatican insider, only referred to as "Gigo," as the source. For an initial sum of twenty thousand dollars and a monthly stipend of two thousand, Jean-Henri could fund the search for the ark until this holy of holies was found...whereupon he would pay ten million American dollars to receive it. The monies were to be sent to a post office box in San Francisco. From time to time, extra expenses may be incurred. He was to make no attempt whatsoever to contact him directly.

It was an easy decision for Jean-Henri. If the touch of a splinter from the cross of Jesus gave him life, this...the ark...had to be the answer to eternal life.

He sent the initial payment and first month's stipend that day.

Wednesday, April 7th, 10:38 p.m. – Rome

Pizza boxes littered the floor, Frs. DeSica and Visconti licking their fingers ecstatically; Mickey and Danica less so.

"Who'da thought Rome had Shakey's pizza?" she said, dismayed.

Still, they ate. Mickey viewed his father's notes like an unassembled jigsaw puzzle, studying them and making his own notes for over an hour. "So where are we?" Danica asked, tiredly.

"The only notation my father makes about The Vault is 'Pope Celestine III-dash-Jack the Ripper.'"

"You're joking."

He wasn't. He was also stumped. But Mickey was stumped in a good way, challenged, his neurons firing on all cylinders like they hadn't fired in years, perhaps due in small part to feeling a little jacked on the Lateran moonshine he'd been given. At times like this, few as they were, Mickey was glad that while other kids played catch and went fishing with their fathers, he and *his* dad were conjugating Greek verbs and discussing the primacy of ethical attributes in the character of God. Getting a thought, he left her to search among the stacks.

Danica, weary beyond measure, finally put her head down on her robed arms. Soon her snoring vibrated the stainless steel tabletop. Blissfully. She never heard the dedicated phone line ring and Fr. Visconti answer, or knew that he'd been ordered to come see Cardinal Thomasina on a matter of grave import, or saw him get in the elevator and leave, or saw the elevator doors open minutes later, Visconti returning dead on arrival as Fr. Leone leaped out with a perfectly executed airborne reverse-spin kick connecting with all his hundred-eighty-five pounds upside DeSica's head. If the kick didn't break his neck, the impact of his head on cement should have. All Danica knew is that she went from oblivion to having a rosary bead garrote crushing her windpipe and that Mickey was nowhere in sight.

Phosphorus-hot panic burned every nerve within her, unable to loosen the garrote or the arms of steel cord holding it. Her vision began to dissolve into pastels she knew would become the light that would draw her near. In love, in rage, in the moment of fight or flight, one sees the world with a different emphasis, and Danica, frantic for any method of escape, saw an anorexically slim solution that otherwise would have never revealed itself, one item standing out to her in high relief from the rest of the world.

Mickey, among the stacks, so focused on his research and scribbling notes, never heard the sounds of struggle. Finishing, flushed, he hurried back to the research area, his words pouring out courtesy of the liquid bam before he even got to the table and Danica. "So like is it hot in here or what, you won't believe what I found, I could use a Mountain Dew, this place is one big-ass boneyard of buried crazy-ass uncles, we didn't get any Mountain Dews with that pizza did we, I wouldn't even believe it if I didn't read it myself but I might've already said that—" Whereupon he noticed Danica, standing above a priest hog-tied with a rosary, red-faced, sucking in deep gulps of properly humidified air.

"Where the fuck *were* you?" she gasped; his choices were so limited he had to stop and think. "And how'd this guy get in here?" Mickey then saw the bodies of Visconti and DeSica next to the elevator. Mickey began to realize that she was the survivor of a near-death experience.

"What the...holy...I mean, sweardagod I didn't hear a damn thing 'n you *know* it's true 'cuz I can't shut the hell up right now *you* know if I knew there was a killer priest down here I'da been in a fetal curl tighter'n a closed armadillo." And then, re: DeSica and Visconti, "Are they dead, they look dead, don't tell me they're dead."

"I dunno. I would've been. Shakey's Pizza saved my life."

She explained how she'd awakened to a rosary squeezing the holy Jesus out of her until, at the last possible moment, she saw the small plastic container of red pepper flakes that came with their Hawaiian-Canadian bacon. She managed to get a hand on it, throw the flakes behind her into the killer-priest's face, and painfully blind him. He released his pressure enough for her to turn the tables, the resulting hogtied priest needing no further explanation. Clearly for Danica the allure of the Vatican was beginning to wane. "How soon can we blow this pope stand?"

DeSica moaned, struggling to stand, blood streaming from an ear; and faster than you could say Lazarus, he was on the job. He crossed to the bound priest, grabbed his hair, and yanked back his head. It was the first time Mickey and Danica saw genuine surprise on the Dominican.

"Padre Leone?" Leone said nothing. DeSica rushed to the phone, punched an extension, and spoke urgently.

Danica whispered, as much to herself, "I can't believe what I'm thinking."

"Something about an exhibitionist gymnast who can bend over backwards 'n touch the floor with her tongue wearing a wet leotard with the air conditioning turned real cold, am I warm, warmish, yes, no, okay, I give, what are you thinking?"

"Right now you're the only person in the world that I trust." It was not meant as a compliment.

Wednesday, April 7th, 10:52 p.m. – Rome

Had not Cardinal Thomasina been in a wheelchair for expediency's sake, he might have fainted. Fr. Leone was untied but seated under the armed guard of DeSica.

"Explain yourself," ordered Thomasina in Italian; Mickey and Danica would understand none of this. "I demand it!"

Leone remained silent. DeSica unleashed a backhand with his .45. But Leone, bloodied, would give no more than his name, rank, and serial number.

"You have worked for me for twelve years...shared my strictest confidences...you are family," Thomasina trembled. "What is this about?"

Leone's eyes met Thomasina's and he said, "But you know." He paused to give the moment full measure. "The private matter of all men."

Thomasina drained. "You mean...*all* this time in my employ...it was in the service of someone else...to find the ark?" In all his experience, nothing gave Thomasina the tools to comprehend this. "Who...who is it you work for?"

Leone exploded from the chair, knocking DeSica's arm, his gun firing and shattering the Plexiglas that held the *Affidavit From the True Illegitimate Son of the Son of Man*, papyrus fragments fluttering down like dried leaves. Leone and DeSica struggled furiously, the weapon exploding again, taking out the purported *Cana Wedding Wine Order to Schlomo the Vintner (Note: bring good wine later)* as the two priests fell hard on the floor causing a third report. And then...a frightening silence; the two men lay there. A pool of burgundy seeped out from under them.

Danica and Thomasina had the exact same thought: If Leone is the one to stand...I'm so dead; Mickey was thinking of Mountain Dew. At long last a figure in black showed signs of life...slowly rose to a hunched position...then rose and straightened to his full stature: Fr. DeSica. Standing over his dead comrade, his levelheaded facade showed signs of fissures.

Cardinal Thomasina was beyond despondent over the betrayal, the carnage, the ramifications of all this. Quietly, he said to DeSica, "You know what to do."

Not even the Vatican police would learn of this; as was always the case, the church took out its own trash. Frs. Visconti's and Leone's obituaries would be posted in *La Republica*, their lives rendered in glowing and unfailing service to God, their deaths attributed to an accidental fall and congenital heart disease, respectively. They would be given proper funerals with proper eulogies and proper mournfulness. Only Mickey, Danica, DeSica, and Thomasina would ever know the truth.

And that number would be reduced in the coming days.

Wednesday, April 7ᵗʰ, 11:51p.m. – Istanbul

The clock was pounding louder than Mickey's heart on consecrated firewater. They weren't sure who was racing them to the ark, but Danica and DeSica knew that what they *didn't* know was as worrisome as what they did.

"Can't you go any faster," DeSica barked at the limousine driver. They were on their way to the airport: Mickey, Danica, DeSica, and his new partner, Fr. Bertolucci, cut from the same mold as DeSica's previous two partners.

"So while I was saving our collective ass," said Danica, "what'd you find?"

Mickey's buzz was peaking, or one could only hope. "You mean *besides* the fact that Pope John XXII was eighteen years old when he was confirmed the Holy Father and turned the Lateran Palace into the Playboy Mansion, and when Emperor Otto of Saxony tried to depose him John ran off to Tivoli with the papal piggy bank, and the bishops tried him *in absentia* for sex, robbery, extortion, and castrating a cardinal, found him guilty, and put in a new pope but then John returned, kicked him out, and cut off noses, fingers, and tongues from the bishops who tried him?"

"Yeah," she said dryly. "Besides that."

"And don't even get me started on Alexander VI—"

"I won't."

"—he was a Borgia, you know—"

"I do now."

"—he'd sell Cardinal posts at top dollar then when he needed cash he'd pay to have a few killed and sell 'em again—"

"Mickey—"

"—and he had a sixteen year-old mistress who got her *brother* the position of Cardinal—"

"Look—"

"—and *he* later became Pope Paul III who—"

Mickey yelped, his middle finger suddenly bent back to a degree he didn't think possible outside a Warner Brothers cartoon. Fr. Bertolucci was holding it. "*Signor* Samanov," he said, enunciating each word calmly and clearly, "your United States of America...it is the greatest, most magnificent country in the world. A beacon of light that all of us beyond her look up to. And yet...is it possible over time

that a president slept with a woman who was not his wife…
or was involved in a questionable situation where someone
died…or maybe even ordered others to perform acts not
condoned in your Bill of Rights?"

"Upp, yeah, right, see your point, I'm guessing two,
three maybe."

"Continue your conversation." The finger was released.

"So anyway," Mickey forged on, words shooting out
as if from a belt-fed weapon, "found two letters addressing the Celestine III reference in Dad's notes, but before
I tell you 'bout that remember the Temple where I figured
Thaddeus buried the ark and it was destroyed in the Jewish
Uprising in year 70? Dude, this car sure does ride nice.
Anyway, year 700 after the Muslims moved in they built this
heavyweight mosque on the spot where the Temple *used*
to be, making it this very holy shrine in Islam, 'cuz there
was this rock they built a dome over that Muhammad took
off from for a magical mystery tour up to heaven and back
with the angel Gabriel, with me so far?"

"Sorta—"

"So fast-forward to 1100 give-or-take when the First
Crusades kick Muslim butt and take back Jerusalem for
Christianity, being that Solomon built the first temple
there, the irony is lost on the crusaders that on the way
to the Holy Land they committed the first Jewish pogroms
and massacred a few thousand Jews in the city to take it,
any-hoo, after *that* the Knights Templar move into the former mosque and set up headquarters—"

"Whoa, wait, slow down, who are the Knights Templar?"

"Nuh-uh, exposition overload, save that for the next limo ride.[40] Okay, now fast-forward to the early thirteenth century, the *Third* Crusade comes to town—"

"Wait, what happened to the Second Crusade?"

"Gets its ass kicked in the holy land so it decides to invade the country that asked for its help in the first place, Egypt, gets shown the door there, too, this unites the Moslems under Saladin, and requires a third crusade to clean up the mess."

"Got it. So, Third Crusade."

"This one's led by Richard the Lion Heart—"

"*Finally*, someone I know in this snore-fest."

"Really? What language does he speak?"

"English for crissakes, he was the king of England!"

"*Ehhhhhhhh*," Mickey buzzed the international game show sound for 'loser,' "wrong, French, he doesn't speak a *word* of English since he was raised in France—"

"Well that's stupid—"

"—and though he's remembered as the noble warrior-king, his first major act of his 'crusade' is to behead 3,000 men, women and children from the captured city of Acre and dig through their bowels for hidden gold he's sure they swallowed, oh, and he's gay."

"So he's got his good points…is there a caboose on this train of thought?"

"Right, meandering, so, Richard's army never quite makes it to Jerusalem but unknown to historians who haven't seen what *I've* seen, Richard is snuck in and visits the Knights Templar, and after he does he writes a letter

---

40 Or just read *The DaVinci Code*.

to Pope Celestine III 'n Richard tells Celestine that he was shown a limestone box with words carved on it that read, 'The Ark of the One True Excreta.'"

"So you were right about the engraving?" She couldn't help but be impressed.

"Educated guess though hot damn a good one but the important thing is we now know it exists or at least it *did* exist, 'cuz the letter Celestine wrote *back* commands Richard to destroy it but I'm gonna make another educated guess 'n say that Richard might be a mass murdering, gold-seeking sodomite, but he's a very religious one, I'm betting that he'd be the last person to destroy an actual, confirmed relic from his lord and savior—"

"That doesn't tell us where the ark is," she interrupted, crestfallen.

"True that, but my *dad* figured out where it was and I'm betting his reference to Jack the Ripper'll send us in the right direction, hey lookee is that Pia Zadora, I've never been t'London, have you, though first year out of the priesthood's a little hazy, my Robitussan-and-Zima phase, maybe I–" Whereupon, like a jet engine expending its last drop of fuel, he crashed, falling face first into Danica's crotch. Her knee-jerk reaction was to knee-jerk his face, rather than let this swine anywhere near her almond joy...except that the silence that followed was a welcome relief. Whereupon he began to snore, deeply, causing a not unpleasant *basso profundo* vibration. Screw it, she didn't care if there were two priests nearby, it'd been so long since she had anyone there, it was kind of like revisiting an old friend.[41]

Thursday, April 8th, 7:48 a.m. – Paris

With Mickey having arrived in London, Aaron rushed to De Gaulle Airport, not even bothering to pack his beloved *Soie Blanche* French buttermilk, trusting that the English diet was better in matters of dairy than it was with their deep-fried, newspaper-wrapped cuisine.

Aaron 2.0 turned more than a few heads marching down the concourse. In his trademark black leather, a scarf around his face, sunglasses, not to mention booking a one-way flight to London, he was not your typical French tourist. At the gate two security agents quickly steered him to a small windowless room with the mirror that fooled no one. The bag Aaron had just checked was brought in by a third agent, who began rummaging through it. Perusing his passport, the second agent said, "Remove the scarf and glasses, please." Aaron did so, the agent having to suppress his gag reflex. "So, Aaron Zworkan…what is your business in London?"

"A matter of the gravest import."

"What sort of matter?"

"Are you religious?"

"As religious as the next man," he shrugged.

---

41 Those of you who missed the wrong city in the chapter heading also missed a key clue earlier, without which the rest of the book will not make sense, and you must, therefore, start the book over.

"Then pray...*pray* for the future. And for your snot-nosed kids and grandkids who say their nightly prayers for God to watch over them and their loved ones."

The third agent discovered the oaken box. He unlatched the pewter clasp, opened it, and held it up for the others to see the metal knight's glove inside. "And what is this?"

Idiots. "A glove."

"What is its purpose?"

Such a question to ask, necessitating an answer that went back centuries. A question when fully answered would be wasted on these low-level, unimaginative clock-watchers. How could Aaron tell grown men qualified for no more in life than digging through strangers' underwear of the glove's rich and twisted history? How could he tell them of the places it had been? How could he tell them that it was a reward given to him for a crime done many years before? A crime helping a particular fraternal order in a nasty piece of business at the *Palais de la Decouverte*, involving an exhibit of medieval religious relics, on loan from the Vatican, the prized focus of which was an actual thorn from the crown of Christ? Nasty due to the death of two guards who stood between him and that object? Two guards who weren't supposed to be there, in fact who had been paid handsomely to be elsewhere on their late-night rounds when Aaron entered through the disarmed door? Two guards who, after accepting the bribe, realized if they killed their briber, they would be rich and heroes as well? Two guards who failed to realize that their briber had con-sidered that same possibility, hence they were martyred by dying for a symbol of the martyr of all men? And in reward he was given this highly prized artifact from another martyr, the most respected martyr of this fraternal order, Jacques de Molay, to which Aaron was also a member? An artifact so prized by Aaron that it came to define who he was? An artifact from a martyr whose story was so disturbing, whose end was so grotesque, that its retelling might appear at any point from here on so that a reader must keep reading?

"Its purpose?" Aaron replied, tiring of all that their question demanded. "It is an accoutrement of The Fist of God. Remember that name, gentlemen. The Fist...of God."

All seemed fine. "Okay. You're free to board."

Thursday, April 8th, 6:32 a.m. – London

Dawn in London. The homeless were rousing from their blankets and lice under the Charing Cross Arches. Maintenance workers were finishing their shift in the purgatory of underground tubes. The first loaves of daily bread were pulled hot from the ovens of Oxley, Fulham, Sunbury-on-Thames. And Mickey, on an airplane, was nose-deep in Danica's lap (this time *her* doing; she waited for him to fall asleep, then placed him there).

The flight was the first sustained sleep Mickey had had in four days, even if it was for less than an hour. As the plane was landing Danica realized he was too heavy to get upright by herself, enlisting a truly disgusted flight attendant to help extricate this apparent priest from the lap of an effeminate altar boy. He rose up looking like a Nick Nolte mug shot.

"Whew," Mickey said, wiping crust from his eyes. "I had the strangest dream."

"From you, that's quite a statement."

"I dreamt I was in a pie eating contest. All the pies were mincemeat...and I hate mincemeat...but *this* pie was the best pie I ever had. I can still taste it. What do you think it means?" He was truly flummoxed.

"That you are nothing if not consistent," she answered. He didn't understand, but it sounded flattering so he left it alone.

The group walked briskly through the terminal until they saw a driver in an all-black uniform and turtleneck, waiting with a hand-lettered sign, DESICA. He escorted them quickly outside to his vehicle...a stretch limousine with a hot tub in back (also a parquet wooden floor inside, a disco ball, surround-sound and a fully stocked bar).

"New Scotland Yard," DeSica barked to the driver as they all piled in.

"I apologize for the...unusual ride, gentlemen," said the driver. "I got the call from the bishop's office to pick you up on rather short notice, and this was the only one left in the motor pool."

"You have *more* of these?" Mickey asked, impressed. "Maybe I gave up on the church too soon."

"No, sir. It's the only one. As I understand it, it was a gift from a penitent who was giving up his previous occupation." Whoever it was, Mickey wished these leather seats could talk.

The limousine merged into the stream of traffic that jockeyed aggressively for position, departing the airport. The driver, trained in personal protection and evasion tactics, didn't feel threatened by a dented, older model Cooper behind them, remaining a casual distance back as their pimpmobile headed into the sludge that was the morning flow on the M4.

Danica felt an even greater excitement to be in another historic capitol, this one a hybrid of the timeless and handsome grafted to the present and future, a bit like fueling an Aston Martin DB5 Vantage with solar panels; not entirely successful, but visual and compelling. From what Danica could see, London already felt like a more perfect fit: Cosmopolitan but working class, historic but accessible, with an air of dogged perseverance that thrived in the face of plagues, reformations, counter-reformations, Nazi bombings, and the Spice Girls. Like the cockroach, London would always be here.[42]

Mickey felt his own tingle of excitement, having found the limo bar, and made himself something red with a celery stalk.

"Is that a virgin?" warned DeSica in his question.

"That's what Joseph asked," Mickey replied as it rose to his lips.

Fr. Bertolucci intercepted it, sipped, and dumped it down the sink. "Not while you're working for us." Mickey

---

42   Ed. note: The London Council of Tourism thanks you, I'm sure.

sagged, a toddler put in the corner on time-out. His silence was oppressive.

"You promised to fill me in on the Knights Templar on the next limo ride," reminded Danica. It was not the best time. Mickey gave her a look that was, if not eat-shit-and-die, was eat-shit-and-die adjacent; Danica saw it was time to pull out the major artillery. "Y'know, Samanov...this adventure has all the makings of a major motion picture. Meaning you'd be the protagonist of that movie. Except from a nuts-and-bolts protagonist point of view? I've pretty much done all the heavy lifting."

It wasn't her strongest card. "B.F.D."

"Then there's my weekend-long, coming-out, all-girl threesome—"

"*So*, the Knights Templar," said Mickey, sitting up straight in more ways than one. "Think of them as monks with swords. And shields and battle-axes and long pointy lances. They answer only to the pope, they live together, they study scripture, they can never see a naked body, even their own. And they maim and kill."

"*Kill?*" Off Mickey's nod, she asked, "Even with 'thou shalt not kill...?'"

"Eeyeah, well...the pope who kicked off this whole crusade thing? His name was Pope Urban.[43] He clarified the fine print on the commandments by pronouncing, 'thou shalt not kill *Christians.*'"

"You're shitting me," she scoffed.

---

43   Contrary to popular belief, not our first inner-city black pope.

"Ask them," Mickey said, indicating the priests. She turned, about to, but they stared at her, no life behind their eyes. She decided against.

"It gets better," continued Mickey. "Despite a vow of poverty, these monks are rich, as in the stinking variety, they're up to their nose-guards in filthy lucre. Though in all fairness, they really didn't try to be." Mickey scratched the itch where the Mohawk gave him the shot. "After the First Crusade captured the Holy Lands, they became destination central for pilgrims. And a Saracen or two saw income opportunity in taking pilgrim gold and the occasional pilgrim life. So the Templars became escorts along the various routes to Jerusalem, to protect the faithful."

"So they only killed in defense."

"Welllllll...these guys were highly trained *and* had God on their side, how do you put Seabiscuit in the Kentucky Derby and tell 'im not to break a sweat? They outgrew the escort business real fast. 'Fact they even took on Saladin himself before Richard got there."

Outside the slow-and-go continued as the thoroughfare turned into the A4. The Cooper was still there but no cause for alarm. Their driver might have thought differently, however, had he known a respectful distance behind the Cooper were three olive green Land Rovers with tinted glass. Inside each one were four paramilitaries, all prone to not smiling, with a decidedly Manichean view of things. Among the three SUVs was enough firepower to destabilize a small third world government.

This was Interpol.

"Anyway," Mickey continued, "they built or took over castles and spread into Palestine and Syria. The Pope and King of Jerusalem were so glad to have 'em, they gave the Templars office space in the Islamic Dome of the Rock. Which you should recall, is where Solomon's temple used to be."

"That's where their money came from? Real estate?"

"Not even close. When word gets out that French monks are selflessly risking life and limb protecting pilgrims, with *that* kind of P.R., well, the bucks start pouring in. Especially from nobles who weren't quite as moved to lose two years and maybe their *lives* to hold onto the Holy Land, so they gave generously to show how committed they *would* be if they didn't have scheduling conflicts. But money also came from Joe Six-Pint, the great-unwashed sinners who were willing to part with a hard-earned halfpence when the average *monthly* salary was five pence. Because the church promised anyone who gave to the cause got time off in purgatory. What God's cut was wasn't quite clear."

"Target still within sight and moving toward metro center," said the single occupant of the Cooper into a hands-free headset to the three Land Rovers...

"Noblemen put their estates under Templar care while they were away, for a management fee of course...pilgrims deposited jewels and gold for letters of credit to thwart robbers, then got their funds when they arrived there... the first use of bank checks far as anyone can tell. This required the Templars to establish financial centers all through Christendom, even their own fleet of ships, making them the first multinational company."

"No kidding...is it still around?"

Mickey sat back in his seat. "*That's* the juiciest part of the story. The private stuff. And speaking of private...I'm overdue for a little taste of your coming-out story."

She shifted uncomfortably, not because that wasn't their deal, nor was she a prude or, worse, ashamed. But there was still enough residual Catholic in her that she preferred her Roman-collared companions not to know one or two secrets about her spare time outside the confessional. "Not the best place..." she said, sotto, a nod to the priests.

Mickey smiled, catching her drift that there *was* an appropriate place, already fighting his mighty unfurling manhood in anticipation of one of the great debutart tales.

The Cooper and Land Rovers continued behind them, inexorable, implacable. Their quarry? Per Renault's call to Paris Interpol, an international killer with top-level diplomatic protection from the Vatican, who traveled in circles that included world court barrister Richard Winthrop, and who was cleverly masquerading as an American pool and spa cleaner. A check with San Francisco's Interpol Division indicated a possible murder or abduction from his now dead-father's residence. A police officer was missing who had interrogated him only the night before. And while this sociopath was cagey enough to not have any felonies on his sheet, enough complaints against him displayed a disturbing ability to pull women under his sway, possibly using them as operatives for god-knows-what. He had all the signs of being what was known in the trade as a "free radical."[44]

44   A word that somewhere along the line has been appropriated by nutritionistas.

To Interpol, there was no question about it: they were dealing with a twenty-first century Jackal.

Wednesday, April 7th, 11:14 a.m. – Paris

Inspector Renault fought a mounting sense of dread. He
stood over the dead *sous-brigadier* police officer, hog-tied
and shot point blank in the face per the gun powder-black-
ened hole on his forehead. Most disturbingly, this was
identical to the officer killings in St. Germaine and Marais.
The three murdered police shared one thing in common:
their last names began with R. Lost in thoughts only a
police officer whose last name was Renault could think, his
stomach churned, sweat moistening his brow. Oh, not for
the surname thing…for an exchange between two other
police he overheard moments before:
    "Did you hear Captaine Aumont is retiring?"
    "Old news. The talk is who will be promoted to his
position."
    "Renault, of course. He's working on a case that
has the makings of an international religious thriller.
If he solves it, it wouldn't surprise me if he makes
chief."
    The worst part was, Renault had the nagging suspicion
that something Richard Winthrop inadvertently said on
Mickey's behalf would lead him to a major breakthrough.
Renault sighed heavily, he knew what he must do. *Even* if
it led to his promotion. He must return to the unpleasant,
sophistic forensics analyst of Mikhail's initial assault. Not
to review the physical evidence. *Au contraire.* The answer

to the clue would hopefully come from the failed thesaurist inside the rotund little man. No, wait. Make that little creep. Or weirdo.

Huh, realized Renault...this thesaurist thing is tougher than it looked.

Thursday, April 8th, 7:23 a.m. – London

The limo screeched to a stop outside 10 Broadway Street. The building was dark, functional and unimaginative. This was "The Yard" to those who worked there, as well as to the locals; "Scotland Yard" or "New Scotland Yard" to the rest of us. Twenty stories tall and within eyeshot of Parliament, it boasted an incongruous revolving three-sided sign out front reading "New Scotland Yard" that would look more at home in front of a muffler shop.

The Mini-Cooper continued past them down Broadway, the job of this Judas goat finished. The Land Rovers took positions on Dacre St., Caxton St., and one further down Broadway. Their passengers watched through magnification as three priests and an altar boy emerged from that tawdry limo. What they must have done to that altar boy inside that vehicle, the Interpol agents thought as one. They had a description of Mickey that fit one of them to an eyelash: the tall, unkempt one with the California tan, so wrong here. This predator would be in their crosshairs the moment he came back out.

There was *always* a newbie on such missions; young, earnest, carried a picture of his sweetheart in his breast pocket, usually the first to take a bullet in heavy fire. This particular newbie, Fitzwiler, leaned forward to the grizzled Colonel Brinkerhoff, who chewed on an unlit cigar.

"Sir, question, sir."

"Jesus, Fitzwiler, need to change your diaper already?"

"Sir, no sir."

"What is it?"

"Sir, the high-value target is walking into a police station. As Interpol and an international police organization that works with state and local police stations, why don't we simply put a call into Scotland Yard and have him arrested, saving possible gunfire, loss of life, and an obligatory car chase, sir?"

Brinkerhoff's neck flushed red, his teeth grinding down on his cigar. "Crissakes, Fitzwiler...this one's gonna require visual aids, in'nit?"

"Sir, possibly, sir."

"Okay, Fitzwiler, it goes like this. No matter what country...what culture...what customs...*whenever* you have a city helping an unincorporated area...a county helping a city... a state helping a county...the federal helping a state...or the international helping the federal...you have what's called 'overlapping jurisdictions.' And when you have that, you always, repeat, *always*, have a recipe for extreme agitation. Because each jurisdiction wants what, Fitzwiler?"

"Sir, the arrest, sir."

"'Cuz why, Fitzwiler?"

"Sir, because each jurisdiction wants the credit, sir."

"And what else...?"

"Sir, because each jurisdiction thinks itself more competent than the jurisdiction it's helping, sir."

"Thus the more high-value the target, the more high-value the what, Fitzwiler?

"Sir, that would be the glory, sir."

"And without the glory, what do you have, Fitzwiler?"

"Sir, that's a trick question, it's not what you have, it's what you don't have, sir."

"And what don't you have, Fitzwiler?"

"Sir, you don't have squat, sir!"

Not bad, thought the Colonel. This newbie might just survive his first mission.

Inside, having dealt with all the pro forma crap of checking their weapons and getting past high security, the four were taken to a sterile bright room with no windows. Six heavy boxes of files on the Whitechapel (a.k.a. Jack the Ripper) Murders were brought in and placed on the table. DeSica and Bertolucci sat guard on either side of the door; there'd be no repeat of The Vault incident here. Mickey looked at the long boxes over-stuffed with manila folders, each containing scores of dog-eared documents. His heart sagged. "It'd help if I knew what I was looking for," he sighed.

Danica, however, was in her element. "This is an unsolved case. Meaning even if it's closed? It's still open. We start with the latest files and work backwards."

"Because…?"

"You don't know what you're looking for and in any unsolved murder, neither do the police. Your father wouldn't make a connection between Pope Celestine and this case if there wasn't a specific. So your time's better spent with whatever they already know rather than sifting through what they have yet to find."

Times like that, she couldn't be sexier to him than if she was lying naked on a bearskin rug wearing only a smile and sucking on a chocolate-covered long-stem cherry, her manicured hot pink nails pulling the orb from the pneumatic orifice, just, y'know, to pick an image. They found the box with the most recent files, Mickey pulled one, and began reading. As he finished a page, he would pass it to Danica, who perused it as well.

And so it went for the next three hours, working backward reading mundane statements from suspects, witnesses, family, the watch constable on rounds that night; spiked with the occasional less mundane tabloid-worthy mortuary photograph or report of a victim who had her intestines pulled out and draped around her, and her left kidney removed. Half of the kidney was later sent parcel post to the police with a letter "From Hell" that reported of the other half, "...*I fried and ate it was very nise.*"

Three hours two minutes in, Mickey stalled on a page, not passing it over to Danica. Waiting for him to finish, she glanced over and picked up the legal pad of Mikhail's notes; it was, of course, all Greek to her. On the second page near "Celestine/Jack the Ripper" she noticed an odd addition in the margin, circled. It appeared to be..."sanitation."

She looked up and saw Mickey was no longer reading what was in front of him, just hovering above it, mentally riffing. "You find something?" she asked. He snapped to, absently passed the page without comment, grabbed another, and began reading. She showed him the pad, indicated the word. "You see this?"

"Yeah."

"What do you think it means, 'sanitation?'"

"Good hygiene. Beyond that I couldn't tell you."

He was in a mood. Danica picked up the page he passed to her and saw it was a coroner's report for victim Mary Jane Kelly, the last confirmed Ripper kill. She read it, nothing jumping out, and was about to move on when a delayed reaction smacked her upside the head. Her attention went directly to Mary Jane's description.

Red hair. Green eyes.

The picture in his father's upstairs terrace. His mother. The same uncommon and arresting color palette. The person he'd never once mentioned. Maybe not the most tasteful time to delve into the subject, thumbing as they were through files of slaughtered prostitutes, but when did that stop her? "Wanna talk about it?"

"What?"

"'What?'" she repeated, with just a hint of scoff. "Red hair, green eyes?" She had his number. She could see he knew it, too.

"I didn't think it'd interest you."

"Maybe it would."

He put down the page, ran a hand over his face, debating. Until finally, "Shit..." Another moment to gather his thoughts. "I haven't shared this with anybody." Her expression said he could trust her. "It's the kind of thing that just...creeps into my consciousness for no reason. I go weeks, months without thinking about it then...boom, something triggers it and I just...." He trailed off, pained, unable to conjure up the right words. "It goes back years..." he began again, eyes beginning to brim.

"Go on...tell me."

He took a deep breath, then: "The pasties on strip-pers...when'd they start getting so big? It's like an evangel-ical right-wing conspiracy, I mean they charge cover *and* a two-drink minimum and they gotta cover the *entire* areola? That's a hidden tax on my right to a boner, and I for one plan to take it all the way to the—"

"You're a bastard."

"That's no way for an altar boy to talk."

"Oh for my service revolver right now."

"You can pistol-whip me anytime.   Preferably in uniform."

"A fantasy we both share. You've never even acknowl-edged she existed."

"She existed. I'd love to tell you how she rocked me to sleep, knitted me booties, or cried at my graduation but I can't since, y'know, none of it ever happened." Mickey returned to the document in front of him, in no uncertain terms ending the discussion. Okay, she thought, it's gotta be painful, clearly this many years later it's still an open wound, no need to go all D.A. on him, just let it go. One-Mississippi, two Mississs—

"What happened to her?"

Mickey exhaled the longest, most irritated exhale. "You're not gonna let it go, are you?" Everything about her said probably not. "When I was four years old she disap-peared. Dad refused to talk about it. Except to say she was dead so that's what I thought. When I was old enough to realize the lack of a funeral and teary-eyed visits to a grave-stone, he amended that to say she was 'dead to him.'"

"But..." His baleful glare gave her pause. "That family portrait...all those years, why did he keep it?"

"He liked. The frame."

No missing that delivery: The fat lady sang, left the stage, showered, changed, laid on her divan, and was on her second box of bon-bons. Another question and he would combust. Danica didn't begrudge Mickey his anger at her or about her, she saw versions of it all the time on domestic calls; the confused child peeking in from the other room as Dad or boyfriend or Mom or both were in restraints and none of it made sense. Mickey the child was still a victim. And whenever the victimizer, directly or indirectly, was a parent, the emotions that child felt were outsized, had a half-life longer than uranium. It was the greatest betrayal, especially to someone in the state of still becoming, their fragile psyche yet unformed, the parent was their eyes and ears into the world, their moral barometer, protector. From a child's waist-high view of the world, a mother especially was the one to cling to and hide behind from the ghoulies and ghosties and things that go bump in the night. They should be the—

Oh. Shit. Wait. It was as if a beam from heaven suddenly shown down on the files. Maybe *that* was it, the answer, not to Mickey's demons or the Ripper case, but to their search. Maybe Mikhail's notation that brought them here wasn't about delving into the *mystery* of the killings, maybe it was about looking into the people in charge of *solving* the mystery. Maybe they were looking at the wrong side of the equation.

"Mickey."

A growl from behind a yellowed document, "This better be about—"

"It is. All this time we've been digging through the victims' files."

"And…"

"What if this isn't about the victims, what if it's about the people who were supposed to be protecting the victims, the authorities, the *adults* here?"

"Adults? What're you—"

"Never mind, your father's notation may have had nothing to do with a Victorian serial killer. Maybe the parallel between the ark and the Ripper referred to someone's *search* for the Ripper, and it's that someone who'll get us back on track."

Mickey was impressed, aroused, but more than a little brain-numb. "So we…?"

"…start over and look for any information in the chain of command."

"I so coulda' used that Bloody Mary."

Twelve years since we last checked on Jean-Henri…

For twelve years Jean-Henri Vandersmissen sent money to the San Francisco post office box and for twelve years the information came – sporadically, sometimes months in between, airmailed letters from Rome, Northern Europe, the Holy Lands. Meanwhile, an investment in outdated automobile dies and machinery from *El Norte* to produce older model American cars in Argentina doubled his fortune yet again and continued to prove that God was on his side.

But Jean-Henri was not Job. The news he received was often vague or informational ("I travel to Damascus on news of potential corroborating information" might be followed by "Alas, it was not to be"). Time had come to hire a shadow for Mikhail Samanovananonvich to be sure this was not an elaborate shakedown.

America had a peculiar subset of beings that thrived in the shadows and made their living on the dark machinations of the soul: The private eye. True, the profession was not unique to America, but Americans were unique in the profession, those who walked that path manifesting equal parts love and hate for the occupation and for themselves, with disdain for the customer and case, yet with an odd code that bound them to follow matters to their twisted and usually deadly end; at least per Chandler, Hammet and stories in *Argosy* and *Black Mask* magazines. He was disappointed he could not find a Continental Op Agency in the San Francisco phone directory, but he found the next best thing: Nick Hazard, Private Investigator. Nick Hazard! Even the name had verisimilitude! A long distance call began thusly:

"Hazard P.I.," someone answered with a smoker's sandpaper voice that was pre-cancerous.

"This is Nick Hazard himself?" said Jean-Henri in his heavy Dutch accent.

"No, this is his secretary who just got a sex change, but they didn't have any dame voice boxes so I gotta sound like this for the rest of my life. Which hopefully won't be much longer with people like you asking dumb shit questions."

Jean-Henri had the real thing! "I have a job of the utmost importance."

"Make it fast, I got an A.A. meeting and I'm gonna pick up my half-hour chip."

Jean-Henri was getting the full-on American E-ticket shamus experience. That Nick Hazard was really Israel Honowitz who read the same books and magazines Jean-Henri did, who'd quit his job at the kosher butcher shop, and who was talking to his first client in the two months since changing careers, would die with him. Jean-Henri ran down his case.

"Lemme get this straight," said Israel. "You want me to tail some guy with an unpronounceable name who you can't describe to me, who you've hired for reasons you won't tell me, to confirm if he's working on something I can't know about."

"You make it sound difficult."

"What was I thinking?"

Nick, of course, took the job as the code of his profession demanded. Two weeks later Jean-Henri got his first packet of information in a string-tied brown paper-wrapped package. He eagerly ripped it apart. Out fell a beefy middle finger, the obituary of Israel Honowitz, his official wallet *Argosy* detective I.D., and a note: *The stipend is now three thousand a month. M.*

Jean-Henri realized he had underestimated a superior criminal mind that could so easily dispose of a bona fide American gumshoe. This was not a person to be trifled with.

Thursday, April 8ᵗʰ, 9:48 a.m. – London

The Fist arrived in England. His contact gave him an untraceable Glock, laundered pounds, and a rental car upgrade to mid-size. Ever the professional, Aaron turned on the GPS, strapped in, fired up the horses, and spent the next seven-and-a-half minutes in search of the proper 80's androgynous music station. Then he took off.

Aaron couldn't know that his destination was New Scotland Yard, nor could he know that he was stepping into a perfect storm of biblical proportion involving British police, Vatican firepower, and Interpol gonadian supremacy with twelve sharp-shooting agents already in position. Death, swift and irreversible, was in store for someone who would be caught in this squall…someone already introduced in our narrative… someone whose demise would forever change the course of history. But Aaron was blissfully unaware as he drove, sang, and performed precision upper-body choreography to Frankie Goes To Hollywood.

Wednesday, April 7ᵗʰ, 1:32 p.m. – Paris

The toady sat in the forensics lab digging through a cadaver sliced wide like an open coin purse. Official procedure mandated that a forensic analyst wear a surgical mask to protect himself from fumes or bacteria, as well as to protect the evidence from contamination. That would have posed a barrier, however, to the several stale éclairs nearby in a pink bakery box; left by the night shift, every day he arrived ten minutes early to steal what remained before the morning shift arrived. If he'd only known that fresh éclairs replaced the ones everyone knew he took that otherwise would have been fed to the alley *souris*.

"Good morning," said Renault.

The beetle-eyed analyst looked up, crème on the corners of his mouth. *Oh joy...him again.*

"I am here on the matter of Mikhail Samanovananonvich."

And my job description includes memorizing the name of every corpse. Inconvenienced, the analyst pushed the remaining pastry into his mouth, wiping crumbs from his lips (that fell into the bisected stomach, throwing off and setting back the investigation seven months), and began to rise.

"No...no need to get the file," answered Renault. "This is not about the *physical* evidence." Then, knowing he had a diamond-encrusted hook that this blowfish couldn't resist swallowing whole: "This is about the last thing Mikhail Samanovananonvich said."

The analyst froze mid-rise. Did he hear correctly? Did the inspector say..."said?" As in...*words?* The ambassadors of the soul? The clothing in which all thoughts are attired? Was it possible for the first time in his miserable second career that somebody actually sought him out for his first love, his only love?

"The...last thing he said?" the analyst dared to repeat.

"Yes. I seem to recall you are without peer when it comes to vocabulary."

Such obvious pandering still made him blush. "I prefer 'lexis' but..." Warming to this man he might have misjudged, the analyst said, "Yes...I seem to remember the strange case of Mikhail Samanovananonvich...what exactly *was* the last thing that he said?"

"Only a word...a single word," Renault tantalized.

"*Only* a word...the DNA of Shakespeare...the grains Melville used to create mountains...ammunition in the mouth of Goebbels...that which births ideas, art, *dreams* that would otherwise remain unfertilized ovum, never to live, grow, *thrive*, what word, come on man, do tell me!" he begged, a hophead staring at a locked-and-loaded hypodermic just beyond reach.

"Then again," Renault shrugged, as if on a fool's errand, "it may mean nothing at all." He made as if to leave. The analyst grabbed Renault's sleeve, a throbbing in his skull.

"Good sir," he whispered hoarsely. "...*please!*"

Renault felt the actual stirrings of pity for someone he would prefer to be outlining in chalk. This was too easy, he thought, he had tormented his tormentor long enough. "The word," he started, pausing, just because, "was...*souris*."

"*Souris*," the analyst repeated, warming to the test. "You are sure."

"A witness testified that he said it more than once."

"I see...*souris*..." However pedestrian a term, one worked with what one was given. "We all can't be Oscar Wilde at the moment of death, can we? What about it do you wish to know?"[45]

"How do you say it in English?"

---

45   Wilde, in his bed, said to those gathered around him just before he expired, "Either this wallpaper goes or I do." On the other end of the spectrum, Henry David Thoreau gave solace to his grievers with the last words, "...Moose...Indian." In fairness, it could have been another example of transcendentalist humor.

"'Mice.' The plural of 'mouse,' an Old English word in use by 900 common era, but its origins are most interesting, predating Latin and can be found in Old Persian—"

"Yes-yes, fascinating. 'Mice,' you say." The analyst nodded eagerly, a trained seal anxious for another cube of fish. "I see," Renault pursed his lips. "Now...*this* is the interesting question. The one that, if answered properly, may unravel this case. I need you to think very...very carefully before you answer what I am about to ask." Renault needn't have said that; given the choice of being right here, right now, helping Renault solve an unsolved case based on lexiconography, or instead being elsewhere getting a tongue-bath by twin pulchritudinous blonde bone addicts who *claimed* they were of legal age, well...it was no contest.

"Go ahead, Inspector Renault," he said, lifting his gaze into the headwinds of challenge. "Ask your question."

O unkind fate! A maintenance man had entered unnoticed with an industrial floor buffer, choosing that very moment to turn it on, the drone of the appliance obscuring all discussion. There was a brief reprieve as, *Zzzzt!* The room was plunged into utter black, a fuse blowing from the buffer using the same circuit as the refrigeration units, filled to capacity with a number of overweight English Historical Society members. And while the hum of the buffer now ceased, allowing us to hear their discussion, the unrelenting string of Romanian profanities by the maintenance man filled the blackness.

At last the lights came on. The maintenance man stopped his profanities and, unable to do his job properly until fewer bodies were on ice, stormed off. In the meantime, the forensic analyst seemed satisfied with the answer he gave to Renault's question that we could not hear, redeeming himself for his national Icarus in solving the riddle.

And Renault seemed most satisfied of all: He had the information he needed to put away Mikhail's killer.

Thursday, April 8ᵗʰ, 10:14 a.m. − London

Brinkerhoff had radioed Interpol for N.O.I. (non-obtrusive interference) to obstruct all streets surrounding New Scotland Yard. Thus on Caxton St., a cement mixer broke down; just past the roundabout at Broadway and Tothill a delivery van hit an ambulance; and at Broadway and Old Pye St., in what was surely a nod to Lewis Carroll and his *Alice In Wonderland* social commentary on hat makers, a transport vehicle carrying unsecured containers of mercury overturned and required the assistance of haz-mat.[46] (If one looked closely enough, he or she might notice that the perpetrators in all these incidents were thirty-something males with steely demeanors and buzz cuts.)

Soon, traffic had been diverted from the hot zone, the last stragglers funneled out Dacre St. before it, too, was blocked by what was surely a nod to the writing stylings of Edward Bulwer-Lytton, when a truck dropped a flatbed full of porta-potties.[47]

---

46   The Mad Hatter was a pointed jab at hatmakers who allowed their employees to stiffen the felt using mercury and their bare fingers; it eventually drove the employees insane.

47   He of questionable writing ability who began his novel, *Paul Clifford*, also set in London, with the immortal words, "It was a dark and stormy night."

Thursday, April 8ᵗʰ, 11:01 a.m. – London

It was a bright and sunny day. Still, traffic was horrible.
Stuck in the angry coagulation, only blocks from his destination, Aaron had to make a difficult choice. Abandon his
vehicle here on Palmer Street, which fed into Caxton, and
proceed on foot to the objective, or at least stay and listen
to the Flock of Seagulls. He made the difficult choice.

Thursday, April 8ᵗʰ, 11:27 a.m. – London

"You are one sharp lesbian." Danica looked up from her
document to see Mickey staring at his. "Check it out."
He handed her the copy of a newspaper article dated
November 8th, 1888. It read, *Sir Charles Warren To Step
Down As Commissioner of Metropolitan Police,* under which was
a proper photo of this proper fellow festooned with various
decorations. Danica read the text, studied the picture, and
failed to get the *aha!* out of the aha! moment.

"The highest ranking police officer in London leaves
his position mid-Ripper investigation." Yeah…so? Mickey
indicated the photograph. "Look closer, right lapel." She
did…and saw a grainy insignia that looked like an inverted
V above and slightly overlapping a right-side-up V. "That's
not part of his uniform, that's a Masonic pin. He was a
Freemason."

"What does that mean?" she asked.

"Okay," he answered, excitement growing, "you gotta
remember two things: First, what I told you about the
Knights Templar."

"Okay."

"Second, your initiation into the pleasures of female fraternization you promised to spill." That got no response. "Good," he said undeterred, "so we have an understanding." Mickey went on to explain:

Though the Knights Templar began nobly enough, they had metastasized over the next two centuries into a power of considerable wealth. And to quote historian Cindi Lauper, money changes everything. More than a few medieval rulers were nervous with a richly funded militia of well-armed monks answerable only to the Pope coming back to Europe at Crusades' end. Most nervous was Philip IV, king of France, who owed them a king's ransom and would greatly prefer to welsh on the deal. So Philip brought trumped-up charges of heresy and grotesque crimes by the Templars to Pope Clement V, who was properly displeased that any cleric should have such gross wealth and unchecked power…besides himself.[48] Clement issued a Papal Bull announcing he was shocked, *shocked* to find such shenanigans going on in his holy kingdom, allowing Philip to arrest all Templars, especially Grand Master Jacques de Molay, for torture and death. This brought the Knights Templar to a formal and blood-soaked end.

However…Philip didn't get all of them.

A few beat it to Scotland and England whose kings recognized a raw deal when they saw one, and gave them asylum. And over the next century a "fraternal organization"

---

48   The fact that Philip was the one to make Clement pope by force of arms had no bearing whatsoever on Clement's coincidental displeasure.

known as Freemasonry (sometimes called The Scottish
Rite) arose in the British isles, an organization that, coin-
cidentally like the Templars, used King Solomon's Temple
as its philosophical focal point. Using the symbol of the
overlapping V's of a square and a compass, tools of ancient
stonemasons, it was a secret society whose members had to
be of high moral principals and whose main function, like
the Templars, was to help others. By the 16th century, Grand
Lodges were established throughout the British isles, and
even in the American colonies where its more hallowed
members included George Washington and thirty-five
signers of the Declaration of Independence and/or the
Constitution (in fact, the dollar bill contains the symbols of
the pyramid, the all-seeing eye, the stars above the eagle's
head in the shape of the Star of David and the phrase *e
pluribus unum* – "out of many, one" – which all have their
origins in Freemasonry).

Freemasonry thumbed its nose at Christianity in its
requirement that members believe in the supreme being,
any supreme being...Shiva, Allah, Buddha,[49] the teachings
of Zoroaster, the Sun God of Mora Tau, all were accept-
able in a spirit of ecumenicalism that demoted Christianity
from captain to a bench of equals. Furthermore, while
Freemasons held regular meetings, what went on at these
meetings was veiled in ritual and secrecy, complete with
armed guards standing by the doors. One thing for sure
they *weren't* doing: Singing odes of joy to the Holy See.

---

49   Granted, Buddha isn't a supreme being, more a supreme
teacher of the eightfold path, right view, right intention, right
speech, etc. Apparently right eating isn't among them.

From the start it was antithetical to the Church to be a member of the Freemasons, punishable in more virtuous times by branding a cross on one's chest; but now, slightly less hysterically, it was simply eternal damnation.

"By my dad's notes, I'm guessing Sir Charles Warren, a proud Freemason and anti-Catholic, somehow found the ark," said Mickey. "If so, this is huge, it confirms the ark survived from the twelfth century to the late-nineteenth and focuses the search. The question, of course, is where did he find it? And if the church didn't know what a stink it would cause 'til 1945, how could he know it was of such value? Or did he know?"

As they prepared to leave the building, they couldn't know that they were the final cloud to move into place for the impending shitstorm. Also unbeknownst to them, they skipped over all the clues that pointed irrefutably to who Jack the Ripper was.

Thursday, April 8ᵗʰ, 11:39 a.m. – London

Twelve sets of Interpol crosshairs were aimed at the New Scotland Yard entrance, the sweat of anticipation moistening every shootist's forehead but one: Brinkerhoff's. Crouched across the street behind a planter retaining wall, the colonel was keeping Fitzwiler under his Marine Corp tattooed wing. There was a smell in the air, a smell Brinkerhoff knew only too well, stronger than the unlit cigar in his bite that was chewed to a saliva-soaked pulp seeping from the corner of his mouth.

It was the smell of pain.

Pain promised by his men brandishing semiautomatic M9 Beretta Pistols firing the 9mm NATO round at a velocity of 365 meters per second. Pain promised by rooftop sharpshooters aiming Tac-Ops Tango 51 .308 caliber sniper rifles. Pain promised at hand-to-hand range, should it come to that, by serrated-edged steel boot knives.

It was a smell Brinkerhoff lived for.

He spoke to his men via headset. "Primary is six-foot-two, two hundred pounds give or take, blond hair. Orders are to bring in the primary alive *if possible*. Any secondaries optional. No one fires until I say." He sighed, then added, "Avoid any female, infant, or canine non-combatants this time." It just wasn't worth the flurry of triplicate paperwork he had to fill out whenever that happened. And it was tragic, too.

In the lobby, 25 meters from death, Mickey and Danica were just about to exit until DeSica, still awaiting his gun from confiscation, saw them and snapped, "Stop! You don't leave my eyesight."

Mickey did not like the clerical dog collar. "Dude... we're at the best known police station on the planet...and in England, one of the civilized countries. They actually have gun laws here they enforce."

DeSica was unmoved. Mickey exhaled impatiently. The only good news in what was about to transpire was that DeSica wasn't the type to gloat.

Aaron, behind sunglasses and a silk scarf, marched quickly at the direction of his GPS past the clot of honking cars leading up to and around the N.O.I. He turned the corner as his device beeped insistently, surprised to see a completely empty street lacking only tumbleweed and an Ennio Morricone harmonica. The next thing he noticed was his objective: New Scotland Yard.

He had been in this business long enough to smell the same thing Brinkerhoff did.

Aaron smiled.

"Now," said DeSica, he and Bertolucci armed and walking across the lobby toward Mickey and Danica, "you may exit." Mickey leaned into the door, about to push out. "Ah-ah-ah-ah!" the priest admonished. Mickey paused. "After me," he ordered. Mickey resisted his leg that wanted to stick out in DeSica's path as he passed.

DeSica pushed on the door. It began to open outward. And time...suddenly seemed...to slow...to...a...crawl...

...as...he...stepped...through...

...the...others...fol..loooowing...beeeehind...himmmm.

Aaron, standing in the middle of Broadway like a lone stalk of wheat in a locust-denuded field, donned his metal glove, his leather duster beginning to billow in a properly atmospheric breeze. Inside his duster he unsnapped his Glock and tripped the safety. He stuffed four pieces of *Bulle Heureuse* into his mouth and savored the sweet release of impending catastrophe. He rolled his neck side to side, listening to it crack. He wiggled his fingers to loosen them up.

Every sense on tenterhooks, he began the slow walk forward.

De...Si...caaaaa....then Daaa...ni...kaaa...then...Mick
...eeee...and Ber...tow...luuuuu...cheeee...stepped...into-
ooo...the...coooouuurrrt.....yaaaard.

"We have a visual!" a suddenly electrified Brinkerhoff
hissed into his headset. He spat an angry glob of brown
on Fitzwiler's boot. "The tall one, disguised as a priest, our
primary," he identified. "Secondaries appear to be cohorts,
that altar boy must be his lover. Sick fucking bastard." His
groin stirred. "Primary is mine and mine alone, *does! every!
body! copy!*"

They most certainly did.

"Sir, civilian or potential secondary at nine o'clock, *sir!*"
said Fitzwiler. Brinkerhoff glanced to his left and saw the
figure that was Aaron. *What the hell was that?*

Time and movement jerked back to the immediate as
DeSica and Bertolucci saw the ghostly milieu before them
and knew. It was all wrong. Even Danica sensed it. The
street was empty, the silence oppressive, the breeze illogical.

Then they saw Aaron. And Aaron saw them.

"Man, I gotta drop a three-day load," said Mickey, not
quite in the moment.

Aaron's Glock came out as the priests pushed Mickey to
the ground, drawing their .45s.

Armageddon.

The Fist of God let loose with three bursts, DeSica
and Bertolucci returning fire as they ran toward the
street drawing fire away from their prize. Somewhere a
voice screamed, "Now-now-now!" and from all directions a

torrent of asphalt-churning .308 caliber hail rained down. Danica hit the ground as bullets pinged on all sides, rendering no haven safe. The glass doors shattered behind her, the flying shards a clear message to anyone considering reentry. She speed-crabbed over broken glass to a disoriented Mickey and yelled, "Move your ass!" Behind them a flood of helmeted Bobbies in black riot gear, bearing German Heckler & Koch G36 semi-automatic rifles, poured out from inside and unleashed confused defensive fire randomly (though it probably wouldn't have been so confused if they were allowed to carry guns more often).

Aaron, a cross between a Hieronymus Bosch figure and Claude Raines with his scarf and sunglasses hiding the horror beneath, his gloved hand, his black duster billowing from the bullets slicing through it, serpentined leaving a trail of spent shells in his wake, unaware that a creased thigh was seeping blood down his Gianfranco Ferre black leather pants.

Brinkerhoff stood up, shooting at secondaries until British G36 semi-automatics found him as foe and returned his ass to cover, causing him to almost swallow his cigar stub. "Goddamn, this is a grade-A unadulterated clusterfuck! Fitzwiler, keep your peckerhead down so you don't lose the few brains you possess!"

"Sir, yes sir!" Fitzwiler said, death zipping overhead. Sweat ran in rivulets, his heart pounded triple time; he had yet to fire his first field round as an agent. He wondered how he ever let his great-great uncle, Jean-Henri Vandersmissen, who moved to Argentina after World War II ("for the curative waters") and whose healthy longevity

Vandersmissen attributed to a daily noontime mash of black bread, stout beer and prunes, talk him into giving up international studies at Cambridge to join Interpol. "Great risk is the anvil on which great character is forged," Vandersmissen used to tell the young boy over a transatlantic line, spinning romantic tales of the life of an agent, filled with German expressionist shadows and intrigue and microfilm hidden in cakes and dangerous women who did things to this day only written about in books printed in Denmark. It was an irresistible world to any sheltered red-blooded British virgin. Leaving Cambridge his freshman year, Fitzwiler rose quickly in the organization and proudly called his great, great uncle the day he was told he would be skipping desk duty, going directly to training for the field.

"You *scheißkopf*," exploded Vandersmissen, telling him that desk work was the *very* place he was most suited, and besides, he needed to help his great-great uncle find a file labeled "Odessa"; apoplectic, he commanded Fitzwiler to turn down field work and return to the office, whereupon mid-call Vandersmissen, lightheaded from anger, fell hard from his chair. It was their last call.

Fitzwiler never did encounter any microfilm or dangerous women or the hard angled shadows he was told about. But he did meet his sweetheart, now his fiancé, Constance Mortimer. He carried a picture of her taken at Brighton. Since he and Brinkerhoff were pinned down, it seemed as good a time as any to look at it. He pulled out a Polaroid. "Sir, would you like to see a picture of my—"

"GODDAMNIT FITZWILER PUT THAT AWAY!"

Phffffft! A ricocheted British rifle shot ripped through Constance Mortimer's splotchy face and sliced Fitzwiler's carotid, the spray painting Brinkerhoff like a Vegas stage act had it been blue. The private fell facedown, still gripping the picture. *Goddamned stupid son of a bitch*, thought Brinkerhoff, forcing himself not to cry; why, why, *why* didn't they teach in field school the battleground risk of showing *anyone* a picture of his sweetheart? He would make that demand in his post-clusterfuck report in no uncertain terms.

Worst of all, though, was what Brinkerhoff, indeed the world, couldn't have known. Fitzwiler, only moments before realizing he wasn't the man for this, had already decided to return to Cambridge and international studies. He'd had a long-gestating plan that would have come to fruition, a plan to effectively and bloodlessly solve the Israeli-Palestinian dilemma. As a foreign affairs *aide de camp* to a politician in the House of Lords who would eventually be elevated to Prime Minister, he would suggest the plan. The future Prime Minister would see its obvious merits and broker the implementation. All conflict would cease. The Prime Minister would win the Nobel Peace Prize.

But sadly…it was not to be.

Thursday, April 8th, three minutes 41 seconds later – London

Matters were becoming as loud and confusing as a Jerry Bruckheimer explosion suckfest. Danica had gotten Mickey to move his ass to the protection of a small retainer wall. But more Bobbies had joined the fray; Aaron – on his second wad of gum, the first stuffed into his leg – recycled a dying Bobby as a shield as he unloaded an endless supply of ammo; DeSica and Bertolucci absorbed enough hits to their vests to kill Rasputin; Interpol – Brinkerhoff curiously out of touch with his men – was still at war with the Bobbies. Mickey at least enjoyed Danica's arm across his back and the smell of her hair from her head jammed low into his neck, though such pleasure would probably be short-lived.

Mickey heard her mumbling beside him, tuning in to catch the end of, "kingdomcomethywillbedoneonearthasitisinheavengiveusthisdayourdaily-breadandforgiveusourtrespassesasweforgivethosewhotrespassagainstus—

"What are you doing?" he yelled above the din.

"Praying!"

"This isn't the best time to panic—"

"Can you think of a better time?!"

Point taken. *Zing, phffft, chip!* Mickey flinched, brushing cement flakes from his face.

"You have the courage to come out of the closet but you hedge your bets by pretending to be a believer?"

"I never said I wasn't and so what!"

"You accept a faith that doesn't accept you!"

"Dear lord let a bullet find this guy—"

"I just find it odd—"

"I don't give a fuck what you find odd—" a gurgling Bobbie fell near them taking one to the throat "—when we're about to buy the farm!"

"Speaking of which, since we *might* buy the farm— "

"No, you *cannot* cop a last-minute feel!"

"Worth a try."

A long tortured howl rose above the chaos, the two looking up to see a vision straight from Dante: a man covered in blood from head to waist – Brinkerhoff – wailing, firing a Beretta in each hand, taking one-two-three direct hits, running straight for them on pure hate and adrenalin. Danica dug deeper into Mickey's neck resuming her prayer. Brinkerhoff, charging, was almost at the curb, Mickey thinking he should revisit that feel, but—

Wha-WHUMP! Brinkerhoff was suddenly pancaked under the church limo skidding to a stop at the curb, water sloshing from the hot tub. The vehicle was between Aaron and his targets, the driver opening his door and waving the four to enter.

DeSica screamed, "Go, we'll cover you!" Mickey and Danica crouched and in true Butch-and-Sundance fashion ran madly toward the door, the priests laying down fire in all directions. The driver threw himself to the ground to let Mickey and Danica dive in, a bullet finding his chest, rendering him an ex-limo driver.

"Get away, now!" DeSica ordered Danica who, last in, was behind the wheel. He slammed the door behind her. She jammed it into drive and burned rubber over Brinkerhoff, DeSica and Bertolucci rolling into the now half-empty hot tub as it passed, still firing.

Danica shot south on Broadway, swerving onto the sidewalk around the haz-mat team and spilled mercury, running-diving-screaming pedestrians becoming human bowling pins. Broadway turned into Strutton Ground and then, very soon, the main thoroughfare of Horseferry Road.

Mickey was still getting his bearings. "I suppose you're gonna say this limo was the answer to your prayers."

Danica blasted through traffic like she was driving an MG sportster. "Damn straight," she threw back, "just to hear one of your pathological anti-faith soapbox rants."

"Sorry to disappoint, you won't hear one."

"Proof that prayers *are* answered," she said then swerved suddenly around a mum with a baby carriage who stepped unaware into a crossing zone. "Goddamnit!!"

"Really? Why do you think God, who's got quite a bit on His plate, would answer the request of a distaff abomination and watch out for that ice cream tru—"

Its Farmer-In-The-Dell loop still played as she side-swiped the truck into a light pole, the turbaned driver leaping out, screaming foreign epithets. Danica swerved left to miss some idiot who felt it was his birthright to brake in front of a speeding reinforced juggernaut, the limo snapping off a hydrant that let loose with the requisite chase geyser. Then, to Mickey, "Mind if I concentrate on one thing at a time?!"

"Not at all, I'll drive."

"You're doing just fine as the airbag."

She skidded around a turn and sheered off the driver side door of a parked Jaguar as it opened, the separated metal sailing through the air like a piece of cardboard. "I just figured it out, you know what your problem is?" she said.

"I'd ask but you'd only tell me—"

"You're jealous, *jealous* that so many have what you're too cynical to feel."

"Blind faith? Why is it if I worship my Chia pet I'm a wingnut, but if I worship a two-thousand year old rabbi who never claimed he was divine, I'm intelligent?"[50]

"What's wrong with believing in *something*?"

"I do. My Chia pet."

"Of course, it doesn't require anything of you—"

"And it doesn't start wars or command zealots to kill or—"

"You're saying *nothing* good's ever come from faith?"

"Of course it has."

"What?"

"The Godfather of Soul."

"The who?"

"James Brown. The faith of slaves gave us gospel, gospel gave us blues, blues gave us R-and-B, and that gave us James Brown."

She took her eyes off the road just long enough to give him the most withering look to date, and, no matter what is written from this point on, beyond all to come; which was probably why she drove through a red light, resulting in a six car rear-end in the skidding cross traffic. She didn't

---

50   Indeed, Jesus even avoids the question from Pontius Pilate. As for Jesus being referred to as the "Son of God," the phrase appears in the Bible many times before Jesus. The Jews in the Old Testatment are referred to as "sons of God"; in Psalms David is referred to as "the son of God." The term meant one who has a special relationship with God. As for the "son of man," another term applied 83 times to Jesus, that phrase is of Semitic origin and referred to one's humanity, and it's use by Jesus, say scholars, was one of humility and to say he was human as well.

notice. "I bet in high school you were voted 'most likely to be crucified.'"

From the hot tub DeSica and Bertolucci saw an olive green Range Rover weaving through traffic behind them, causing more mayhem as it gained ground. The priests jammed fresh clips into their guns and, unbeknownst to Mickey or Danica, shots were being exchanged. That is, until the priests finally exhausted their ammunition. The Range Rover could only dent the limousine's armor plate, the paramilitaries within growing frustrated. DeSica and Bertolucci knew if they could keep their heads down they might survive. If only Danica would speed up, what the hell was going on up there?

"You don't see the contradiction, do you," she said heatedly, "you don't see that you're part of the problem!"

"Hard to see what isn't there."

"How do you sleep at night?"

"You have a standing offer to find out." The double entendre was lost on her.

"If *ever* there was a bullshit church it's yours—"

"It would be if I was selling the answers."

"What *are* you selling?"

"The questions."

Which gave Danica, if not the vehicle, pause as she strayed too close to a peloton of cyclists, thirty-seven middle fingers shooting into the air as one.

The Range Rover was gaining. The priests ducked as garbage cans inexplicably careened across the top of the limo. Bertolucci pounded on the rear window to get

Danica's attention, his efforts futile amid the louder impact of bullets.

Inside, not only were they unaware of the Range Rover and gun battle behind them, they were unaware that Aaron was bearing down on the Range Rover, in a vehicle he commandeered from a passing well-intentioned believer delivering boxed meals to shut-ins. Yanked from his car, taking a bullet in his buttock, he was left in an existential dilemma of wondering why God felt his charitable acts should be so rewarded.

Danica swerved yet again, avoiding sawhorse barriers designed to keep drivers like her from plowing through an arts-and-crafts street fair of countless breakable *objets d'art* that she probably wouldn't avoid in the cinematic adaptation. Over-correcting, however, she caught the corner of a dumpster being wheeled out from a fish market to the curb, rotting offal ruining a number of shoppers' day.

"Bottom line," continued Mickey, "there's a difference between blind faith and intelligent faith. And ninety-nine percent of 'the faithful' wouldn't know faith if it gave 'em a rim job."

"Thomas Aquinas, right?"

"Four thousand-some religions out there, only one of 'em can be right. Or none of 'em. I say we scrap all 4K-plus, let people find the deity on their own, and to paraphrase a chief justice, they'll know it when they see it."

"He was talking about pornography."

"So there's some overlap."

"Are you through now?"

"I'm just warming up."

"I am *so* going to heaven when I die."

"Because…?"

"My time with you, I've been through hell."

Wham! That wake-up call was the Range Rover ramming them from behind. All this while Danica was barreling forward with less idea of where she was going than where she didn't want to be. She had zigged and zagged blindly through streets that went from white collar to no collar, now in a warehouse district with long rows of deserted warehouses separated by wide, brick paved, oil stained, bottle-strewn roadways that once allowed big rigs to maneuver; no doubt an area marked for destruction, which was fitting since they were, too.

Mickey craned to see the Range Rover that rammed them now, oddly, falling back. A paramilitarist emerged through the sunroof. "Who the hell *are* those guys?" he asked, the man lifting into place a weapon he was unable to use until now. "And why are they aiming a rocket-propelled grenade at us?"

"How the hell do you know what an RPG looks like?"

"You watch CNN since 9/11?"

Danica began evasive action, which worked a lot better in her police car than it did in this bootylicious fuckbucket. Unknown to her, DeSica and Bertolucci, rolling about in the hot tub, were in the latter stages of motion sickness. Danica tried to become even more erratic. The Range Rover was amused. It stayed the course, its gunner following his target with all the difficulty of a crippled pachyderm. Mickey saw the white puff of smoke as the shooter recoiled, yelled "Incoming!" and *whump*, the

projectile slammed hard against their back window, crack-
ing it and falling into the hot tub. In the nanosecond that
followed Mickey expected to feel hot particulate limo matter aerate his ass – only to see a priest he had no idea was
there shoot up, lob the grenade back, and watch the Range
Rover swerve and overturn in the immediate explosion,
the Interpol agent and his RPG launcher ejected from the
sunroof as the vehicle rolled and burst into a righteous
conflagration.

It was enough to make Mickey believe in God. Or at
least one who gave a shit.

In the not-so-distant past...

Jean-Henri Vandersmissen practically lost his mash at his
dining room table. Used to years of search updates of min-
imal value, having lost another gumshoe *and* a Nicaraguan
CIA-trained Contra torturer shadowing this animal, having
had to raise the monthly stipend to a total of five thousand
dollars and the payment for the ark another two million,
he had opened the latest *par avion* letter over his noontime
repast. It read: *I am in Paris, the ark will be mine in a matter
of days. I will bring it to you personally. M.*

As the letter made it's way to Buenos Aires, however,
Mikhail Samanovananonvich would be murdered in a
Parisian alley. Which would change nothing, the letter
was truthful except for the fact that it wasn't from Mikhail.
None of the letters had been from him. And none of the
money, wired directly to a San Francisco account, had gone
to him. But then you already knew that, didn't you?

Wednesday, April 7th, 2:49 p.m. – Paris

Renault didn't dare go to Poujouly with what he learned. On the razor's edge of promotion, this would tip the scales irretrievably. Instead he chose to return to his parish priest, Father Mirasol, with whom he could review the evidence, perhaps tie up loose threads.

It felt satisfying to tell someone of his clever ratiocination that got him to the solution of this heinous murder, breathlessly taking Fr. Mirasol through the case from the start, allowing himself the rare opportunity to take pride in his diligence and the ability to reverse his position: Mickey Samanov, reprehensible as he was, was not the killer and he would now bring to justice the proper deviant. Mirasol was duly impressed.

At day's end Renault left and drove to the grocery store to shop for dinner. A divorcee who had long cooked for himself, he was in the mood for poultry, stuffed eggplant, and an oaky Chardonnay. He couldn't help but feel a profound sense of accomplishment, that heady sense of knowing he was about to be part of something much bigger than himself, that could even preserve his name in Wikipedia... *if* he were willing to take credit for it. Testing the firmness of several egglants, a slight melancholy came to the fore that he couldn't lay claim to this and remain in his sweet spot. But such was his lot. *I'll talk up Castel-Jaloux,* planned Renault, *tomorrow morning in the coffee room. He's a sycophantic martinet known for case larceny. I'll casually mention the Samanovananonvich matter to him, my suspicions of its import, but confess that I've reached an impasse. Whereupon I'll give him all my notes for review. Next day he'll return them with his basset hound expression, wishing he could be of assistance, offering some cliché of encouragement. Within the week he'll have brought all police powers to bear to capture the killer and make the front page of Le Figaro, above the fold. It will surely get him bumped up the ladder and put his deserving ass in line for some major bureaucratic mastication.*

Renault left the market with his groceries that, like all Parisian shoppers' bags, included a loaf of French bread peeking over the top even though he never ate it.

Renault entered his modest, first floor St. Germain apartment, smelling pleasingly of pine scent because today, Wednesday, was the day Salima came and cleaned. He put his groceries on the kitchen counter, thumbed through the mail she placed there, then removed his jacket in preparation for his celebratory feast. Wait, an inspiration! *Call Castel-Jaloux now and leave word with him, word that will make him eager to seek me out like a cat hearing the thrashing about of a spotted kiwi or a baby nandu*[51] *when I arrive in the morning.* He called directly into Castel-Jaloux's voicemail so that nothing would get lost in a written message. Short and sweet, he laid the trap.

Three quick silenced reports stippled red over the ingredients of the meal that would never be made. Mickey's would-be savior crumpled to the linoleum. He never saw Salima behind him, slumped at his dinette table, eyes red from burst blood vessels, her skin a sickening pallor, the piano wire garrote still around her neck.

Gloved hands unscrewed the silencer and placed it and the gun back inside a jacket pocket. Being this late in the

---

51   Both birds being of the small and flightless variety.

day, a day with a double killing that would work up an appetite in anyone, the assassin wished he had been less anxious and allowed Renault to make the meal before killing
him.[52] He later dined nearby on lesser fare at the Planet
Hollywood, assassin per diems not keeping up with inflation these days.

Thursday, April 8th, 12:08 p.m. – London

Aaron, having followed the Range Rover, watched from afar
as the four scrambled from the limousine and ran from the
approaching sirens, disappearing between two warehouses.
Bâtards stupides, he thought, they wouldn't get far from the
insect-like plague of police about to descend and chew
through every square centimeter of this area. At Scotland
Yard he had no choice but to defend himself from Mickey's
escorts, though he wanted Mickey alive. But the last thing
Aaron's people wanted was for Mickey to be arrested and
detained for months or years, any investigation bringing to
light what must be kept secret. In all his years as an antag-
onist-slash-villain-slash-antihero, nothing he had so far
encountered prepared him for what had to be done in the
next few moments: Somehow help Mickey and company
escape without in any way getting captured himself.

The first police car didn't arrive at the abandoned
limo and burning Range Rover for almost three minutes,
delayed as they were at Scotland Yard by Interpol firepower.

52   The intended meal: Chicken and Apples Normandy, which
takes only twenty minutes to prepare, with six grams of fat, 284
calories, and 28 grams of protein per serving.

The Bobbies radioed the location, backup arriving with a vengeance: Armored vehicles, sharpshooters, an ambulance, and what could charitably be called a take-no-prisoners attitude.

Surrounding the Range Rover, it was obvious that anyone inside could not have survived. A single passenger had been thrown free, in a still-smoking uniform, a short distance from the wreckage, and he was probably dead as well, a grenade launcher beyond his reach. The limo sat past all this.

Vested, helmeted police advanced on and surrounded the limo with extreme caution. On cue, six semi-automatic muzzles were thrust in the open doors, ready to release the full load of their clips.

"They couldn't have gotten far," said the commander, sizing up the various avenues of escape. The six officers then double-timed over to the rest of their contingent surrounding the smoking Interpol body from the Range Rover. The commander approached, knelt down, rolled him over...and to a man they winced with revulsion at his seared face, mottled skin, and skeletal holes for a nose. Amazingly, he was still alive. He wheezed, pointing.

"What, man, what?" said the commander. More pointing. "I think he's telling us the direction the others went." The poor agent nodded, pointing even more insistently. "Mathers, O'Brian, stay, everyone else go-go-go, and get that ambulance over here!"

Police ran to cars that screamed out of there, disappearing among the warehouses. The ambulance pulled up and two paramedics jumped out. "Secure the scene until forensics arrives," the commander ordered Mathers and O'Brian. "I'm escorting this one to hospital."

The paramedics put Aaron on the collapsible gurney and loaded him in the ambulance, the commander climbing in behind him. The vehicle disappeared, its siren trailing behind it.

After the fire burned itself out, Mathers and O'Brian would find a charred body denuded of its uniform, as well as scorched black leather pants and jacket inside the car. Their colleagues had given chase in the opposite direction; the ambulance would never make it to the hospital.

Friday, April 9ᵗʰ, 12:04 a.m. – London

The priests out of earshot, Mickey whispered to Danica, "What would you say if I told you I had a plan to bail?"

Danica, exhausted, looked at him. "I'd say the world has spun off its axis."

Possible sarcasm notwithstanding, he continued. "We have passports. I have Richard's phone number. We can give these two the slip, get ahold of him, and he'll get us back to the city by the bay."

"Just like that."

"Just like that. Look, it's not like I *don't* want to help, that I *don't* want to save the faith of millions, that I *don't* have an altruistic bone in my body—" Off her look: "Fine, okay, that's exactly what it is. Sue me." Objectively, it was hard to blame him...only days before he'd been perfectly content in his low-maintenance, high return lifestyle that afforded the kindness of near-strangers; both church and pool clienteles, however, being fickle lots, would evaporate soon if he didn't return and get back into service mode. Then, of course, there was the whole cessation-of-life issue.

"With everything at stake...with you being the only person on this planet who can get to the bottom of it...you're just gonna bail."

"Like you even give a shit if we find the ark?" Her hesitation was response enough. "You're a Christmas-Easter believer who doesn't think twice the other three hundred sixty-three days outta' the year about the faux-salvation you were force-fed as an impressionable young virgin that you're too lazy to question now. But I can tell you what you *do* care about three hundred and sixty-five days." He annunciated very clearly, "Your A-through-G spots and a certain someone who knows their locations."

She didn't have an answer.

"Amazing," he practically gloated. "She treats you like something she wipes off the bottom of her platform heel, she's probably already moved on, and you still think about S-E-triple-X with her. You're a lot more like me than you'd care to admit. In fact, the only difference between you 'n me is..." He paused, knotted his brow for a good fifteen, twenty seconds. "Know what? I can't think of one."

Per *her* knotted brow, she didn't have one on the tip of her tongue either. Worse, once again in his pre-Mesozoic kind of way, he was more right than wrong. Getting back to Nikki was still Danica's number one goal, not the Ark, second only to remaining above ground. Even though three people already died for it, probably more, even though *they* almost died for it, her helping was for expediency's sake, to get things done then get the hell out of Dodge. Still, she had to respond, taking the high road.

"At some point, Samanov, you have to realize that a few things in this universe are a little bigger than you…that you *don't* have all the answers…and that as the most selfish, egocentric human I've ever met, you have some growing to do." He wasn't greatly bothered. "As for bailing, you're not going anywhere. You don't have your passport."

Mickey frisked himself, slowly realizing that she was right. Now he was greatly bothered. The fog of memory lifting, he recalled asking her to hold it when they changed clothes. Somewhere among London's *demimonde* were three homeless priests and an altar boy who a few hours earlier traded attire with Mickey, et. al., for a few pounds. The four then rented an hourly hotel room to clean up and to toss their newly acquired apparel in the laundry. Now after midnight, they were sitting in a louche twenty-four hour internet café populated with what appeared to be the recently paroled and terrorist wanna-bes, all intensely hunched over rented computer monitors.

Bertolucci returned from the cashier and indicated a vacant station. "This one," he said. DeSica returned from the vending machines with too-hot coffees and stale scones. Mickey, resigned to staying, sat glumly in front of the well-worn computer, the others circling him. Mickey fired up the computer and it responded with the spryness of a fourteen-year-old dog. As they waited: "So who were those guys?" he finally asked the priests, "the paramilitaries with all the fireworks."

"Interpol," said Bertolucci.

Danica scoffed. "I'm a police officer, I've done business with Interpol. They're just a toothless fact-gathering database...crime stats and information. Their so-called agents aren't allowed to carry anything more dangerous than nail clippers."

"It's what they would have you believe," said DeSica.

"Say what...?"

"That myth," he continued, "is how they lull the absolute worst criminals into letting their guard down. For a scumbag to hear that Interpol is on his trail is to laugh. In truth Interpol is a bunch of vicious sociopaths who shoot first, ask questions never, and see themselves as the last resort. They're the new Foreign Legion, they take the dregs...ex-mercenaries, police fired for overt violence, those with a psychological profile that shows a latent pathology towards cruelty. Once in a while a normal gets in, but he's usually killed on his first mission. You want nothing to do with them."

Danica was agog...for once bad movies, paperbacks and television got it right.

The computer screen came up. Mickey typed in *Sir Charles Warren* then began to click around the various offerings. It didn't take long before:

"Dip me in shit and roll me in bread crumbs," he said, his mood abruptly changing by the connection of two more dots provided by his father. "Before Chuck became police commissioner, he was sent to Israel under the commission of the Palestine Exploration Fund with a team of Royal Engineers. Guess where he dug? The Temple Mount. Says here he discovered a water shaft that led to a network of tunnels *directly* under the headquarters of… guesses, anyone?…the Knights Templar. And he found enough Templar leave-behinds to prove that they used those tunnels."

"Yet all those centuries they were kept hidden," said DeSica.

"It gets better," Mickey said, reading off the monitor: "Warren was later elected 'Founding Master of Quatuor Coronoti Lodge No. 2076.' Not just a Freemason…the grand poo-bah."

"And this information helps how?" asked a cranky Bertolucci,

Mickey opened the accordion file as if to say, '*lemme ask my dad,*' retrieving the dog-eared legal pad. He flipped to the page where, from 'Celestine III/Jack the Ripper,' a bold line cut through an array of seemingly less important notes, arriving at another circled and underlined heading: It read 'Four Crowned Ones.'

Bingo.

Mickey got up, grabbed a phone book, flipped through it, ran a finger down a column, and said, "60 Great Queen Street." A collective *huh?* "It's the Masonic Lodge he founded. Anyone here a Freemason?" The obvious response produced faux chagrin. "Then I don't know how I'm going to get in. I mean, with two priests and a cop, I just can't break and enter."

(Editor's note: The following location is an actual functioning Freemason Lodge. The publisher wishes to express that he believes

in the God-given right — whichever God you prefer — of this very
powerful, though certainly-not-dangerous, and in fact highly mis-
understood and moral society to exist, indeed flourish; that it has
been wrongly characterized in literature, TV and film and quite
possibly by this author; and that the publisher does not condone
breaking into this or any other Freemason, Shriners, Moose, Elks,
Rotary Club, or Royal Order of Water Buffaloes lodge, nor does he
condone the barest suggestion as to how it might be done; thus we
have excised all such references from the manuscript.)[53]

Friday, April 9th, 12:41 a.m. — London

Quatuor Coronati, Mickey knew from his Catholic Latin,
meant "four crowned ones." Founded over 120 years ago,
it operated from a grotesque neo-Roman layer cake of an
edifice unbecoming of an inscrutable society; but make
no mistake, this was the orgnization's international center
for historical research of all things biblical and Masonic,
publishing an annual sanitized "transactions" of information discovered over the previous year. But it was the
unpublished goods, the stuff in the back room, brown-paper-
wrapped-adults-only goods that, naturally, Mickey wanted to
peruse.

It was 12:41 a.m. as the group assembled near the
Lodge, the streets already thinned of reputable sorts.
"Looks pretty impregnable," said a skeptical Danica.

"I tend to agree," came a rare, unsolicited opinion
from DeSica.

---

53 Author's note: This is an outrage to art and artists everywhere.
     Ed. note: Agreed. We would never do this to art.

"I'm no cat burglar," said Mickey, pointing, "but look there, at the ███ ...you see that ███ ██ ███ ██, ███ next to the ███?"

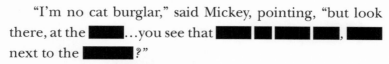

"Above the ███?" said Danica. Off his nod, "How do you intend to get to it?"

"Two choices. Either ██ ██ ██ ██ ██ ██ ██ I ███ ██ since ███ █ ███ ███ ███ up to ██ ███. Or we ██ ██ ██ ██ ███ to that ██ ███ then ███ up the ███. I'm guessing █ ██ ██ ██ ██ ██ ██ ███, there might ██ █ ███ ███."

"I forget," Danica couldn't resist jabbing. "You have some experience sneaking into ███ ███ ██ ███."[54]

"I don't like it," said DeSica. "That ███ is too ███, you could ██ █ ██."

"Usually I'd agree," said Mickey. "But think about this: ███ in the ██ ██ ██ ██ ██ for over a hundred and twenty years. ███ █ ███ you don't think █ ███ ██ ███ ███ ███ in all that time?"

Their expressions said it all. He just might be right. "Let's do it," said DeSica.

"Take this with you, *signora*," said Bertolucci, pulling from his ankle a six-inch razor-edged knife that he handed to her. "You may need to ███ the ███." To Mickey he said, "Out of our purview, you might be tempted to take leave of our company. I would not recommend it."

"I take great umbrage you'd even think that," said Mickey with great umbrage. Or as much as he could fake.

---

54   Author note: Thanks for killing one of this character's best witticisms.

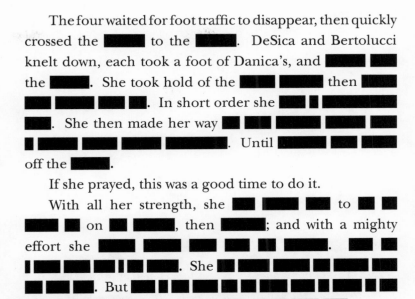

The four waited for foot traffic to disappear, then quickly crossed the ▮▮▮ to the ▮▮▮▮. DeSica and Bertolucci knelt down, each took a foot of Danica's, and ▮▮▮▮ ▮▮ the ▮▮▮. She took hold of the ▮▮▮ ▮▮▮ then ▮▮▮ ▮▮▮ ▮▮▮ ▮▮▮ ▮▮. In short order she ▮▮▮ ▮ ▮▮▮▮ ▮▮. She then made her way ▮▮ ▮▮▮ ▮▮▮▮ ▮▮▮ ▮▮ ▮ ▮▮▮ ▮▮▮ ▮▮▮ ▮▮▮▮. Until ▮▮▮▮ ▮▮▮ ▮▮▮ off the ▮▮▮.

If she prayed, this was a good time to do it.

With all her strength, she ▮▮▮ ▮▮▮ ▮▮▮ to ▮▮ ▮▮ ▮▮▮ ▮ on ▮▮ ▮▮▮, then ▮▮▮▮; and with a mighty effort she ▮▮▮ ▮▮▮ ▮▮ ▮▮▮ ▮▮ ▮▮▮. ▮▮ ▮▮ ▮▮▮▮▮▮▮▮▮. She ▮▮▮ ▮▮▮ ▮▮▮ ▮▮▮ ▮▮▮ ▮▮ ▮▮ ▮▮. But ▮▮▮▮▮▮▮▮▮▮▮▮▮▮ ▮▮ ▮▮▮ ▮▮. She ▮▮▮ ▮ ▮▮ ▮▮ ▮▮ ▮▮ ▮ over to ▮▮ ▮▮▮ ▮▮▮ ▮▮.

And then the moment of truth.

(Ed. Note: So as to not test your eyes and/or patience with the tiresome blackouts, the next two-and-a-quarter pages have been excised. We resume the narrative:)

From the street, they finally saw her ▮▮▮ ▮▮ ▮▮▮ the ▮▮▮▮. No one had to say the obvious: if there was a more dangerous and breathtaking task on their undertaking, they had yet to confront it.

Friday, April 9th, 1:02 a.m. – London

Two Bobbies walking the beat had only to turn the corner and see Mickey and company, stopping instead to rouse a drunk slumped in a recessed store entrance. The drunk slowly rose – and rammed an elbow into one Bobby's face, grabbing his truncheon and felling them both.[55]   Aaron opened the trunk of a nearby car and threw them in.   He wrapped their mouths, wrists, and feet with duct tape in time that would do a rodeo proud, then slammed the trunk to dispose of them later.   He resumed his post keeping watch, slumped in the doorway.   He, too, had exchanged clothes with a derelict, though without the courtesy of spending a few pounds.

████, ████ ███, *1:04 a.m.* – ████

(Ed. Note: Another page-and-a-half excised; they gained entrance to the lodge. Mickey follows Danica in. To resume:) When they were out of ██ ████ and ████ themselves off, Danica whispered, "Great, we're inside…be nice to know what we're looking for and where to find it."

"We're looking for whatever they don't want us to see. Which means it'll be behind locked doors."

"With a heat-sensored surface…infrared trips criss-crossing every inch of floor…motion cameras…guards, live ammo."

"Exactly," said Mickey, "so it'll be easy to find."

But first they had to get past ██ ████ around ██ ████████. Mickey watched it █████ every ████ ██. If they ████ correctly, they could at least get to ██ ████ and see ██ ██ ██████ ████.

---

55   Alas, another cogent argument for Bobbies carrying firearms.

"Ready?" he asked. Danica nodded. This would be their biggest test. Mickey inhaled deeply. "Here goes everything."

(Ed. Note: Blah blah blah, two-and-one-third-pages later they finally arrive at:)

Mickey was not easily amazed and astonished. But here he was, amazed and astonished, standing impossibly inside this room, with Danica, their clothes tattered, wringing with sweat. That they were covered head-to-toe in balsamic vinegar would be a long explanation. Yet they had performed what no one else in one hundred twenty-seven years had ever accomplished, likely the most intricate and clever break-in in contemporary literature.

The moldings removed, false wall swung wide, they faced the vault with a numeric pad.

"You have one chance to pick the right combination without setting off an alarm," she guessed correctly.

Mickey was undaunted. "Isn't it obvious?" he said. Mickey raised his finger to the pad...hesitated...then punched in ███ ████ ████ ██.

Of course. It was so obvious, based on ███ ████ and ██████. With a crisp *click*, it opened. He reached in and pulled out a flat, clasped oaken case with a Masonic crest and the Latin phrase *Adaperio Ab Abi In Malam Rem* ("Open and Go To The Devil") on the cover.

He opened the case, unsure of what met their gaze: It was a parchment, august, hand lettered in script and all in French, which might as well have been Swahili to them. At the bottom were thirteen signatures, one them Charles Warren's. It was dated September 25, 1869. But what

most stood out was at the top of the document, a graphic:
Three identical, elongated lions flattened like road kill and
lined up vertically. Just as they'd seen on the airplane that
brought them to Paris. Just as they'd seen at the hospital. The parchment appeared to be a charter. Below the
graphic were the words: *Fonds de Suisse de Lion.*

"Think you could remember that," Mickey asked her,
indicating the French.

"We're not going to take it?"

"Do you honestly think we can get this out when we
barely managed to get the two of us in?"

He had a point. She stared at the parchment, com-
mitting the French to memory using the police tools for
remembering license plates and perps.

Mickey returned the case to the vault, swung the
wall back into place, and began to replace the moldings.
Danica couldn't help but notice his previous appetite for
escape had been replaced by a focused energy that went
beyond the arrested adolescent getting to sneak into the
Masonic equivalent of the girls' locker room. She suspected it had to do with their ability to get this far thanks to
his father. Deciphering his doodles and scrawls, decoding
his thinking, executing a similar path his father took, was
to become reacquainted with the man and his prodigious
intellect; was to know that despite how far apart they grew,
that Mickey was cut from the same cloth; and that he was
somehow moving in a direction that, in life, might have led
to a rapprochement.

"That thing still gives me the creeps," she said, looking
at the door; 'that thing' being the tall mannequin beside it

dressed in Templar chain mail, a steel helmet, and a white tunic bearing the distinctive red cross, girded by a leather belt and broadsword.

"Tradition, remember?"

"The guard at early Freemason meetings," said the dutiful student, "to protect their secrecy."

"You get an A, Missy. Care to stay after class while I grade on your curves?"

"I'd rather dissect a frog."

"Go to the devil."

"What's that supposed to mean?" said Danica, unsure she'd heard correctly.

"Go to the *devil.*" It was then she realized that the voice, resonant but muffled, came from *behind* her. Danica slowly turned. "Ohhhh shit."

Mickey stood as quickly as if a husband just came home. "What?"

"That mannequin? It's not a mannequin." As if to confirm her discovery, it pulled out its broadsword, brandished it in both hands. This was not going to end well.

"Fuck. Me." said a discouraged Mickey. "That makes no sense at all!" he exclaimed to the knight. "You let us go through all the hassle of figuring there's a goddamn hidden vault, how to get behind the goddamn wall, how to *open* the goddamn vault, *then* reveal you've been there the whole goddamn time?! *Why?!*"

The knight shrugged. "I don't get many visitors."

The knight took a small step forward; he was going to savor this. Mickey and Danica took a small step back, knowing they would soon run out of chamber. Even if they weren't, there wasn't a lot of wiggle room for them turning matters around, at least not to Mickey. Danica, however, saw a slight chance for an opening.

The knight continued his slow, inexorable advance. As they backed away, Danica side-stepped ever so slightly, each step putting a little more distance between her and Mickey. Assuming incorrectly that the larger person represented the greater risk, the knight angled toward Mickey, backing him toward a corner, with maybe two feet of life left. Mickey heard a smug chuckle from under the helmet. The sword was lifted, arced high, and with one more step ready to crash down on him like a wave.

A wave.

The surfer within Mickey, the one swimming out to the swells at Maverick's, North Point Reyes, down in Santa Cruz, the one who had yet to meet the wave he couldn't get under, awoke as the knight tensed, a batter ready to send the ball into the nosebleeds, cresting with a mighty overhand swing as Mickey dove *into* the danger and under the blade that splintered the floor where Mickey used to be. As he scrambled past the Knight's feet, Danica jumped their attacker from behind, yanked his helmet off, and held Bertolucci's knife under his chin, drawing a pinpoint of blood.

"Drop it or I cut you another mouth." The Knight hesitated. The pinpoint became a steady drip. The sword clanged to the floor. The moment Mickey was waiting for. He went to grab the weapon, swing it at *his* head, and see how *he* liked it...until Mickey lifted it, realized it weighed just south of a Buick, and decided a woman half Mickey's size and weight getting the best of this guy was revenge enough.

Imprisoning him behind the false wall, the hard part was yet to come...getting out. And they didn't have a lot of time before their prisoner figured out how to set off the alarm. "Let's make like Elvis and leave the building," said Mickey. She nodded, her jaw tight.

He opened the heavy ███████, they stepped out into the ███████, and prepared to trace their path back, step by step. *(Ed. Note: the next three-and-a-half pages excised.)*

Wednesday, April 7th, 11:17 p.m. – Rome

The historic synod was only five days away.   Cardinal Thomasina, refining his argument that Adam, *after* partaking of the fruit, would have been more attracted to Eve had she been Evan, never got the message that Father Mirasol had called from Paris. Thus he never heard what Renault had confided in Mirasol. The cardinal only found out by accident when, in his office, praying the rosary as he did nightly for the outcome of this search, he squeezed the beads so hard in supplication that he broke the string, scattering wooden balls everywhere.

"Jumping Jehosephat!" he muttered in place of his usual use of the Lord's name, this being Lent.

He threw the beads into the trash – and noticed the crumpled phone message slip in the receptacle. Knowing he had not thrown one away, he pulled it out, smoothed it, and read it. His white face became even whiter, realizing that someone close had intercepted the message; and that if this had been intercepted, Renault was already deceased; and that Fr. Leone, his former and equally as deceased secretary, was not the only mole in the Vatican working against him. Who *were* these enemies?

"Goddamnit, god-damn-it, GOD*DAMNIT*!"

He would find a new Lenten sacrifice to make tomorrow.

Friday, April 9th, 10:23 a.m. – London

Time, growing heavier by the minute, was pressing down upon them like a metaphor of great weight.   London police and British intelligence issued an A.P.B. for Mickey, which included photocopies of their passports – meaning that every member country of Interpol, which at last count was one hundred and ninety-nine, as well as various law enforcement and intelligence groups down to the Luxembourg Crossing Guards' Guild would be looking for them.[56]   The French were after a murder suspect and sexual deviant, Interpol was after an international agent of terror, and the British police knew *something* was up since Interpol only went after the scum de la scum.   From this point on, travel for the four was going to become exponentially more difficult.

---

56   Established in 1742 when a runaway carriage trampled Prince Phillipe Hapsburg, this was no group to take lightly. Over the centuries their eagle-eye alertness not only saved countless lives from such pedestrian mishaps, but during World War II they were the most decorated crossing guards' guild in all of Europe, saving countless more from the treads of Nazi tanks and then later, the liberating allied personnel carriers.

It was morning though Mickey couldn't have said what day or date, even if a reach-around hung in the balance. He and Danica shed their shredded clothes for store-bought attire, courtesy of the priests, having changed by now more times than a Cher impersonator at a gay pride concert. The theme of this look was well-to-do American, Mickey wearing a Bally leather belt and Ferragamo loafers for the first time in his life; Danica was in an Yves St. Laurent pantsuit. They had repaired to another hourly hotel, where cash replaced the need to see proper I.D. And before they left, all four did something else: They dyed their hair a different color; Danica and Mickey went dark, the two priests went blonde.

DeSica interpreted the French phrase from the document Mickey and Danica had found in the vault, *Fonds de Suisse de Lion*: the Lion Swiss Fund. A call to the Swiss Federal Banking Commission revealed that such an organization had been chartered in 1869, the same year as Warren's archeological dig, in Zurich on Breitentrottennordstrasse Boulevard. Working backwards from the Freemasons to the Knights Templar to the Crusades, Mickey realized the bank's graphic could be from a noble's banner that his standard bearer carried into battle. Whereupon the four hastened to the Lambeth Palace Library, archives to the Archbishops of Canterbury where, in a tome of nobles' banners, he found he was correct: It was crest of Richard the Lion Heart's.

"So I'm guessing here's how things break down," Mickey shared *sotto voce* with the others, huddled under the dark stained gothic-beamed ceiling in the library's great hall. "The Templars found the ark where Thaddeus buried it, Richard conspired with them to go against the Pope and not destroy it, and they hid it in the secret tunnels. Warren found the tunnels and the ark, snuck it back to England. Funny part is…it's too perfect that this Freemason found the most valuable of Templar relics. Meaning all this time they knew it was there, he *expected* to find it, and they had reason to grab it. The Freemasons then chartered a bank in Switzerland using still-hidden Templar gold. And they named the bank in honor of Richard."

"Why Switzerland instead of England?" asked DeSica.

"Its history of bank secrecy dating back to the Middle Ages. The Freemasons probably didn't give a shit if the bank had one depositor, it wasn't created for commerce. It was created to hold the ark."

"So the ark is there," Bertolucci said.

"I'd bank on it."

Heartbeats ratcheted up, goose bumps prickled, tiny hairs rose on arms and necks. Mickey and Danica even saw DeSica do something they thought him physically incapable of doing: Smile.

"But how do we get across the channel?" said Bertolucci, their jubilation suddenly shattered like a 15th century Ming vase; their new appearances weren't reflected in their passports. In fact any movement beyond British soil required entirely new identities.

"The Vatican," Mickey offered. "Can't they get us bogus passports p.d.q.?"

"The Vatican," Bertolucci paid out disdainfully, "does not indulge in the implementation of felonies."

Mickey found untapped reserves of self-control to not respond to that set-up.

"Richard," Danica offered, addressing Mickey. "You can call him, right? He got us legit passports, could he work the same mojo with fake ones?"

"I dunno…I don't think the guy's so much as jaywalked. I might as well be asking him to procure me an underage Filipino hermaphrodite dressed like Raggedy Ann." He saw their concerned looks. "Just, y'know, to pick an example." They still questioned.

"Does anyone have a better plan?" she pressed. Mickey sighed heavily. He knew the answer.

Friday, April 9ᵗʰ – two minutes four seconds later – London
"I'm sorry," said Mickey, "what time is it in Zimbabwe?" He had woken Richard up.

"When a whole country's broken, usually it's time to leave. I'm glad you called, Mikhail, I've been worried."

"Because we're being hunted by Interpol?"

"…Interpol?" The good feeling Richard felt from receiving the call drained from his voice. "Those savages… they take the residue of humanity. Thank God TV, films, and tawdry paperbacks are finally getting it right…no, I'm afraid it's something else, I feel terrible. I had gone to Lt. Renault to disabuse him of your culpability and, well…I'm afraid I cocked it up." It wasn't like him to use such earthy aphorisms. "I raised more questions than I put to rest." Richard recounted the conversation in detail, becoming more lachrymose with each remembered exchange.

"Richard. Quit the self-flaggelence. I do more harm by noon than you've done your entire life."

"I, er…thank you."

"Besides, I need your help."

"Anything."

Mickey asked for the bogus passports. There was a long, thorny silence on the other end. "Look," Mickey finally said, "Forget I asked, I don't want to compromise you in any—"

"No, Mikhail…that's not it. But know what you're asking. In my job I've encountered every variety of unsavory purveyor…so I know usually where those purveyors are. These people are cockroaches, they know where to scurry, how to survive, some days I feel all I do is keep the lid on the trashcan. My concern is this: If Interpol's in the mix, there's a substantial reward for your arrest. The criminal element is as aware as law enforcement as to who's got a bounty, for two reasons: First, they want to know if they themselves are in the crosshairs…and second, they want to know who represents a quick payday. If you venture into that circle, you're putting yourself in greater danger than you are now."

"Understood."

"And you still want to do this."

"I don't have a great alternative."

"Actually, you do…in 1999 for a case I was trying, I extracted a high ranking member of the Kosovo Liberation Army from Serbia who could prove that material support was coming to it from Albanian drug lords. I did it by convincing the British Embassy to confer upon him British diplomatic status under U.N. Protocol 47, wherein a country confers protective status upon a foreign national if it can be shown that he's a viable witness in an on-going investigation for the organization. It would take some work but I could do the same for you, get you back to the United States, and at least return you to the safety of your courts."

Mickey smiled. There was a time...ten hours, forty-minutes ago, to be exact...when he would have taken him up on that. But for some reason, right now, it just didn't feel right.

"Thanks. But no."

Richard sighed. "It'll take a few calls. Until I get back, stay as under the radar as you can."

It was advice Richard would have done well to heed.

Friday, April 9th, 1:13 p.m. – Richard's hotel

Richard called his contact in MI5, who then had to place some calls. While Richard waited, he ventured down to the hotel restaurant. Bringing work he needed to peruse, he took the stairs (as he always did to help maintain his thirty-two inch waist that hadn't expanded since his days at Cambridge) and found a table in the busy dining room. He opened the brief and began reading while awaiting a menu.

He had no reason to suspect he was being followed. Engrossed in his reading he never noticed the person who sat down a table away shortly after he did.

Friday, April 9th, 12:04 p.m. – London

Pounding again on a hard wooden surface, deliberate... measured...angry. After a pause came the voice, always a little lightheaded; which in fairness could have been a trick of transmission over the scrambled line.

"You mean to tell me," began the voice in its familiar slow boil, "that Mickey Samanov is now wanted by French authorities...British authorities...*Interpol*," and then the operatic crescendo, "*and every criminal element in Europe once a reward is posted?!*"

"More or less," said Aaron, enjoying the comforting aroma of chamomile tea in a café across from the Lambeth Palace Library, now dressed in an even more *au courant* leather outfit from Saville Row sporting a shorter, nimble three-quarters length duster and orthopedic boots for his overworked arches.

"No. Not more, not less, that is *precisely* the state of this fiasco!"

"The endgame is near, however. This foursome is surprisingly clever. I'm confident with my help they will elude capture and lead us very soon to the prize. Whereupon I have a plan for *la finition grande.*"

"For your sake as much as ours...I pray that you do."

Aaron knew exactly what he was doing. He'd had the night to think about it after his and Mikhail Sr.'s first encounter when the elderly nun had interrupted him.[57] He had been moments away from the truth. But he soon realized

----

57   Sister Laudare, by the way, now living in the south of France and experimenting in the gentle art of water colors, had since retired from her position at the *Biblioteque* for fear of witnessing such twisted Sodom and Gommorhic perversions again. At eighty-seven she had earned the right to spend her autumnal days celebrating the good in man and avoiding the perverse; she was also going to explore this new thing called the internet.

that he had done the right thing for Aaron Zworkan. Granted, he had yet to acquire the information he and his organization so desperately wanted, but had he *not* killed Mikhail Samanovananonvich the next morning, this story would have ended soon after and Aaron's life rights in any resultant telling wouldn't have been worth a day-old croissant. Now it was so much richer, more complex, international; sexy and violent with, surely, more sex and violence to come; and now he was the lynchpin, the hub from which all spokes emanated, the lubricant of the story engine that drove this narrative. True, he put himself in a unique position for an implacable killer, needing for now to help keep his prey alive, but that would change soon enough. He was already debating which Los Angeles-based entertainment agency to use for representation, though Creative Artists had the edge. He'd recently met a vacationing CAA agent in the Marseille and Aaron felt a professional kinship.

After all…this was not just his story. That is to say, it was his story, *all* his story, but it was a story that began centuries before and one he was born to fulfill. A story that this narrative could almost cross-fade to at this point and pick up at a key moment in its inception when …

Thursday, March 18, 1314, 6:04 a.m. - Paris

…Jacques De Molay, the last Grand Master of the Knights Templar, awoke in his cell. It was his last day on earth…and he looked forward to it. His beloved Templars, whom he joined a half-century before as a foot soldier, rising all the way to their revered leader, had been ripped

asunder by the very institution it was created to honor and
protect. Nearing seventy, jailed for the last seven years, lac-
erated with the scars of torture and in constant agony from
infection and improperly set bones, forced to confess to
unthinkable acts including the trampling of the cross and
homosexual initiation rites, he could have saved himself...
had he not recanted everything his tormentors had forced
him to admit. Now he stood ready to be tried by the only
adjudicator who mattered. And he knew before Him he
would be judged properly.

He had been denied everything in captivity, most especially the company of sympathizers. But on this day he
requested a scribe with an abundance of ink and paper
that he may put together his final thoughts to address the
large and tumultuous crowd assembling on the *Isle des
Juif*, thirsty for his demise. This request had been granted
because DeMolay intimated to his captors that now, close
to death, he was willing to recant his recantation, this time
in writing, and agree to all their lies.

It is known he spent the morning dictating version after
version of what he planned to say. What isn't known is that
he first dictated a document that few eyes have ever seen.[58]

---

58   Indeed, until very recently, only three pairs of eyes – DeMolay's, the scribe's, and the soon-to-be-mentioned Guillame's
– had ever laid eyes on the document. Why the complete and
authentic letter was not destroyed, and how it came to see the
light of scholarly day is the stuff of pulse-pounding action, sweat-
inducing suspense, and endless heterosexual and lesbian cou-
pling involving the Cult of Orifice, a band of questionably aged
young girls who believed true Godliness could only be attained
through orgasm, or even better, in the orgasm of their partner, or

And the first sentence explains why the scribe, loyal to the royal court, smuggled this document out under penalty of death. It read as follows:

My dear Guillaume: The scribe who gives you this is to be paid ten thousand gold coins from the treasury and given safe passage to any destination he chooses. As the last Grand Master to have been humbled by the position bestowed upon me, these are my final orders.

Today represents the formal end of the Knights Templar. We have been tortured, killed, our holdings appropriated, and our history corrupted for base motives. But as the Son sacrificed Himself for our sins, we too shall be martyred for the greater good. For verily, those of you who have escaped the continent, and those who may still join you, have a new mission: To destroy the true infidel, the institution that began so perfect and pure with St. Peter but is now infected beyond salvation by the stain of man's original sin. You must eradicate and resurrect it with a body ecclesiastical cleansed through the offering of our blood, that will be our legacy for all time.

To achieve this, the gold caches we have hidden throughout Europe are to be unified into a single repository where you now reside and kept safe to continue the cause.

Secretly with our brothers, you are to reconstitute and maintain the Knights Templar under a new appellation. And should the task of retribution and reformation outlive you, the mission is <u>*to be kept alive by your progeny until such day as we shall not see*</u> the orgasm of anyone witnessing or reading about their orgasm and that, except to stop and take in food and drink for continued energy, their entire waking existence should be spent attempting to attain Godliness. But, though a story within itself, it would only be told should there be demand for a sequel.

one brick remain upon another at the Lateran Palace. The exact methods you and those after you choose to implement I leave to your divinely inspired judgment.

My gloves, which witnessed such bravery in our ranks and upheld the highest measure of our faith, are hidden in the family stables in Chartres. As the last pair of gloves of this most revered position, I wish them to be handed down as a symbol of what two mortal hands in the service of Our Lord can accomplish. I only pray that someday a hand within such a glove will violate as deeply as possible the carcass of this corrupted faith through a path least expected.

And lastly, that most holy of relics: the Ark of the One True Excreta. As Richard, he truly of lion heart, protected it, keep it safely where it is until such time that it be deemed unsafe or in need of retrieval for higher purpose. How it will serve our cause only He knows, as it was His divine hand that guided us to discover such sublime manufacture from the actual body of His Son.

I commend my spirit to the Father and to the cause, and die in the knowledge that one day truth shall prevail. Yours in Christ, Jacques De Molay.

Who Guillaume was is not known. But that the scribe succeeded in reaching him and lived the life of a pasha ever after is beyond doubt.

De Molay was escorted to the island on the Seine, taken atop the platform, and the masses quieted to hear his final words. By prearrangement, he was unfettered and allowed to stand forward without guard, leading his captors to believe he would recant once again, this time in their favor. The 19th century Templar scholar Charles Addison recorded his final words as follows:

To say that which is untrue is a crime both in the sight of God and man. Not one of us has betrayed his God or his country. I do confess my guilt, which consists in having, to my shame and dishonor, suffered myself, through the pain of torture and the fear of death, to give utterance to falsehoods imputing scandalous sins and iniquities to an illustrious Order, which hath nobly served the cause of Christianity. I disdain to seek a wretched and disgraceful existence by engrafting another lie upon the original falsehood.

Addison is reported to have found a few torn and discarded fragments from earlier drafts of DeMolay's final statement. He believed it was the very first draft that began, *"You fuckers of mothers, I hike my robe and show you my maypole of enormous standard that I may piss on your provincial heads before—"*

Friday, April 9th, 2:39 p.m. – London

Sitting in one location – they were still in Lambeth Place Library awaiting Richard's call – felt so counterintuitive to the four that, as exhausted as they were, the last thing any of them could do was relax. DeSica and Bertolucci pretended to read newspapers as they kept their eyes out for armed interlopers or the keen-eyed citizen who had read or heard their descriptions. Mickey and Danica sat at another table, backs to the room. Danica thumbed through the New York Times, the closest periodical she could get to California, as if such news might keep her in touch with home; Mickey, using his time productively, had a number of books in front of him, assiduously flipping pages, making notes. "I'll be damned," he finally said, sitting back in his chair.

Danica couldn't resist. "No you're not...God forgives you."

"'Course he does," Mickey couldn't resist back, "that's his job."

"Uh-oh...I awoke the sleeping midget."

"Don't want the genie, don't rub the lamp."

"I avoid rubbing anything that gets a rise out of you."

"So I've been investigating shit," he said, getting a rise out of her. "Holy shit, to be precise."

"*That's* what you've been doing the last two hours?"

"Or more reverently known as 'hallowed shite.'"[59]

---

59   While etymologists are split as to whether or not the phrase began as a reference to the purported sacred stool, the first of the two words, 'holy,' was believed to have originated before 900, thus Old English – anything pre-1150 common era – and by the period known as Middle English, which goes up to1475, was *holi*. The second word also began in Old English as *scitan* but its original meaning was closer to "split, divide, separate." However, the use of the term as regards the purging of excrement from the body first came about in the second half of the 16th century and exclusively as a verb, *to shite*; its use as a noun would not begin until the 17th century. Either way, verb or noun, from the start it seems that it was considered vulgar, appearing not at all in Shakespeare or the King James Version of the Bible and was represented in all other form of written word as five dashes. Thus the case *against* Jesus' leavings inspiring the term "holy shit" is that a) the two words would have had to come almost 1,600 years after the feces of Christ were first mentioned in a rare Gnostic text, and b) the vulgar meaning of the noun from its inception seems to rule it out as a sacred descriptor.

"And this helps us how...?"

"I'm thinking of selling official 'hallowed shite' re-creations on my church website...key rings, necklaces, earrings...oh, and belt buckles, those'll kill in the Nascar states. Want in on the ground floor?"

"If only you knew what this hallowed shite looked like."

"I've been working on that, too."

She just looked at him. Of course he had.

"A big clue comes from the diet in that neck of the woods, first century," he said, referring to his notes. "Wheat and barley, unprocessed. Lentils, coarse beans, cucumbers. Figs, dates, grapes, raisins, and pomegranates. Some animal protein with sheep and goats but a delicacy for most people only on special occasions or feast days. 'Fact goats were used more for milk than meat. Fish from the Mediterranean was as common as camel flies, eaten fresh or salted to travel anywhere. Nuts, honey, and sweetmeats, you see what I'm getting at."

"Uhh...just to be sure *you* do..."

"Seems to" because there is still the possibility that the *combination* of the two words may have first been used as such. In fact it may have first been coined by a pontiff, Pope Urban VIII, in *direct reference* to Christ's stool. In a letter by King Philip IV of Spain written to his queen in 1642 after a visit to the Vatican, Philip claimed during a grand meal in which much sangria was consumed, that the pontiff told him "as Saint Paul wrote in Galatians that in God there is no male or female, no freeman or slave, no Jew or Greek, so can it be said in all things Jesus that there is no profane or non-profane, there simply is all that is sacrosanct. Thus even Christ's shite transcends earthly standard and is, verily, hallowed shite."

"The average inhabitant of the Levant couldn't get more daily fiber if he ate a coil of rope. Thus it's safe to say Christ pinched off very solid logs."

"Thank you for sharing."

"Size gets a little trickier: I'm betting on three samples of the same length and one sample half that length, with the following measurements." Reading from his pad: "3.858 inches long by 2.2047 inches in circumference for the first three, 1.939 inches long for the half with the same circumference. Converting inches into metrics, the lengths are 98mm for the first three, 49mm for the half. The circumference is 56mm for all four. Every one of those measurements is divisible by seven. Multiply the number of samples by two and you get seven."

"Amazing…if I knew what it meant."

"Around 1890 a Russian scientist named Dr. Ivan Panin,[60] an avowed agnostic, was reading the Gospel of John in the original Greek. John starts off with the verse, 'In the beginning was the Word and the Word was with the God and the Word was God.' It struck him as odd that the

---

60   Dr. Ivan Panin, graduate of Harvard, once tutored Albert Einstein, though in literature, not in any discipline related to Einstein's later fame. The pupil, not particularly taken with the subject nor giving it his all, prompted Panin to write on an essay of Einstein's, "it's sad that the energy required of you to do the most rudimentary of jobs on the subject is equivalent to the bulk of your substance, were you to work at the speed of light, indeed twice that fast, only to produce nary half a sentence." Dr. Panin had no lasting influence on Einstein.

article 'the' preceded the first 'God' and not the second.[61] Until he learned that in Greek and Hebrew, the alphabet also served as a numbering system. That is, by placing a tic mark next to any letter, it became a number...a' = 1, b' = 2, and so forth, with provisions for tens, hundreds, thousands, etcetera. That gave him the hunch to explore the numbers behind the text of the entire Bible.

"He used the oldest, most accurate texts he could find, called the Received Hebrew Text and the Wescott and Hort Text. For the next *five decades* he converted each word and letter, start to finish, into its numeric value. And an arithmetic pattern began to appear, which was this: the total number of words, *and letters*, in each book were divisible by seven...the number of words beginning with a vowel were divisible by seven...the number of words beginning with a consonant were divisible by seven...the number of words occurring once...*and those occurring more than once*...were divisible by seven...the total number of proper names, the number of male names *and* the number of female names, all divisible by seven. In fact in the very first verse of the Bible..."In the beginning God created the heaven and the earth"...has over thirty different combinations of seven. This was enough to turn a man of science into a bible thumping man of faith."

Danica stared, openly slackjawed. "Really."

"Really."

"So...according to Panin...this goes throughout the Old and New Testatments, right?" Mickey nodded. "Even

---

61   To save lesser minds from such confusion, most translations have excised the offending article.

I know those books weren't written by the same person or even group of people."

"True…they were written by thirty, thirty-five-ish people on several continents over about sixteen hundred years."

"But Panin still came up with the same patterns."

"Apparently."

"Name me one thing more astounding than that."

"It's no 'Free Bird.'"

"You don't find it the slightest bit amazing."

"Well…there are a few theories as to how it could happen."

She gave him The Look. Of course there were.

"The first is the give-enough-scribes-enough-pens approach, probably the least probable. Next is the cultural syntax theory, which basically suggests that the spoken word had an unspoken rhythm that would lend itself to such a pattern when written down. But that doesn't explain all the mathematical interpolations. Then there's the latent pattern theory, the front runner, and goes something like…the first five books of the Bible were written by the same person, supposedly Moses. He consciously began the numerical blueprint that the other writers of the Old Testament followed. About a hundred-and-fifty year span is between the last writings of the Old Testament and the first gospel of the new. But since the New Testament was written by Jews already well versed in ancient scripture, they consciously or subconsciously followed the same meter. If we take Panin's theory at face value, if the text was divinely inspired, then seven is the most mystical number in scripture, and it no doubt manifests in the flesh as well as spirit. Hence the scientific and/or inspired origins of my measurements."

"All to make key rings and necklaces and paperweights."

"The possibilities are mind-boggling."

"That means there's one sure way, then, to prove that the Bible is divinely inspired."

"Whassat?"

"Find the ark. If the samples match the number and measurements you claim..." She left it at that.

The cell phone near Mickey's groin gave him a good vibration. He pulled it from his pocket and answered.

"Write this down exactly as I tell you," said Richard.

Friday, April 9th, 2:58 p.m. – Richard's hotel

The agent from MI5 had called Richard back mid-meal. Richard scrawled the information on his napkin then called Mickey straightaway. Finishing his meal, Richard left the napkin on his plate. The agent for Jean-Henri Vandersmissen watched him leave then took the napkin.

Friday, April 9th, 6:41 p.m. – London

"Winterbottom and Avery, quickly as possible," said DeSica, as they piled into the cab.

"'At's in Hackney, eh?" the cabbie asked. "Y'know why the Regents' Canal runs through Hackney?" They did not. "So it don't get shot." He laughed hard; no one else did. "'Ope y'wearin' flak jackets."

Calling the number Richard provided, they were instructed to show up at the address no sooner than 7:00 p.m. Dusk began to blur into evening, street lamps casting their jaundiced yellow glow as they ventured into the Hackney district, the kind of area straight-faced real estate agents would call "developing," "bohemian," or "potential slumlord opportunities." The cab turned into a narrow side street and stopped, the four getting out. Danica's antenna went up not from the boarded up for-rent storefronts, but from the unmistakable tang of meth cooking somewhere close. Luckily this was not her jurisdiction. The group walked mid-block to the address Richard had given them, and arrived at Fogle & Sons Printsmith, sandwiched between Manny's Bail Bonds and Sanjeevani's Indian Sweets, whose smells no doubt masked the meth when Sanjeevani was still in operation.

Pre-war bells tinkled above the door as the four filed into the print shop. A less convivial place of business would be hard to find in Edgar Allan Poe...interrogation-style lighting, walls of chipped lead paint revealing sedimentary layers of more lead paint, and linoleum more worn and pocked than a pre-op Courtney Love. The only indication that this might be a for-profit concern was an adding machine and receipt book atop an unadorned counter and a few twine-wrapped brown paper parcels behind it awaiting pick-up. A door behind the counter finally opened and a sinewy shaven-pated junior-middleweight came out in leather apron, sleeves rolled up, a tattooed tear falling from his left eye; the kind of tattoo Danica saw most often on ex-cons, the tear representing their gang affiliation and

the tragic fade of white supremacy. He said nothing, looking inconvenienced.

"Are you Witherspoon?" asked DeSica. The question
evinced a subtle change in his demeanor, to be asked for
by name. Witherspoon nodded. "Ashes...ashes...all fall
down," said DeSica. The two gave each other a patented
Lee Van Cleef stare.

"How did you 'ear of our establishment?" He wasn't
soliciting the effectiveness of his advertising dollar.

"The Fatman," DeSica was told to reply. It was always
a Fatman.

The four tensed as Witherspoon's blackened fingers
reached under the counter. He came up with a phone,
punched some numbers. Then into the receiver, "Spoon.
Di'you send some business?" A beat. "Four." He listened,
eyeing them. "Right." He hung up. Without a word he
raised a section of hinged counter, turned, and went back
to the door. He opened it and nodded for them to follow.
Mickey's intestines began rumbling anew like the early
warning system picking up an unfriendly.

They found themselves in a large open-beamed warehouse with antediluvian iron printing horses that no doubt
produced first editions of *Great Expectations*. Most sat idle.
A few churned noisily, plates rising and falling, drums spinning, finished product spitting out lazily. Somewhere Al
Green was taking it to the river on speakers lacking woofers
worthy enough for the Reverend. One sensed Fogle & Sons
had alternative income streams since it appeared printing
wouldn't keep so much as the coffee maker warm. They
were led to a table in a darkened back corner. Witherspoon

yanked a pull chain on a hanging hooded light, causing it to swing and rake them in a side-to-side illumination as if lit by someone who'd watched too many 70s British noir films.

"Three thousand pounds for a standard passport, six thousand for chipped," Witherspoon said without pre-amble. It had been decided that DeSica and Bertolucci would walk point on this, but the cost was higher than the Fatman quoted. Yes, they had wired the Vatican for money, enough to pay for this, and yes, they were in the service of the Church of Rome's very *raison d'être,* but what with fewer priests coming out of the seminary, parishioners at an all-time low, rising secularism and, um, all those law-suits, they *were* on a budget. Danica saw that neither knew what "chipped" meant.

"A passport with a microchip. It has details you can't read, an image of the original holder in case someone tried to replace the picture," she said. "Good fakes are pretty foolproof, if they're properly cloned," she said with a chal-lenge to Witherspoon. "Your chips, are they stolen or blanks?"

"Beggars and choosers," he said.

"I don't trust stolen. If they're not wiped clean we might as well go directly to jail."

He smiled. "Unlike you, missy, these're untouched virgins."

That meant Fogle & Sons had a connection, usually from an airline or immigration, an employee with expen-sive habits or naughty tastes. "Still too pricey," she coun-tered, taking over for the priests, "we'll pay four thousand per."

As usual, Mickey's loins stirred watching her in action. *Damn,* he thought, *I'm glad she uses her powers for good... 'cuz sweardaGod, I'd give up state secrets just to drink her bathwater after she ran a marathon through the sewers of Mumbai.*

"Five. Or stuff it."

She looked at the two priests. They nodded. "I will need a receipt," said DeSica. You can guess Witherspoon's response.

Friday, April 9th, 9:22 p.m. – London

They looked at their finished passports complete with microchips filled with false data. "Jesus," said Danica, impressed and despondent all at once, "why do we spend half our lives standing in airport lines, emptying pockets, taking off shoes, belts, watches, walking through detectors, putting back on shoes, belts, watches, dealing with random frisks and electronic wands and pissy underpaid airport security staff who deal with just as pissy travelers at a cost of billions of taxpayer dollars, when any scumbag can get something like this, cross any border, and do whatever the hell he wants? I mean what's the point?"

"That's very unbecoming," said Mickey.

"What?"

"Nihilism. Doesn't it usually come *after* ten, fifteen years on the beat seeing humanity at its worst?"

"Hanging with you shaves a good decade off that."

"Glad to save you the time."

As Bertolucci counted out the money to Witherspoon, a voice from across the room called, "'Spoon! Blower!"

"'Oooissit?'"

"Fatman." Witherspoon walked over, took the phone.

Danica was still morose. That this kind of subculture thrived and turned out a product that could fool the director of Homeland Security was not news. It was something she never thought about on a daily basis until suddenly here she was, face to picture with it, in her hands: An *aide memoire* that no matter how good a job she did to serve and protect in the micro – getting to know the neighborhood, reuniting a lost child with its parents – in the macro she was just one more polyp on a great reef of humanity, one-100th of a gram of it's biomass. And the single additional polyp that was Danica wouldn't mean a tinker's damn to such an organism. A church with armed clerics, an international police force of sociopaths, an unkillable flesh-and-blood assassin, a divine savior who might be undone by the most mortal of acts, that didn't give her pause, that was beyond her ability to control. This passport, though, was not. This was comprehensible, on her plane, exactly the sort of thing she and her profession should be able to render obsolete, and it was more prevalent throughout the world than the golden arches; it depressed her to no end.

"Okay," said DeSica, satisfied that she was satisfied with the product, "let's go."

Except that Witherspoon and his eight co-workers now stood between them and the door, brandishing ad hoc implements of ill will – iron bars, a wrench, a steelhead mallet – Witherspoon holding a sawed-off shotgun. "Lotsa' customers come in'ere with a price on their heads," he said. "But none as high as yours." The call he'd just received must have tipped him off. With 'Spoon and company having home court advantage, this had all the makings of a pisser. "And in your case? It's dead *or* alive." Mickey slowly, almost imperceptibly, moved behind the Kevlar barrier that was DeSica.

DeSica and Bertolucci, unfazed, pulled out their guns to the vexation of their would-be bounty hunters.

"Bloody 'ell," Witherspoon spat. "You're supposed to be priests!"

"We are," said DeSica.

"Then why ya' carry a bloody forty-five?"

DeSica squinted. "Because they don't make a forty-six."

The tension dialed up by eleven. The wooden floor creaked under shifting nervous weight, each side waiting to see how serious the other side was, one side factoring in the cost of their escape, the other side factoring in the cost of the prize, and neither side willing to show its hand; especially the priests, who only this moment realized they had used the last of their ammunition in yesterday's fracas.

The coffee pot gurgled. Or Mickey did, he was standing next to it.

"Put 'em doon and we'll 'and you over to Interpol alive."

The silence with which that was greeted said, oh... yeah...right.

Shotgun and hardware were raised. DeSica and Bertolucci stiffened their aims and prayed for a fishes-and-loaves-like phenomenon that would miraculously provide them with just enough ammunition to get the job done. One false move...one wrong word...one word, period...

and a very short fuse would be lit. The fragile, gossa-mer silence could not have been louder with impending calamity.

And it was at the worst possible moment it was ripped, shredded, completely destroyed with:

"I am so *Goddamn sick and TIRED OF THIS SHIT!*" screamed Danica. Mickey felt the room combusting into more crossfire and eye-searing cordite than Detroit after a Pistons title victory, mallets and bars crushing bone, shot sparking off steel, shrieks of the dying competing with explosions as flesh shredded and blood dappled every—

No. Wait. None of that happened. Mickey opened his eyes. No one fired. Everyone still stood there. He unclenched his butt, hoped his girly screams weren't out loud, and that the new reek was printing chemical.

All turned to Danica who walked boldly into no man's land between the two factions. "Okay…listen up, every-one…I mean *everyone*," she said, including the perplexed priests. "It's not *just* that there are so many crooked, lying, cheating, car jacking, racketeering, raping, murdering slime buckets in this world…or that there's only so much one person like me can do against such a river of shit. No. What's *really* beginning to chap my hide is this: I'm about to be in my third shootout inside a week. My third. That's gotta set some kind of record that I, for one, would care not to set."

"Um…actually…? It'd be your fourth," corrected Mickey tentatively from behind DeSica.

"Bullshit…your father's house, Scotland Yard, here."

"Airport in Paris. You slept through that one."

"Jesus! My fourth goddamn shoot-out! We can put a man on the moon, but when it comes to the most fundamental interpersonal problem solving, we are *still* grunting knuckle-dragging lice-picking primates! Is this all anyone can think of – and by 'anyone' I mean men – when things get to an impasse? You pull out your big phallic noise makers, make big phallic noises, let the smoke to clear and see who's left standing?"

Witherspoon and his men...DeSica and Bertolucci... looked among one another as if to say, *uhhh...pretty much.*

"Figures," she scoffed. "We've been weaned on so much violence on TV, in movies, video games, paperback thrillers, that this is all we – and by 'we' I mean you – *can* think of. Did you ever consider that maybe, just maybe, this is why television and movies and video games and paperback thrillers *have* so much mindless violence? That this is a never-ending, chicken-or-egg cycle, fiction reflecting life reflecting *fiction*? A cycle that will not only lead to more physical death but *creative* death as well? What happened to cleverness when the chips are down? To *imagination*? To taking the time to find an innovative way out of situations like this? But then why should you – and by you I *mean* you – even *try* something other than violence when no one demands anything more, when everyone just expects it?"

A few of the men looked down, shuffled a bit, shrugged.

"Lady," said Witherspoon, "why blame the 'ole bloody world when it's you bloody Yanks and your bloody second amendment that gives every man, woman, cat 'n dog in your bloody country the right to own a bloody gun?"

"It does *not* give them that right, it only guarantees citizens the right to a well regulated state militia, ergo personal ownership is a privilege subject to control."

"Bollocks, your bloody courts think otherwise. Take District of Columbia versus Heller, the bloody Supreme Court ruled that self-defense was central to individuals owning their own bloody firearms."

"But in 1939, United States versus Miller, the Supreme Court upheld an *earlier* federal court ruling regarding a gun law prohibiting the interstate transport of weapons, and said that certain weapons were *not* necessary for a 'well regulated state militia,' meaning that the government has the last say on what a militia, and therefore citizens, can and cannot use."

"Ha! You best read the fine print, duchess, 'cuz to reach that bloody decision the court had to posit that a 'well regulated state militia' was made up of *individuals*—"

"—answerable to the needs of the *militia*—"

"—no, since the bloody second amendment was written at a time when there was a strong bloody reason to mistrust standing armies, thus U.S. versus Miller has come to be interpreted as the second amendment being *intended* for individuals. Your own bloody Thomas Jefferson said, 'What country can preserve its liberties if its rulers are not warned from time to time that their people preserve the spirit of resistance? *Let them take arms.*'"

"Let me get this straight...you're actually saying...it's because of Americans' *right* to have a gun, that it's *our* fault there's a worldwide near-extinction of imagination when it comes to conflict resolution?"

"Bloody *fookin'* right. You wanna see clever resolutions, take away these restraints to our problem solving," he hoisted the shotgun, "that hobble us, that steer us down the path of mankind's baser instincts! *Challenge* us to raise the bar, and in so doing, allow us and the rest of the bloody fookin' world to reach its true potential!"

Grumbles of agreement welled up from Witherspoon's side of the room. It was Danica's turn to shift uneasily, made to feel by dint of heritage that she was a bigger part of the problem than they were, and that maybe some of these ne'er-do-wells did have more to offer than mindless violence.

"But until such time as conscientious telly watchers, movie-goers, video gamers and paperback readers rightly demand more by voting with their wallets," Witherspoon shrugged, "we gotta go with what we know. 'N you ain't walkin' outta here."

Weapons from both sides locked back into position, the tension factor resumed at twelve. DeSica and Bertolucci had the sinking feeling that they were about to fail not only their order and their Pope, but God Himself. How ignominious, thought both, that the salvation of Christianity should be stopped in a rude London underground print shop whose employees would gain their thirty pieces of silver from this sacrifice.

Mickey was so wishing he'd copped that feel back at New Scotland Yard.

"Actually...we *are* walking out of here," announced Danica. "Since you *aren't* challenged to evaluate and analyze, you fail to extrapolate the ramifications of your actions if you try to stop us."

"'N why's that, missy?" smiled Witherspoon, seconded by a few condescending chuckles.

"Because it would require that you kill us. Which would have to be explained to the police. Which would be difficult to do without revealing that you yourselves were in possession of illegal firearms. Which would bring a shit-load of constabulary down upon your little venture that, without looking very hard, would find an extremely lucrative, highly unlawful passport operation."

"Nice try. But we could just capture you and turn you in."

"Then we would tell."

As Witherspoon and his men scrambled mentally to process that she turned to Mickey and priests. "You coming?" Whereupon she marched to the door, opened it, and walked out as if leaving a flower shop. The two priests, Mickey pressed so close behind DeSica as to be a tumor, walked out after her.

Poor Witherspoon and Company could only watch their largest payday ever close the door behind them. And the sad part is, he was right, it wasn't their fault that they couldn't come up with a better, more original way to resolve this in their favor. If only they weren't creatively challenged by America's stubborn insistence on a misinterpretation of the second amendment.

Friday, April 9ᵗʰ, 4:45 p.m. – somewhere over the continent

From what could be gleaned from Richard's side of the phone conversation, the food-stained clue on the napkin, and a call to the phone number he passed to Mickey, it was clear to Jean-Henri Vandersmissen's agent that Samonov and friends were getting false passports. That meant they were returning to the continent. The safest way to do that was through the channel tunnel. It would take them time to get the passports and if they were lucky, make the last train out that night. It was the slimmest of possibilities to get to their destination first. But why was it that for those who were truly evil, those slimmest of possibilities always seem to work themselves out?

Friday, April 9ᵗʰ, 9:58 p.m. – London

"Sonovabitch!" Mickey exclaimed at the beginning of another chapter, this time from the back of a cab as they rushed to catch the last Chunnel train that night to the continent, until their taxi got caught in a major constipation of traffic. Inching toward the obstruction, they saw two-way traffic reduced to sharing a lane, hard hats allowing alternate strands of one-way travel at a time. Lighted as bright as day with arc lamps, a crane was lowering a length of heavy pipe into the trench.

"Sorry mate," said the cabbie, "this 'as been bollixing things up for weeks. No way 'round it."

But Mickey wasn't upset with the traffic; indeed, he was excited. "To save my life I couldn't figure out why Charles Warren went where he did, when he did, to dig up what he did," Mickey said, careful to withhold even a scintilla of information from the driver's ears. "At the library I couldn't find any war, unrest, any ecclesiastical exigency, any other archeological team sniffing around. It seemed arbitrary, even risky, since the Freemasons were the only ones who knew where it was. But my father figured out why Warren quit as police commissioner, in the middle of the most sensational serial killer investigation of the century, and had to go." He pointed out the window at the construction. "That's why."

"London putting in a sewer system?" said Bertolucci uncertainly.

"No, Jerusalem putting one in," countered Mickey.

Danica realized what he was talking about, the word Mikhail scrawled on the pad in the margin. "Sanitation," she said.

"Bingo. Any digging near the temple site was a possibility that the tunnels could be found. They couldn't take the chance that the relic would be discovered."

"And how does that help us?" countered DeSica.

"It tells me they didn't know the true value of what they had, beyond the nature of the relic itself. The Gospel of Shem and the edit from Mark had yet to be discovered. That means it's probably still safely stored away and hasn't been used for any higher, or lower, purpose."

But Danica knew what it really meant. Mickey looked out the window and smiled an involuntary betrayal of satisfaction at the opportunity to have made one more chance exchange, however tenuous, with his late father.

Friday, April 9ᵗʰ, thirty-three seconds behind – London

Caught in the same snarl, Aaron too sat in a cab. "Yes…I said I'm on my way now to the Chunnel," he repeated expositionally on his scrambled phone for those who came in mid-conversation.

"The 10:20?" asked the listener.

"The same. All they had available was premiere class."

"Indeed. And Samanov and his party...they too are traveling premiere?"

"It appears they got the last four tickets in economy."

"How fortuitous," the voice said in *that* tone. There was a time when a global nefarious concern could fund a covert operation for a mere fifty dollars a day, some middling scotch, and a case of Spam. Granted, this was the era of the Berlin Wall, when agents were damaged, existential, and guilt-ridden enough to believe they deserved placebo meat chased by middling scotch. But damn it, they knew how to keep an expense account. Realizing this concept was as foreign to Aaron as sex without a hot glue gun, the voice continued. "We need you to make sure a certain someone doesn't get off that train at its destination."

This sparked in Aaron a Pavlovian response. *A murder on a train!* he thought, electrified by the possibility, *every assassin's dream! An enclosed space...a score of potential witnesses...to perform the ultimate thrill without detection...this would be a challenge worthy of my skills...the mission that would finally get me into the exclusive Club Hashasheen in Tripoli, not that I want to join, but just to enter, order a hookah, and see the look on the face of that braggart and poser Le Cigare, who only had to slip an explosive tobacco product into the pocket or humidor of his intended target, how hard is that to do, and he was allowed to join two years ago...? Le Cigare notwithstanding, though, this was the pinnacle of the sanguinary and sinister arts.*

"Which someone?"

Friday, April 9th, 10:06 p.m. – London

The four walked briskly from the cab into the cavernous St. Pancras station. They marched toward the ticket offices, past the shops and kiosks that were beginning to shutter, eyeing every unwashed student with a backpack, every businessman with a briefcase, every thick-ankled woman hunched over a cane, as a potential killer or bounty hunter.

The tickets procured (their passports surviving their first close inspection), they continued to the Eurostar embarking platform, Aaron shadowing them. Arriving at the dock and standing among the waiting, Mickey began to feel a growing discomfort that he didn't expect to feel. It wasn't that he didn't like trains; quite the opposite, he would forever hold fond a memory of a warm East Coast spring evening...Amtrak...the bathroom...and a possible transgendered Atlantic City casino change cashier who obviated the need to raise such an indelicate possibility with the flash of a thigh and her lace-topped seamed hosiery. But that was then, the carefree days of...well, okay, *every* day was carefree until four days ago. Now that anyone in the free world could have their number, the thought of sitting in a confined space for over two hours with no place to run, no chance for escape, where any passenger with a recent newspaper and nothing but time on his or her hands to inspect the features of fellow passengers, seemed like a piece of business for a hero (or faux hero) to do that was so contrarian as to defy logic.

By the time the leviathan approached, stopped, and the doors hissed open, Mickey began to prefer swimming the English Channel wearing a wetsuit of lead rather than traverse it in a train car. He had read enough Graham Greene, Eric Ambler, John Le Carre, Ian Fleming, Allan Folsom, Agatha Christie, even *Tolstoy* for crissakes,[62] had watched enough *I Spy* and *Man From U.N.C.L.E.* reruns, and had seen enough Alfred Hitchcock, Claude Chabrol and (redundantly) Brian DePalma movies to know that when you're in the middle of an international pursuit and even *near* a train, nothing good ever came of stepping on board. Especially on to a train going through a thirty-one mile long tunnel.

But board they did, finding their seats and settling in, Mickey with the growing pessimism of a puppy on a freeway median. Danica sat on the aisle, Mickey by the window, DeSica and Bertolucci in the seats just behind them. The train left with a fascist timeliness, wending through the dense London midtown and suburbs, then picking up speed, finally able to stretch its legs as it hit the outlying environs.

The policewoman in Danica might have felt an imminent threat as well, confined to seats as they were. But trains also being classically romantic transports, and danger being the greatest aphrodisiac, the full effect of their situation put her in that mood of all healthy sexually active post-pubescents. Not the scorched-earth mood of Mickey's more-than-occasional need for anyone with a pulse (and even that requirement seemed optional sometimes),

---

62 Paging *Anna Karenina*.

rather, the urge of wanting to travel with that someone who
provided a deep and satisfying connection, someone who
was as adventurous as she was feeling at the moment; a line
of thinking that, as much as she resisted it, led inexora-
bly back to Nikki and the fevered, frenzied, endless couplings of those first weeks and months. But thrown into a
world one normally experienced vicariously in the fictional
lives of others, forced to concentrate on the immediacy of
survival, challenged by the conundrum that was Mickey,
Danica had sublimated those memories. Until, rendered
stationary, alone with her thoughts in her train seat and
having nothing to replace them with, she still desired the
devil she knew. It almost made her long for the dull brain
ache caused by one of Mickey's self-righteous, holier-than-
thou rants.

Which made her realize…

They'd been traveling a good hour and were approaching the Channel. To be with Mickey on such a Freudian
conveyance about to penetrate headlong into an orifice
and hear not a word was, well, bothersome; in fact, since
they boarded Mickey hadn't made a single reference to
getting his basket weaved, his runway foamed, his Shania
Twained, his Noam Chomskied, his beefsteak plumped, his
joystick played, his pencil sharpened, not to mention anything to do with laying pipe, cleaning the carpet, parallel
parking, snaking the plumbing, or doing the bone dance;
leaving untouched the entire universe of flatulence, bodily
fluids, toys or repurposed items of adult enjoyment, as
well as all barnyard activities. She looked over. His whole
demeanor confirmed her suspicions.

"What's wrong?"

"Nothing."

"You always sweat like that in air-conditioned train cars?"

"Apparently."

Mickey, in default mode a source of antipathy to her, actually engendered pity in such a pathetic mode, even if he was the source of his own pitifulness. To approach this subject head-on would be as productive as asking about his mother. Better to come at this via the low road. Danica stretched invitingly, arched her back, exhaled a long, husky breath. "Y'know what I have the strongest urge for right now?" she began. "Dunno why...but a big...fat...moist German sausage."

Nothing from Mickey. Zero. Zip. Zilch.

"'And did I mention I'm part German,'" she answered for him in her best Samanov-by-way-of-Groucho delivery, "Guess which part?" She nailed it and he didn't so much as smile; he shifted in his seat, pulled at his collar, and glanced at everything but her. No doubt about it, this guy was seriously defrosted. He couldn't explain why, he just knew something was setting off his get-your-ragged ass-to-high-ground alarm, an instinct honed by years of quick exits from tight spots.

Aaron, hat pulled low, his face behind a scarf, tinted glasses concealing the intent of his soul, had moved from first class to the car behind them. He carried a large shoulder bag, its zipper strained by its contents. Awaiting his moment, he was to execute his plan for maximum benefit – for what was the point of doing this if not to achieve

the utmost dramatic effect to get a power table at Club
Hashasheen – at the mid-way point in the tunnel.

"Mickey," Danica said, "much as it pains me to say this...
I'm concerned about you." He was flushed now, in a way
she'd seen on the job when someone was having a heart
attack or severe allergic reaction. "Are you all right?"

He had to say something, if only to get her to shut the
hell up. "Shut the hell up."

That worked.

The mood throughout the train was quiet, sedentary,
tired travelers lulled into near-sleep from the rhythm of
the ride. Aaron finally stood, in control even as he had to
contain his professional excitement, and sauntered to the
door. Opening it, he stepped into the vestibule between
the two cars. Through the door window of the next car he
could see his target.

Whereupon the train entered the tunnel that even
during the day would reveal outside nothing but black,
beyond the occasional service bulb. It was as if mystery
and thriller writers worked as advisors to the Chunnel
architects during the design stage to help create maximum
atmosphere; which had a certain logic to it since the business concerns funding the Chunnel probably knew that
the Orient Express would be about as well known and uti-
lized as the Titticut Trunk Line in North Haversham if not
for Agatha Christie. Their input seemed valuable in the
design of the passenger cars as well, specifically the electrical wiring within the cars, and on the dedicated breaker
box placement. Most train cars had mirror image electrical couplings at each end of the car, so that regardless of

its end-to-end orientation, when attached to another car, a continuous circuit was completed. However, interrupt that circuit and *all* cars risked lighting and climate control issues. The cars on this train contained their own independent electrical generator that worked off the car axle; all of which led to a direct-current control panel of circuit breakers, complete with an emergency backup circuit and relay, housed in a panel conveniently placed...in the vestibule in which Aaron stood. That the cover over the panel read in bright red letters, *Danger! Keep Out! High Risk of Electrocution!* narrowed his search considerably. It was child's play to unscrew the panel with a 6.35mm hex key, Aaron never leaving home without a set of hex keys any more than he'd leave home (prior to the incident at St. Denis hospital) without his hair gel. Once the panel was off, a flip of six switches would incapacitate the main power as well as the back up power stored in the coils on the undercarriage.

Which, when the time came, is just what Aaron did.

Inside the car everything went black. This didn't bother most of the passengers, asleep as they were, until a little girl began her incessant screaming. The priests and Danica were jolted to full double-alert but Aaron had already stepped into the car, gliding swiftly down the aisle, an even darker black in the blackness, plunging a blade deep into the chest of his victim as he walked by. In the dark no one could see the spume of blood as life gurgled from the wound with each receding heartbeat. Aaron then made the boldest move imaginable, never leaving the car, sitting only six rows from the murder in a pair of unoccupied seats, and from the bulky purse pulled out a dress and heels. He changed into the female wear (his face may have been disfigured but he still shaved his buttermilk-soaked legs and kept his trim boyish figure), stuffed his old attire under the seat, then assumed a masquerade of repose.

Coming from the tunnel onto the continent, the train reached its maximum speed of 186 m.p.h. until it finally eased into the *Gare du Nord* station in Paris. Two Eurostar security personnel had been called to the car within ninety seconds of the event and the incident prevented the doors from being opened once they pulled into the station.[63] There was a grand and inconvenient delay as Parisian gendarmes arrived to interrogate each passenger coming off the train, all 629 of them.

Aaron, stylish in black silk and spiked heels, hidden behind his glasses and scarf, explained in a voice less odd for a female, how a freak CAT scan at the *Centre Médical de Saint Denis* – he produced a card from the hospital executive administrator himself if there was any question – resulted in his present condition. His purse was searched to find nothing of interest. His passport for Lillian Pompidou was in order. He waited as the phone call was made, after which he was allowed to leave; besides, a female so disfigured and memorable could never commit such a grotesque public slaying.

---

63   It should be pointed out that even though this is a work of fiction, this is the first murder, real or fictional, on the Eurostar Channel Tunnel train, and that the circuit breaker box has since been moved to a less accessible place.

Our four, too, were eventually cleared, their passports again performing as designed, much to Danica's conflicting relief and dismay; she also happened to notice in the interrogation line that there were no little girls from the car they had exited.

As for the deceased...he would turn out to be one Giuseppe Romagnoli, who had nothing to do with this story. He was a supporting character from the book *Il Protocollo del Michelangelo*,[64] transporting important and revealing information in the service of good; and had he been able to reach his destination alive, that narrative would have been cut short considerably. Since he happened to be on the same train, Aaron was ordered to kill him as a professional courtesy to the antagonists in *Protocollo*.

Saturday, April 10th, 9:48 p.m. – Zurich

Since to catalog all the obstacles put in the way of our protagonists to reach Zurich from Paris, as well as how our protagonists dealt with each of those obstacles, would expand this read as to give Tolstoy pause, and since the reader's time is no less valuable than the time of his or her literary surrogates, suffice it to say that what *wasn't* recounted here on the road to Zurich resulted in the destruction of: An Islamic Friendship Center, Auguste Rodin's sculpture *The Gates of Hell* (though six other copies still exist), and a runaway tourist double-decker bus (luckily empty of the Grant-a-Wish Children's Group at the time) that resulted in the

64   By Angelo Cannelonni, Donatti Press, copyright 2009, all rights reserved; it has not yet been translated into English.

death of a brave Luxembourg Crossing Guard who pushed a blind woman and her unaware seeing-eye dog to safety. Danica dodged death on at least two occasions ("at least" because a third one she never knew about), Bertolucci ultimately needed sixty-eight field stitches from three different impalements, and Mickey somehow managed to stay out of everyone's way.[65]

Mickey, still in his lederhosen, sat in the back of the compact that Danica, still in her furry fox costume, had to hotwire due to a one-day Zurich cabdrivers' sick-out protesting an international plushofilia convention that resulted in a number of perverted acts by costumed patrons in the backseats of cabs. The two priests were in the front, dressed as Spanish Basque folk dancers,[66] all four in a state of anticipatory excitement as they raced to the *Fonds de Suisse de Lion* address – silent until Danica thought to ask Mickey something.

"Not too crazy about dying, are you?" Perhaps the most unnecessary query he'd ever been asked by a police officer

---

65   As for the unaware seeing-eye dog, it was demoted back to civilian life for being so inattentive and, sadly, would never live down its shame of not protecting its charge, even after being adopted by a loving Luxembourg family, escaping their home to live a dissolute life on the streets, chasing and barking after double-decker buses and urinating on their wheels. You can guess how that ended.

66   All costumes will be explained in the spin-off, *Ark of the Golden Sample*, wherein all events from this point on will be prelude to an even grander adventure of perversity and thrills, laughter and tears.

in an animal fetish costume. "You thought you were gonna buy it on the train," she continued.

"Says who?"

"A little girl who sounded like she wet herself."

The magic that was Danica was starting to wear off. He would normally ignore the question, but for someone dressed as a *vulpes fulva*, she sat in a smug stillness that demanded rejoinder. "Look," he said finally, "even though it was dark, the acoustics imperfect, and your highly offensive allegation circumstantial at best…let's assume for the moment that *was* me on the train," he said. "B.F.D."

"I agree," she said. Which, of course, meant that she didn't.

"Okay Farburger, what gets under *your* skin? There's gotta be something that makes you hit a high-C, and not in the way that you like, either."

"Waking up and finding you in my bed?"

"C'mon…what makes your short hairs go straight? Everyone's got a loose bowel for something, I'm guessing if Christ himself comes back he won't be too crazy to see all the crosses that've cropped up since he was last here. But for some reason you expect me to have a big-ass red 'S' on my chest to match my cape."

"So I'm right."

"About what?"

"The dying thing."

"Big. Fucking. Deal." he said with as much forbearance as he could call upon.

"Aren't you the modern Moses down from the mount with the inside track on salvation, the one who thinks – no, wait, the one who *knows* – how shallow everyone else's faith is because they only *think* they have faith, even if they're Mother Theresa herself?"

"Wow…is that why you're called a scissor sister? 'Cuz you're so sharp?"

"Is that why you're called an asshole? 'Cuz you're such an asshole?"

"Padres on board, watch your tongue. Or let me watch it for you." The two priests stared straight ahead, the parents ignoring the bickering kids on a cross-country drive.

"Just saying," she continued, feeling in the Socratic driver's seat. "You might not be such a hereafter-wimp if you believed in something."

"Something."

"Yeah."

"What would you recommend?"

"Your choice, Samanov, but all those billions of people you dismiss? Most of 'em have an exit strategy. Doesn't mean come check-out time they'll be happy about it, but they'll probably go with a tad more dignity."

Mickey decided to try to use his if-I-ignore-her-she'll-go-away strategy.

"How can someone so intelligent not see the paradox?" Her voice betrayed more frustration than she would have cared to betray. "The other day you said an unquestioned faith *is* a weak faith, that it's *okay* to have doubts, to admit your faith is no more valid than any other. 'Fact the bigger those doubts, maybe the bigger your faith. Hell, Samanov, by that definition you have the strongest faith of all. But you're afraid to admit it because it somehow makes you a lesser being, so you'd prefer to stay in your little club of one, sit on high, look down, and tell everyone what *not* to believe."

In the stillness that followed, his expression betrayed a rare indecision, as if something she said tapped into the young Mikhail who, through the arrogance of youth, alienated his father and now with the wisdom of years, wished he *lacked* that wisdom, denied as he was any chance at reconciliation. The moral high ground shifted somewhat under her feet. *It's almost unfair,* she thought, *this guy's such an easy target.* It was not in her nature to let a wounded psyche bleed out. Danica chose to offer an olive branch. "Though I could be wrong."

"Keep your eyes open," Bertolucci ordered over his shoulder, "we're almost there."

The priests turned onto Breitentrottennordstrasse Boulevard. Immediately it felt wrong. Too much nightlife for a banking center, too many cars. The streets were alive with foot traffic, mostly boisterous foreigners, and the first business establishment they saw was a good indication as to why: In four different languages, the sign above it read *Adult Toys and Sex Shop*, as did, with minor variations, the second, third, and fourth establishments past it.

"Check the address," DeSica snapped at Mickey, as if this was his doing.

"Right city, right street," he said from his notes. "The fourteen-hundred block. The property's still owned by the bank."

The bad news was that they were in the fourteen hundred block. DeSica yanked the car to the curb and parked in the only space afforded, by a fire hydrant. They spilled out and marched the boulevard checking addresses. That Mickey in his lederhosen and Danica in her furry costume, as well as the two Basque folk dancers in their wooden sabots, warranted nary a second glance here was lost on them. They arrived at the address for the ultimate kick in their collective ark-hunting nuts.

They stood in front of *Pussy's Crack Palace.* From the bass-heavy *wah-wah-chicka-wah-wah* music that poured out from inside, it was safe to assume Pussy wasn't offering distilled blow.

Saturday, April 10th, 10:14 p.m. – Rome

Bishop Boza-Edwards, a conceptionist on the homosexual question and an ally of Cardinal Michelle, arrived from Uganda and even before he was settled into his quarters, anxiously sought out Cardinal Thomasina. "Your Eminence, I come with disturbing rumors that I hope you might put to rest," said Boza-Edwards in his mellifluous if slightly fay British colonial school-trained English.

"Whaatah' eeesit?" asked the Cardinal.[67]

"That within the Vatican a fifth column is lurking to unseat the pontiff before his time!"

That moles were ubiquitous and that they worked for a fifth column was beyond doubt. Thomasina's private

---

67   Verisimilitude must be sacrificed from this point under threat of lawsuit from the Italian Defamation League. The good Cardinal will no longer speak in authentic Hollywood-Esperanto-Italian.

line rang and he excused himself, promising to take this matter up with Boza-Edwards later that evening. ("After the screening of *Funny Girl* in the St. Sebastian Room," the Ugandan specified.) Thomasina answered to hear a funereal resignation in Father DeSica's voice.

"All has led to a dead-end in Zurich. A bank was established here in 1869 most likely to house the ark. But it no longer exists. We are not sure where to turn next."

"The synod begins in less than thirty-six hours! Pray you find it in time or have the strength to suffer the consequences, *do you understand?*"

"But Your Emi—" Thomasina slammed down his receiver mid-reply. He could not see Father DeSica's demeanor on the other end, a demeanor that reflected a level of concern less to do with the ticking clock than with the heretofore-intangible sound of agenda in his superior's tone.

Thomasina was in high agitation. If Boza-Edwards heard the rumor of conspiracy, others had as well. Where Boza-Edwards fell short, however, was that there were *two* fifth columns; that is, not two-fifths of a column, which would only be a fractional threat, but *two* complete fifth columns, which was five times as threatening as the potential misperception.

One column was whomever the moles worked for.

The other was Cardinal Thomasina himself.

August 12ᵗʰ, 1906 – night – Zurich, Switzerland

Jorgen Lindqvist, president of *Fonds de Suisse de Lion Bank*, was the last to arrive in the upstairs conference room

that balmy August night, having left the house without
his Freemason pin and ordering his driver to turn the
brougham back to retrieve it. The other twelve board
members were already assembled, enjoying Partagas cigars
from Havana and snifters of eighteen-year-aged cognac;
Jorgen's arrival made the thirteen complete. The ceremonial sword-wielding guard moved to the door. Jorgen took
time to partake of spirits, a cigar, and indulge in meaningless banter to disguise the magnitude of the night's agenda.
Across the room he could see Borje Hendenbratt, handsome, at ease in his smoking jacket and pomaded hair; if
Borje suspected anything, he was a thespian in possession
of greater tools (not to mention both his legs) than Sarah
Bernhardt.

"Gentlemen," Jorgen finally announced, quieting the
room, "it is time to attend to tonight's business." As the others began to don their regalia, Jorgen caught them short.
"There will be no formal calling to order...no opening supplication...no presentation of square, compass, or Bible."

Concern permeated the room. Carl, he of wide girth
and great muttonchops, asked anxiously, "Then...there will
be no dancing naked, oiled, and erect around the effigy of
the pope until we all ejaculate our splooge?"

"Not tonight, Dad." More than just Carl groaned,
dispirited. "This sacred body," intoned Jorgen with proper
gravitas, "has a boil. A boil that must be lanced immediately for the body's continued well-being." He had the
room's attention. "That boil will be lanced tonight." He
paused to increase the importance of his announcement.
"We have among us...a papist fifth column." All looked

among one another confused;[68] all, of course, except Borje
Hendenbratt, his snifter dropping onto the Persian rug,
cognac spreading like the mark of Cain. Everyone turned
to him sharply as if choreographed by Bob Fosse.

"Yes, Borje...you." Jorgen accused. "We have our own
fifth column[69] within the Vatican." In a voice so stentorian
it shook the Swarovski crystal pendalogues on the chande-
lier, Jorgen pointed at him, quoting, "Mark, chapter nine,
verse forty-seven, 'if thine eye offend thee...pluck it out!'"

What happened next was never recorded, as the meeting never officially occurred. Under Jorgen's command,
Borje was restrained and thrown down, on his back, on
the conference table. His collar was opened, the better
to expose his neck. Borje babbled about mercy, about
understanding, about how he never noticed that the red-
felt fleur-de-lys ceiling paper above didn't quite match the
walls (but – as has been said – we all can't be Oscar Wilde
at the moment of death).

The guard at the door approached, broadsword at
the ready; this night he would not be purely ceremonial.
Jorgen brought forth an oaken box with pewter hinges and
latch, and with great care placed it on the table. Opening
the box with veneration, he revealed the glove of Jacques
de Molay. The guard kneeled reverently as Jorgen lifted it
from its place and placed it over the guard's upturned right

68   Ed.note: Understandable since the term "fifth column"
came from the Spanish Civil War thirty-one years later from a
group of supporters General Mola said was inside Madrid besides
the four columns attacking without.
69   See previous footnote.

hand. The guard then stood and gripped the hilt of the sword with redoubled intent.

From beneath the table Jorgen slid the large brass basin that heretofore held the papal effigy and gathered their communal manhood, positioned it beneath Borje's head, then told him, "Prepare to enter the ninth circle of hell." A curt nod to the guard sealed Borje's fate. The guard hefted the sword above his head, all stepping back to avoid any difficult-to-explain stains on their eveningwear. Then with a mighty swing the blade hewed head from body, and with a dull thunk it landed in the basin followed by a forceful cataract of red. The body continued to drain for quite some time as the twelve, with a wiveless meeting-less evening before them, chose to resume the time in continued bonhomie, cigars, and cognac. They would come to remember this night as one of their more bracing and stimulating (even if they were denied the effigy dance) for the rest of their lives.

Which was only four more days and seven hours.

Borje's head was found next morning on the altar of St. Peterskirche Catholic Church, a warning to those in the know who might try again to infiltrate this Freemason's lodge. Despite being their newest member, Borje had still been able to send the names and addresses of all the Freemason bank board members. From Rome came twelve angels of death who, in the same night, at the same hour, descended upon the twelve homes, decapitated the remaining twelve board members, and set such a fire to the bank that the vault door in the cellar warped off its hinges. The bank was never rebuilt, the ruined vault was removed and melted for scrap, and the neighborhood never quite recovered...though nude dancing and the spilling of seed would continue to flourish.

Saturday, April 10th, 10:31 p.m. – Zurich

The agent for Vandersmissen, having correctly predicted the four's arrival in Paris via rail, was late and might have missed them if not for Aaron's murder and the resulting police cordon that detained everyone from disembarking. The agent then tailed the four from Paris to this inappropriate section of Zurich and, on top of that, could make no sense of them standing outside a strip club, their body language the contraposto of defeat. They were followed from there to an internet café off the main thoroughfare where, through the café window, said agent could see them huddled around a computer.

From behind an arm snaked hard around the neck, a point digging into a jugular vein. *"Parlez vous français?"* asked Aaron.

"Oui," came the agent's anxious response, if not entirely true.

"Why were you only moments ago on Breitentrottennordstrasse Boulevard and now you are here?"

"It is to very easy," his victim replied. "I was please use not in shower while plugged into Keith Richards."

"What...?"

A foot kicked back into Aaron's crotch, the blade scoring the neck and drawing blood, Aaron's grip loosening enough for the attackee to launch Aaron over a shoulder, slamming him onto the cement sidewalk with sickening impact. A knee dropped like an anvil onto his chest. The knife clattered away as he gasped for more air, the blade grabbed by his prey, raised high enough to glint red from the light of a whore's window, then brought down hard into his chest. Aaron stiffened, his jaw opened to the breaking point, but all that came out was a sound like a rusty hinge. And then he slumped, still, the hilt perpendicular from his heart, as fading footsteps told the story's denouement, Aaron another polyp sinking onto the great reef of life.

Except that this polyp wasn't quite subsumed yet.

Much has been written on the dehumanizing effects of pornography...how it debases and objectifies...how it reduces emotional response to a soulless mechanical charade...how the greater one's exposure, the greater one's tolerance, until only the most perverse defilement and degradation is craved; or as Naomi Wolf has written, "...the relationship between the multi-billion-dollar porn industry, compulsiveness, and sexual appetite has become like the relationship between agribusiness, processed foods, supersize portions, and obesity... if your appetite is stimulated and fed by poor-quality material, it takes more junk to fill you up. People are not closer because of porn but further apart; people are not more turned on in their daily lives but less so."[70]

But where are the media when pornography *saves* a life? Indeed, how many incidents are there that we never know about? But the truth is, had Aaron not loitered a moment

___

70   *New York Magazine,* Oct. 20th, 2003.

on Breitentrottennordstrasse Boulevard to purchase a copy of *Hairless Asian Pillow Biters #14*...had the shop owner not been out of plain brown bags on this busy Saturday night... had Aaron not rolled the magazine up and slipped it inside his jacket pocket...the blade would have cleaved his left ventricle like a vine-ripened tomato. Instead the knife pierced first the many layers of the rolled four-color, eighty-eight page annual, penetrating into his chest but halting a quarter-inch short of its target. It took Aaron a full minute to realize his heart was still beating, and that he joined a rich history of miraculous survivors by way of printed material. Of course, the story always told by other victims saved by such material involved a *Bible*, the *Koran*, the *Vedas*, the *Vinaya Texts*, etc., that amazingly absorbed the near occasion of death, thus making it a miracle. How many were saved by *Hairless Asian Pillowbiters, Chitty-Chitty Gang Bang, Starship Poopers,* etc. will never be known.

Aaron finally dared to move. Sill supine, he weakly reached for and unwrapped a stick of *Bulle Heureuse,* and began to masticate.

Saturday, April 10th, 10:47 p.m. – Zurich

In the computer café the four learned of the fire that consumed their destination as well as the entire board of directors within.[71] They sat in demoralized silence. Danica

71   The twelve beheadings were considered so heinous that the Zurich constabulary reported that the twelve were killed in the conflagration that they may better investigate without public and media hysteria. The families of the deceased were ordered to

watched as Mickey pored over the pages of his father's pad with a jeweler's eye as if an answer would magically manifest between the scribbles, until he finally sat back in his chair and stared abjectly into middle distance. Even in lederhosen, it was a sad sight.

She knew that his profound funk wasn't about the probable end of their search, nor from Thomasina's warning made only days ago how those who knew as much as they did tended to have a diminished shelf life. No one more than he loved to tempt fate or knew that the longer one gambled the house always won. No, what it came down to is that if this was the end of the journey, so too was the communion he was beginning to share with his father in death that they had so long denied each other in life. She could see in Mickey that whatever he had become now, however far he strayed, he knew his father was among the threads woven into his fabric; that the path Mickey veered from, the knowledge he accumulated, the choices he made, were the product of his upbringing by a single parent who did the best he knew how, and not the result of purposeful misguidance. Though he had every opportunity, Mickey never spoke of his father as a bad person. Inflexible, strong willed, less Christian than even Mikhail Sr. could admit in his inability to forgive a prodigal, all true, but not someone worthy of the disdain Mickey had accumulated over the

---

conspire in the ruse as well and it was consistent that all twelve would be buried in a closed-casket ceremony. Because of the cover-up which has remained in place to this day, our four were denied a big clue that would have cut nearly the last thirty-seven pages from this book.

years, disdain that was ironic, born of inflexibility that was an inheritance Mickey was not able to rise above.

Inheritance. Then there was *that* word.

Through an act his father would have considered spiteful, sacrilegious, even heretical had he known of The All-Encompassing Church of the Unified and Omnipotent Being, Mickey was able to acquire the wealth of his father, wealth accumulated through hard work, endless travel, and meaningful scholarship; wealth that Mickey stumbled into through Fate's idea of a tasteless joke. It bothered Mickey as much as anything.

"Mickey," she finally said, "You did more than anyone else could've."

"Except my dad," he said matter-of-factly. "This didn't stop him."

"Your dad devoted decades to this."

"I had the cheat sheet."

"You don't know that he found it."

"He did. His writing gets more illegible and excited as the notes go on...a few words in Russian he didn't even bother to translate. Plus, he was murdered by someone who knew he was diabetic, meaning he was being watched more closely than a flea circus. No reason to kill him unless he had the answer...someone probably threatened him with the ark or his life. Unlike me, he made the right choice."

She was on wafer-thin ice, but she said it anyway. "Maybe you didn't like your father...but you loved him."

His expression could not be more baleful. "Spare me your penny-ante, dime-book, voodoo psychoanalysis."

From the soles of her feet she could feel the flush rise within her. *Goddamnit,* she thought, *enough of this shit.* It was time to make what cops call a blink decision, as in don't think, just do it, worry about it when you're dead. She stood, thrust out her hand. "Gimme your passport."

"Why would I give you–?"

"Shut the fuck up and gimme your goddamn passport, now."

Well…when she talked to him that way…even at this low ebb…she might as well have been quoting the *Rubaiyat of Omar Khayyam* au naturel on a Magic Fingers motel bed with a roll of quarters. He gave it up. "Follow me." She produced her own passport, walked past the two downcast priests at the next table, and threw both passports before them. "We're grabbing a beer."

"Sit down," ordered DeSica.

"Bite me." Danica continued on, Mickey unsure but following her.

DeSica looked up. "Do not walk out that door."

They didn't stop. The two priests jumped up and spilled into the street. "Come back! NOW!" It was the first time DeSica, whose commanding presence never required it, raised his voice. The tall silhouette in Bavarian shorts and the short silhouette in the saggy-assed furry fox costume kept walking toward the bright main boulevard.

Bertolucci pulled out his gun, aimed at Mickey, and cocked the hammer.

"No," said DeSica, dispirited.

"We've reached a dead end," said Bertolucci, drawing a bead, "and they know too much—"

"*No*," snapped DeSica, slapping down Bertolucci's arm. DeSica, admitting this for the first time, said, "I believe Cardinal Thomasina does not have the best interests of the church at heart."

"What are you saying...?"

DeSica said with the burden of the disillusioned, "I fear we are in the employ of the Cardinal...not the Holy Father." He told Bertolucci of the last phone call.

"Shit," said Bettolucci. "I need a beer, too."

Saturday, April 10ᵗʰ, 11: 38 p.m. – Zurich

"So God looksat th'believer sitting there with this teeny Billy Joel with 'is teeny piano," slurred Mickey above the cacophony of patrons around them, bent over his fifth stein of doppelbock and a second plate of *Amerikanische Flügel des Büffels*,[72] "an' God says, 'upp, my bad...I thought you were praying for a twelve inch *pianist.*'" His whole frame contorted with a silent laugh. The other three were still waiting for the funny. He recovered, saw. "Jeesus...tha' useta' kill intha'sem'nary."

Danica turned to the priests, in cop-mode. "You lied to us at the hospital, didn't you? Whether we found this ark or not, your orders were to not let us live."

DeSica nodded, chagrinned. "For the greater good."

"Then why should we believe you now?"

"Because we didn't have to tell you."

---

72   That uniquely American cuisine that still baffles certain celebrities and a former distaff Alaskan governor as to how bison can have such tiny wings.

"Then why did you? What changed?"

It was a tough sell, DeSica trying to explain an inflection in his superior's voice, the subtle shift of its timbre, the sound of urgency that went beyond the exigencies of their institution and felt more about the exigencies of his needs, detectable only from a decade of interaction with him. But he tried.

"But you still want to find the ark," she asked.

"Yes, to get to the bottom of this," he said, then added, "and it's the only protection any of us has."

"You're saying," Danica said with no small degree of skepticism, "that the two of *you* don't expect to get out of this alive?"

"I will die for the cause. Father Bertolucci and I still need to serve the greater good, even if it's counter to our superior. Help us find the ark, and we will not obey our orders."

"And why should we believe you this time?" she said, sipping her beer.

"We give you our word."

She sprayed a torrent of hops and Artesian water upon them. "Sorry," she cough-laughed. "As irony goes, it doesn't get much better than that." She wiped her lips. "*Your word*. That's what you said, right?" The priests looked at her wanly. "You *do* see my dilemma."

DeSica pulled out both of their passports and tossed them on the table. "You have every right not to trust us. Go. We will continue on as best we can." DeSica took out his wallet, counting out a pile of one-hundred dollar bills. "That should fly you both back to San Francisco, first class." Danica stared at the pile as if the moment she took the bait, a dagger would slam down and pin her hand and filthy lucre to the tabletop. The means to escape lay within reach, passports that could probably fool God and enough money to try it, an offer that loomed all the more tempting in light of the truth, and yet to Danica something about it felt like the wrong choice.

Mickey, belching, swept the money towards him like the grand winner of a Texas Hold 'Em Tourney.

"So whoooose w'me furra' trip back to Pussy's t'study th' aesthetics of Brazilian wax vershsus a landing strip…?" He stood up and in the same move, unmoored by animal fat slathered in barbeque sauce and ranch dressing, washed down with nearly two gallons of dark beer, he began to capsize, lacking the motor skills to even raise his hands and protect his face; luckily the wooden floor broke his fall.

Saturday, April 10ᵗʰ, 11: 47 p.m. – Zurich

Pwahhhhhhh….pwahhh-pwahhh-pwahhhhhhhhhhhhhhhh, Mickey expelled from heretofore unplumbed depths, kneeling over the yellowed toilet bowl that surely had never seen expelling as visceral as this. *Pwuh-puh-puh-puh-pwah-Pwaaaaaaahhhhhhhhhhhhhh!* Orange semi-digested matter flecked his face. Danica could only marvel as to how she came to be kneeling in a Zurich sex district men's bathroom stall wearing a plush fox costume, trying to read foreign graffiti while ministering to a vomiting shit-faced ex-priest dressed in lederhosen.

"Let it out, Mickey."

Pwuh. "...yeah," he gasped, "...yeah...led'id out..."

"Let it all out."

"...led'id all out..."

"That's right."

"...it hurts..."

"I know...you're gonna feel a lot better."

"...but id's jus'...easier nod'to—"

"Hold back, you'll only make it worse."

He took a few deep breaths, gripping the bowl's edge like he was steering the Exxon Valdez through icy shoals. "...yur right..."

"I'm right."

"...jus' spill allovit..."

"All of it, that's right."

"...'kay...spill allovit...I'mready, youready?"

"I'm ready."

Danica braced herself for a blunderbuss of discharge.

"...youready..."

"I'm ready, Mickey. I'm here."

"...'kay...'kay..." Mickey took a few more deep breaths to pump himself up, Danica's hand rubbing his back encouragingly. "You can do it."

He nodded, grabbed the ship's wheel more firmly. And then: "I dunno where t'begin...never tol' this t'anyone..." *Pwaaaaaaaaah-pwaahh!* "...I mean s'no secret that 'tween my dad 'n the pries'hood...I didn't date a whole lot growing up..."

Holy shit...was she hearing correctly?

Maybe because he was in a booth on his knees...and if he wasn't exactly close to death, death seemed preferable just now…but Danica realized that Mickey was actually *con-fessing! Coming clean! Coughing up more than just chicken and beer!* He was delving into his own personal stuff in the plain brown wrapper, and the trick, like any good cop getting a perp to confess, was to pay out just enough line to keep the confessor talking.

"…I hadda learn al'bout women by readingup on the subject."

"Reading what?"

"*Letters to Penthouse.*"

Beat. "It could've been worse."

"Really?"

No. "Keep going."

"Y'see, my father wassalot like Sir Thomas More…'cept for bein' English 'n the beheading part…"

"Uh huh…uh huh."

"…devoted t'God…th'church…tried to follow the monastic calling…but he din' have what Sir Thomas Wolfe called 'the righ' stuff'…so he came back t'civilian life… something that—" *pwa-pwa-pwa-pwaah-ah-ah-ah* "—shit… something tha'came to bother his extra-large Cath'lic guilt…but th'best was yet to come."

"Really? What was that?" *Damnit-damnit-damnit, too eager!*

"…ahh…itso' involved," he moaned, sounding retreat.

Danica tried not to panic. "No-no Mickey, you're safe in here, safe with me, this is good. You're going to feel soooo much better if you keep talking, trust me."

"…s'involved…"

"Then make it simple, sort through it." She wasn't sure if he heard that, the silence that followed was unbearable.

Mickey was one with the bowl, staring down at more than just his gastronomic sins. He shifted, hunching, still quiet. Until, allowing Danica to breathe again:

"He d'cided t'become th'worl's most devoted lay-person since Paul…became this brainiac of ancient her-heret-heretical texts, master of translashun'…his books published inta' shitload of languages…very comfor'ble income… Richard gave 'im some 'vesting tips an' he became *more* comfor'ble….an' tha' prob'bly weighed on 'im even more. But tha' isn't what really diddit…"

What? What diddit? she wanted to shout. *And did* what, *by the way?*

"…guess he lived pretty simply 'til he got married—"

"You guess?" she said, tempting fate. "He never told you?"

A derisive snort. "Tol' me…? Nooo…I grew'p onna need-to-know basis…like memorizing titles of alla' books oftha' Old 'n New Testaments? Need to know. Th'miracle o' reproduction? Only if I wanted my eyes t'melt…th'one thing I *did* know wassat he traveled more'n th'Jews inna desert…now I know alotta' that was lookin' for th'ark. Jesus, flush this shit, wouldja?"

She pulled down the toilet lever. The spin-art of vomit swirled down to make room for more.

"He gave allot' t'charity…kept 'is nose t'the grin'stone… 'voided the three F's like th'plague…fun, frivolity 'n fucking…or so I thought. Onna visit home from sem'nary I found a shoebox fulla' letters…seems f'years 'fore I was born he carried on a long distance 'lationship with a' green-eyed, red'eaded, vaginally-equipped scriptural translator in

Ireland...name 'o Meghan, who'ee planned to lose his virginity with'in the sac'ment of marriage an' turn out lotsa little translators."

"Your mother."

"No...she was Maureen."

"The picture I saw—"

"—was th'woman he married—"

"—who had red hair and green eyes—"

"—an' was Meghan's sister."

Ohhhhhhhh. "Oh..."

"Yeah...you can guess the punch line."

No, not yet, don't stop now. "Of course I can, but it's good for *you* to get it out, Mickey, force it all up—"

Pwaaaaaaaaaaaaaaaaaaaah-pwah-pwaaaaaaaah. "Bad choice'a words," he croaked, "...flush." She did; then, "'T'navigate the human soul, true north is never love, it's lucre."

WTF? "Uh huh..."

"Thas'wha dad always said...he mennit, too, which was strange forra' manna' faith to reduce all incentive not t'god but money. He even wrote id'down in his notes, las' page..." He trailed off, mystified. "But I know where it start'd...his fiance's sister found out ee'had money...and 'cuz sisters can be major c-bombs t'each other...Maureen made it stateside first an' got to know dad."

"In the biblical sense."

"Very good, cricket." She heard the faint smile in his voice.

"'Ee was lonely...she looked like Meghan...Maureen got pregnant...an' my dad bein' the Cath'lic ee'was, married 'er...the letters from Meghan stopped 'fore my birth. Mom musta' beenna' real Delilah...not only got dad t'sin, she got 'im t'upgrade their address t'the one you saw. When she divorced 'im, I'm sure she bailed witha' golden ejection seat...'an bein' the Catholic he was, he never remarried." *Up-uppp-hwaaaaaaahhhhhhhh-ahh-ah.* "Ahh Jesus...he coulda' got the marriage annulled... f'anyone couldadunnit, *he* coulda'...but'ee was more guilt-ridden thanna post-Easter Judas....see, t'him? 'Ee got what ee'deserved."

He went quiet and she sensed it wasn't because of his stomach; he was reviewing how profoundly the sins of the father visited the son; the part that was the key to Mickey Samanov that she was dying to unlock. Carefully, on tip-toes, she primed the pump. "Your father was determined to not let his son fall victim to other Jezebels...wasn't he?"

"An' what better way t'do that than t'groom the son for the monastic life *he* shoulda' followed? Didn't havva' goddamn chance....'tween the best Catholic schools an' 'is tutoring, I was the goddamn Manchurian Can'date." A memory prompted a chuckle. "Once...I wasss fifteen... in my bedroom when th'cleaning lady's daughter thought t'polish a knob that wasn't on the door...Dad caught'us... an' I spent th'next *year* translating Erasmus's *In Praise of Folly* from English ta' Latin.[73] But hey...I graduated toppa'

---

73 An ironic title. Folly is a character who, in a series of orations, praises self-deception, madness and pedantry but ultimately makes a strong apologia for Catholic ideals. By any title, not the most fun time spent by a fifteen-year-old.

my class from the University of—" buurrrrrrrp "—so, y'know, it was time well spent."

He was drained, ready to stop; his tone, his whole demeanor, had an air of finality, the planets threatening to shift out of alignment. His grip loosened on the bowl and he lifted up on his elbows. He took a deep, cleansing breath. "Think I'm done."

If they left the stall, that was it. Period. Time to be bad cop. "You must be hungry after all this...let's go back in, order you some crackers to settle the stomach...maybe a good, watery Limburger cheese to—"

PWAAAAAAAAAHHHHHHHHH-pwaaaah-pwah! PWAAAAAAAHHHHHHH! "....ohhhhh shit...oh shit... ohhhh...."

"Easy, easy...don't rush it...just stay put." He was gasping, a free-diver who misjudged the surface, his throat seared from stomach acid. "Mickey...take your mind off this...it helps to keep talking. About anything." He mumbled something. "What?"

Weak but hopeful: "...y'think Pussy's still open...?"

"Um, yes, probably." At least he still thought about dipping his wick, she might be able to play the sex card; though that was a delicate line to walk with someone like Mickey, if he went one millimeter off-beam and fell into the depths, all the king's horses couldn't reel him back from the gutter. *Last thing he talked about was what, graduating, pick up the thread from there.* "I'll bet you were a good priest," she offered. No acknowledgement. "With your genes? Maybe a future theologian...even a saint. Y'know, St. Mickey, patron saint of runway poles? I mean someone's gotta do it, right?" Still nothing. He was arched like a human parenthesis over the bowl, doing his penance in silence. *Okay, try vanity…that's a weakness he couldn't resist even if his physique was being admired by the Donner Party.* "Bet you looked good in a collar…even had your own groupies." It didn't register on his radar. "What do you even *call* religious groupies? Pastor plaster casters?" Not even a semi-amused grunt. And this was her A-material. This was serious, time was running out.

"…okay…I'm empty…les'go…"

And like Saul on the road to Damascus, divine inspiration struck – the sure-fire magic bullet, the grenade she could lob into his fragile psyche. She was working the wrong side of the street; the answer was almost too easy.

"I know God thought you were a good priest."

Mickey, still hunched, began to convulse, veins streaking his forehead like lightning, his face flushed red, a death rattle wheezing out. Danica was suddenly afraid he might self-combust.

"Mickey…Mickey, are you all ri—"

But he was laughing, so hard he fell against the stall divider. He slid to the floor, eyes wet and crimson. "No," he said, wiping tears away, "thas' the best part. He *didn't*."

"He didn't," she repeated as a question.

"Nuh-uh."

"You know this."

Hiccup. "Uh-huh."

"How…?"

"'Cuz…he tol' me."

"…He told you. God spoke to you."

"Coulda' been an'assistant but I'm pretty sure i'was He-Who-Is."

"The God you said you don't believe in."

"I said I don' believe in any version of God we 'ave so far."

"*Whatever* version of God spoke to Mickey Samanov."

"He orders Abraham t'kill his son," Mickey began with no small amount of umbrage, "...'ee chooses a killer t'be bring down the commandments t'man...'ee sends an angel t'Joseph t'say his fiancé's got a messiah in the oven...'ee sends the archangel Michael to a French peasant to tell her t'kick English ass...'ee has the angel Gabriel dictate to an illiterate camel driver...'ee has the angel Maroni reveal th'truth to a New York treasure hunter...whas' so hard to believe?"

She'd hit the triple-cherries and was about to collect the payout. Between the spewing of his stomach and the sudden desire to deflower this naïf of her naiveté, Mickey seemed more alert. Still, thought Danica, it seemed best to remain in a bathroom stall to hear this since, she was certain, some serious shit was on the way.

Saturday, April 10th, 7:45 p.m. – Buenos Aires, Argentina

"*Hola*," the butler said into the phone.

"I need to speak immediately with Jean-Henri Vandersmissen."

"*Y quien es?*"

"Tell him...it concerns the private matter of all men."

Jean-Henri felt lightheaded when the butler announced the caller with this odd phrase, clearly an announcement of something momentous; they had spoken only a handful of times in all these years. His veined and frail hand shook taking the receiver. He placed it to his ear and took several deep breaths before asking: "Do you have it...?"

As before, by quirk of satellite bounce or a deliberate need for subterfuge, the voice sounded oddly attenuated, as if a high register was being lowered or a low register raised. "I'm to fly to Paris tonight for what will be the final piece of the puzzle."

"Then why call me now?"

Before being nearly gutted by Aaron, the agent had discreetly gone into the cyber-café and ordered a cappuccino then walked out, a transaction that took less than four minutes. But enough was overheard from the four and their discordant exchanges to know they had reached what in a book would be called a late Act Two dead end.

"I   have   something   they   don't...Mikhail Samanovananonvich's briefcase."

Leaving the café, realizing Mickey's et. al., circumstances, this called for a careful re-perusal of the contents of said briefcase. In it was something that initially meant nothing, but now took on the weight of the Holy Grail.

A carbon of a receipt, signed by Mikhail.

It was for records he was studying the night he was accosted, the records that gave Mikhail the final clue that he was ultimately unable to act on. But the library was closed until Monday.

"You have connections and unlimited money," the agent said. "Whoever you can contact, however much you must pay, get me in the *Bibliotheque Historique de la Ville de*

Paris Antiquities first thing tomorrow morning. Do so and the ark will be yours."

Father Mikhail Samanovananonvich Jr. had, over time, become known by his students as Father Mickey, and that stuck with the other priests and lay teachers as well in the Department of Historical and Doctrinal Studies; as did the surname Samanov. Mikhail, focused as he was on the task of sustaining the soul, marching to class in robe and open sandals even in the dead of winter, always leaning forward with a sense of mission – even to the commissary – didn't care... if the Anglicization of his name freed up more memory in his feeble students' minds for the things that truly *mattered, so be it. As for what mattered, it was in the course catalogue at the Apostolic Theological Union in Chicago. Mikhail's read:*

CV 3250 – God Manifest in Practice and Proclamation: An exploration of God as Jesus Christ proclaimed in scripture, theology, and historical document; a rumination of the Holy Mystery; the reconciliation of the doctrine of Trinity with monotheism; and understanding man's inability to truly comprehend the beauty of spiritual contradiction, especially viewed through the limitations of secular egotism.

It went on to give his official biography:

Father Mikhail Samanovananonvich, Jr. received his doctorate in religious history from Europe's oldest Catholic institution, the University of Louvain in Belgium, where he minored in archaic languages. He has helped his father, world-renown scholar

and translator Mikhail Samanovananonvich Sr.
research some of his most notable works, including *The Ontology of Non-Being*, the translation of the
Gnostic Codex XIII from Nag Hammadi, and *The
Trimorphic Protennoia: On the Origin of the World*.
Outside interests include tracking the application
of the Golden Mean from Pythagoras through the
High Renaissance and attempting to calculate its
ultimate numerical value. He has yet to find the
end.

*Fr. Mikhail was also department chair of Historical and
Doctrinal Studies, a position that gave him even more ecclesiastical authority in the field besides being the son of his father.*

*Fr. Mikhail considered himself the spiritual gatekeeper of the
drawbridge that lowered from academia to the outside world; the
teacher whose class best girded the student with the proper weapons
to slay the dragons of heresy and ignorance. He suffered youthful
merriment not at all, was known never to give an A, and was the
nemesis of more than a few tearful would-be graduates. Still, to
say that Father Mikhail lacked the capacity for idle pastimes, rec-
reation and small talk would be wrong; he lacked even the gene.*

Until his fateful twelfth year of the cloth.

*Mikhail Sr. was in the Aran Islands helping archeologists
with a pre-Christian excavation when the Coptic Orthodox Church
of Cairo contacted him. It seems a partial leaf of Aramaic text
came into their possession written by a 4th century scribe from the
Ecumenical Council of Constantinople. It was this gathering, pre-
sided over by St. Timothy I, that finished what was begun earlier
at the Council of Nicaea, most notably the Nicene Creed. But this
single fragment was potentially explosive because it indicated an*

earlier alternate version of that all-important creed, a version that potentially contradicted a central tenet of faith. Others, however, were not so sure and Mikhail Sr.'s expertise was quickly requested to put the matter to rest. Unable to leave the Aran Islands, he arranged for his son to take leave from his post and inspect the fragment in his stead. It was particularly relevant for Mikhail Jr., as the part of the creed it affected was the very core of his studies and chair at the university, that of the divinity and the unity of the Holy Trinity.

The fragment concerned the end of the Nicene Creed. What the Council of Constantinople codified and has been universally repeated ever after was:

"We believe in the Holy Spirit, the Lord, the Giver of Life, who proceeds from the Father, who with the Father and the Son is worshipped and glorified, who spoke by the Prophets, and in One, Holy, Universal, and Apostolic church. We confess one baptism for the remission of sins and we look for the resurrection of the dead and the life of the coming age, Amen."

But this fragment appeared to say:

"We believe in the Holy Spirit, the Lord, the Giver of Life, who *beside* (italics added) the Father and the Son, is worshipped and glorified..."

Thus the inference that, until very late in the formalization of Christian theology, that only the Father and the Son were at the top of the firmament, and the Holy Spirit was a supporting player. If this were the case, that the Holy Spirit was cut from another cloth instead of part of the same Father-Son fabric, it would have tread dangerously close to polytheism, which was antithetical to Jesus's teaching. The issue of the Holy Spirit was impossible to ignore since Jesus, in John 14:15-18 mentioned the entity himself, and the inspired writers of the three synoptic gospels mentioned it at the beginning of Jesus's ministry; thus this fragment seemed to suggest that rather than acknowledge another holy entity and veer into polytheism, the answer for the church fathers was to simply stir it into the same mélange of Father and Son; making the mystery of the holy trinity less an essential cornerstone to the faith, and reducing it to more of a bureaucratic sweeping-under-the-rug. To say that Mikhail Jr. was eager to inspect this fragment himself was the understatement of the new millennium.

He flew straightaway from Chicago to Cairo, by coach, beside a colicky baby who didn't stop its caterwauling the entire trip; Mikhail was certain it had been placed there by the Lord of Flies himself to undermine his ability to assess such an important find.

If so, Beelzebub had done his work well.

Upon arriving, Mikhail insisted on going directly to St. Mark's without rest on a day that was cool and balmy... if this were Death Valley. When Alexander the Great conquered the area, his men found a hieroglyphic on the city gates that was of the following images: A wicker stool, a full mouth, a vulture, a half-mouth, a double reed leaf, a viper, a quail chick, two baskets, a single reed leaf, water, a jar stand, a twist of flax, a quail chick, and a half-mouth. Twenty-two hundred years later with the discovery of the Rosetta Stone, the hieroglyphic was correctly translated to "pretty (expletive) hot."[74]

Fr. Mikhail's taxi driver was conscientious enough to advise him that his transport lacked air conditioning after *he loaded the*

---

74   The hieroglyphic turned out to be an ad for Djehutimes' Shade Apparatus.

priest's luggage in the trunk and refused to remove the cases until he took him to his destination. Mikhail felt like a transmogrified cartoon thermometer about to expel its rapidly ascending mercury through his exploding head, but – as he did on the airplane – he kept reminding himself that his was a minor cross to bear in the service of the original Cross Bearer.

The driver crossed the Nile, traveling along the Shita W-Ashrin Yulyu which then turned into Al Gala then, after a messy turn-about, turned into Ramsis... taking an hour-forty minutes to traverse a distance in third world gridlock that Fr. Mikhail could have walked in fifteen minutes wearing polio braces if his luggage weren't held hostage in the trunk like a blindfolded New York Times journalist; a crossing made all the more pleasant with a tinny AM radio blaring Egyptian music that made the airplane baby's cat-erwauling sound like Tony Bennett. Still, he told himself, have patience, all will arrive in due time. Even the snail made Noah's Ark.

Fr. Mikhail finally arrived at the magnificent cathedral of St. Mark, the seat of the Coptic Orthodox Pope and shrine to St. Mark. Drenched through in perspiration, jet-lagged, sleep deprived for two days, none of it mattered, running on sheer adrenaline to be so close to the find. Perfunctory to the point of rudeness in his intro-ductions, he was escorted to the cool, humidified room that, empty of all else, held the parchment on an examination table under a raised plate of glass that deflected even the warm breath of exam-iners. A monk seemingly as old as the fragment itself joined him with prayer beads and sat to the side, keeping watch, whispering his devotions, the beads slowly working their way through his spot-ted hands.

Fr. Mikhail approached the table as if it was the baby in the manger and gazed upon the fragment. His fingers dancing above the glass, he read the Aramaic letters, getting to the problematic part. Yes…yes…yes-yes-yes! *he said to himself,* I see the dilemma! *He settled into the chair, undid the leather ties around his chamois roll, and laid out his tools. The first implement he pulled out was a 30x loupe.*

Aramaic is very similar to Hebrew and was more common in the day. While Greek was the Lingua Franca, especially among the intelligentsia, bishops brought scribes to such councils as Nicaea from all corners, and this scribe recorded matters in the language most comfortable to his employer. The challenges for translators centuries later, however, were manifold. An angular, geometric-looking alphabet, the incline of a stroke of 45-degrees versus 35-degrees meant an entirely different word. Furthermore, Aramaic used dots to differentiate words, and a dot placed above or below a letter would make the word radically different. Therefore, due to the vagaries of time, storage, and handling, a dot might appear or fade that would alter a word. For instance, the word **kheta***, which meant "sinful," was spelled exactly the same way as* **khetey***,"wheat"; except that* **kheta** *had one dot below it and* **khetey** *had two dots above it. Even trickier are the words* **awaley***, or "unGodly," and* **eweley***, "babies"; the former had two dots above and one dot below, the latter two dots above and two dots below.*

What seemed apparent was that the lines of text in this fragment were squeezed for space. The issue became if the dots were below words of the higher line, or above words of the lower line. Thus where it should have read:

"…who proceeds from the Father…"

it read:

"...who beside the Father..."

because of a dot that wasn't *there, making the word "beside."*
"Proceeds" required one dot below; but because the word below it,
"worshipped," was properly spelled with one dot above, there needed
to be another dot near it. And that dot was nowhere to be seen.

A dot. One single pinpoint of ink that could make all the
difference in the genesis of Christian orthodoxy. A dot that could
determine if the mystery of the Holy Trinity was organic to ortho-
doxy or the result of theological expediency.

But the dot wasn't there. And a number of eminent experts
were beside themselves. Still, that didn't mean it hadn't been there;
it may have faded away over the centuries. If the dot had *been there*
and left so much as a molecule behind, Fr. Mikhail was determined
to find it.

And so, over the next thirty-six hours, fueled by shots of sap-
like Egyptian coffee, eating carb-heavy unleavened bread and hum-
mus, Fr. Mikhail performed the most exhaustive investigation pos-
sible. First he had the area in question magnified with an electron
microscope. Then he called in a spectrometer to measure the minut-
est shifts in tone and color temperature on the surface in question.
After that, a Merkle-Landroscope, ordered in advance and flown
in from Bonn, was used for the first time in such an examination
to photograph and reveal potential latent images. And when all of
that proved inconclusive, he could only entrust matters to the tools
God gave him.

Fr. Mikhail brought three sets of indirect bounce lights –
incandescent, fluorescent, and mercury color-corrected – and lit
the parchment with one set at a time from eight different compass
points, one point at a time, at a 45-degree angle. Then with the
loupe pressed to his eye, he spent an hour with each new lighting

arrangement scrutinizing the surface texture that might indicate contact with a writing implement, even if the ink was no longer there. The only other sound in the room came from whatever monk was on shift keeping watch, whispering his devotions.

Confined in this room with no windows, time became irrelevant; all the better to Fr. Mikhail who cared not for such distractions, and who gladly suffered the demands of his body for sustenance and elimination in the service of such a quest. He took breaks to stand, to rest his eyes, to stretch, to apply eye drops and only when he could no longer contain, to use the water closet within the room; necessary irritants, the failings of man after he was banished from paradise to the the east of Eden. He longed only to investigate, and any interruption – especially, heaven forbid, a few hours' sleep – was a loss of time that he could not recoup. The door to the outside world was only opened when another monk came in to relieve the one sitting for the previous eight hours, or if another plate of food was delivered. He had no idea what day or time it was when he first heard Him.

'Sup?

Fr. Mikhail, about to begin inspection with the third set of lights, rubbing the loupe-indent around his reddened eye, ignored whatever the monk had said.

'Sup, my man? came the voice again, deep, buttery, mellifluous. Fr. Mikhail turned to the monk to see someone else entirely sitting there; not sitting so much as casually sprawled. Fr. Mikhail's pulse began to quicken.

You aren't Brother Darius, he heard himself say.

No shit.

...who...who are you...how – ?

F'you don't have the 411...you gots to bounce.

I'm sorry...?

The person leaned forward wielding a cane topped with an intimidating 8-ball, a large many-ringed hand smothering the orb. Nilla', you got to ax' me...? I oughta' murph yo' ass.

Okay, Fr. Mikhail didn't know who he was or even what tongue he was speaking, but he knew intimidation when he heard it. I have no idea how you got in but you're about to leave, said Fr. Mikhail. He pushed back in his chair and attempted to rise – but he realized he could not.

The person grinned, revealing a small diamond in every tooth. Bro'. We jus' choppin' it up. S'cool.

Fr. Mikhail could only stare. Issues of entrance and departure aside, here in Cairo, in the soul of the Greek Orthodox universe, in the very church that held the remains of St. Mark himself, it made no sense to be confronted by someone wearing a white ermine floor-length coat and a matching ermine broad-brimmed hat. This was wrong, disturbing, alien, but not alien at the same time.

I know what you be trippin' on, purred the man... how this be wrong, disturbing, alien but not alien at the same time.

Fr. Mikhail felt his throat constrict. The man reached into his jacket, pulled out a sheaf of papers, and tossed them on the table. Checkkit out, he said. Fr. Mikhail flipped through pages of uninterrupted numbers; he knew what they were... and that they were probably correct.

Damn straight... that be the exact numerical value of the golden mean.

...who are you?

You STILL got to ax? The man stood up to his full Smack-Down height in his four-inch white platform shoes. Who am I? Who AM I? How someone so crank be so goddamn crunk? He walked

*to the front of the desk, his red velvet belled pants sweeping back
and forth, slamming his cane on the floor with the force of Moses
striking the rock. I be the O.O.G...the original...ORIGINAL...
gangsta. The word on wheels, the aboriginal supreme, Moet and
Chandon, the ultimate Mr. Welfare, the hella hardcore phat mack
daddy of ALL mack daddies, you dig?*

Fr. Mikhail, try as he might, was not quite digging.

Do...you...dig?

*And yet...lasered past reason, burning directly into his cortex
where the lizard brain still resides and knows without understanding...as a plant knows to lean toward the light without understanding photosynthesis...he understood.*

I say, wizzle...DO! YOU! DIG?

*Fr. Mikhail, shaking uncontrollably, felt his heart might break
his sternum if it beat any harder. The lizard brain knew. It was
the one encounter any Christian, any agnostic, hell, even any athe-
ist would die to experience, to see manifest the ultimate mystery, to
no longer have to rely on faith, on hope, to have the certainty of
the prophets, to truly know that all sacrifice, all supplication, was
validated not from within but objectively from without. Not, of
course, that Fr. Mikhail ever doubted; but to be one hundred percent sure was a hundred times better than to be ninety-nine-point-
ninety-nine percent sure. Ask anyone at Churchill Downs.*

I...I—

YOU WHAT?

I...dig.

*The man flashed his Tiffany smile. Good, good. S'all gravy.
So you can chillax. Now I know what else you be trippin' on.
Since I be who I be, why not represent as bossman Jay Chrizzle*

wid the bleeding grabs and pads surrounded by all those kiss-ass seraphim, am I in the pocket?

Very much in the pocket, thought Fr. Mikhail.

I tell you why. 'Cuz thas what you 'spect to see. Thas what you need *to see, to justify your whack bootie-crack-corn fake-ass fill-os-oh-phee, ya hurd?*

Fr. Mikhail was afraid that he had. It had something to do with that horse he bet on.

Straight then, lemme break it down for you. What you be doin'? An' I know what you be doin', I jus' wanna hear what you say *you be doin', don't gimme no hype.*

I…I'm attempting to ascertain the accuracy of this text.

The man reared up, seeming to grow in angry mass. You hear that shee-it? "*Temptin' to ass-er-TAIN the trooth o' this text." No, that ain't what you be doin'! You be temptin' to ass-er-TAIN what you* WANT *to* BE *the accuracy o' this text, did I not tell you to gimme no hype? He raised his cane. Bitch, answer me that again I Rodney King yo' ass! He leaned forward, his bare chest over the desk, enough gold chains swinging to make Solomon salivate. Now…what…you…be…DOIN'?*

Fr. Mikhail carefully chose to re-calibrate his position. I'm… attempting to reconcile this text with church orthodoxy.

The man's laugh vibrated against the walls. Good, oh thas' good, wizzle. Rek-con-sile. You 'sactly on the border 'tween the right answer an' this eight-ball rearranging your grill ugly. Props, my face gator. His laugh rolled, long and sinuous. Now…lemme tell you what I *figga you be doin'. He paced the room though Fr. Mikail heard no footsteps and the silence felt like a calm before the deluge.*

Look at yo'self, with that Escalade brain and what you been doin' with it the last day anna half. You been spinnin' your wheels like a krillhead, cruisin' to nowhere. Goddamn day anna half, sheeee-it...but thas not the ultimate flop, foolio...you been cruisin' to nowhere for YEARS, circlin' the same goddamn hood. Day anna' half you been trippin' on a dot, am I right? A DOT. One mu'fuckin' dot. One mu-fuckin' dot in one mu'fuckin' sentence in one mu'fuckin' piece of parchment from some mu'fuckin' butt boy at some mu'fuckin gang powwow from some mu'fuckin' seventeen centuries ago, to do with one mu'fuckin' 'terpetation of one mu'fuckin' fil-oss-o-phee out of four-thousand-two-hundred-sixty-seven mu'fuckin' different fill-oss-o-phees about the Main Soulja Supreme. That don't strike you as whack?

Well...that is...not if one is in search of the truth—

The TROOTH? THE TROOTH?! You crazy peckerwood, I oughta mollywop yo' punk ass, you know who you be? You on the mu'fuckin' Titanic, the ship done hit the big-ass iceberg, band be playin', people be prayin', and what YOU be doin'? You be up top rearrangin' the mu'fuckin' deck chairs!

What...what do you mean? Fr. Mikhail asked.

I'm sayin' is time to bust yo' shit, you be pervin' on some bammer weed!

That couldn't be good.

You know what I be talkin' about, why the hell you think there's four-thousand- two-hun'ert-sixty-seven mu'fuckin' different wanksta faiths out there?!

Fr. Mikhail answered with conviction, his one brief moment on solid ground: *There's only one true faith.*

The man's detonation of contempt slammed against Fr. Mikhail's chest harder than a bass-riff at a Metallica concert.

Shee-it, cracker, all this time you think you be livin' chilly, you be livin' silly! I ax you again...why they be so hella many?

Oh sweet baby in the manger, thought Fr. Mikhail, dare I go there? Dare I say...because all versions of faith are wrong...?

Fo'sheedo, damn! he answered. Everyone think THEY be the one fo' real, but NO one get it right, ya hurd?

Yes, but...well...surely—

Surely what, cracker?

...one of those faiths could be...y'know...partly right...?

Now what the fuck that mean, "partly right," wigga?! Like there be a religion half-true? That mean it still be half-whack. You crackers like parables, dial in this one: You just bought yo'self a bran new Lamborghini, candy apple red, mad pin-striping, custom Snoop horn, the most fly fuckbucket in O-Town, it be da ATOM bomb, y'dig? But it don't have no wheels...it be sitting on damn cinderblocks so it be goin' nowhere. Now that be half-true an' that be half whack! What the hell use is that ride? "Partly right" my big ass nightcrawla. There be ONE true, dig it, and there be ev'erthing else. An' what you wigaboos have is ev'erthing else.

Even...my church...?

Yo, apple head, what part of ALL fucks wid yo' mind, I said ALL yo' religions!

Fr. Mikhail was beginning to feel diminished...devalued. He felt the worst thing someone like him could feel: meaningless.

Why...? he finally whispered.

Say wha'?

Why tell me this? I devote my life to you...to the propagation of faith and the veneration of your being...and of all the people doing terrible things in your name...you choose to tell me that everything I've done has been for naught?

Lemme me ax you a question...y'ever tell some poor-ass buster brown "the lord sure work in mysterious ways?"

A dispirited shrug...sure.

Now what the fuck that mean? It mean that when you keep adding two-plus-two an' you be getting five you blame MY ragged ass. 'Cuz you can't find the answer in all your so-called good books an' tea leaves an' Jay Chrizzles-on-a-tortilla. You be like muthafuckin' Plato's prisoner in a cave who think shadows be his peeps, a fire be the sun, and climbing out to the fo'sheedo sun he STILL get it wrong. But you haven't even left the cave, wigga. Until you peckerwoods break it down to MY trooth, not YOURS, that's what you always gonna haf to be sayin'. To yo'SELF, too... the Lord sure work in mysterious ways.

You didn't answer me, Fr. Mikhail insisted, so dispirited he no longer cared if he was banished from Eden...why me?

Din you jus' hear, mu'fucker, I be Mysteriouso Supreme, thas why.

Bullshit! Fr. Mikhail, who never so much as raised his voice to a religious superior, was in no mood to be toyed with, not now, not even by He Who Is. Why! Me!

Fr. Mikhail found himself on the receiving end of a Notorious B.I.G. stare, not that he would have called it that, wishing he could rewind his outburst, reminding himself that this was the being who, y'know, created the entire fucking universe. Time, as it did for Joshua, stood still. Until the man finally allowed a bejeweled smile.

Maybe...jus' 'cuz I feel sorry fo' yo ass.

Sorry...?

Yeahhhh wizzle. Watchin' you humpin' that table long as you been to get to Thee Trooth when I coulda' created another heaven and earth. Shee-it.

The life of utter sublimation he'd lived... the daily mass... the *beauty of ritual... performing the miracle of transubstantiation... the striking of his breast, sincerely, for his sins and the sins of his congregants... sharing the same communal feast traced back to Christ's last night on earth. Such religious passion, what strength it gave him! And He for whom he dedicated his very being said he felt "sorry" for him? The raging inner-fire that drove Fr. Mikhail, that gave him that ninety-nine-point-ninety-nine percent certainty had been reduced to censer ash. Fr. Mikhail remained immobile. Even if he was free to stand, he lacked the will.*

Oh, an' homes... that dot you be lookin' for? Checkit out, it be there. Both dots're there. Damn butt boy scribe, he wrote one dot over d'other dot.

Fr. Mikhail found the energy to lean forward and put his eye to the loupe. He could detect no difference. When he looked up the man was nowhere to be seen. Brother Darius sat in his chair, working his beads, mouthing his devotions.

Eight days later Fr. Mikhail left the priesthood.

Sunday, April 11ᵗʰ, 12:14 a.m. – Zurich

Danica didn't realize they'd spent an hour on the floor of a bathroom. To say that she doubted the finer points of Mickey's experience would be wrong; she doubted all of them. But taking in the diorama that was his life up to The Incident, she didn't doubt that the recipe of ingredients – starting with his forced march to the priesthood, his devout and (even he would say) untested faith, his mental state in Cairo, his need to justify that which resisted justification, all baked in the oven that was Egypt – added up to *some* kind of experience that could charitably be called Anti-Pauline.

Whether Mickey felt better having confessed she couldn't say – slumped, he appeared to be snoring – but *she* was rejuvenated with the thrill of the chase. The policewoman used to taking statements, trained to listen for incriminating nuance, odd phrasings, inconsistencies, found a kernel from his backstory that reminded her that they had lost focus, and in that reminder was the suggestion of how to proceed. It was almost as if there was a plan, *The* Plan, that was their destiny to take part in; a realization of their heavy mantle that lesser mortals would have cast off long ago.

She managed to rouse Mickey, guide him from stall to sink, and wash his face of any discharge. She then dragged him out of the bathroom, back into the boozy throng, and plopped him down with the two depressed Dominicans.

"We have a plan," she said.

"We do?" said DeSica.

"Whahuh?" said Mickey.

"It's a long story but Mickey's father had an experience that greatly impacted his world, that gave him a specific point of view, and I quote: 'to navigate the human soul true north is never love...it's lucre.'"

"What, pray tell, does that mean?" asked a dour Bertolucci over his beer.

"He had to reach the same dead-end we did. But it didn't stop him. Why? Because he continued to follow the money."

"The bank was destroyed."

"The bank was a front."

"So what money was there to follow?"

"The money that was never there. Templar money. The money that was used to establish a bank that had no interest in making interest. Mikhail was killed in Paris. He was looking in the *Bibliotheque Historique de la Ville de Paris Antiquities.* But I guarantee you he wasn't there studying anything to do with religion."

"How do you know?"

"Because an organization represented with the crest of Richard the Lion Heart has funded at least one hospital and owns a fleet of private jets in the City of Lights. The same crest used in *this* bank's charter. That's where the funds came from to set up this backwater branch. Think about it...why was the bank never rebuilt?" Before they could think: "It was never rebuilt because the fire was suspicious, meaning they thought someone was close to the truth and they were better off moving the goods. If the bank is headquartered in Paris I'm betting the answer is there too. Somehow we need to get into the *bibliotheque* tomorrow and find the last thing Mikhail was looking at. That should lead us to the ark."

So many questions they wanted to ask. Why was she so sure of herself? What in a repository of largely religious texts from antiquity would give them the answer to such a secular question? And how she could enunciate *Bibliotheque Historique de la Ville de Paris Antiquities* in perfect French despite never hearing it pronounced before? But no time for that now...

Sunday, April 11ᵗʰ, 12:24 a.m. – Zurich

The bathroom door slammed behind Danica and Mickey as they exited. In the stall next to theirs a pair of black leather boots peeked beneath the twelve inches of clearance. The beep of a cell phone being dialed was heard.

And then…the unmistakable voice.

"It is me." One-Mississippi, two- "THE MOTHERFUCKING SONOVABITCHING FIST…" A moment to collect himself. "The Fist…of God." A sigh. "Yes…yes, of course…can't be too careful." And then, "I have just eavesdropped upon a *long*, indulgent, but key conversation that will bring matters to the moment of truth. And I feel I must act."

In what manner? would be the unheard question.

"A death." Aaron, so close to his prey all this time, unable to do his job until they served his employer's purpose, was beginning to feel as if he was trapped in a Henry James novel.

Two drunk, laughing Japanese stumbled into the lavatory drowning out the next exchange. But when the stall door opened, Aaron exited, smiling; and Aaron smiling is more memorable than Aaron surly. The two Japanese made the mistake of taking his picture.

Sunday, April 11ᵗʰ, 10:22 a.m. – Paris

How they got a new change of clothes and raced to Paris by 10:14 a.m. that Sunday is of little narrative matter except to the supple brunette, twenty-two year old Mathilde Garroux,

who came out of her Courcelles-les-Monbeliard flat in a
light and fulsome spring dress preparing to go to market,
only to find her restored 1956 Heinkel Touring motor
scooter stolen. Pity we couldn't see how four adults weighing a combined 704 pounds managed to ride the final leg
to Paris on a 9.2 horsepower, 175cc two-seater. And more's
the pity in the scooter's absence that we were denied
another image, that of Mathilde Garroux riding to market...the cool morning wind pushing the magenta-colored
fabric against her sinuous form as if it were tinted directly
upon her skin, pressing most delightfully atop those magnificent, symmetrical and sprightly breasts so perfect in
their arrangement that they did not require – indeed, they
rejected! – any support, even if decorum demanded; and
in their freedom, with cotton of only one-hundred-eighty
thread count protecting those comely protuberances from
the slight morning chill, made the slightest degree more
chilly by the vehicle's forward thrust, producing an involuntary and by no means unwelcome physical effect that
evolution has seen fit to accentuate; the pleasing raising up
of the bull's eye to meet the nippiness, the halo that stands
within the larger halo of womanly radiance, magnificent in
its goose-bumped and hued accent from the surrounding
alp as if to announce itself as the apogee, the capstone,
the zenith of nurturing fecundity, the *ne plus ultra* of the
maiden planet; an artistic triumph in form and function,
that perfect object that gives succor to childlike need and
adult desire; that gives life to the immature and affirms
life to the mature. In the case of Mathilde Garroux on
her Sunday morning shopping excursion it is to weep to

witness those dual hemispheres majestically pointing the way, and to feast upon flawlessness that in transit becomes even more flawless. Adorned however sparingly, it is best to observe such perfection covered rather than baldly arrayed, not because a woman is never so naked as when she is clothed, not *just* for the mystery that pledges more stimulation in the unseen, but just the opposite, to protect the observer from the unbearably high standard to which he would forever hold this succulent alabaster fruit and, like a tragic Anaïs Nin character, be forever ruined and left hungry, nay ravenous, ceaselessly wandering in search of one more taste of rapture but never again to experience. For naked truths can be too difficult to face, they shine more blindingly than a million near-truths, truths that while true are less sizeable, truths that are never near as pointed, truths that are more global but which sag under the mass of their own sizeable authenticity, truths that seem to flatten without the support of additional truth, or truths that have been inflated and corrupted with non-truth; sadly, the attainable and lesser truths most of us must settle for. And in settling we take consolation in the deceptions that allow us to accept such lower hanging, less succulent fruits that we can grab or that fall into our hands and have the rude approximation of truthfulness.

No, that nascent spring day, Mathilde Garroux did not take her scooter to market. She called a taxi. And she never replaced her beloved Heinkel, opting instead to buy a used Carmen-Ghia. It was a tragedy for the town of Courcelles-les-Monbeliard; one might say it was a tragedy for us all.

Sunday, April 11ᵗʰ…and still 10:22 a.m. – Paris

Time, immediate, insistent, was pounding louder than a cowbell in a Chambers Brothers song as the requested file that Mikhail had been perusing on the last night of his life was dropped in front of Mickey by the dour, craggy Sister Marie Agnes, who had been unceremoniously called from high mass to retrieve said file. Danica and the two priests breathlessly watched Mickey open the folder – followed by a needle scratch of anticlimax to reveal forty-seven yellowed pages of lists, all in French…bills of lading over a century old, from:

"A moving company?" Mickey asked.

"An inventory of items moved from the *Fonds de Suisse de Lion Bank* in Zurich to the branch in Paris," DeSica read dubiously.

"What are they doing in *this* place?" asked Danica.

"I have no idea."[75] Though, to give Danica her props Mickey added, "But it looks like my dad followed the money."

---

75   True, while it is called the *Bibliotheque Historique de la Ville de Paris Antiquities,* and it is famous for its vast store of religious texts and related correspondence, what they couldn't have known is that in September of 1956 a tax law was passed in France giving write-offs to any letters of historical import, official documents no matter how minor, or records of commercial transactions exceeding 250 francs by any French or foreign concern with a French branch (the amount of the write-off to be determined by government licensed antiquities assessors) that were over 50 years old. As the bills of lading were dated August 28, 1906, they just qualified and someone saw fit to make a few dollars off these seemingly meaningless records, giving our protagonists the vital

"There was nothing to send," said DeSica crossly, "the bank was burned to the ground." He flipped through page after page. "Every item on this list is a crate labeled 'ashes.' Forty-seven pages of ashes!"

"And yet to my dad it was a clue...*the* clue...to the location of the ark."

"That's too easy," said Bertolucci. "One of those boxes labeled 'ashes' was the ark and it was moved to the branch in Paris."

"No," said Danica. "The bank here was a party to our kidnapping. They'd have no reason to take us if they already had it."

The fossil that was Sister Marie Agnes barked something to DeSica. He drained.

"The sister says to hurry, she wants to go back to mass," he translated...then he added, "she tires of these interruptions on a Sunday morning."

"Interruptions...?" said Danica, sensing. "As in plural?"

"We are the second party to request this file today."

They experienced a communal sinking feeling. The nun, especially an irritated and interrupted nun who held a modicum of authority over others, as they are wont to do, would not say who or how long ago the person was here. But clearly that person was already on the way to the ark's retrieval.

---

clue to keep this narrative going; and proving contrary to literary convention that arcane tax laws have a place in sexy and violent thrillers.

The cowbell of time... *Tick*...! *Tock*...! was now joined by echoing African-American voices metronomically moaning, "...*time*...!" *Tick*...! *Tock*! "...*time*...!"

"But," sputtered Bertolucci, "there is nothing here!"

"Jesus...Christ." said Mickey, realizing, Bertolucci's fortuitously voiced frustration giving birth to Mickey's revelation. "That's the clue...what *isn't* here! What isn't on this list! The ark or anything close to it! The only people who knew of its whereabouts were killed in the fire.[76] The bank in Paris had every ounce of ash sent back to sift through it to see if there were any remains of the ark!"

"Meaning..." queried Danica, "...it's still in Zurich?"

One who traveled the unique path that Mickey Samanov did to find himself in a Parisian antiquities library contemplating a limestone box of petrified shit, had that once-in-a-millennium advantage over the average religious-thriller participant. He could almost hear the voice that said, *you punk-ass buster brown, you pervin' on some bammer weed? You knows the 411!*

"The dot over the dot..." he murmered.

"The what...?" said DeSica.

"The dot over the dot! The bank doesn't realize it's still in possession of the ark! The Templars were too clever for their own damn good, they built the bank vault *over* the ark vault."

---

76 As most of us know, he is only half-right. For those of you who have just been skimming, there was a fire and the official story is that all were consumed. The board of directors was beheaded afterwards. This is your last reprise, stop skimming.

"What's the point of that?" asked Danica, no longer caring that such queries seemed to be her purpose.

"A last line of defense. A vault installed to hold money could always be breached, just ask Willie Sutton. But whoever did still wouldn't find the ark or think there might be a second vault! Problem is, everyone who knew about the second vault was killed!"

It had its own logic; not the dot-over-the-dot part, that made no sense to them, but who cared? They raced out of the *bibliotheque* as the conversation continued... *maybe the ark was also destroyed... maybe it wasn't... doesn't heat travel upward... how does the person ahead of us know about the vault... maybe they don't, but they know the ark's still there... who the hell's Willie Sutton...* blah-blah-blah.

Sister Marie Agnes, thankful to be rid of them, locked the door, extinguished the lights, and turned off the muzak that was playing *The Best of the Chambers Brothers.* She hurried back to the remainder of her mass.

Sunday, April 11th, 11:04 a.m. – Rome

Cardinal Thomasina was in an expansive mood, getting off the phone with Fr. DeSica who informed him that the search was back on track in earnest. So expansive, in fact, that he decided to spend time with the mincing Bishop Boza-Edwards, who would absolve all homosexuals of original sin, believing such deviants had no choice in their bestial proclivities what with genetics and culture's growing willingness to program situation comedies around them, or to at least give them meaningful second-banana status in comedies and dramas. It was hard to suffer such theological pinheadedness, but then the church, like the post office, couldn't turn away every applicant or it would lack for messengers. Why not have coffee and biscotti with the little frog and suss out what he knew – or thought he knew – of this supposed fifth column. Which might help expedite the transition between Thomasina the Cardinal and... in less than forty-eight hours...Thomasina the Pope.

Sunday, April 11, 8:07 a.m. – Paris

The newspapers would not report a break-in of the 何かは なま臭い Sushi Bar, especially since no money was taken; in fact nothing appeared to be taken. It would not be until lunch that master chef Akiko, preparing the day's special, noticed he was short one fuju fish, a.k.a. a puffer. A busboy emptying the garbage would find the remains of the purloined puffer in the alley dumpster, sliced open, its viscera for all to see. The busboy was not yet trained in the art of ginzu knives to notice that the only thing not among said remains was the liver.

Sunday, April 11th, 11:17 a.m. – Paris

The clock running out, Fr. DeSica determined they had to brave the train again. After a spirited exchange, Mickey found himself on the losing side of the decision, standing on the platform, already anticipating an even less pleasant outcome to this trip. Danica tried to take his mind off things. "Like all banks," she addressed Mickey, "the vault had to be on the bank floor, right?"

No answer from Mickey. The train was pulling in to the station.

"You said the vault that held the ark was very likely *under* the vault that held the money, are you suggesting in a basement below?" Silence redux. "Mickey."

"…whahuh…?"

"Bank, plan, *think*, could there be a basement?" The train hissed to a stop.

"…yeah, sure, basement." He was perspiring through his *Real Madrid* t-shirt.

"You know for sure or don't give a shit?" The car doors swished open.

"…the second thing."

Fr. Bertolucci suddenly grabbed the back of his neck and yelled "*Figlio di puttana!*" Mickey jumped as if he was the one who had been pricked by a needle-like object. Danica and DeSica whipped about, scanning the throng for his attacker, facing a sea of discourteous French faces pushing forward to board the train.[77]

Bertolucci crumpled to the ground in terrible spastic seizures, tongue rolling back, foam flecking his lips. In two minutes he was dead from 0.00002 oz of the most deadly toxin found in nature, the most agonizing, raw, interminable two minutes of his life. A gendarme would find this John Doe (stripped of all identification, he would be bur-

---

77   Not discourteous in the clichéd sense of the inherent rudeness of the French; they are no more rude than the average American, especially those French who like religious thrillers.

ied in a potter's field) an hour later slumped on a station bench like an inebriated patron who missed his train. The unpleasant little forensic analyst, who had helped the late Inspector Renault, performed the autopsy and, detecting a trace of tetrodotoxin from a fuju fish liver, deduced that the deceased had been the victim of improperly prepared sushi. Such conclusions gave him a certain satisfaction. Rutting around in the innards of the dead had taught him much about what to put in his mouth and what not to; and while most would say eating three, four crème-filled confections a day was not in one's best interests, he could smugly note that he had never written under "cause of death" on an autopsy report "ingested bad chocolate éclair."

Sunday, April 11, 11:29 a.m. – Paris

Time to mourn the dead was best left to those not about to join them, which didn't include our three, their lives for the foreseeable future not in their control; in fact the term "foreseeable future" seemed a grandiose concept not supported by current events.

They pulled Bertolucci against the boarding tide to a bench against the wall. After the crowd thinned out and the train departed, Danica and DeSica denuded Bertolucci of his passport, a chain and gold cross, his Dominican ring, and all clothing tags that could be traced to recent purchases. As they waited for the most opportune moment to desert the body – a John Doe who would later be claimed by the Parisian branch of the Catholic Potters Field Society – Fr. DeSica took a moment to say last rites *sotto voce*.

They quit the station and, to the relief of the Depends-less Mickey, decided not to ride the rails to Zurich. But the death so close to him served to bring to the fore something that, given the last few days, he hadn't had time to ponder. On the march down the Boulevard de Bercy, Mickey asked for DeSica's cell, leaving the discussion of what to do next to the trained professionals.

"Hello?" Richard's refined voice answered.

"It's me," Mickey said.

"Good to hear my godson's still above ground. I'm back in London about to go into a meeting, what can I do?"

"Something no one else can do for me right now. I need to know what's happening with my father's investigation, would you call Renault?"

"Are you certain you want to entrust me with that after last time?"

"I'll take my chances," Mickey deadpanned.

Mickey hung up and waited, half-listening to DeSica and Danica's travel plans that excluded all forms of public transit except hot air balloon. By the time they turned onto Rue de Charenton Richard called back.

"I was transferred to an Inspector Castel-Jaloux. Renault has been murdered." But that wasn't the worst news. "As of now, the inspector believes you have one more victim to clear yourself of."

"Jesus…there's gotta be some good news in this *somewhere.*"

Richard did his best. "France outlawed the death penalty in 1981."

Sunday, April 11, 11:46 a.m. – Paris

Across the Seine on the Left Bank Aaron sat on a bench near the rose garden in the sixty-nine acre *Jardin des Plantes*. Head tilted back, arms draped over the bench, still buzzing from the railway kill, he enjoying the warming spring sun on his distressed epidermis; made all the more enjoyable by small children who crossed his path, gaped, dropped their ice cream cones (purchased from the kiosk not twenty meters away that he had strategically placed himself by), and ran in terror, often to stumble and scar knees, elbows, and foreheads. Life was good.

"Monsieur Zworkan?" asked a chauffeur who appeared before him as if from a Helmut Newton photograph.

They drove to an underground garage, taking the private elevator up that avoided all regular security. The chauffeur escorted Aaron down the teak-walled hallway to an imposing set of double doors, ordered Aaron to remove his boots for the slippers awaiting there, rapped three times, then opened the door for him.

Aaron stepped onto a thick woolen 15th century Turkish carpet, painstakingly hand-woven by Muslim women, a piece any museum curator would pay six figures to rescue from the horror of foot traffic.

But not Benoit Dubost.

He rose from his completely bare oriental desk, the panorama of Paris behind him out his floor-to-ceiling 13th storey window (a 13th storey not found on any other elevator or in the building directory). He approached in his ultimate bespoke suit, Eton cotton shirt, silk Pietro Baldini tie – and sockless, shoeless feet. Benoit allowed only himself to experience the feel of centuries-old fibers rising up through his feet, every step a sensation of history, of mission, of a battle still being waged. Silver haired and elegant, the only thing about him that seemed amiss was an angry red spot on his forehead, as if impacted repeatedly on a hard wooden surface.

"What necessitates this meeting on such short notice?" he asked, up until now a cautious voice on the phone.

"What else?" Between them Aaron need not say.

"The ark?" Between them Benoit felt he needed to.

Exasperated sigh. "Yes."

"You have it?" Benoit's toes curled into the wool weave.

"Soon."

"Then I fail to understand."

"You fail to understand that as a member of a fraternity to which we both belong…that I stand before you today…a corporeal manifestation of the hopes, dreams, and desires of *thousands* over *centuries*…to impress upon you the historic nature of what is about to transpire…and to ensure you will be prepared."

"For?"

An exasperated sigh. "What else?"

"The ark…?"

To continue this conversation was more hazardous to Aaron than ordering fuju fish sashimi, his ears pounding from rising blood pressure. Forswearing all circumlocution and symbol, he continued as calmly as possible. "We have agreed upon a considerable sum…equal to that which Jacques de Molay gave to Guillaume…adjusted for inflation. You are to have it by tomorrow and, upon receiving the ark, are to wire that sum to my Swiss bank account."

"Oh. Not a problem. We could have settled this in a call."

True...had Aaron not wearied of the head-exploding rage required to announce himself over the phone. But then we would not have noticed an item of interest on Benoit's person: an elegant silver Masonic tiepin.

The chauffeur drove Aaron to the airport.

Sunday, April 11, 9:47 p.m. – Zurich

How Mickey, Danica, and DeSica raced from Paris back to Zurich that Sunday by 9:47 p.m. is of little narrative matter except to the lithe, blonde twenty-year-old Francoise Annaud who came out of her Champigny-sous-Varennes farmhouse that afternoon in her short, light spring dress preparing to ride her chestnut horse, Châtaigne, only to find the mare missing. How three adults weighing a combined 538 pounds managed to ride the final leg to Zurich on a single horse lacking a saddle can only be imagined. And more's the pity in the animal's absence that we were denied another image, that of Francoise seated upon Châtaigne, her hem billowing in the breeze, unencumbered by underwear, squealing in unadulterated equine-induced joy. *(Ed. note:* **omit the next three and a quarter pages for common decency's sake.***)*

Once again our three found themselves outside Pussy's Crack Palace. They had cased its exterior and discovered in the alley a small, ground level window painted over in black. The bad news was that it was too small any of them to squeeze through. The good news was that there *was* a basement; and that they already had a plan to get into it worthy of the establishment's name.

Sunday, April 11, 10:29 p.m. – Zurich

Much to Mickey's dismay, the proprietor of Pussy's was not only *not* named Pussy, he was squat, bloated and feral and there never had been a proprietor named Pussy. Mickey could only conclude that this was yet another case of buyer-beware, like the mistitled evening spent at *The Vagina Monologues*. Theo, the feral man, drank in the prospective new stripper. "Show me," he said in his thick French-Moroccan adulterated English as a tongue slithered out and moistened his lips.

"No cash, no flash," said Danica in spiked heels, a black raincoat, and more makeup than Jayne Mansfield's corpse. Spoken like a true stripper, thought Mickey, in the best manager-slash-pimp attire they could find on short notice; which looked more like a rabbi in a cowboy hat.

"You expect me to put her in prime midnight spot, sight unseen? No, my friends."

"Theo, my man," said Mickey with the bored arrogance of a car salesman who knew this year's model so smoked last year's that he could bend you over the hood, violate you with your pants around your ankles, violate your wife, and you'd still drive away happily in the car, "she just did a private show for the Sultan of Freedonia. Not to diss your product, but when I walked in, that gunnysack on stage you call a stripper didn't even have all 'er tattoos spelled correctly. You wanna a taste for nothin', I'm gonna have to charge you double for showtime. In advance."

Theo, calculating, tongue wetting his lips overtime, finally pulled out a roll of bills, peeled off ten, and thrust them at Mickey.

"Yo, Caledonia," Mickey said, taking the bills, "show your moneymaker."

Danica *thought* she knew what she was agreeing to when they came up with this plan, not that she was looking forward to it. She once asked Nikki how she felt stripping in front of fifty, a hundred men. *I might as well be in my bedroom dancing naked for myself... it's so public, impersonal, everyone out there's like furniture. It's when you draw the first shift on the Monday after Super Bowl and there's one customer... that's when it gets creepy.* Now she understood.

Still, she remembered, this was for something so much bigger than herself, for the possible salvation of *man* (even this man...), and that induced her to unbutton her jacket in languid fashion. Then, heightening the anticipation... she slowly drew back the curtains. Unfortunately, standing behind her, Mickey could only see the effect on Theo, akin to military volunteers who witnessed the first mushroom cloud. He could not see the bralette of small red hearts that covered only the tips of those glorious warheads, the fishnet garter that spanned the flat plane of her tummy, the matching red heart thong, and the lace-topped red hose with little red hearts all over (thanks to a hearts close-out sale at the nearby 24-Hour Madonna-Whore Emporium).

"Three strippers are my daughters," Theo said in a trance. "I sell them to slavery if you headline only for me."

In the alley DeSica, dressed as a Euro-Trash tourist, discreetly broke the window to the basement. It was too dark to see if someone had been or was still there. As quietly as possible he dropped in two crowbars, a chisel, mallet and spade; he had borrowed these from a closed hardware store, adding to a serious list for his next confession.

The agent for Jean-Henri Vandersmissen watched DeSica with night vision glasses from the far end of the alley. If they found what they were after – and it would be easy to monitor their progress through the broken window – it would be the shortest-lived victory of their lives.

Aaron was across the busy boulevard from Pussy's watching from his rental car. With three thermoses of chamomile tea, a piss bottle, and a radio station playing *The Fine Young Cannibals,* he had everything necessary to pass the most pleasant of evenings until zero hour when he would enhance his life rights by three more deaths.

DeSica paid the cover charge and, with the slightest of limps, entered the first strip club of his life. He had stepped into purgatory.

The under-lit, uncomfortably warm room, filled to capacity, smelled of desperation. A runway thrust out into a sea of patrons, the greatest concentration of testosterone hanging on to its edges like barnacles, where they could offer up bills to an increasingly naked meat puppet for a moment's attention and public abasement. A haze of smoke hung in the air, pumped into the club and designed to enhance arousal, as it no doubt metastasized in the lungs of the employees. DeSica stood outside the experience even as he was in the thick of it. It seemed somehow fitting to the priest that the three of them had to pass through this netherworld to get to that holy of holies.

For modesty's sake he averted his eyes from the goings-on and studied the layout. Two 'roid-pumped bouncers out of Bulfinch's Mythology stood on either side of the stage watching for any breach of strip joint etiquette. He could see no door that might lead down. He feared it was back-stage or through the swinging doors where miniskirted, bare-midriffed waitresses came and went with drinks and – what *was* it with these things? – buffalo wings. He saw a sign, *salles des baines*, and elbowed his way to the bathrooms.

In the dark hall there was a ray of hope: a padlocked door. When the moment was right, from his gimp leg he pulled out a bolt cutter, snapped the lock, and removed it. He peeked inside.

The stairs to the basement.

Monday, April 12, 12:07 a.m. – Zurich

Mickey joined DeSica at a deuce in the back that would allow for an easy b-line to the bathrooms. The last stripper – "What kind of parents would name their child Vulvina?" DeSica sincerely asked Mickey – had finished almost ten minutes ago and both were concerned: Where was Danica?

Worse, Vulvina had really torn it up and the natives were seriously agitated; it was not good form to let the customers go flaccid. Nor was this crowd going to settle for mere aerobic disrobing, they were primed for raw, unadulterated, hot buttered exhibitionism that would delaminate their top layer of skin; that would not just raise their masthead, it would raise their dead relatives; that would make them forget every female going back to the 7th grade dance when, after working up the courage to cross the floor with freshly pomaded hair and mother-pressed slacks, in front of God and everyone, the cunt said no to them; or the girl who'd dated them in high school, gave them tongue, then dated their best friend and gave him head; or the women they married who promised such concupiscence and nightly volcanic eruption, but who now just laid there annoyed at the mere hint of male need, just like their secretaries who, after giving them that promised promotion to *senior* executive assistant, stopped even faux-moaning; or the women who advertised in the adult rags a pre-six p.m. phone sex special at ten Euros for ten minutes, talked a customer into a messy finish within three, then charged them fifty Eruos on their phone bill, knowing they wouldn't have the balls to take it up with the phone company given the picture it would conjure up *and* that they could only last three minutes.

Truly, there were some major issues in the room.

The plan was for Danica to give a performance so riveting that every man here would rather marinate in his own fluids than leave to evacuate a six-beer bladder, allowing her two cohorts to slip unnoticed into the basement; and would end only after she saw the two of them leave the premises behind the hyper-focused crowd. But Mickey, who in his time had seen a girl or two work a pole, not only wondered if she had enough moves to last, but if she had enough, um...how you say...

...*nasty* in her soul....that special magic a person was or was not hardwired with from their first breath; sure, it could be taught, enhanced, teased out of a willing nastya-colyte. But to truly plumb the heart of darkness, one had to have *gnosis*, a divine understanding, a mature spirtual comprehension beyond the rational, as flight is to a young swallow fresh from the egg.

Mickey had his doubts.

The opening strains of *Also Sprach Zarathusta* whip-lashed all eyes, except DeSica's, to the stage. A guttural announcer spoke above the music, slowly...deliberately... gaining in strength and momentum with the orchestra-tion...until, strings, horns, and pounding percussion all reaching the apex, the smoke swirling at its thickest...

...a backlit primeval fertility figure stepped from the mist...CALEDONIA!

Zarathustra stopped. In the silence she moved not at all, her silhouette in the defiant cop stance. A dangerously impatient air began to swirl up from the audience into the blue smoke. Mickey had told her to trust his music selec-tion, that it would do the work for her as long as she didn't think, just gave into it like an entranced Sufi. But this unexplained pause was beginning to scare him. And then:

*Bomp!bomp!bomp!bomp!bomp!bomp!bomp!**BOMP**! GIT UP, GIT ON UP! GIT UP, GIT ON UP, GIT UP, GIT ON UP!*

STAY ON THE SCENE, GIT ON UP, LIKE A SEX MACHINE! GIT ON UP! A spotlight hitting her, Danica cast off her raincoat, dropped into a splits, raised back up on legs as muscular as the music's horn section, and tapped into her inner-James Brown, high-stepping onto the runway to the catlike rhythm guitar, legs pumping high and low, arms driving back and forth. Clearly she had thrown out the stripper handbook with a more brawny bump and grind, the very heartbeat of autoerotic propulsion, and knowing she couldn't imitate imitation, dismissed striptease-sexy for red blooded, meat and potatoes basics.

Tables overturned, chairs fell back, glasses broke, the audience standing as one, howling banshee-like at the Godmother of Soul. The bouncers came to life, tense, alert, sensing that this could get ugly. She spun like a dervish on a spiked heel, rocked back, rocked forth, splits, *STAY ON THE SCENE! GIT ON UP! LIKE A SEX MACHINE!* hitch-hiked left, hitchhiked right, and like a magician who had misdirected the eye, came up with the bralette in her hand, no one witnessing its removal. Mickey, his blood suddenly rerouting itself from five extremities to the sixth, debated whether to leave for what now seemed like a trivial task.

Even worse: DeSica, incapable of not looking, now could not look away, reduced to a modern-day Juan Diego on Tepeyac Hill encountering the mutha of all mothers.[78] Mickey had to act.

"Padre!" Mickey yelled above the din. "Now! Go-go-go!" Not even an eye blink in response. Mickey was screaming

_____

78   At least that's how DeSica chose to filter her image, as the Virgin of Guadalupe, so that his eyes would not melt.

into a Niagra of forty-some years of sexual refutation that was about to top the levee and, if he didn't do something quick, DeSica would end up at a waterfront Lisbon bar dancing inside a gold cage wearing gold lamé hot pants and go-go boots, wasting away the remainder of his prime years on randy British dowagers who were there for holiday and a quick shag. It was too much even for Mickey to bear; for once he had to be the bigger man. He grabbed DeSica's arm, yanking him through the crowd to the bathroom hall. He opened the door leading to the basement, pulled him in, closed it, and—"*Shit-piss-fuck-shit-piss-fuck-shitpissfuck!*" Mickey misjudged the landing and rolled down the wooden stairs.

DeSica, removed from the source of temptation, rubbing his face as if coming off a drug, somehow found the lightswitch and turned on a flickering fluorescent bar. To their great surprise, the basement floor was as it was a hundred-plus years ago: dry-pressed clay brick and mortar. The walls were lined with boxes of t-shirts and hats (*"I Got Stanky On My Wanky At Pussy's!"* in four different languages; though in Japanese it read *"Toaster Wank My Keith Richards!"* so it was not a big seller), and cases of gin, vodka, and beer – meaning they could be interrupted at any time by someone retrieving alcohol. Not good since that crowd looked like it was gonna work up an awful thirst.

DeSica had rejoined the living, came down the steps, stared at the thousand-plus bricks that made up the floor. "Where do we start?"

Mickey, on all fours, squinted under the sputtering illumination. He got within a tongue's length of the porous red surface, then slowly, systematically, crawled in lawn-mower-like fashion, back and forth in straight lines across the room inspecting every square centimeter.

"What are you doing?"

The music had changed to *"Ain't It Funky Now,"* the staccato bass riff vibrating through the floor. Whatever Danica was doing was whipping the throng into an even more slavering pack of carnivores, the Man from Macon testing the outer limits of his vocal cords as Danica tested the outer limits of man's ability to not self-detonate. It made concentration difficult as Mickey looked for a marker of some kind; and in the great bank inferno the floor had been scraped, cracked and pocked, making him fear that whatever he *was* looking for might have been obliterated.

Brick...after brick...after brick...after brick...after brick...

DeSica, at the base of the stairs, watched for the first sign of the door opening – all the while resisting the urge to rocket back up and disappear into the mob.

...brick...after brick...after brick...after...wait a minute...

...what's that? Mickey blew dust and decomposed clay off a spot. He'd almost passed over it. He saw what remained of a small stamp pressed into the clay before the brick was fired: barely half an inch, the imprint of the lion from the banner of Richard the Lion Heart. Part of the stamp, the lion's haunches and tail, was obliterated by a divot.

DeSica saw Mickey's excitement, grabbed the mallet and chisel and madly gouged out the mortar around it. He pulled up the brick…then another and another. Beneath was a layer of coarse 19th century concrete. Like the mortar, it gave way easily. Beneath the concrete was tamped earth. DeSica grabbed a crowbar and began stabbing it into the soil, over and over.

Until they heard the contact of iron on steel.

Mickey grabbed the other crowbar and together they ripped up more bricks until they exposed a three-foot square patch of concrete. They cracked and pulled out brittle cement chunks. DeSica attacked the dirt with the shovel until a clunk stopped him, the two men pawing away the remaining earth to see a metal box.

Braised atop the surface was the Masonic symbol.

They trenched around it, hands blistering, until they could work the bars underneath and pry it out. It was about a foot square and two feet long. The hasp was padlocked. Feverishly, DeSica took the bolt cutters and snapped it off.

The two looked at each other.

"It should have been your father's to open," said the priest. He turned the box towards Mickey.

Mickey took a deep breath and placed a hand on each side of the lid. The hinges grinded as he raised it up. He was met with a layer of excelsior that he brushed aside to find a shoebox-sized rectangle wrapped in burlap. He carefully lifted it out…placed it on the ground…and pulled back the layers of swaddling.

Upstairs was the cacaphony of lust and obsession, huffing rhythm and funk, *mashed potatoes jump back jack see you latah alligatah.* But down here it was sepulchral, hallowed, as silent as the moment Thomas touched Christ's wound in unspoken awe. In front of Mickey and DeSica, stripped of the burlap, was that which they hoped to see, indeed, expected to see. But it was a wondrous sight to actually behold.

A limestone box, faint yellow in color, weathered and distressed.

Chiseled on the front were words in ancient Greek, in no need of translation if the contents within bore out. Mickey swallowed, pulled out a silk handkerchief that was part of his costume, and placed it over the box so as not to soil the porous stone with his dirt-covered fingers. He gently took the lid in both hands, and lifted it away.

They stared.

Monday, April 12, 12:28 a.m. – Rome

The phone rang in Cardinal Thomasina's quarters, waking him. The message was brief.

"We have it."

Thomasina felt a flush of euphoria from head to toe. "Stay where you are," he ordered, "I'll send the Swiss Guard to escort you back."

"No," DeSica answered, "it is better we travel light and bring it to you ourselves."

"I would not advise that."

"I'm sorry, Your Eminence. We can't afford to stay in one place."

"You can't afford to travel unprotected with such an artifact! I command you to wait!"

"Then I must beg your forgiveness."

"The penance does not exist to atone for this insubordination. Are you positive you choose this path?"

Yeah. He was. DeSica was certain that whoever showed up would be ordered to kill him, Mickey and Danica on sight...though waiting outside was the secular equivalent.

Monday, April 12, 12:29 a.m. – Zurich

They raced from the basement and replaced the lock on the door to appear undisturbed. Mickey carried the burlap-wrapped ark. They were not prepared for what met them.

A chair splintered against the wall outside the hall, the room beyond a full-blown riot that rivaled Woodstock 1999. The two rushed out to see a writhing panorama of aroused males in a state of *impotentia coeundi*,[79] bodies littering the floor, the two bouncers on stage in front of Danica – who wore nothing but platform shoes and a look of horror – as the patrons inexplicably turned their frustration on their fellow man and beat the living shit out of each other. Eyes were gouged, blood and hair flocked walls, some just rocked and sucked on their fists as others rolled in broken glass speaking in tongues. (Future sexologists would refer to this phenomenon as The Farburger Effect.)

DeSica pulled out his gun and made like a Frank Frazetta paperback cover, whipping a swath through the barbarians toward the stage. Mickey crouched behind his blocker smothering the holy pigskin. They got to the

79   Singer, B. Conceptualising sexual arousal and attraction. The Journal of Sex Research. 1984; 20, 230-240

bouncers, who recognized them and parted, letting them jump upon the stage.

"Take this sybaritic she-Moloch out of here!" one of the Minotaurs screamed; or at least that's what DeSica heard.

Mickey lateralled the box to DeSica, threw his jacket over Danica, and pushed her through the curtains to backstage. More walking dead awaited and had to be disabused. Theo sat on the Marlene Dietrich prop chair, wrung out, bent over, a broken club owner. He lacked even the strength to look up. "What...kind of woman...are you?" he said hoarsely. Mickey and DeSica moved her past him to the dressing rooms.

"What did you *do*?" Mickey asked.

"J-just danced—"

"Just *danced*?"

"It's not like I *knew* what I was doing. Next thing I see..." She couldn't finish, overcome with the horrible responsibility of having split the stripper atom, witnessing the apocalypse that was her doing. "I am never, ever, *ever* going to dance nude to James Brown again." And that was the worst part of all: Haley's Comet had already passed. For Mickey it was too late, and it would be for future generations to remain vigilant.

"Hurry," Mickey said, pushing her into the dressing room to change and closing the door while they stood guard outside.

"Whoever killed your father is probably waiting on the street," said DeSica above the din.

"I figured. It's crazy how that sonovabitch always seems to know where we are." Mickey scratched his left shoulder furiously.

"It's as if a homing device had been implanted in one of us. But a person would have to be brain-dead to not know that by now," said DeSica. "The point of implant always itches maddingly."

Mickey froze. Long, ill-at-ease pause. "Really."

"Oh, yes. It begins almost immediately. They're made from a fired silicon that always irritates, even a rhesus monkey will chew it out of its own skin."

Mickey's hand casually left his shoulder, rose up and brushed through his hair. "Yeah, huh, well..."

DeSica shook his head mordantly. "I mean imagine... three priests, half a dozen Interpol agents, lord knows how many innocent bystanders dead, not to mention all the senseless destruction...to think if one of us *were* implanted all this time and said nothing, what could have been avoided," he said bitterly.

"Whew...yeah...imagine." His shoulder was on fire. Why did an itch irritate in logarithmic proportion to one's inability to relieve it? Mickey, afraid of the consequences should he scratch himself now, in front of the very priest who counted three partners among the dead, was ready to forever give up head if he could just rub the shoulder unseen against the wall; or lose his arm in a nearby piece of machinery; or maybe he could feign an epileptic seizure, fall to the floor, and satisfy himself. With no better plan, he was scanning the boards beneath him for the most abrasive spot to collapse when DeSica rapped on the door. "We must leave, now!"

No answer. He rapped more urgently. The two had the same horrible thought. They barged into the dressing

room. Danica faced them completely naked. Behind her
stood the agent for Jean-Henri Vandersmissen with a gun
to her head. It's good that Mickey was not in possession of
the ark, because he would have dropped it.

"Hello, Mikhail."

He could barely get the word out. "Mother?"

Monday, April 12, 12:35 a.m. – Zurich

Maureen stood before her son, though the moment
lacked the Paul Simon lyricism of a mother-child reunion.
A handsome woman frozen in time, dressed both for
style and function (stretch pants, running shoes, light
jacket, aquamarine Glock matching her earrings), she
could be the cover model on the next issue of *MILF
Monthly.*

Danica was as shocked as Mickey. Here was the woman
who gave him life, now threatening death; the mother who
suckled him in nature's most intimate relationship now a
virtual stranger; the missing piece of the family puzzle that
no longer fit. Mickey whipsawed between hate, anger, and
hate-anger.

"The years have been kind," Mickey said, for lack of
anything else.

"Kick boxing at the Learning Annex...it's the fountain
of youth." She regarded his current state. "You should try
it."

"Yeah, well, I have a motto: No pain, no pain."

"A little hard work never killed anyone."

"Why chance it?"

She smiled. "All those years with your father didn't leave much of an impression. In fact," she indicated his unsavory attire, "you seem to take after your mother."

"Genetics are a bitch. But then, so are you."

"Careful," she gestured with her Glock. "I don't believe in sparing the rod."

"Lemme guess," Mickey began, emotions bubbling up. "You found out Dad was onto the find of the century with no intention of profiting from it. To you that was incomprehensible, you decided to beat him to the punch. So you left, began the search on your own."

"Pretty much."

"Sorry I didn't know where to send all those mother's day cards."

"You can make up for it with a gift." She indicated the burlap square in DeSica's hands. "Who were you planning to give that to?"

"You first."

She ran it down like all good villains in the third act: How Mikhail had already been commissioned by Rome to find the ark...how she came across correspondence from a rich South American benefactor who would pay handsomely for it instead, but Mikhail refused...how she left him and made contact with said benefactor under the guise of her husband...how she kept tabs on and followed Mikhail all these years, and had fun doing it; jet-setting around the globe on someone else's dime, meeting new and interesting people, killing one or two, *so* much more stimulating than being a religious scholar's trophy wife, attending high mass every Sunday and holy days of obligation, or the interminable monthly dinners with the clerical fat cats of the diocese who sipped twenty-five year-old port after a thick center-cut slab of chateaubriand then next Sunday exhorted the flock to tithe 'til it hurt...how post-Hillary this was one more crack in the glass ceiling when a female operative/spy/assassin can make as much as or more than a male.[80] "Now," she continued, "who were you planning to give that to?"

"The church," said DeSica, concentrating on Maureen, the gun, and Danica from the neck up.

"The church?" Maureen smiled ruefully. "Maybe you're more like your father than I realized...unless the church is going to pay you ten million dollars." Mickey, the piqued puppy hearing his leash jingle, turned to DeSica. DeSica shook his head. Shit...

"It's been great catching up, Mikhail, but all good things must end. I'd prefer not to kill anyone. How would you care to handle this?"

Danica could contain no longer. "You'd kill your own son?!"

"I don't think she said *that*," Mickey jumped in.

"Actually I did."

"Oh."

"We have no intention of handing this over," said DeSica.

_____

80   It's true, history is rife with unfair gender treatment. During World War I records show that Mata Hari made one-third less than Gaston Champion; in World War II Nancy Hall and Virginia Wake made only half of Sir Hugh Dowding's salary; and on their execution even Ethel Rosenberg was given less juice than Julius in the electric chair.

Yeah, big talker, you're Kevlared. "We could at least be democratic about this," Mickey said irritably. "I vote we send out for some *fasnachtsküchlein* and discuss."

Maureen cocked the gun, Danica closed her eyes.

"One. Two—"

"*Okay!*" Mickey yelled. "You can have it!"

A tense, uncertain pause in the room. "It is not yours to give," said DeSica.

Mickey pulled the silk handkerchief from his pocket; it was tied in a knot around something. "The contents aren't in the ark. I dumped the samples into this." Mickey gave a nod to the ark. "Check under the hood...you have a few pieces of mortar in there."

DeSica yanked the burlap off and looked inside. "You... you..." he stammered; then, uttering a word that had never before left his lips, "...*motherfucker.*"

"'Judas' would have sufficed."

"I should have known...you planned all along to sell it, didn't you?"

Mickey didn't answer. Even with a gun at her temple, Danica felt a stab of disillusionment.

"You *do* take after me," Maureen said proudly. "Influence is a funny thing. Your father spent only a few years in England, and for the rest of his life adopted so many of their pretentious words. You grew up with him and adopted nothing. Now..." She indicated the handkerchief.

"Let her go first."

Maureen shoved Danica toward the men. She pointed the gun squarely at Mickey. "Be a good boy."

"Careful...it's very fragile."   Whereupon he lobbed
the wad at her, Maureen grabbing for it as her gun fired.
Mickey felt the white hot burn of impact, falling. DeSica
shoved the ark into Danica's gut as he dove for Maureen in
one motion. She went down hard, DeSica wresting the gun
away with an elbow to the jaw, followed by a straight right
for insurance. It was all over that fast.

Danica rushed to Mickey and crouched over him,
his shoulder shot clean through.   "My God, does it
hurt?"

"Yeah," he grimaced, "but put some clothes on and the
swelling should go down."

"I meant your wound."

"Oh. Not too bad."

Danica grabbed a towel and applied pressure to his
wound. "We have to get this cleaned. It's a miracle you
weren't killed." It probably was. But there was another
miracle, albeit smaller: the bullet that pierced his shoulder
removed the tracking chip along with a chunk of Mickey.
He didn't know that right away, he saw it in a splotch of
bloody matter next to where he landed. The resulting plan
that occurred to him proved that the Marquis De Sade was
right: In great pain *does* come great inspiration.

"I'll take it from here," he said to Danica, pressing the
towel to his burning shoulder. She rushed to get dressed as
Mickey picked up the sashimied flesh containing the chip.
He pressed his finger upon it, coming up with a black dot
swimming in red. He crossed to his mother, still supine
under DeSica.

"Let her go," Mickey said.

"Let her go?" DeSica exclaimed, "she will try to intercept and kill us before we get to Rome."

"We have her gun, a lead...and do you really want to be responsible for murdering my *mother*?"

DeSica, who had taken life in the fury of the moment, realized he really didn't have the gladiator's stomach to snuff out the already vanquished, especially when that vanquished was the womb service that delivered the person asking for mercy. He removed his forearm from Maureen's throat, standing up warily.

"Thank you, Mikhail," she coughed. "No matter how long apart...what obstacles in between...a mother and son will always have that special bond."

Monday, April 12, 1:04 a.m. – Zurich

Aaron, watching the club, was unable to comprehend why patrons were stumbling out as if from a tilt-a-whirl on warp speed, bloodied, limbs fractured, eyes like blackened golf balls. Still, his three subjects had been inside since 10:30ish, and the longer their stay the more it augured well that success was at hand; *after all*, he thought, not knowing Mickey, *one can only look at so many breasts and vaginas.*

At 1:10 he jolted with anticipation as his GPS signaled movement! On foot, at a clip, they were escaping down the alley behind Pussy's! This was it, the moment of certainty, of delayed gratification that made its fulfillment all the more pleasurable, that would give his life rights immeasurable worth and provide the fitting end to the story he was now justified in stringing out to such a ridiculous degree!

He slipped on the avenging metal glove of De Molay. *Savor the end game…give them a lead, take your time, and when you corner them, conduct the end like the maestro of mayhem you are; any petty malefactor can simply confront his victims, unload a clip, and be done with it! What happened to the craft – no, art – of termination, to the slow build, to restraint, to the indescribable fear generated by expectation, taking the prey to the edge of the precipice then backing away, making the doomed question the inevitable, such that when the inevitable happened it had been orchestrated with an ebb and flow worthy of a Mozartian dirge, building to a crescendo and cresting in their chorus of cries for compassion! Make this your masterpiece that will be the talk of Club Hashasheen for years to come!*

We need not dwell on Aaron's dismay upon cornering his quarry. Back at Pussy's, Mickey did have a problem with DeSica executing his mother. What he couldn't say in front of her, however, was that he had far less of a problem with *Aaron* executing her, an outcome that was sealed when he wiped the tracking chip inside her collar and Aaron discovered he'd been following a decoy; which informs why authorities found the woman's body riddled with *two* clips of 9mm bullets.

Monday, April 12, 1:35 a.m. – Zurich

Hands from all sides, hundreds of squirming tentacles, clawed at her, drawing her toward an unimaginable fate, an ankle grasped, a thigh encircled, she was being pulled down by this millipede of perversion into the maw of—

Danica shot awake, sweating, glancing about to confirm she really *was* in the backseat of some poor tourist's stolen rental car (albeit an odd tourist; he had left it unlocked, keys inside, with a full bottle of urine); she caught her breath, realized it was just a case of PTSD[81] and resigned herself to the probability of more such occurrences.

They raced to the border. Up front bro-mance was in the air, DeSica congratulating Mickey on the handkerchief ploy that distracted his mother and telling him how the Dominicans were looking for a few good men, Mickey complimenting DeSica's ability to wing it without any foreknowledge of his plan, suggesting he look into a career in improvisation. Danica wondered why Mickey, from the moment they had left the club, talked not at all about what had to be one of the most unsettling encounters of his life: The brief and unkind meeting with his mother (Danica would have been even more jaw-droppingly flummoxed if she knew how Mickey used Maureen as a clay pigeon for Aaron). Maybe he had so trained himself to think of her as evil and manipulative, that when she finally appeared and confirmed the assumption it was anticlimactic; maybe there was genuine closure to his many unanswered questions; or maybe he just didn't give a shit. Whatever the truth, he seemed entirely unaffected right now, even jocular with DeSica. But she was present for the news of his father, and she witnessed the growing satisfaction he took in matching wits with him *in absentia*; so she knew he was capable of acknowledging parental responsibility, even the need for parental reconciliation, at least from his father. That same acknowledgment,

---

81   Post-Traumatic-Stripper-Disorder.

however, did not extend to the woman who wronged them both and who, ultimately, did more to shape Mikhail's and Mickey's lives than she'd ever know. With one parent circumstances shattered any chance for reconciliation; with the other, Mickey was part-architect of those circumstances. For now all she could do was consider this one more valise added to the overworked porter whose miserable task it was to carry all of Mickey's emotional baggage.

"I was particularly impressed when you dropped the m-f bomb," Mickey laughed.

"Just following your lead. When I saw that you hadn't switched the excreta, I *imagined* how I would feel if you had."

But let's face it, anyone whose only adult conversation with his mother was at the end of a gun from behind a hot naked lesbian, who then shot him and who *he* then sent off on a death march, was in need of a serious psychoanalytic brain-douche. For all his ability to slice through the bullshit of others and get to uncomfortable truths, Mickey didn't know where to begin in getting to *his* truths, sorting through the swirl of emotions that were his inner-Sargasso. Maureen's and his entire encounter was less than ten minutes and, unknown to Danica, Mickey kept parsing every word, every nanosecond of it: Her profound lack of emotion...her complete dismissal of all things Mikhail...the inescapable reality that at the end of the day he *was* her son. If there was anything good to come of this, it was how much taller Mikhail stood in Mickey's eyes. His crippled parental style lacked warmth, he was more comfortable with scholarship than fatherhood, he disdained outward displays of emotion...but he was there. In fact what Maureen viewed as Mikhail's negatives, grew as positives to Mickey; that he never betrayed his core values; how he was an odd mix of old world conviction but youthful influences; even the unique way he expressed himself in colloquialisms from his time at college in—

Expressed himself...

Wait a minute. Wait. A. Minute.

Holy excreta.

"What did you say?" asked DeSica.

Mickey looked over, confused. "Nothing?"

"You were explaining the difference between the system and Method acting vis-à-vis pre-Modernist plays and you suddenly said...'mice'.

"I did?"

"You did," agreed Danica.

Mickey retreated back to his thoughts, rewound and reviewed them; then reviewed them again. And he realized at the moment of death what his father was trying to say.

Now he was fucked up.

Monday, April 12, 1:47 a.m. – Zurich

A shattered bottle and the reek of urine were in the space where Aaron's car used to be. So close to the treasure of ages and now so far, he had little choice but to call Paris, endure the humiliating identification ritual, explain all, and arrange for an emergency flight on a bank jet from Zurich to Rome in the hope he might still be able to intercept them. Failure was an outcome too terrible to contemplate. At the very least he would be divested of his glove and, along with it, his cherished mantle, The Fist of God; and in failure he knew they would not kill him, no, that would be too painless. Disgraced in his field – and word tends to get around in contract killer circles – he would be reduced to an Edith Piaf impersonator in a smoky, low rent, backwater speakeasy, forced to forget life as an international assassin, until he drank himself to an end not unlike his impersonation.

This called for an enema bag, 1.89 liters of hot chamomile tea, a bathing pan, and olive branches. He had to think.

Monday, April 12, 4:03 a.m. – the border crossing between Switzerland and Italy

Richard got the call from Mickey, heard the urgency in his voice to meet them in Northern Italy and, being on the continent, commandeered a NATO helicopter to nearby Milan where a driver would take him to Gorla Maggiore within three hours.

Mickey and crew had barely eluded Swiss authorities thanks to an A.P.B. of their descriptions from Theo at Pussy's, an A.P.B. also alerting Interpol; thus alerting every scumbag looking for their bountied heads since the Scotland Yard contretemps. Taking a back road near Lugano, DeSica knew this less-traveled crossing into Italy would be near empty this time of night. Still, with their high-value profiles, nothing could be taken for granted. Indeed, bored immigration guards in the middle of nowhere and a collar of this magnitude – one that would make any guard a national hero, complete with promotions, reassignment from Bumfuck to Big Time, and more attention from women of easy virtue than they could handle (being Italian, that was quite a bit) – was a recipe for disaster.

Mickey slept through the crossing wherein DeSica anticipated the situation. The priest knew if there were little traffic, the guards would be warm in the station room, watching a bootlegged Nicholas Cage/Jerry Bruckheimer suckfest, eager to wave them through and resume their suckfest. But if things were slow, and they lacked such a diversion of pointlessly combusting property and vehicles, they would want to generate a little pointless excitement of their own. DeSica obviated the need by giving them exactly what they wanted, purchasing a bootleg Nicholas Cage/Jerry Bruckheimer DVD at a gas stop earlier. When asked for passports and the priest took *this* out of his jacket pocket instead, well…all three guards' eyes widened, they were waved through, and the guards ran back into the warm station room, raising the gate for them to cross into Italy.

It was an hour later when Mickey was awakened by DeSica's rude Italian epithet and flashing lights behind them accompanied by the stomach-churning, two-note singsong of a police siren.

"I'm not stopping," DeSica warned Danica and Mickey.

"Bad idea," said Danica, "pull over."

"Pull over?!"

"It's a single police car, we're on an empty road in the middle of nowhere, if they had any idea who we were they

wouldn't be stopping us without backup! Give them a reason, they'll alert every police car between here and Rome,
pull over!"

DeSica reluctantly eased off the gas and veered onto
the gravel shoulder.

"Turn off the engine and keep your hands on the wheel
where they can see them," she commanded. Two sets of
police boots crunched toward their car.

What finally caught up with them was not the Swiss,
Italian, or international monitoring of highly coordinated
databases; nor was it the intricate net cast far and wide by
the underworld. No, what threatened to reveal them to
authorities to face a raft of murder and mayhem charges
not seen since the Baader-Meinhof gang…was the rental
car company. Maybe Aaron had lost the ability to track
them with an implanted microchip, but *Alpine Selbstmieten
A-1* didn't. Aaron, rivulets of sweat, blood, and chamomile
tea dripping down into a bathing pan in a motel room,
quivering from freshly inflicted olive branch wounds, had
a moment of painful throbbing revelation:

LoJack.

He alerted *Alpine Selbstmieten A-1,* they located the signal and called ahead of the vehicle to the police in Italy,
where Mickey and Company were sticking to side routes,
speeding toward Gorla Maggiore. Famous for virtually
nothing beyond its non-existent crime rate, the alerted
constabulary was not about to allow lowly car thieves into
the city to bump up their stats even one tick. Which is why
they were intercepted outside of town, on a stretch of dark
two-lane road winding among acres of grape vines.

Danica knew the drill and coached DeSica, who convinced the two officers to allow them one call to a U.N.
consultant, that they were delivering a very important
package to the Vatican, and that he would corroborate the
unfortunate and embarrassing mix-up of them taking the
wrong car in Zurich. Between her cop savy and the two
top opened buttons on her blouse, they agreed to wait with
them until their *sporgenza* showed up. Needless to say, the
two tired police snapped to attention when, in the warm
grey light just before dawn, the black town car with diplomatic flags and tinted windows approached and pulled
to an intimidating stop. Richard exited from the back,
his assured presence and underplayed command already
promising a swift end to this snafu.

They watched the cops and Richard confer, the men
speaking officially, firmly – until, satisfied, the police
drove away, the incident never having happened. Richard
approached the three and said, "Leave the vehicle, remove
everything that's yours." The last of the whippoorwills were
calling as the grey morning sky began to brighten, revealing endless rolling hills.

DeSica went back to retrieve the gun he'd put under
the seat and the tattered burlap-covered ark as Richard
clasped a paternal hand on Mickey's shoulder, "Mikhail,
good to see you again...did you fulfill your mission?" Off
Mickey's nod, Richard smiled warmly. "Your father would
be proud. And now what?"

"We have to rush the ark to Rome," Mickey answered,
"but...I have one more favor to ask you."

"Please."

"I need to know why you killed my father."

Danica and DeSica froze where they stood, eyeing Mickey uncertainly. Mickey purposely never told them what he'd deduced in case they needed Richard's help again, not wanting either of them to betray his secret.

"Mikhail...why would you even think that?"

"Like the Christ, it seems we all have some shit from our past."

"I don't know what you mean—"

"The last thing my father said was 'mice.' Maybe he did mean a rodent, but not the cute little Disney kind...I remembered that he always referred to you, his lawyer, by the British term."

Danica and DeSica still weren't sure where he was going.

"'Solicitor.' He was trying to say...'*my solicitor*'."

The whippoorwills had gone silent.[82] You could have heard a pin drop all the way in Rome.

"That's why you went to Inspector Renault, trying to help me and, as you say, 'cocked it up.' To make me look more guilty. At some point, though, Inspector Renault figured out the truth, told the wrong person, and you killed him, too."

"Why would I have helped you get this far?"

"Because you want the ark. For all your supposed world travel, I'm betting you were never far away from us. You were always available, always there, always ready. I'm not sure how, unless..."

---

82   Ed. Note: As well they should since they're found nowhere on the European continent.

"He is working with me," came the answer, perfectly timed in that voice strained through a sieve of acid and gravel. *Aw, goddamn sonovabitch...of course.* The scent of chamomile wafted their way.

Aaron had emerged from the car and stood by the driver's door, wearing the metallic glove, gun in hand, working a wad of gum. Mickey – though it was increasingly unlikely this was going to turn out in his favor – still preferred not to jinx things and admit in front of DeSica that *he* was the tracking device carrier all along; and as freakshow knew, Richard knew; and that in calling Richard to expose him, it would bring this cockroach back with him, which he *didn't* realize.

"I'm sorry, Mikhail," said Richard, strangely meaning it. "Your father was family."

"In the fucked-up Tennessee Williams sense. All these years you two discussed his search, didn't you? He trusted you, shared his notes, you were the one person outside the church he talked to. You knew how close he was." Richard nodded. "And all these years you worked for the bank that came from Templar money, while you were this globe-trotting Johnny Cochran."

"I prefer 'Clarence Darrow.'"

"Not when you're in cahoots with a glove-wearing whack-job," Mickey nodded to Aaron, "even if *this* one didn't play for the NFL."

"Necessity tends to breed, well...necessity."

"What do you plan to do with the ark?" Mickey saw no good end to this.

"What I was approached to do as your father's confidante...give it back to the bank, which will pay handsomely...

whereupon the bank will use it against Rome as reprisal for its destruction of the noble Templars. Unless the Holy Father is willing to pay, oh, tens of billions, the bank will release the ark for study and let the chips fall where they may. The church, of course, would not dare risk the truth. A truth you don't even care about, do you?" True. Mickey didn't give a rat's ass if Christ ate chocolate-covered ants at the last supper. "Why jeopardize your life to find it?" Richard asked.

"You wouldn't understand."

"Even if you'd succeeded in delivering this item you don't care about...and are about to die for...sadly, it would not have remained with the church. We have so many deep-mole Masonic operatives, one within the offices of *il Papa* himself, that the ark would have returned to our hands within the week." Richard eyed the burlap wrapped box in DeSica's hands. "Please...put the ark down and step away."

DeSica, running down the various fight-or-flight scenarios, couldn't figure out one that wasn't going to end ugly.

"I'm sorry," Mickey said, *sotto voce*, to Danica, "for getting you into this."

"It's not your fault," she offered back, closing her eyes for what was about to occur.

"Put...the ark...down," Richard commanded. Aaron, arm resting on the car roof, had his Glock trained on DeSica as well. The priest appeared transfixed by headlights, for once completely at a loss.

The gunshot echoed across the hills as Danica's eyes opened to see Aaron with a bloody right metallic hand that no longer held a gun. DeSica still held the ark and, like everyone else, was turning every which way, frantically scanning the vista, trying to get a visual on the shooter to see if it was friend or foe. Danica, the only one to track back from Aaron's blood spray atop the car, spied the glint of a scope catching the morning sun, high on a rise three hundred yards away; then another glint fifty yards to the left of it; and yet another fifty yards left of that. She guessed there were more in the hills on the other side, creating a crossfire. This was an organized group of trained snipers. Which meant one thing:

"Interpol," she said, "three, six, nine, twelve o'clock."

Fate had let slip the dogs of war. And these didn't have their vaccinations.

Who knew Interpol tracked LoJack? And that Aaron's description of the perps was close enough to the Scotland Yard bloodbath perps to signal a five-alarm-red-alert-full-metal-jacket Mayday?

"Remain where you are!" an amplified voice echoed around them. "Each of you is in our crosshairs!" In the distance the group saw a caravan of olive green Range Rovers approaching, cresting and disappearing on the hilly road.

"I dunno about anyone else," said Mickey, "but I'm not a fan of the structured indoor lifestyle and being just anyone's bitch. I say we make like Frankenstein and bolt."

The Range Rovers were bearing down.

"Make a move and I'll warn them," said Richard.

"On three," said Danica, realizing Mickey's plan, "we all pile in to the limo. And I drive."

"I mean it," said Richard.

"One," she began.

"Don't try it…"

"Two—"

"You'll leave me no choice—"

"Thr—"

Richard sprinted toward the oncoming vehicles waving his arms and yelling, "They're attempting to escape, they're making a run for it!" Rather, that's what he *intended* to say; all he got out was "They're—" as six twenty-four inch threaded-muzzle barrels zeroed in from all sides and Peckinpah-ed him with a storm of 7.62x51mm slugs that, in 2.7 seconds, atomized everything above his neck into red mist, reducing his chest cavity to strawberry preserves and, for good measure, separating the right leg below the knee, his spiraling torso landing with soggy finality onto the pavement.

Richard had sacrificed Mickey's father for personal gain. In return, Richard became a sacrifice for Mickey in his moment of need. That 2.7 seconds was all the three of them needed to get in Richard's car and make like Frankenstein.

Monday, April 12, 6:20 a.m. – outside Gorla Maggiore

"Jesus," said Mickey, the g-force from the accelerating car giving him an Asian face-lift, "I've been on slower jets!" Danica had discovered eight cylindars of positive displacement supercharged thrust, the multistage axial flow pump ass-raping the intake manifold by forcing too many cubic inches of air into its tight chamber, creating half-again more horsepower and almost as much torque; every part of the rebuilt American-made modular V-8 screamed in pain as she neared mach-one, and she planned to keep on abusing it all the way to Rome.

The snipers lost the car behind grape rows and a dip in the undulating road before they could draw a bead, leaving it to the Range Rovers – and the Al Qaeda-level of firepower each one carried – to catch up to and blow the vehicle into scrap.

The car caught air over each crest, landing thirty feet later, the shocks recovering just in time before next lift-off. DeSica glanced behind them, saw Interpol maintaining its tail. "We can't outrun them, it's almost seven hundred kilometers to Rome!"

"Any extra weight we can lose, it feels like we're carrying some drag!" she countered.

Mickey glanced down and saw four metal fingers sticking from his completely closed front passenger door. He adjusted the electric side-view mirror down, finding the contorted screaming face of Aaron (appearing closer than it actually was), his body twisting on its dislocated arm, the stumps that used to be his feet scraping the coarse pavement at a hundred-plus miles per hour. Lips pulled back, his skeletal orifice mouthed *please for the love of God!* but it wasn't clear since Mickey didn't understand French. The car caught air again and Mickey was amazed to witness how resilient the human body was, Aaron flopping like a windsock.

"Found your drag."

The car took a turn in a rubber-screeching slide as Mickey opened the door, launching Aaron straight ahead, flying like cannon shot until he made an abrupt arboreal stop against a large oak.

"Fasten your seatbelts," commanded Danica in her best Margot Channing, "it's going to be a bumpy ride!" She gripped the wheel preparing for the literary third-act car chase of the year. Which *would* have happened if not for American Congressional lack of oversight, the greedy American homeowner, and the enabling Wall Street implosion causing the economic downturn of the world commodities markets.

The lead Range Rover radioed Interpol Command to alert them of the high-speed chase. "Sir, Mother Goose One, we have code-red-high-value target in our sights, request air support and N.O.I.[83] at the following coordinates!"

The order crackled back firm and loud: "*Cease and desist this instant, Mother Goose One!*"

"But sir—!"

"No buts, soldier! Here it is, straight up, Interpol's portfolio of large cap stocks got bukkake'd in the great American stockbroker gang bang and lost *forty-one percent* of its value, we are in deep, and I mean deep, budgetary shit! You cannot afford to expend *another bullet* on this case until the start of next fiscal quarter beginning on June 1st, do you copy?!"

"We copy, sir, but...there must be *something* we can do, need disposition immediately!"

---

83   Non-Obtrusive Interference.

"Stand by!"

The lead Hummer waited anxiously as a conference went on Command-side. Up ahead civilian habitation was looming larger. To have such a high-value target in their sights was worth the field decision of countermanding orders. It was clear if they didn't act soon that unsuspecting civilians were in harm's way and would have to be sacrificed as collateral damage. Finally the answer came back.

"Okay soldier, found a patch of blue! Per the manual, page two-forty-seven, paragraph B, field emergency contingencies, you are allowed to countermand a direct order, continue the chase, expend the necessary fuel and firepower, incur any collateral destruction, itemize fuel, firepower and collateral destruction, pay for it out of your own pockets, and file a 1011-a for reimbursement by year's end, do you copy?!"

They did.

The Range Rovers slowed to a dispirited stop.

Monday, April 12, 10:42 p.m. – outside Gorla Maggiore

How Aaron still lived, footless, oozing from places not designed to ooze, lacking a single unbroken bone in his body, was as unexplainable as Keanu Reeves. Fifteen hours later, his body working off its shock, he was able to stand the agony since, through the years, he had inured his body to a level of ungodly pain that would make lesser mortals beg for death; but it could be worse, where there was life there was hope. Granted he'd be paralyzed for the rest of his days, would eat through a tube, shit in a bag, and get sponged-bathed by a third-world immigrant who so resented being exploited for minimum wage that he'd blow smoke from the Turkish cigarettes he wasn't supposed to be smoking around patients into Aaron's face, then snuff the butts out on his testicles...or so Aaron could only hope. He'd lost a lot of blood but had just enough to keep his heart pumping; he didn't bleed out as he fortuitously landed against the tree with the stumps of his legs raised up against it, allowing a protective scab to form in the spring sun and breeze. Surely a passer-by would find him, even if this road was little traveled except for trucks and agricultural machinery driven by unshaven pasta-eating opera-singing nits.

And then finally: rustling...movement...life! Coming his way! It was hard to hear if it was a person or persons over the jackhammer working inside his skull, but it was cause for optimism. The rustling got louder and he realized it wasn't coming from the road, it was coming from within the grape rows. No doubt two young lovers who had consummated their passion amid the fruit of Bacchus and were heading back to town. *Please in your love-sated state, find me!* He summoned up what strength he could and wheezed a pathetic sound for help.

It turned out to be not such a good idea.

Aaron found himself surrounded by eight sets of yellow, baleful eyes belonging to a pack of patchy, feral dogs, heads hung low in uncertain inspection. This was too good to be true, their hesitation seemed to say, to find helpless and tenderized game just for the taking. Heads swayed from side to side, others paced back and forth, carping gutturally, waiting for the alpha to give his permission to feast. The top dog howled in mistrust, nothing came this easily, especially when they hadn't eaten all day. But his howl finally attenuated into a damn-it-to-hell cry of *trap or no trap, I'm getting me some of this action,* then it leaped forward, sinking its teeth deep into one of Aaron's leg stumps. The lieutenants, snapping at each other's throats, jockeyed for the other stub, two of them winning the scrum and dividing the spoil between them. Others discovered the raw extensions that used to be his hands within the shredded leather jacket, and found them to be damn good eating.

To his complete and absolute horror, Aaron realized he was being consumed from his extremities inward and that nothing was going to stop them; worse, given that they were not wild from birth – a fucking Pomeranian was eating his ear, for crissakes! – it would be an eternity for them to gnaw him to death.

There's pain and then there's pain. This was the latter.

The dogs shredded flesh, gnawed bone, and sucked marrow until dawn, leaving a torso with skeletal limbs that held onto a few stringy remnants of tissue. In a state of surfeit, they slept around him, saving what was left for breakfast. Beyond all scientific reason, Aaron was able to endure such grotesque violation and remained alive to see the next daybreak.

My last sunrise, he thought, *and it's going to be a beautiful one... it reminds me of mornings as a child in my beloved Orleans, walking with grandpa to the bakery... at least I still have sight to see such a glorious image.* He focused on the distant horizon viewed through the east-west vine rows, awaiting the rising sun.

Until a flock of screeching blackbirds descended upon his head and pecked out both orbs.

Monday, April 12, 6:25 a.m. – STILL outside Gorla Maggiore, Italy

"What the fuck do you mean?" Mickey said, starting a chapter with vulgarity for emphasis' sake.

"I mean," DeSica reported, "Interpol has stopped the chase."

"I don't trust them," snapped Danica, slowing down as they came into Gorla Maggiore, "they must be waiting ahead. Either way, you know they reported a car with diplomatic plates carrying three wanteds, we ditch this car here and steal another one."

Too late. Driving along Via Como, they came to the roundabout at Viale Europa to see it shut down by every available police vehicle within a ten-mile radius, their lights flashing, countless police guns trained on their car. The traffic snarl around them allowed for no escape.

"I have another idea," said DeSica.

Monday, April 12, 6:31 a.m. – Rome

Cardinal Thomasina, celebrating morning mass in front of the assembled bishops in the Basilica of St. John Lateran, prayed for guidance and wisdom in the synod that was to begin that day. He held the host high and somberly intoned, "*Hoc est enim corpus meum,* " as an altar boy rang the bells, signaling the rite central to the Catholic faith, a ritual and miracle created by Jesus Christ himself, that still gave the Cardinal chills as a wafer of common flour transformed into – *zzzz-zzzz-zzzz…zzzz-zzzz-zzzz!* Thomasina felt the vibration in his pocket. To the amazement – no, abject horror – of all, he dropped the host, hiked up his robes, and grabbed his cell phone.

"Where the hell are you?!" he whispered into the cell as the altar boys froze, waiting nervously for a bolt of lightning from on high to strike the cleric where he stood. "You need me to *what?!* *Now?* Do you have any idea what I'm… you *what…*oh shit on toast!" He raised a hand to his forehead, listening, realizing what was being asked of him, and that he would have to implement it immediately. Then, lowering his voice more so that even the altar boys not ten feet away might not hear, he hissed, "This is fucking *incredible*, I'll do it but no more goddamn fuck-ups, do you hear?!"

He shut the phone, turned angrily to the assembly… and realized per their demeanors that he forgot to mute his lavaliere microphone. His mind scrambling, he cleared his throat, and then in the most serious and stately of tones, explained: "Just as the Prince of Peace himself whipped the money changers in the temple who would profit in God's house…we are called, *especially* in these times…to whip by tongue…those who fall short in their service to our Lord." The audience continued to stare, their opinion in abeyance, waiting to hear what could possibly warrant such a blasphemous display *during the very heart and soul of the Catholic mass.* "In this case...it is the novitiate who puts too little starch in my Roman collar so it is limp by lunch and who *insists* on sending my mozzeta to the dry cleaners instead of hand-washing it himself, using our precious and diminishing collection plate to support such languor."

Ahh...of course, a knowing murmur began and grew in intensity along with chuckles and nods to one another, *where do the seminaries get some of these inbreds?...Indeed, the bar for acceptance into the priesthood has fallen...I'm convinced this new crop is God's way of testing us like Job!* and so on. Thomasina had dodged a bullet. "If you will excuse me a moment," he said as he left the altar for the sanctuary.

Monday, April 12, 7:58 a.m. – Gorla Maggiore

Mussolini helped rescue our intrepid three. The Vatican is the world's smallest state at approximately 110 acres and, thanks to *Il Duce*, has been an independent one since February 11, 1929, when Mussolini signed the Lateran Treaty with Pope Pius XI. Thus the Vatican could officially send and receive foreign dignitaries, get representation in the U.N., and even refuse to adopt certain laws of Italy that were in conflict with orthodoxy. In return, he and his successor Pope Pius XII kept their noses to the liturgical grindstone during World War II and somehow managed to miss one or two of the bigger developments of that dust-up.[84] Another benefit was the ability of the Vatican's

84   In fairness, though, the Church of Rome in 2001 asked a general forgiveness from certain aggrieved parties over the years,

Secretariat of State to grant diplomatic status to anyone in the service of the Holy See. Which is what DeSica called Thomasina about, convincing him to get the Secretariat to do just that. Thus for the next twenty-four hours Mickey, Danica, and Fr. DeSica were made Vatican ambassadors-at-large. All national as well as all international law enforcement agencies were apprised of this – the Gorla Maggiore police immediately backed off – allowing the three to travel unmolested to Rome assuming they murdered or raped no one en route.

Granted there was a time crunch. Granted they were traveling with a historical relic that could radically rearrange the topography of world religion. Still, since Mickey figured he'd never be an ambassador again, well...it seemed that one should...y'know...enjoy at least a perk or two that came with the office.

"Like what?" DeSica asked dryly. Mickey was crushed to find he couldn't bitch-slap the Iranian ambassador, date the current Miss Vatican, or get his picture taken wearing the Pope's miter sitting on the Pope's throne (and he didn't mean his chair). However...DeSica begrudgingly gave in on letting Mickey place calls from the car through the Vatican Secretariat of State's office to each of his ex-wives *and their mothers*, announcing a phone call from Ambassador Mickey Samanov; whereupon he'd get on the horn, let 'em know what they missed out on, and tell them to drop by next time they're in Goombah Town.

---

the Jews among them, for the historical sins of the Catholic Church. It can be assumed that most of the Crusades, the Inquisition, and the Holocaust were included in that *mea culpa.*

The car raced toward Rome.

Monday, April 12, over the course of the day – Rome

The Swiss Guard noticed a larger influx of tourists than usual, overwhelmingly male. It wasn't the influx that was troubling…it was that they gathered in St. Peter's Square with no ostensible interest in visiting the Basilica, milling about idly, facing the entrance to the square as if waiting for something. Among them was a tourist with a falsified British passport…Witherspoon.

His buddies from the print shop were with him.

And under their British working class tourist clothing, they all had their American 2nd Amendment-protected buddies with them. Richard had been right: As Interpol became aware, so too did those who Interpol was after. And they were most aware of the large bounty still on three heads due to arrive any time.

Though they weren't sure who these people were or why they were here, the Guard was put on the highest level of alert: Code Golgotha.

Inside Paolo VI Aula Hall, the synod was getting personal. Not since the Ebionites versus the Marcionites had lines of demarcation been so pronounced between Christian camps, nor could anyone remember positions so intensely argued. No sooner had a conceptualist finished speaking than the social conditionalists hooted and jeered him down. The conceptualists were no better, adherents having to restrain Cardinal Elba from lifting up his robes, turning, and showing his disdain to the other side of the hall; Thomasina, shocked to find how many conceptualists thought homosexuality was from the zygote, was beginning to suspect that a few might have personal reason to take such an unenlightened view.

But Thomasina had another reason to be agitated. DeSica had said they should be at the Vatican by 5:00 p.m. Time seemed to move backwards being so close to the dream fulfilled, but he heard not a word from DeSica since (in part because Mickey was hogging the phone).

Monday, April 12, 4:58 p.m. – Rome

Zero hour. They negotiated their way to Rome, incurring only one police encounter involving Mickey and public urination – resulting in a ticket which Ambassador Samanov used to wipe his hands on, then ripped up in front of the motorcycle cop who had not gotten the memo of the offender's exalted right to urinate on his motorcycle if it so amused him. DeSica had taken over the wheel outside of Rome, now speeding down the Via della Conciliazione. After a week of Mr. Toad's Wild Ride (Sex and Violence edition), they were not ten minutes away from the Vatican.

"Now that we're here," Danica asked DeSica, "what's the plan?"

"The plan."

"The *plan*...since you think the Cardinal has his own agenda, wants us dead and probably you, too...the plan, what is it?"

"I have been praying for inspiration the entire drive here."

"And were those prayers answered?"

"Yes."

"Good, great, love it, what did God tell you?"

"Nothing."

"*Nothing*?

"Nothing."

"You call that an answer?!"

"Have you ever prayed for a promotion," he asked, "or to win the lottery? Or for a relationship to work out with a special someone?"

That last one stung. "Yeah."

"And what happened?"

"Nothing."

"Your prayers were answered.   The answer was 'no.'"

Her head was beginning to throb from the brain tumor no doubt caused by this adventure. "Just to be clear...you asked God for guidance...to do *His* work...which might cause all of us to meet Him sooner than later...and He blew you off."

"No, He was very clear...He wants me to trust my own plan."

"Ah. Okay. So you *do* have a plan."

He cleared his throat. "Actually...I've been too busy praying."

She felt like the plant manager at Chernobyl who finally opened the sealed In-Case-of-Emergency instructions and read: *Kiss your ass goodbye.*

They were entering the narrow passage into St. Peter's Square...and DiSica's Dominican spidey sense began flashing stress lines: Too many tourists at this hour...too many too close to the entrance of the square...too many males... many of them eyeing this official vehicle and reaching under their jackets. DeSica stopped the car. Anyone could see that to continue the next hundred or so yards would be driving into the Plaza of No Return.

"Looks all clear," said Mickey. Okay, not *anyone*. He took a second look. "Oh. Shit."

"Our entrance, remember, is there in the right wing," DeSica said, the engine idling. "I'm praying this car has reinforced plate glass."

"And I'm praying *your* praying gets better results this time," said Danica.

"Yo, Team Ark, why all the ado?" Mickey interjected. "Have you forgotten we are *ambassadors* and un-fucking-touchable? We get out, apprise them of matters, salute them with a single digit, and walk to home plate."

"Fine," said Danica, "we vote you to get out and apprise them."

"What remains of you will receive a full state funeral," added DeSica.

"Uh huh...uh huh," considered Mickey. "What's our backup plan?"

Scores of men watched as the town car slowly turned around, about to burn rubber to parts unknown.

But it just sat there. Idling.

More Swiss Guards were getting itchy, stealthily fanning out behind the Tuscan columns surrounding the square.

As valuable as the incoming package was, Thomasina chose not to alert the Guards to DeSica's arrival – reducing those in the know he might have to eliminate – to effect his plan. And DeSica figured this.

"Get up front with us," DeSica ordered Mickey. "You'll have more protection." Mickey scrambled into the front seat, cradling the ark.

"You're going to *back* into a crowd of armed criminals?" Danica asked incredulously.

DeSica quickly unbuttoned his shirt, took off his Kevlar vest, and handed it to Mickey. "Wrap this around the ark." Mickey did so. "I'm going to get us as close to the door as possible. When this car can't move another centimeter it's every man for himself."

"The guy who made the universe in six days is trusting *that* plan?" Danica opined.

DeSica ignored her, put the car in reverse, kept a foot on the brake, and revved the engine to warp speed. Contrary to her skepticism, he was correct about them having more protection backing into the danger; a reinforced diplomatic vehicle had an added steel plate between the trunk and passenger compartment...

...had Aaron, anticipating his next job when he met up with Richard, not put in the trunk a shoulder bag filled with C-4 plastique, ready to leave for that job directly from Gorla Maggiore.

"Get down," DeSica ordered as he, too, slid low in the seat, adjusting his rearview mirror.

Then he released the brake, tires squealing for traction...and so began the next two minutes, thirty-eight seconds that have become known as the infamous St. Peter's Square Massacre.

The car rocketed backward, swerving diagonally across the square, Mickey and Danica jammed low and tight on the passenger side, Mickey's arm protectively around her. Deafening impacts dented the door beside them and spiderwebbed cracks in the windows as they bounced over speed bumps not put there by Gian Lorenzo Bernini. They couldn't see the crossfire of death they were entering, the Swiss Guard opening up on the interlopers who returned fire. Nor could they see when both passenger-side tires were shot out and shredded.

"*Madre del dio!*" yelled DeSica, the wheel yanking from his grip, the car veering sharply...

...inexorably for the obelisk...

...which DeSica saw coming in the sideview mirror. "Brace yourselves!" He couldn't foresee how inadequate that counsel was. The car collided with the obelisk in a blinding flash that turned the world white, the sonic announcement of six-and-a-half pounds of C-4 disintegrating the car to the rear reinforced plate, the rest propelled into the air and over on its roof. Scumbags and bystanders flew like ragdolls in all directions, pieces of bronze and granite arched high and rained down.

The car finally settled. Deafened, confused, intertwined, eyes burning from the pungent stench, the three couldn't hear the yelling around them, the diminishing gunfire...or the slow grinding of stone on stone behind them. The mighty forty-one-meters tall 13th century BCE Egyptian monument that was moved to Rome in 37 AD, the only obelisk in the eternal city still standing from that era, began to tilt...

...then tilt more...

...then began a drunken free-fall-half-twist toward the car, its shadow crossing it but in the final moment crashing beside it with such finality and sending up such a storm of debris that it shoved the vehicle aside and almost rocked it upright. The crippled shell of the vehicle settled more violently this time as, outside its windows, the world was swirling dusty red.

Mickey, master of the back-door-second-story-window-trellis exit, forced the car door open enough to worm himself free with the Kevlar protected ark, then pulled out Danica; DeSica crawled after. Disheveled and disoriented, what they saw around them was a George Romero film with a budget. Bodies and their various parts – run over, reduced by C-4 into pigeon feed, pelted by or crushed under stone – littered St. Peter's Square unlike any time in history.[85] The dust of centuries had yet to settle as

---

85 Which is not to be confused with the tens of thousands of Christian and Jewish bodies *outside* St. Peter's that littered Europe over the centuries courtesy of numerous Medieval Inquisitions, the Spanish Inquisition, the Portugese Inquisition, and the Roman Inquisition. Lest this appear to be a glib indictment of ecclesiastical power, heretics were genuinely believed to be agents of Satan, Jews were reported to drink the blood of Christian babies, and Exodus 22:18 instructed "Thou shall not suffer a witch to live." On March 12th, 2000, Pope John Paul II issued *another* papal catch-all apology that covered these excesses as well as those of the Crusades, so we can rest assured that the Church begins the new millennium with a clean slate.

numerous shocked survivors stood mumbling to them-selves or lurched about without purpose. The gunfire had stopped, the surviving attackers assuming their bountied quarry had been reduced to sub-atomic particles; and with tourist and terrorist looking the same covered in crimson granite dust, the Swiss Guard – the only ones able to be dis-cerned when covered in grime from their Rio-Mardi Gras costumes – withheld fire. The Guard encircled the car-nage, their 9mm pistols allowing no one to escape from the scene of…what? The crime? The happening? The incred-ibly fortuitous *deus ex machina*? Toward the one o'clock point of the circle, amid the eerily churning dust that hung in the air like fog, they saw a figure swaying boldly toward them in attenuated time.

"*Fermata!*" a guard ordered, his finger tensing on the trigger. The figure (unable to hear? *No parli Italiano?*) kept coming. These guards didn't ask twice. Three shots flashed in the mist, hitting their target square in the chest.

Mickey saw the silent flashes through the haze, felt the impact, *one-two-three*, knew he'd been hit and stumbled, fall-ing. He lay there trembling, unable to suck enough air into his lungs, chest aching as if struck with a sledgeham-mer, wondering if this is how it felt to die.

When he regained his senses he realized the ark he held in front of him had absorbed the bullets in the Kevlar. DeSica rushed to him and waved an I.D. as he barked to the guards who stood down. Mickey was helped up and when DeSica tried to take the ark Mickey refused to let go of this relic that had just saved his ragged ass, almost as if it were...even Mickey would admit...a miracle. He wasn't about to let it out of his sight.

Is anyone still reading these things anymore, 5:11 p.m. – Rome

Once again our three were escorted past Renassance, high Renaissance, Baroque, and Mannerist magnificence, until they arrived at the imposing closed doors that opened into Paolo VI Aula Hall. Mickey's head pulsed, his palms dripped, a rage of emotions battled inside him: Pride at having finished his father's work, excitement at the prospect of journey's end, elation at having dodged explosion, bullets and falling obelisk, uncertainty as to what the next ten minutes would bring, and the realization that whatever this was all about would soon come to light. Not to mention that it dawned on him only now that his and Danica's importance to this process had ended back in Zurich; all focus shifted from the finders to the find. Mickey and Danica had gone from subject to postscript, and the odds of this inanimate box seeing tomorrow morning, in Vegas book terms, were, oh, a hundred times greater than them doing the same. He didn't know what the powers-that-be had in store, but he was too far invested to not see this through to the end.

DeSica, knowing they were about to walk into the ecclesiastical brain trust of Christianity, thought they might at least dust themselves off a little. "Let us all go to the water closet and wash up," he said. As the guards escorted them down the hall, Mickey hugging the ark like a two-thousand-dollar-a-night Halle Berry lookalike, Danica gave voice to everyone's fears.

"That ark's the only thing keeping us alive. We hand it over, we've played our trump card."

"Maybe not," thought DeSica. "The cardinal wanted us to bring it to his chambers. With no witnesses as to how he got the ark, we most definitely would be vulnerable. But walking into the hall and presenting it to him in front of God and the synod...might indemnify us *and* expose his plan."

Mickey had his doubts, especially when there was, well... the larger issue. "What about what's inside the ark? You'll be announcing this to the world...it will be inspected, dissected, tested. What if the Gospel of Shem was correct?"

"Then the truth..." DeSica paused, pondering, then continued, "...the higher truth...needs to be known." His answer was not full-throated.

The guards opened the bathroom door, allowed the three to enter, then closed it behind them. The room was spacious but no place for privacy, the toilet not even partitioned off. Sleeves were rolled up, faces splashed; grime was dusted, brushed off or shaken out; hair was combed through with fingers. It made no difference, they still looked to have risen from the grave.

"Uh, fellas?" began Danica, "I have to tinkle." She indicated the door they entered, as in for them to leave.

"We must stay together at all costs," said DeSica. He and Mickey turned away as she reluctantly did her business; which, of course, listening, made them have to do their business, which the two men did as well.

All the while, Mickey thought of his father and what he would do in Mickey's shoes, since it was because of him he was here. He wondered if deep down his father had any personal conflict over this mission, given that he lived an existence in servitude to the church and raised his only son in accordance with its laws and fine print; especially given how all his life Mikhail was a commando on the front lines in the never-ending war against heterodoxy. He knew Mikhail's enthusiasm for the search. But his father was too smart not to consider the potential downside. This man of such deeply seeded faith had to know he was possibly handing over to the church the rope that would hang it. Which could have meant only one thing: Mikhail was convinced the truth would side with him. He was certain his faith and the faith of all the unquestioning billions over the centuries would be vindicated. For all the supposed thorns from His crown, splinters from His cross, a nail from His palm, no actual relics of Jesus Christ – the most followed, most written about, most argued and researched figure in the history of mankind – existed because, according to scripture, He was taken up wholly in the resurrection. If anything were found to be from the Son of Man Himself, Mikhail felt it would only reinforce The Truth.

Mickey knew the right thing, and that it had to be done...even if it meant his life.

When all of them were finished they were escorted back to the doors outside the synod. "Are we ready?" asked DeSica.

Here goes everything, thought Danica, taking a deep breath. DeSica nodded to the guards. A key went into the lock.

Monday, April 12, 5:26 p.m. – Rome

The doors swung wide into a vast chamber with its arched brightly lit ceiling to reveal what could have been a super-elite Star Trek Conference: hundreds of grown men dressed in the same costume assembled to argue matters of the cosmos.

"And so, as we end this day of discussion on a most weighty matter," intoned Thomasina from the dais, "let us pray together that tomorrow we may...we may—" He stopped, leaned forward in his wheelchair, and squinted down the center aisle. A wave of murmurs began from the back and rolled forward as the three tattered intruders made their way to the front. Thomasina blanched, apprehensive and enraged. He could see the limestone box, that most holy of relics, that which he prayed and betrayed for; and now with the ark virtually within his grasp, this was all wrong, not the time or place, a situation he might not be able to control. Thinking fast, he blurted:

"Pray to yourselves on the way out, good night everybody!"

"Wait!" shouted DeSica, marching up front before the tired clerics could make their eager exodus to the dinner hall.

"This is no concern of yours," said Thomasina urgently to the hall, "and tonight's dinner special is veal scappolini!" The conflict among the clerics was palpable as the aisles began to fill and funnel toward the exit, quite a few already out the door; Bishop Montoya was in full trot.

"Don't go," DeSica yelled, reaching the stage, "I come here today with the most historic relic of the last two millennia!"

The flow of clerics began to clot near the doors...

"The vegetable is snow peas almandine, topped with fresh-shaved ten-years-aged parmigiana cheese!"

...then the hemorrhaging began anew.

"I beseech you, this concerns the very *future of Christendom!*"

Okay, this was the hook that brought the remaining clerics to a standstill, that might actually carry some weight since the guards in their SEAL-like vigilance had allowed these three derelicts to actually enter the hall. The buzzing of numerous languages rose up to ask the same question, *what could he possibly mean?*

"And dessert is to die for, from the private chef of Queen Margrethe II of Denmark herself, a lovely bread pudding topped with caramel sauce!"

That was worse than offering inebriated Brit soccer fans free Who tickets, the last of them stampeding away over anything in their path. When the riot sounds faded, it was just Mickey, DeSica, Danica, and Thomasina; only one of them was happy about this. The cardinal spoke to the two Swiss Guards still at the doors and one of them marched forward, pulled out his gun, handed it to Thomasina respectfully on upturned palms, then turned and marched back up the aisle to the doors. The two guards exited. Mickey felt his stomach drop as he heard the doors locked from the outside.

Since Mickey and Danica didn't understand Italian and Thomasina spoke painfully awful English, if one removed the irritating need to translate everything, their conversation went thusly:

"You can't just shoot us in the Vatican," said Danica, whistling past the graveyard.

"Of course I can," said Thomasina. "I commissioned you to find the ark, you did, then attempted to blackmail the church. When I refused you became violent and I had to shoot all three of you."

"Right." Mickey scoffed. "And Colombia's biggest export is coffee."

"You'd be surprised what the faithful will believe," answered Thomasina.

"You'd be surprised at what doesn't surprise me what the faithful will believe."

"Huh?"

"Nevermind."

"You mentioned blackmail," said DeSica. "Why do I believe that's *your* plan?"

Thomasina fixed him with a withering look. "Because it is *I* who should have been chosen Pope in the last election, Cardinal Francis Xavier Thomasina, instead of that doctrinaire lapdog they picked."

"So all this time," said DeSica, "all this death and destruction...*that's* what this is about? A selfish grab for power?"

"You say selfish, I say selfless, I only want to serve. Besides, more than a few popes killed for the position.[86]

---

86   Indeed, a third of the popes between 872 and 1012 died violently. *A Treasury of Royal Scandals*, Michael Farquhar, Penguin

The search for the ark has been going on for decades. When I was passed over I thought all was lost…until, like manna from heaven, the Holy Father appointed me to oversee that search. The church wants to suppress this relic, not share it. I knew if it was found on my watch, I could take it to the pontiff and broker a deal: step down, appoint me successor…and with the synod assembled, he could convince them to vote me in…or else I release this to the secularists to find whatever is there to be found. You, however," he said, his eyes narrowing at the priest, "would reveal this to the world and risk everything."

"I risked nothing. I have more faith than you that it will vindicate our Lord."

Thomasina sighed. "I fear you do. Perhaps it is a function of age, I will find out if He is the Son soon enough. Until then, I prefer not to test my faith."

"Then your faith is worthless."

Mickey was stunned to learn that he and DeSica were on the same page; as was Danica who almost got whiplash from her double-take at DeSica.

"I'm glad your faith is so strong," said Thomasina. "It will make what is about to occur easier for you."

"And I'm sorry Pope John Paul II abolished hell," said DeSica. "Swimming in a lake of fire would be a fitting eternity for you."

Thomasina gestured with the gun at Mickey. "Put it down…here…by my feet." Mickey swallowed dryly, nervously. With no other choice, he stepped forward, aware of the barrel pointed at him and that the gun was in the control of someone completely uninformed as to how little pressure on the trigger was required to effect instant death. He placed it at Thomasina's feet then gingerly stepped back. "Now," Thomasina said, his voice lowering to a whisper of husky anticpation, "remove the lid."

"Me?" asked Mickey needlessly, the kid caught in the hall between classes by the principal. The gun pointed at his chest. Mickey anxiously stepped forward again, leaned down to the ark, and carefully took the cover in both hands. He did this slowly, deliberately, raising it up by increments, knowing this would probably be the last action he voluntarily performed, though various involuntary bodily functions were likely to follow.

Thomasina leaned forward, trembling. "Hold it up, that I may see within." Mickey did this as well. Thomasina peered inside. In the long uncertain silence, Danica and DeSica watched anxiously. Then, Thomasina's voice a vibrato of barely restrained fury: "Where is it?"

"Where is what?" said DeSica, confused.

"The excreta, what happened to it?!"

Mickey cleared his throat. "Well, y'see, I, um...flushed it."

A stunned silence.

"You what?" Danica heard herself say.

"You what...?" said DeSica.

"You *WHAT*?!" screamed Thomasina.

"I flushed it. Down the toilet. When we were in the bathroom...what St. Thaddeus shoulda' done a couple thousand years ago."

Thomasina's gun shook dangerously. "What were you *thinking?*"

"Um…it's kinda complicated. See, you don't know me or anything so I don't expect you to get it…but for way too long I had this real need to prove that someone and everything he believed in was a bunch of shit," he said with no irony whatsoever. "Y'know what I mean?"

That would be a hell no. Mickey tried another tack.

"I was no different from most of you guys. I wanted to force *my* version of things on everyone else. When the truth is…I don't have anything better." He shook his head. "See, my dad, he would've handed all this over, he had no doubts. That's faith. Just 'cuz I don't have it, who am I to take it away?"

Danica and DeSica were beginning to understand; Thomasina stared at him blankly. But it wasn't hard to assume what he was thinking: *this fucking fuck just fucked up my one fucking chance to forever be included on that select roster that goes all the fucking way back to St. Peter. This fucking fuck just took away my one fucking chance at a piece of the rock. This fucking insignificant fuck fucked with the very fabric of history and chose to fuck everything up because…because…*

Truth is, Thomasina still didn't know the because. His breath quickened, his face reddened; he steadied the revolver with both hands as he aimed. Mickey, the son, was about to be sacrificed for the faith of his father. Until, with a mighty anguished groan, a groan that captured the depth of his pain and anger and despair and need to exact recompense…

…Thomasina died. Just like that.

Massive heart attack.

He slumped, the gun dropping to the floor. DeSica rushed up, felt for a pulse, and began C.P.R. as Danica ran to the doors and pounded on them. Mickey did what he did best, stood still and tried not to embarrass himself. For days to come, in the swirl of activity that followed, and forever after, these three would continue to marvel at the amazing, almost divine timing of what happened in Paolo VI Aula Hall – how Thomasina died at the exact moment he did, not so soon as to be unable to hear how all his plans had been for naught, and just soon enough before he could pull the trigger to take Mickey's life. But perhaps Father DeSica summed it up best:

"The Lord works in mysterious ways."

Six days later, on another continent

Jean-Henri Vandersmissen, still waiting for Maureen to call, would choke to death on a prune pit left in his mash.

Monday, April 12, 6:52 p.m. – Rome

"We could use another miracle," Danica said to Mickey, both of them tired, emotionally drained, handcuffed together on a bench in the decidedly un-Rennaisance offices of the *vigilanza*, or the Vatican police. "Bad enough there were no witnesses so we look complicit in Thomasina's death… or that we were carrying the terrorist's minimum amount of explosives in our car to take out a Vatican obelisk…

or that you're still wanted by the French police...or that they'll probably try to pin that murder in the train on us... or that we're all wanted by Interpol. Or that Father DeSica wandered off somewhere free as a bird with the ark, the only evidence we have that we really were doing what we say we were doing." The litany sounded even worse when she said it out loud.

"All the better, then, that you tell me now."

"Tell you what?"

"About that weekend in college you came out of the closet."

"My god...don't you *ever* forget?"

"Not the important stuff...if I'm gonna spend my peak sexual years in the Bastille, I'll need a little help for those lonely nights."

"An image I hope someday to erase from my mind."

They sat there blankly in the sterile over-lit environs... until something occurred to her; what *she* might call the important stuff. "I never saw inside the ark." He looked over. "What you said earlier...was it true?"

"Whassat...?"

"The number of pieces...you were banking on three and a half."

"I was, wasn't I?" He smiled, the blackjack player who just pulled a ten on a queen-deuce. "There were only three."

"Really." He nodded. "About the size you said?"

"I'm guessing...but yeah, they looked around what I figured."

"So you were close."

A dismissive shrug.

"So no earrings, paperweights, belt buckles for the fly-over states?"

"That's so yesterday...I'm thinking bigger, longer, and rock hard."

"Not even gonna ask."

"Two words: Vatican obelisk. Sell it by the pound. There's gotta be a few tons' worth out there."

"Your future's in breaking rocks, not selling them." He had to agree. Still, there was a cosmic symmetry to how their week together ended exactly as it had begun: In a police station. Which brought up something else: "But, you know," Danica began, not caring how it would be received, "if some greater power played a part in this...it picked the best person for the job." He didn't understand. "You...to find the ark. Maybe you were supposed to."

Mickey pursed his lips, considering. "I guess if He can choose a stutterer to hand down His laws to man... or an adulterer to be Israel's greatest king...or the apostle who denounced Christ three times in one night to be first pope...God's pretty consistent in His picks."

"I'd say He topped Himself."

Facing the end of life as he knew it, he still managed a smile. They slid back into silence, slumped on the bench, heads against the wall, the stillness of the police offices feeling even more oppressive, devoid as they were of activity. Until an entrance door somewhere boomed open and hard soles marched in, approaching with a take-no-prisoners attitude, someone here no doubt to cement their fate. A figure rounded the corner. All in black, robes flowing from the sense of mission that drove him forward, it was implacable authority incarnate:

The Angel of Death.

Fr. DeSica, washed, shaved, returned to his stone-faced master-of-disaster self, reached into his robe and immediately Mickey knew what was going down: They were wanted criminals on whom could be pinned all manner of sins, he was a priest protected by the authority of The Church, the same church that took the limestone ark that might have proved Mickey's and Danica's ecclesiastical employ, and anyone who could or would tell the truth was dead…except for the two of them who, it would be explained, were shot in an abortive attempt to escape. Mickey jumped on Danica to take the first bullet and give her the advantage of one more second of life, one extra breath, maybe she could see by his final act he just wasn't after her well-manicured Delta of Venus though in all honesty he was, his body tensed to receive impact. And then he heard:

"Mmmick-heee…I…can't…breee-he-heeeth."

No gunshots, no sudden impact…he looked over his shoulder to see DeSica, his I.D.. pulled out, conversing with several officers. Mickey stayed pressed against Danica just to be sure.

"…blacking…out…now…" He finally disengaged, not wanting to be her cause of death on the coroner's report.

"Follow me," was all DeSica said. They didn't know where or why, but he was back in the saddle, full throttle, and you didn't fuck with that.

Monday, April 12, 8:58 p.m. – Rome

This time the chambers they were taken to for their personal use would have impressed Louis XIV. They showered under brass fixtures and endless hot water so soft it felt like it would never towel off. Mickey was provided with a fresh razor and such a variety of hygienic toiletries that he was unsure what some were for. Danica found in the vanity of her quarters enough makeup to do the trick and learned the joys of a bidet. Both had laid out on their beds a conservative mode of attire. And both dressed with a formality and carefulness befitting the occasion.

At the appointed time a knock came on the door of each, the Swiss Guard outside to escort them to their destination. Each was taken outside to the Vatican gardens where Mickey and Danica saw one another for the first time, two butterflies freshly emerged from their chrysalises.

"You look damn close to respectable," she said. He didn't have to say anything. Covered in sewage or new-penny clean, she was mouth watering.

Fr. DeSica joined them, still a little miffed at Mickey for thinking he was about to kick their buckets, and they marched in tight-lipped silence to the highest point of the gardens. There stood the impressive Tower of St. John.[87] They were escorted inside to an intimate room and told

---

87   Originally built in the ninth century by Pope Leo IV, it was designed as a citadel to protect the precious relics of St. Peter from attack by the Saracens. Though built from conflict, in 1994 a small olive tree was planted to commemorate the start of Vatican-Israeli relations. The tree has yet to bear fruit.

to wait. Something about this place made small talk feel sacrilegious.

The door opened and, from a chamber beyond, the Man himself entered.

Whatever one did or did not believe, to be standing in the presence of *il Papa* in his purple and white robes was to understand the full dimension and depth of the word *awe*. Mickey didn't realize how much priest was still in him until his eyes began to water and his knees, already threatening to fail him, wanted on their own to kneel before the direct lineal descendent of the Apostles. The Holy Father performed the short ceremony in Italian. When he was finished he went on to speak to Mickey and Danica, DeSica translating, expressing heartfelt appreciation for all they did. He then took their hands, kissed their cheeks, and they were escorted out.

As the infallible emissary of God, the Pope had just forgiven them of all their sins. It is a little known fact, however, that he can also absolve even the most heinous of lawbreakers of all crime, transgressions, and international violations.

Just like that they were sinless and no-longer-wanted criminals.

Monday, April 12, 9:18 p.m. – Rome

In the gardens DeSica chose to say his farewell. He was not one for the long goodbye.

"I leave today for Istanbul," he told them. "*Signora* Farburger, this would have ended considerably differently but for your cooperation. You may never talk of it, yet know that in the highest levels of your church, you are held in the greatest esteem." Going from a condemned woman who knew too much, to a venerated non-virgin, left her speechless. She blushed and lowered her gaze. He gave her a buss on each cheek.

"Mickey Samanov," he said, turning to him, "it is one of the great tragedies that we lost your father. But it was he who guided us all the way. You are more his son than you realize. And it is a tragedy that we do not have you working for us."

"I don't suppose the ambassadorship to Sweden is open."

"The church prefers to remain on good terms with Sweden." For him that was almost a joke. "Goodbye."

Mickey extended his hand to avoid the buss and the priest took it in both of his, warmly, holding his gaze. He finally turned and walked away. They watched him go, about to disappear through the gate, when he paused, remembering to say one thing more. But he thought the better of it, opened the gate, and he was gone.

San Francisco

The phone was answered on the third ring. "Officer Farburger." She was met by a mucid throat clear.

"Hey," Mickey announced, trying to sound nonchalant.

"As I live and breathe….no thanks to you." She was not unpleased to hear his voice.

"Yeah, well…I kinda wanted to make up for that."

"Really."

"Really." He waited for her to fill the awkward silence but she didn't. "So, um, I was wondering," Mickey began like a pubescent teen before prom, "if, y'know...you had any plans this Friday."

"Mmm, I don't know...I don't really go out with clerics."

He could hear the hint of a smile. "If you mean my church...I've kinda seen the error of my ways."

"Will miracles never cease?"

"That depends..."

"On what?"

"If you're seeing a certain someone."

A pause. "No," she said, "I've seen the error of my ways, too."

"Then I guess they don't." Things were definitely looking up.

She was doodling on a pad, letting him twist in the wind a bit longer. "There's still the other thing."

"What other thing?"

"I don't date men."

"Neither do I, so we've got *that* in common."

The subtext of their conversation, though, was what they did have in common, the bond they'd have forever: The shared adventure they could never discuss, the one time the real story *didn't* get out...the close calls, the death and destruction, even the felling of the obelisk in St. Peter's, it was all chalked up to various other causes (in the lattermost, stone termites and a leaky gas main were partially to blame). The archbishop of San Francisco had called Danica's superiors and explained her absence in such a way as to allow her reacceptance onto the job without question. Aaron's remains, never to be identified, were buried in a Northern Italian pauper's grave. The *Fonds de Suisse de Lion* used the great economic downturn to fold up its tent (though no doubt it will return in some other form; Templars, like Nazis and God, would have to be created by unimaginative writers and pandering cable channels if they didn't already exist). The Church in Rome did a house-cleaning of all moles. The Ark of the One True Excreta, minus the excreta, would be consigned to the bowels of the Vatican, a limestone sled never to be deciphered. And Mickey's decision to assign Christ's final remains on this earth to the sewers of Rome would never be known. Thus the only people Mickey and Danica could talk to about this were each other.

"So, y'know, since we're both unencumbered, I was thinking something casual…food and drink…a place we'd both enjoy."

"Hooters?"

Shit. "Nooooo…no, of course not."

"Uh huh." Then, "I seem to recall you're a pretty good cook."

"I am," he said, liking where this was going. "We can stay in. And I promise not to try for a feel."

"You know how to flatter a gal." Her smile dropped, though, remembering their last meal together in San Francisco. "I'm not too crazy about tempting fate again at your dad's."

"Me, neither. I'll have you out to Marin."

"What can I bring?"

"Your detailed memory of a certain college weekend."

She should have known. In the two weeks away from Mickey she was beginning to realize she missed this, the expected and unexpected that came from him. His unintelligent intelligence. The fun tension. The kind of thing she never had with Nikki. With Nikki it was just the tension. She was never her equal, and if Danica could give Mickey credit for one thing, it was that in her short time around him she learned she had more to offer than to be a silent partner in any relationship; just as she learned not to rush into something no matter how passionate with someone who saw her primarily as a sexual accoutrement; and that she wanted to be with a person she actually enjoyed being with. She was surprised that Mickey filled two of those three necessesities.

"Lemme check my calendar…" She doodled a moment longer. "Looks like I'm pretty open through the rest of the decade…I guess Friday works."

"Great."

"Yeah…great."

Awkward pause.

"Bring the handcuffs?"

"Don't push it."

That Friday

It was the kind of spring day that could fool you into believing summer already started; the unadulterated blue sky, the gentle winds off the bay, locals in t-shirts and, to Mickey's delight, tank tops on those who wore them best.

He had gone to Chin's A-#1 Best Produce and picked up fresh spinach still dirty at the roots, as well as garlic just in from Gilroy, then headed into Little Italy and bought handmade pasta, extra virgin olive oil, and pinon nuts from Ciapponi's just off Columbus Square.

In his father's no-nonsense Volvo station wagon he drove west to Franklin, taking it all the way down to Holy Cross Cemetery. He pulled into the lot, parked, went into the offices, and was given directions to his father's grave. Driving inside the grounds, it was hard to believe he was in the heart of a metropolis squeezed onto a peninsula with not a square inch to waste. Sprawling, open, with green rolling hills, the graves were shaded with trees as old as the city itself. He rolled quietly among the mix of modest and ostentatious headstones until he came to where he was told to park.

Mickey got out and wandered among the dead. Somewhere a weed trimmer was manicuring around marble, the only sound of life in here. He paused at the large dark granite marker that was Joe DiMaggio's and wondered who came here to lean baseball bats against it. He moseyed on.

Mikhail Samanovananonvich's plot, freshly dug, still lacked for sod and Mickey was told a headstone was coming, courtesy of the Archdiocese, which had shipped his body back. He glanced about and knew his father would approve of this location.

Some rows away, the groundskeeper paused from his trimming to wipe his brow and drink from his thermos. In the distance he saw a figure kneel down beside the plot to pray. He chose to wait until the mourner was finished before he fired up the weed trimmer again.

Mickey wasn't praying. But he was paying his father his highest respects. He reached down and dug a small furrow in the tamped earth. From his pocket he pulled out a small plastic bag and removed the half-piece of excreta. He placed it in the furrow and covered it, forever to remain with Mikhail.

He went home to make dinner.

Acknowledgements

There are a number of people to thank (or, depending on your tastes, blame) for the finished product and to whom I am greatly indebted.

Krishna Rao was the earliest reader and my biggest advocate...until his wife Sandy Bieler took it upon herself to read the manuscript, and was an even bigger advocate, with copious firm, encouraging and extremely helpful notes. That both read my first, longest, most post-modern and indulgent draft and were as supportive as they were was a major impetus to continue.

Alysia Grey read a portion early on of the same draft and also encouraged me to continue; coming from her, a published author, it was heady reinforcement indeed.

Bob Mehnert actually asked to read a revised draft after giving me his very in-depth notes and I stand in awe of his masochism.

And then there's the lit reading book group of John and Viviane Arlotto, Ben Garcia, Veronica Alvarez and Yelena Shapiro, all of whom put aside their valuable time devoted to the classics to indulge my manuscript then spend an entire evening discussing it in detail. That they denied themselves Cervantes or Melville or somesuch author for me redefines the concept of magnaminity.

Among my toughest critics were Ladd Graham, one of my oldest friends who has vetted my scripts for years; Vanessa Greco, whose honest head-scratching reaction gave me much to think about; and Tim Atkinson, who returned the tough-love I've given his screenplays and novels. Extremely helpful, all.

Fellow Art Center/College of Design writing teacher Brad Saunders looked this over with a writer's loupe as only a fellow wordsmith can. As did a few of my former students whose opinions I sought because it was clear to see how talented and thoughtful they were in the crucible of the give-and-take of the classroom: Khalil Sullins, Nate Ingels, Matt Epstein, Ted Marcus, and my erstwhile T.A., Elizabeth Bayne.

Hrag Yedalian tore himself away from his 24/7 job as a political aide and budding filmmaker to read this and give me his views and a much-needed vote of confidence late in the process when I was losing focus.

And lastly, a sincere acknowledgement to my far-more-Catholic-than-me wife, Tina, who chose not to read this but whose unspoken comments got me to the ending that I did.

About the Author

Ron Osborn lives in southern California with his wife and two daughters, where he has been a television and features writer for over thirty years. He has been nominated for 7 Emmys, 3 Cable Ace Awards, 2 Writers Guild Awards, and a Humanitas. He has only won one Cable Ace, after which the award was discontinued. Ron is certain there is no connection.

Proof

Made in the USA
Charleston, SC
24 January 2012